SCOTTISH

RITE

Maggie Devereaux Mystery #1

STEPHEN PENNER

RING OF FIRE PUBLISHING

ISBN-13: 978-0-6155778-3-8
ISBN-10: 0-6155778-3-0

Scottish Rite

Published by
Ring of Fire Publishing
Seattle, Washington, U.S.A.

This is a work of fiction. Any similarity with real persons or events is purely coincidental. Persons, events, and locations are either the product of the author's imagination, or used fictitiously.

Cover image by Istvan Benedek. Cover design by Stephen Penner.

To everyone who's encouraged me over the years.
Thank you.

This one is special.

SCOTTISH RITE

1. Scottish Rite

Annette Graham pulled her jacket tight against the chill of the evening fog and quickened her gait. She turned from St. Machar Drive onto High Street and passed the rows of shops, all of which were already closed up for the night, their merchants long gone home. It was just before nine o'clock. The late September sun had set some time ago and the streets were dark save the circles of light cast by the streetlamps and the faint glow from the dimly lit store windows. Although Annette felt much safer walking the night-darkened streets of Aberdeen than she would have back in Montreal, nevertheless she was uneasy and looked forward to completing her errand and returning to the relative safety of her flat.

Soon she reached her destination and pulled three envelopes from her coat pocket. After double-checking that she had affixed enough postage, she dropped each into the postbox in turn. The letter back to her parents in Cape Breton. The letter to her friend at MacGill. She held the last letter in her hand, but hesitated.

"*Il faut avoir du sang froid,*" she reminded herself. 'One must have cold blood.' Then she dropped the envelope into the mailbox.

Her mission accomplished, Annette turned and walked

slowly back up High Street. The entire business was starting to make her a touch paranoid; her eyes darted back and forth, trying to catch a glimpse of someone who might be watching her. Although there were a handful of people milling about nearby, she could see no one who appeared to be surveilling her, and she relaxed a bit. As she continued up High Street, she came to one of the many entrances to the college campus. She had avoided walking through the campus on the way over. She had wanted to appear as any local resident, not necessarily a student, whose comings and goings were inextricably linked with King's College. She paused. It would be considerably shorter to just cut across the campus to her flat on Don Street. And it was getting late. She glanced over her shoulder once more. Then she turned toward the college grounds. She was sure no one had seen her.

She was wrong.

Annette quickly reached the large courtyard behind the Edward Wright Building—the one she always cut through on her way home from her classes. She had walked to it out of habit. But rather than the bright, sunny field packed with busy, vibrant students, a recessed vault of blackness stared back at her. With no residential quarters in this area of the campus, the buildings were dark except for a single office window, illuminated by a light either left on by a forgetful member of the faculty or turned on by a diligent member of the cleaning staff. The fog was thicker back away from the street and the only other light in the courtyard was from four widely spaced lampposts along a thin stone walkway. The lamps were at least twenty meters apart by Annette's estimate, leaving vast areas of blackness between their protective oases of light.

Annette stood at the edge of the path, her heels still illuminated from the street behind her. She looked back the way she had come. It was only a short walk back to the well lit High Street. On the other hand, it was a considerably longer way home and did go by the pub, where someone she knew might see her and ask what she was doing out so late. She might even run into the recipient of her local correspondence. That wasn't something she was ready for just yet. Turning again to the poorly lit pathway through the courtyard, she steeled herself for a very quick walk to the safety of the other side. All she needed to do was hurry from one lamppost to the next and everything would be fine.

"Remember," she reassured herself, "this is Scotland."

She took a deep breath and looked up at the sky. Through the patchy fog she could see a few stars, but there was no moon visible and thus no moonlight to help illuminate her way. Shoving her hands into her coat pockets, Annette lowered her head and hurried away from the light of High Street into the darkness of the courtyard. In a minute or so she would be across the black abyss and onto the floodlit sidewalk of St. Machar Drive. In five more minutes she would be safely in her flat, the unpleasant business she was engaged in locked securely outside.

She reached the first lamppost in short order and relaxed slightly. The noises of High Street, such as they were this time of night, had faded and the quiet of the dark courtyard enveloped her. It was surprisingly peaceful, she thought, as she continued on to the next island of light. Her shoes clacked hard against the stone path and almost, but not quite, covered the rustle of bushes to her left.

Her heart jumped at the noise but her brain decided to argue that it was nothing—probably just a rabbit, or maybe a squirrel. Nevertheless she quickened her stride and did not pause as she passed through the glow of the second lamp.

The next sound she heard came from behind her and off slightly to one side. She didn't turn to face it, but it was a combination of the rustle of fabric and the pounding of slippery footsteps on wet grass. Any doubts Annette might have had that the noise was from a person running at her were violently dispelled as the wire wrapped itself around her throat and she was driven to the ground.

Despite frantic clawing at the cord clamping shut her throat, it was only a matter of some seconds before Annette Graham was dead.

Waiting several more moments to be sure the wire had done its job, the assailant finally pulled it from the flesh of the young woman's neck and wrapped the bloodied coil in a rag. This rag then neatly tucked away in one overcoat pocket, a gloved hand produced from the other pocket a four-inch long scalpel.

The light of the third unreached streetlamp reflected off the blade as the killer kneeled over Annette Graham's lifeless body and looked to the sky.

2. Grandmother's Funeral

"'Marvel not at this: for the hour is coming, in which all that are in the graves shall hear His voice, and come forth,'"

Reverend Gregory Tilbury's voice strained to fill the sanctuary of Seattle's Trinity Parish Episcopal Church, but the vaulted ceilings rose too high. The stained-glass saints could only gaze down from the corners of their meticulously etched eyes and strain to hear the dying echoes of his sermon.

"'They that have done good unto the resurrection of life;'"

The Reverend stared down austerely from his pulpit. Despite his seventy-two years on God's green Earth, his white hair was thick and his shoulders stooped only slightly as his wrinkled, spotted hands held the sides of the lectern in an iron grip. He had been preaching from that same dais for over fifty years, and as his piercing blue eyes gazed out from beneath their bushy white brows onto the congregation he had nurtured and led for the last half-century, he was thankful that the Lord had led him to his true calling. He sincerely loved being a minister.

"'And they that have done evil, unto the resurrection of damnation.'"

But he hated eulogies.

"So said our Lord Jesus Christ. The Gospel of St. John, Chapter five, Verses twenty-eight and twenty-nine."

He mopped his wrinkled brow with a starch-scented handkerchief and took a deep, slightly labored breath.

"And so we can take some small comfort that Kate, having done so much good in her life, shall hear His voice and shall be called forth unto the resurrection of life."

'Kate.' Catherine NicInnes Ingram. Kate Ingram had been a member of the congregation when the Reverend had first arrived so many years ago. He had liked Kate from the moment he met her. She was a friendly and intelligent woman with a magical smile. He would truly miss seeing her face in church each Sunday. He would even miss their wonderful disagreements—and occasional agreements—over the nature of God's creation. Kate had been a vital member of the congregation and to a large extent, the Reverend Tilbury could mark his tenure there by the events of her life.

He hadn't presided over her marriage to Joseph—that had happened prior to his arrival at Trinity—but he had had the happy duty of baptizing their daughter and only child, Ellen NicInnes Ingram. He had also presided over Ellen's marriage to David Devereaux, and soon thereafter the baptism of their own daughter. But the Reverend had also had the unhappy responsibility of eulogizing Joseph Ingram at the still vibrant age of 63. And the even unhappier duty of eulogizing his daughter, Ellen Ingram Devereaux, when she passed away at the tragically young age of only 34, leaving behind her husband and daughter. Now he was eulogizing Kate Ingram as well. And the only daughter of the only daughter of Kate Ingram sat next to her father in the front pew of Trinity Parish Church. Entering the last minute of his eulogy,

Reverend Tilbury let his gaze fall from the beautifully decorated ceiling of the sanctuary to the beautifully soft face of Kate Ingram's only grandchild, Margaret NicInnes Devereaux. Maggie.

The eulogy stretched out to the mourners, but it passed by Maggie Devereaux's ear like a warm summer breeze; she was aware of it but paid little notice. Through insurgent tears and her small glasses she stared at the blurred starburst of color high in the stone wall behind the minister. Her gaze drifted softly over the sunlit rainbow above the altar, as her thoughts trudged sluggishly through the dark sadness in her heart. She was genuinely surprised at just how sad and empty she felt. Grandma's death had not been a surprise; she was 81 years old and had had a prolonged bout with colon cancer. Eventually everyone, including Grandma herself, had realized that the battle would soon be lost. The doctors had done everything they could, but despite several surgeries, increasingly longer regimens of radiation and chemotherapy, and increasingly shorter periods of remission, there came to be nothing to do but make her grandmother comfortable and let events run their course.

What surprised Maggie the most was that given all of the time she had had to think about Grandma's death and how she would feel about it—all the talks she and her grandmother had had about what was happening—none of that seemed to make it any less painful. She had actually believed that she had prepared herself emotionally for this day, but sitting in the church and hearing her grandmother being eulogized had destroyed any pretence to somber resignation. Sadness filled her heart and ran down her cheeks. She had thought this time would be different. Different from that unjustifiably sunny afternoon when Maggie was eight wonderful years old and she sat in this same pew and listened to a younger Reverend Tilbury tell the congregation of the virtues of her dearly departed mother.

Maggie had known, of course, that Grandma's funeral would bring back memories of her own mother's death. As she stared at the flaming colors behind the preacher, her thoughts slid painfully back to the evening her father had told her the news she had feared with every cell of her young body. Maggie's mother had also had a protracted illness before she died. Heart failure was the official cause. Heart failure at the age of 34. She had spent her last month in bed, and the last few days at the hospital. And although Maggie had known that her mother was sick, and had known it was serious, she had not really been able to conceive of her mother actually dying. She had encountered death before, but from a safe distance. Death on television or in a book isn't real. Even the death of a pet is insulated by the gulf of species. But when her father had come home from the hospital that night, his eyes as red as blood and the flesh hanging gray from his cheekbones, Maggie had known—and had jumped from her grandmother's lap and run up to her bedroom, slamming the door behind her. When her father finally came up to her room, she screamed and cried at his words, and she hated him for telling her what her eight year old heart simply couldn't bear.

And then she just cried. For days. She was inconsolable. She cried until her eyes couldn't cry anymore, and then her heart cried alone. And eventually, when her eyes had stopped crying, and her heart had stopped crying, and her soul had stopped crying, she was left with the far too real fact that her mother was still gone and she was still there. As her young mind struggled to understand the not-understandable, she blamed everyone she could find in turn. Except her mother. Because even as she blamed herself and her father and the doctors, one thought lurked in the darkest recesses of her mind. And young Maggie Devereaux refused to allow it to escape those dark recesses to step foot into the light of conscious thought. But it was there nonetheless and it colored her other thoughts and stalked her dreams. And even from the dimmest nooks of her unconscious, it racked her with guilt. For try as she might, Maggie had not been able completely to fight off the horrible, hateful, intolerable conclusion that her mother had simply not loved her enough to stay alive.

Maggie wiped a tear out from under her glasses. The Reverend was saying something else about her grandmother, but she wasn't listening. She glanced down at the silver pendant her grandmother had left her and which hung now, shining and silent, atop her black sweater. It was in the shape of a circle, designed to look like a leather strap, buckled on itself at the bottom. Inside the leather circle was the head of a boar, its lower tusk jutting up above its snout. Written on the strap, arched across the top of the pendant, were the words, 'BE TRAIST.' Middle Scots for 'Be true.' The crest of the Clan Innes. She closed her eyes and succumbed to a sad smile.

Maggie had half-expected her grandmother to fade from her life once her mom had died. Instead, however, Grandma had become even more involved in her life. When Maggie was eleven, she went through a phase where she wanted to know everything she could about her ancestry. Obviously an attempt to connect with her dead mother. But rather than counsel Maggie against opening old wounds, or lash out at her for the wounds it must have opened in her as well, Grandma had seized the task with zeal. She helped Maggie trace the family back for generations. Maggie would later learn that Grandma had already done the genealogy and knew at least some of their ancestors back to the 1600s. But rather than simply give her the family tree, she had let Maggie research it, providing information only after Maggie had found most of it herself, or occasionally when discouragement threatened to end the project for good. When they had finished, Maggie could not have told you even who her father's grandfather was, but she knew thirteen generations of mothers and daughters across two continents whose middle name was 'NicInnes'—'daughter of Innes'—and in some small way, being part of this larger, centuries-old family helped to ease at least some of the pain of her loss.

Of course, the interest in genealogy would fade, others rising to take its place, but eventually her interest in her Scottish ancestry would return. When she started high school she had known she wanted to study languages, but she had been unsure which to take. Her choices were Spanish, French, German or Latin; but she knew which language she truly wanted to learn. So just before her freshman year, Maggie had found her grandmother out in the back yard, painting the sunset, and had said simply, "Teach me Gaelic."

Grandma had smiled, then set down her paintbrush and crossed the lawn to the patio table where she had placed, earlier that evening, the Gaelic reader she had first used to teach her own daughter the language. She picked it up and handed it to Maggie.

"Gaelic," she began, pronouncing it 'Gah-lick' like a native speaker, "is one of the six Celtic languages..."

From that point on, Kate Ingram played an increasingly active role in the education of her granddaughter. Other languages had not been rejected, simply reprioritized. She could learn German at school and Gaelic at home. And college would be a fine place to learn French—at least a reading knowledge of it—and Latin too of course. But the choice of college would ultimately come down to the study of Gaelic. Maggie and her grandmother spent countless hours investigating and comparing potential colleges, even visiting a few the summer before her senior year. Finally, Maggie had settled on the University of California at Berkeley. The selling point, aside from the fact that it boasted the oldest degree granting Celtic department in the country, had been its exchange program with the University of Aberdeen.

While Maggie had originally intended to study in Scotland during her junior year of college, it had quickly become apparent that while a Ph.D. in Celtic Languages might, maybe, secure her a professorship teaching that same subject to the next generation of gaelophiles, a simple B.A. was going to provide exactly zero professional opportunities. If she was to be serious about her studies, and her career, she had to accept the fact that she would have to earn a full Ph.D. Ironically the inevitability of this additional schooling had stripped away any sense of urgency from her study abroad plans. Grandma had not been pleased.

"I thought you said you were going to Aberdeen next year?"

"I did," Maggie had replied with a disinterested shrug, "but there's just too much going on right now. But don't worry. I've got plenty of time. Aberdeen will just have to wait."

Kate Ingram had looked down at her wrinkled and spotted hands. "Wait," she had repeated. "But for how long?"

In the event, four more years, as Maggie first completed her B.A., then studied for and passed her Master's exam. Only then, as a full-fledged doctoral candidate, was she ready finally to study abroad. She had been accepted at Aberdeen and would enroll directly once she arrived. Berkeley's Celtic Department agreed to give her a year's credit, so long as she authored a 100-page thesis on her area of focus. And Grandma had known of a Scottish-American foundation, 'The Ladies Albannach,' which had provided her a sizeable fellowship grant—and which Maggie suspected consisted of little more than her Grandmother's own circle of friends. Finally, in case she needed additional funds, Grandma had also known someone in the British consulate who had helped Maggie obtain a work permit. Everything was all set.

And then Grandma took a turn for the worse.

Maggie looked past Reverend Tilbury to the maple casket which held her grandmother's remains. Although she couldn't see the body from her pew, she could imagine her grandmother reclined peacefully, eyes closed and hands folded on her chest. Just as she had laid in the hospital bed the very last time Maggie had visited her, a week before she was supposed to leave for Aberdeen.

Maggie had pushed the door open as quietly as she could and thought that perhaps she hadn't awakened her grandmother.

"Come in, Maggie." The bedridden woman's eyes didn't open and her lips barely parted.

"Hi, Grandma," Maggie croaked, her voice blocked by the brick in her throat. "How are you feeling?" What else was there to say?

"Not too bad," Grandma breathed, her eyes still closed. "All things considered."

"The doctors said—" Maggie stopped. The doctors had said her grandmother would not survive. The cancer was back, and it was too widespread now. Even if they could remove most of it, she couldn't withstand any more chemotherapy.

"I know, Maggie." Kate Ingram opened her eyes and gazed up at her beloved granddaughter with a pained sigh. "Come sit down next to your grandmother."

Maggie complied, her throat constricted.

"Grandma, I—" but she didn't know what to say. She could speak Gaelic and German fluently, and English of course; she could read and write French and Latin, and she even knew a little bit of Russian her ex-boyfriend in college had taught her. Still words failed her.

"Hush." Even in its raspy tone, her grandmother's voice carried authority. "I'm not very long to this world, Maggie, and I have some things to tell you yet."

"Oh, Grandma." The tears were welling in Maggie's eyes. "Just rest."

"I said hush," her grandmother repeated, "and listen. Maggie, your poor dear mother wasn't able to raise you, so I did what I could to help. I've tried to teach you about yourself, about your heritage, and about what's right and what's wrong."

Kate Ingram's body was then racked by a coughing fit, but Maggie just sat silently, knowing her grandmother hadn't finished yet.

When the coughing subsided, Kate continued, "I love you Maggie, like my own daughter. But try as I might I can't stay here with you for very much longer."

"I love you too, Grandma," Maggie whispered.

"But Maggie—" Again a cough. "Maggie, remember the things I've taught you. Remember who you are. Remember where you come from. Remember right from wrong." She wheezed a long, deep breath. "And know this: as long as you stay true to what's right, I will always be with you."

And with that, Kate Ingram used up the last of her strength and closed her eyes. She would not open them again.

Maggie squeezed her grandmother's hand one last time.

"I love you, too, Grandma," she repeated. "Thank you."

"And thank you all for coming."

The Reverend's voice seized Maggie roughly and dragged her unceremoniously back to the church sanctuary. The eulogy was over and the mourners had started to rise. Maggie too stood and looked up at her all too mortal father as he rested his hand on her shoulder.

"You okay, hon?"

Maggie blinked, releasing a tear down either cheek. "No, Daddy. I'm not."

And they turned to file out into the unjustifiably sunny afternoon.

3. Half the Fun

Maggie looked out the plane window, beneath heavy eyelids. They had been in the air for less than an hour, and her internal clock assured her it was only seven o'clock, but it had been a long, draining day. She hadn't been able to postpone her flight again and so had had to spend the day at the funeral and burial, only to rush home, finish her packing and race to the airport to catch her red-eye, over-the-Pole flight to London. She was tired.

And the motion sickness pills weren't helping any. '*May cause drowsiness*,' she thought as her eyes fought to stay open. The airplane wing was illuminated almost entirely by its own lights now, the sun intent on completing its descent into the horizon on the other side of the aircraft. Out Maggie's window, no moon was visible over the soft wool of the clouds.

Maggie unfurled her blanket, covering her legs but leaving enough on her lap to pull over her shoulders once she was ready to sleep. She had buckled her seatbelt loosely over the blanket so as not to be disturbed by the stewardess should they encounter turbulence during the flight. The middle-aged man next to her, in seat 14B, was similarly belted and in fact was already asleep, plastic neck-pillow fully inflated.

She leaned forward and unzipped her carry-on. She had
three choices of reading material: the in-flight magazine filled with
photographs of celebrities she didn't care about and already
completed crossword puzzles; the latest installment in her favorite
mystery writer's series; or one of the books her grandmother had
left her. She pulled the hard-bound book from her grandmother
onto her lap. In part to justify having shoved the heavy tome in her
carry-on bag, in part because she actually wanted to read it, but
mostly because, despite her sincere interest in Middle Gaelic
literature, she thought it had the best chance of lulling her off to
sleep.

Her grandma had actually left her a total of five books, each
a collection of Modern and/or Middle Gaelic prose and poetry. Four
had made their way into her checked luggage, while this volume—
the most interesting of the lot—had landed in her carry-on. So the
pendant had helped her travel wardrobe and the books would help
her travel reading. The final bequest would also aid her in her trip
to Aberdeen. Grandma had survived not only her husband, but also
their only daughter, Ellen, Maggie's mother. Maggie too had been
an only child, meaning that she was Grandma's only surviving
descendant. Grandma had of course been aware of this and had
formalized the arrangement by providing in her will that Maggie
would receive, after various charitable bequests and the like, the
bulk of her estate—on the condition she complete her year in
Aberdeen. This condition was made all the more significant by the
fact that the estate apparently included a quaint little cottage on
Seattle's trendy Queen Anne Hill which had approximately
quintupled in value since Grandma and Grandpa had paid off the
mortgage several decades earlier. The end result was that when the
year was done, Maggie would be looking at a nicely stocked bank

—and a healthy monthly stipend in the meantime. She supposed she wouldn't need that work permit after all; she could focus fully on her studies. Even when, she considered as she gazed down at the 400-page collection of Middle Gaelic literature, those studies were used to lull her to sleep.

Clicking on the overhead light, she paused for a moment to ensure this hadn't disturbed Mr. 14B. Then she cracked the book open to any page. Her Middle Gaelic was pretty good—not as good as her modern Gaelic or her Latin—but she was able to recognize most of the words and had a good feel for the short story she found herself reading. She quickly surmised that a young man named Diarmit had been selected for the priesthood only to fall deeply in love with a young maiden named Catrìona. The excerpt Maggie was reading appeared to be Diarmit's musings on the nature of love, the spirit, and service to God. It was structured as a sort of catechism, with Diarmit posing questions which he would then answer to the best of his ability.

'How does one best serve the Lord?'

'Cannot one serve the Lord by loving one of His creations?'

'Has not the Lord created man and woman to live together as man and wife?'

"Would you like anything to drink?"

Maggie looked up at the stewardess with a start. The broad smile she encountered revealed large white teeth, as well as several reluctant wrinkles around its owner's mouth and eyes. Maggie wondered whether the woman had come late to stewardessing, or was simply a seasoned veteran in the field.

"Um, no, thanks," Maggie replied. "I think I'll probably try to sleep soon."

The stewardess nodded approvingly and then cocked her head to look at Mr. 14B. By all indications he was still fast asleep.

The stewardess smiled again at Maggie, eyes squinting happily and a finger to her lips. She looked like someone else's mother.

As the flight attendant turned her whispering attention to the passengers across the aisle, Maggie looked around and observed that the cabin was dark save a small handful of overhead lights like hers. Confirming that the woman behind her had already tilted her seat back, Maggie followed suit, snuggling down as best she could, and resting her head against the plastic wall to her left before returning her attention to her reading material. Diarmit didn't seem to be getting anywhere with his question and answer period. The words began to blur and Maggie squeezed her eyes shut to refocus them. Then she pulled her glasses off and tucked them loosely in the pocket of her blouse while she rubbed the bridge of her nose. She yawned deeply and closed the book on her thumb to mark her place while she closed her eyes for a moment. And after that moment she was asleep.

* * *

The rolling Scottish hills gathered themselves up to rise majestically into two towering crags, which in turn merged into a single granite peak. Tucked at the base of the green hills, where the valley came together in a perfect 'V' under the watchful eye of the mountain behind it, was a small loch, perfectly still and reflecting the dense Scottish clouds overhead. In the center of the loch was a small island which was almost completely covered by the stone castle which had been erected centuries before. Although boasting towering granite turrets at each corner, connected by impregnable stone walls with nothing more than thin arrow slits in their facades, the castle was nevertheless dwarfed by the majesty of the landscape which surrounded it. The island of the keep was connected to the mainland by a single long, narrow, stone bridge. Where the bridge ended, a rutted road curved lazily from the loch, winding slowly along the rolling landscape and rising invitingly to greet Maggie as she walked toward the castle for her coronation.

The sky ahead of her was relatively light, albeit still gray. But as it arched over and behind her head, it gradually darkened and the wind at her back confirmed that a storm was on its way. Maggie looked down at her arms and observed that they—and in fact her entire body—were draped in a vibrant tartan, red with thin bright lines of white, yellow and blue. Her feet were bare and although the air was cooling and the wind was blowing, the earth was warm beneath her feet.

As Maggie approached the bridge, the path ahead was flanked on either side by four pairs of young women, all approximately Maggie's age, and each pair dressed in a different vibrantly colored tartan: the first pair wore yellow, the second green, the third a pale blue, and finally the fourth pair, whose tartan matched Maggie's own. The wind was strong at Maggie's back now; it cut through the wool wrap and chilled her skin, pulling the plaid from her limbs and plastering it to her back. The sky behind her had fully darkened and the castle too had been thrown into the shadows of its mountainous protectors. A cold rain started and it cut across Maggie's face as she marched toward the bridge. As she came even with the first pair of gaily dressed women, she noticed them looking past her, seemingly oblivious to her presence, eyes wide and tears running silently down their cheeks. As she walked by and they passed from her view, she heard their screams rise and then fade as they were swallowed by the storm which was now on Maggie's heels. The next pair of women, dressed in green tartan, were devoured by the storm in the same manner. Maggie quickened her gait and pulled the scarlet tartan close around her shoulders. By the time she reached the pair of blue attendants, the sky was entirely dark except for a small halo of medium gray directly behind the castle—the castle which was still too far away. As the screams of the third pair were smothered by the now roaring din of the storm, a swatch of Maggie's plaid peeled away and flapped wildly behind her. She began to run.

As she neared the fourth pair—those wearing the same tartan as she—the loose swatch pulled taut behind her and she fell to her knees. The rain had turned the path to a thick muck and she struggled to return to her feet even as the storm yanked on the plaid. She looked up; the bridge was only a few feet away. The sky was completely black now as she struggled against the pull on her wool wrap—only the glow from the open portico of the castle cast any light. Maggie knew she had to reach the castle. The two maidens in red had disappeared, but without a scream. The black storm wanted *her* now. Rain sliced at her face as she raised herself to her feet and sprinted across the bridge toward the main gate of the castle.

The storm pulled again at her tartan and it unraveled from her body as she sped across the bridge. The storm was right behind her and slashed at her naked back like an animal. The wind and rain smashed away at the stone of the bridge under her feet and she raced to keep one step ahead lest she plummet into the icy loch below. Ahead of her the glowing courtyard burned brightly, but for the first time she noticed that the light shone through the lattice squares of an iron gate which blocked her entry into the castle.

Maggie knew her only refuge lay inside the castle, but just as certainly she knew the only force powerful enough to tear down the iron gate was the very tempest she fled. With no time to reflect, she threw herself at the ground before the gate and covered her face with her arms. The storm pounced on her, slicing at her naked, unprotected body. The gate was giving way, but so too was the flesh being torn from her bones. She looked up toward the courtyard in desperate agony, hoping for some miracle to save her. Inside the keep she could just make out the outline of a figure—a figure of someone she felt she knew. Maggie stretched a bloodied hand toward the woman—just before the glow of the courtyard exploded into a blinding ball of light.

Maggie jerked awake and the book flew off her lap, landing on the floor of the airplane with a graceless thud. She squinted against the sunrise streaming in through the plane window. Her brow was damp with sweat and her heart was still racing. She glanced over at the man next to her to determine whether she had perhaps cried out in her sleep. Although he was now awake, he did not seem in anyway concerned or alarmed or really even interested in her presence. He also appeared to have had more pleasant dreams than she. Except for one upturned lock of hair behind his left ear, he seemed remarkably put together for someone who had just spent the night sleeping in an airplane seat.

She leaned forward and picked her book up off the floor. Her still foggy brain was trying to decide whether to shove it back into her bag, or just set it on her lap while she woke up more. The latter won out. She closed her eyes and stretched her back. Sleeping upright was not terribly comfortable and it had been less than eight hours, but she had gotten at least some rest—despite the dream. She could feel her heart slow to a near normal pulse. It jumped again at the stewardess' voice.

"Good morning!"

Maggie glared out the corner of her eye at the all-too-perky flight attendant. She didn't always wake up in a good mood and nightmares followed by smiley stewardesses didn't help matters.

"We should be landing at Heathrow in a little over an hour," the smile explained. "Would you like something to drink? Orange juice, mayb—"

"Coffee." Maggie rubbed the drying sweat from her temples and put her glasses back on.

"Okay then. Cream or sug—"

"Black." She looked groggily at the stewardess. "Thanks."

The coffee came with a bagel and in a little over an hour, the bagel and coffee having been successfully ingested, Maggie was standing, crouched over, waiting for Mr. 14B to move his well-rested butt into the aisleway so she could exit the plane.

4. *Ceud Mìle Fàilte*

It was late afternoon as the train approached the outskirts of Aberdeen. It snaked its way along the North Sea coast, to its left the Grampian Highlands and ahead of it the mouth of the River Dee at the center of Maggie's destination. As they entered Aberdeen, Maggie was struck by the stark beauty of the rows of slate-roofed townhomes. She could also see the ships in the harbor, looking so much like the vessels she had always seen on Elliot Bay back in Seattle. The train station was down near the docks and the oldest part of the city, and as the train pulled through the town, she could see the bustle of the Aberdeenians as their work day drew to a close. The train began to slow as it approached the station and Maggie's pulse began to quicken as her stomach filled with both excitement and anxiety. Her trek would finally be over and she would set foot in Scotland, but she was also about to meet her 'aunt' and 'uncle,' Lucy and Alex MacTary, for the first time. Technically, they were some degree of cousins, thrice removed or so, but 'aunt and uncle' was going to be a lot simpler, and regardless of the exact familial connection, she was going to be living with them—at least for the first semester—so she hoped deeply that she would like them, and they her. She looked at her watch. 5:49. Only three minutes late as the train slowly rolled to a stop at platform six.

The nearly empty train unloaded quickly and in as much time as it took to pull on her coat, grab her bag, and follow the two young backpackers off the train car, she was standing on the blustery platform, tucking her thick, straight hair behind her ears and scanning the faces of the people there for some expression of recognition.

"Maggie?" A woman stepped toward her and smiled. The woman had short black hair with loose curls blowing around the edges of her round face. She shared Maggie's petite stature and wore a simple, but obviously high-quality brown overcoat which covered all of her clothes save the hem of her gray skirt and her black leather shoes. Maggie guessed her age at about 45. The woman offered a tentative wave. "Maggie Devereaux?"

Maggie smiled, almost as tentatively. "Aunt Lucy?" Then, looking at the smiling man behind the woman, she ventured, "Uncle Alex?"

The couple stepped forward and the woman embraced Maggie in an uncertain hug.

"Welcome to Aberdeen, Maggie." Her Scottish brogue bathed each word. "I'm your Aunt Lucy. And this is your Uncle Alex."

Uncle Alex pushed forward a hand in greeting and Maggie shook it warmly. He was a large man, at least six feet tall, and probably a few years older than his wife. His hair was thick and brown, dotted with both red strands and white streaks. He too wore a coat, a red wool affair, but it was smaller and unbuttoned, flapping in the wind to reveal a tan sweater and brown trousers. "Welcome, Maggie."

"Thanks," Maggie said simply, not sure what etiquette

required when one meets distant relatives in a foreign country for the first time.

"Er," Alex mirrored her awkwardness. "That is— Well, we were sorry to hear about Kate."

Maggie frowned sharply. Her grandmother's death had slipped her mind in the excitement of her arrival. She felt bad for that. "Thanks. Me too."

"She's in a better place," Lucy offered.

Maggie smiled. "I'm sure you're right."

Not sure what else to say as they stood on the now deserted train platform, Alex pointed at Maggie's carry-on bag, "Is that all your luggage, then?"

Maggie looked down at the bag. "Oh, no. Of course not. I've got three other bags, but I checked them. They've probably been unloaded already."

Sure enough, a quick glance around the platform revealed her bags standing unobtrusively against the wall behind Alex and Lucy, next to the entrance to the station lobby and under a large sign marked, 'BAGGAGE.' From the side of the station extended a cast iron fence with a gate hanging open to the parking lot.

"Good Lord, girl!" Uncle Alex exclaimed with a laugh as he spied the luggage. "You don't think I can carry all that, do you?"

"Hush, Alex," Lucy chided. "If she can bring them all the way from the States, you can certainly help bring them to the car."

She turned to her niece. "Don't mind him, Maggie. He's just an old man who likes to grouse. And he hasn't been himself lately anyway. All the preparations for your arrival, I expect."

The three of them walked over to the suitcases and Maggie quickly arranged them into two two-bag combinations so that she and Alex would be able to roll them easily enough to the waiting car. Uncle Alex pulled his suitcases toward the iron gate, Aunt Lucy at his side, but Maggie stopped for just a moment to look around. She was there. She was in Aberdeen. She'd done it. But then her smile turned to a soft frown. Somehow she had pictured herself being able to see rolling Scottish hills from the train station, but no such luck. Squat brick buildings were the only scenery visible from where she stood. Still, as she gazed around at her surroundings, she felt a surge of nervous accomplishment that she was actually, finally, really there.

She looked up at the sign over the train station door.

'WELCOME TO ABERDEEN. *CEUD MÌLE FÀILTE CHUN OBAIR DHEADHAIN.*'

'*Ceud Mìle Fàilte.*' 'A hundred thousand welcomes.'

Maggie smiled, the wind blowing her hair across her face again. It would be a good year.

She rolled her suitcase toward the gate. Lucy and Alex were already well into the parking lot. As she approached the gate herself, Maggie looked up and around, trying to remember as much as possible of what she was seeing. But she was so busy looking up that she didn't notice the newspaper that blew by her feet and pinned itself to the iron fence as she walked by. And as she stepped through the gate, she completely failed to notice the newspaper's headline:

'FEMALE   STUDENT   FOUND   BUTCHERED   AT UNIVERSITY'

5. The Pursuit of Knowledge

The drive from the railway station to the MacTary's house was a quick one and their home was as nice as Maggie's grandmother had described. Unfortunately, Maggie had been exhausted, and the comfort of family—even distant and previously unmet family—had only served to increase her sleepiness. As a result, Maggie noticed little more about the house than that it was green as she dragged herself up the stairs to the front door. After a brief tour of the downstairs, Aunt Lucy had taken Maggie upstairs to her room and encouraged her to lie down before dinner. Not needing much cajoling, Maggie had dropped her bags near the door and crawled onto the bed, surrendering to sleep almost as soon as her head hit the pillow.

When Maggie finally awoke, she was thoroughly surprised to find that it was the next morning. She had slept through dinner and indeed all through the night. She was still in her street clothes, although someone had placed a warm quilt over her during the night. The clock on the bedside table showed 7:15, and the dawn was just beginning to break.

Maggie sat up in bed, simultaneously groggy and rested.

The air in the room was cold and she pulled the blanket around her shoulders as she swung her feet off the bed. As she came more to her senses, she realized that she heard muffled voices echoing around the room. Looking around in the relative dark of the chamber proved unhelpful, so Maggie clicked on the lamp next to the clock and the room was illuminated by a soft yellow glow shining through the well-aged lampshade.

The room was a little larger than she had remembered from the night before and was decorated in a comfortable, if perhaps overly cute style. The double bed was centered in the room, a multicolored floral bedspread over it and its dark wooden headboard pushed against the wall opposite the door. Against one wall was a rather tall wooden chest of drawers and an even taller wooden wardrobe. Against the opposite wall was a fine wooden writing desk with a roll top. That left the corner between the desk and the door to be filled by a comfortable looking reading chair with a small table next to it, a standing lamp next to that, and two waist-high, and quite full, bookcases hiding against the walls behind them. On the other side of the door, toward the wardrobe, was a second door, slightly ajar, through which Maggie could see a small sink.

Ah, she thought, *the bathroom.*

She rose from the bed and crossed the hardwood floor with a purpose. On the way she found the source of the muffled voices: an air vent in the floor between the chest of drawers and the wardrobe. Crouching over it she could now clearly hear Aunt Lucy and Uncle Alex engaged in light conversation.

"... wake her up?" Aunt Lucy was asking, her voice echoing metallically through the vent.

"Nae, love," was Uncle Alex' reply. "Let the lass sleep."

"But she'll miss breakfast."

"Aye, perhaps. But she's obviously tired. Let her get her rest first. There'll be time enough to eat later."

It was quiet for a moment, then Lucy tried, "Well, what if she wakes up and doesn't know where the loo is?"

"Lucy," Alex replied. "The loo is connected to her room. If she hasn't already found it in the middle of the night, then I expect it will be the first thing on her mind when she wakes up."

Well, that's certainly true enough, Maggie's thought. As she walked to the bathroom, she could hear Alex' voice trailing off, "And you've already put out fresh towels for her. She's a smart lass, studying at the college and all. I wager she can figure out how to use the fixtures..."

As Maggie entered the small but adequate bathroom, she made a mental note to close that vent in the event she ever needed some privacy. She was sure voices would travel both ways.

Soon, Maggie had fetched her toiletries from her luggage and taken advantage of the small shower shoved into a corner of the bathroom. Once cleaned and dried, she pulled on the smart new outfit she had bought for her first day in Aberdeen, set her small glasses squarely on her face and bounded downstairs, fully rested and eager to be a more considerate guest than her exhaustion had allowed the previous night.

"Good morning, Maggie." Aunt Lucy was waiting at the foot of the stairs. "I could hear the water running so I knew you'd be down soon. You're just in time for breakfast. Come on then."

"Great," Maggie replied, but her efforts to apologize for her failure to visit with them the night before were met only with warm rebukes.

"You can't help it if you're tired after two days of travelling," Uncle Alex said as Maggie and her aunt entered the dining room; he had obviously overheard Maggie's protestations. "Besides, the rest will make you that much more lively company for breakfast."

"Come, lass." Lucy pulled a chair out from the already set table. "Sit here. I'll go fetch the food."

Maggie did as she was told, wishing to be as polite as possible. She felt a twinge of guilt as she looked out over the elaborately set table. It was large enough to seat eight comfortably. Its legs appeared to be cherry, but the remainder was hidden under an enormous cotton tablecloth, which boasted an amazingly intricate floral design of green, lavender and gold. Two separate flower arrangements graced the table as well and scattered among the plates and bowls were a sugar bowl, a creamer, a butter dish, and three different jars of marmalade. As Maggie surveyed the tabletop she noticed for the first time that there were four places set.

"Is someone joining us for breakfast?" she asked her aunt who was just walking in with a basket of rolls.

"Aye," was the answer as the rolls descended onto the table near the butter dish. "Mr. Grant. He's the manager of our store. He usually breakfasts with us Monday mornings so he and Alex can go over the books and such. He's a good man. We're lucky to have him."

"Is there anything I can do to help?" Maggie offered.

"Oh, no. Just stay seated, dear. Breakfast is ready. I'll just bring it out. Alex will help me." She looked at the small wooden clock on a table near the window. "Mr. Grant should be here any minute now."

Aunt Lucy disappeared for a moment then returned with two platters of food and Uncle Alex in tow with two more. Soon they were all seated and Lucy offered Maggie a platter of oatcakes.

Taking one, Maggie asked, "Should we wait for Mr. Grant?"

She wasn't sure what the etiquette was at this point, but did not want to experience the wrath of a hungry old Scottish store manager, should he take offense at their having started without him.

"Nae, go ahead and eat, lass," Uncle Alex exhorted. "The man will be along soon enough. He can't expect others to go hungry waiting for him."

This settled, Maggie took a generous bite of one of the oatcakes. Looking desperately for the marmalade, her thoughts on the epicurean value of oatcakes were cut short by the sound of the doorbell.

Alex rose from his chair. "That'll be Iain," he said simply and disappeared toward the front door.

Readying herself to meet another local, Maggie sat up straight and brushed the crumbs off her chin. She wondered absently whether Mr. Grant also had wisps of gray in his hair like her Uncle Alex. Looking up as the two men entered the room, the answer was definitely no.

Iain Grant was no more than thirty. He stood a good bit over six feet tall and his body hung loosely, but pleasantly, from broad shoulders. Also hanging from his shoulders was a thick black wool sweater. His hands were in the pockets of his tan pants, which extended down his long legs to his large black European shoes, and a newspaper was tucked under one arm. His sweater accented his thick black hair, which fell lightly over his bright blue eyes despite obvious efforts to comb it back from his strong, clean-shaven face.

"Iain Grant," Alex waved toward Maggie. "Our niece from the States, Maggie Devereaux."

Iain Grant flashed a disarming smile. "A pleasure to meet you, miss." His soft Scottish brogue hung magnificently on the 'r' in 'pleasure.'

"Yes, it is," Maggie replied to the blue eyes.

Iain raised an eyebrow. Alex smiled.

"I mean," Maggie corrected, slightly embarrassed, "it's nice to meet you, too."

"Well, come now lad," Alex laid a hand on Iain's wide back. "Sit yourself down and have your breakfast. I'll get you some coffee from the kitchen."

"Sit yourself, Alex," Lucy said, rising. "I need to fetch more marmalade anyway," and before Alex could argue, Lucy had slipped past both men, adroitly snatching Iain's coffee cup on the way. Alex' "Thanks, love" followed after her toward the kitchen.

Iain pulled his chair out and sat down opposite Maggie. They each smiled again, and then uncertain what else to do, Iain pulled the morning paper out from under his arm.

"So, have you seen the news then?"

"What's that?" Alex was spreading marmalade across an oatcake. *Smart man*, thought Maggie.

"About that poor girl."

Alex didn't say anything.

"What girl?" Maggie asked.

"Come now, lad," Alex started, "that's hardly—"

"I know," Iain apologized only half-heartedly. "But you have to admit it's a bit unusual to have a murder like that right at the college. And so sensational. The state the police found her body in—all cut up like it was Jack the Ripper who'd done it."

Maggie's eyes widened at the story. She noticed Aunt Lucy standing in the doorway, more marmalade in one hand, coffee in the other, and a look of horror on her face. A glance at Alex revealed him to be staring intently at his eggs, his face contorted into a grimace, like a patient in a dentist's waiting room trying to ignore the sound of the drill within.

Iain looked at Maggie. "It's not the sort of thing one expects in Aberdeen, is it? And her being all sliced up like that. Obviously the work of some madman. I mean, that's the sort of thing one might expect in America, right, Maggie? But not Aberdeen."

Maggie just grunted noncommittally as she watched over Iain's shoulder as her aunt's face flushed.

Iain turned back to Alex, "And what was she doing out alone at that hour anyw—"

"Iain Grant!" Aunt Lucy's voice cleaved the room.

Iain turned straight around to face Lucy. Alex dropped his fork on his plate a bit too loudly and sat up in his chair, but he said nothing.

"You'll not talk of that poor girl like that in this house!" Lucy's face was entirely red now and coffee spilled onto the saucer held by her visibly shaking hand. She looked urgently at her husband. "Alex?"

Alex MacTary nodded his head slowly as he dabbed his mouth with his napkin. "She's right, lad. Mustn't speak ill of the dead."

Iain's face showed his mortification at having offended his employers, albeit inadvertently. For her part, Lucy seemed more upset now with Alex' half-hearted admonishment than at what Iain had said.

"Come along, lad," Uncle Alex added quietly as he stood from his seat. "It's time to head in to the store anyway. Breakfast is over."

The clock on the table confirmed that it was nowhere near time to head in to the store. However, despite Alex' half-full plate and Iain's never-filled plate, the two men walked out to the foyer, and in the amount of time it would take two men to grab their coats and keys, Maggie and her aunt heard the front door slam shut. The episode having thus ended, Aunt Lucy seemed to regain herself. She crossed to the table uncertainly, the flush draining from her face, leaving it blotchy and tired-looking. Maggie sat quietly, not wanting to be the first to say something.

Aunt Lucy set the coffee and the marmalade on the table with two clacks.

"Forgive me," she said as she slumped into a chair. "It's just—" She shook her head.

"It's all right, Aunt Lucy," Maggie tried to reassure her. "Iain probably shouldn't have been talking about it." Although Maggie wasn't sure it really warranted such a harsh reaction.

"No. No, it's not all right. Iain's a good man. It's just— I mean—" She stopped and took a deep breath. "No matter what she'd done, she didn't deserve to die like that." Then with conviction, she added, "*No one* deserves to die like that."

Maggie agreed earnestly, although she knew nothing of the murder beyond what little Iain's comments had revealed. Aunt Lucy was silent, lost in thought, and Maggie was starting to feel a bit uncomfortable. Suddenly, her aunt reached out and grasped her hand.

"Promise me," she implored. "Promise me you'll be careful. I can't—I couldn't stand to lose kin."

Maggie's eyes widened. It had been a strange morning.

"Sure," she agreed. "I'll be careful."

This having been settled, Aunt Lucy relaxed and the two of them finished a hearty, if sometimes quiet breakfast. What conversation there was danced delicately from subject to subject until it was agreed that once the breakfast dishes were done, Maggie would head into the college for the morning, then meet her aunt and uncle at the shop to go out to lunch together. They agreed to meet at 12 o'clock. Give or take. Maggie had a habit of being five minutes late for everything. Might as well get that out in the open from the start.

* * *

The MacTary's house was southwest of the college by some distance, approximately halfway between the Old Aberdeen campus and the city's modern center. By the time Maggie was ready to head into the campus at nine o'clock, the city's streets were filled with activity. Overcoming Aunt Lucy's initial concerns, Maggie had succeeded in convincing her that she could in fact walk safely to the college. Maggie wanted to see the city and could think of no better way than a pleasant stroll from the nice residential neighborhood to the campus. The MacTary's woolens store was also within walking distance of the college and so it would be no problem meeting them for lunch at noon.

The walk proved interesting enough, as Maggie took in the sights and sounds of residential North Aberdeen. Rows of townhomes began to give way to shops as she approached the college. A cool but pleasant autumn breeze sent leaves scurrying past her feet and tussled her auburn hair playfully. While still several blocks away, Maggie could see the unmistakable top of the King's Tower, its stone crown visible over the shorter residences and shops. Seeing this reminded Maggie once again that she was finally really there. She was finally going to spend her year in Aberdeen.

The university actually consisted of three different campuses strewn across the city in a manner not entirely unrelated to its historical development. Farthest away was the modern Medical Institute located quite a distance northwest of the city center. In the heart of the city, down near the waterfront, sat the Marischal College campus. Originally founded as Marischal College in 1593, its enormous gothic stone building—at one time the second largest such building in the world—was later acquired by the University of Aberdeen and came to be used primarily for lectures and concerts.

And approximately two miles due north of the Marischal College, straight up King Street, lay the original Old Aberdeen Campus.

Nestled between King's Street and Bedford Road, with High Street splitting it down the middle, the Old Campus consisted of thirty odd buildings for students pursuing subjects from agriculture to zoology. Located at the center of campus, snaking its long crooked way between High Street and Regent Way was the Taylor Building, home to all of the modern languages, including the Celtic Department, and also the Elphinstone Institute on the Culture of the North of Scotland. Across Regent Way stood Elphinstone Hall, which in turn was connected to the original King's College Building. In this building was housed the university's historic collections, including ancient manuscripts in the original Gaelic and Latin. The King's College building also could boast the university's most recognizable landmark, a large stone crown sitting astride intersecting stone arches at the pinnacle of the King's Tower. The crown Maggie had spied over the building tops as she approached her new school.

As Maggie turned from Bedford Quay to High Street, she got her first good look at the university. The King's Tower stood ahead on the right, followed by rows of gothic architecture which simply looked like a college should look. An irrepressible smile beaming on her face, Maggie crossed High Street and entered onto the Old Campus of the University of Aberdeen.

A directory map stood at the curb and although Maggie had looked at maps of the campus when she had applied several months earlier, she had no recollection of exactly where the Taylor Building was, at least not as it related to her present location. She would also need to know where the University Office was. A brief survey of the board suggested the quickest path lay straight up High Street, with a right turn after the King's Tower. She started on her way, eyes darting happily from interesting architectural feature to ancient tree to students walking past her speaking in that distinct Scottish burr. The other students about that morning didn't seem to be staring at her, confirming that her time spent thumbing through mail order catalogs of average priced British department stores had not been wasted. While she knew she probably still looked like an American, at least her appearance didn't scream it. And her effort to blend in, she assured herself, was an attempt, not to hide her nationality, but rather to show respect for the culture whose ancient languages she would be studying. Really.

The Taylor Building was actually a series of five long halls, connected at their ends in a zig-zag fashion, so that the narrow end of the first structure abutted High Street, then receded to meet the end of another hall which stood parallel to High Street. This pattern was repeated until the fifth and final hall which stood next to the Regent Building, home to the languages center. Maggie stepped from High Street and followed the Taylor Building back toward its end. The University Office was located behind Taylor and Regents, so she was heading in the right direction. As she came around the first corner, however, her eyes were drawn not to the disappointing non-gothic architecture of the halls, but to the blue-and-white tape cordoning off a courtyard which lay between two buildings to her left. Maggie looked around. She could see some activity in the courtyard. She walked over.

The tape blocked entry to a large courtyard tucked between a 'J' shaped building on the left and a shorter, more compact one to the right. Through the other side she could see a parking lot and a road beyond it. The other entrances to the courtyard had also been tied off with the same blue-and-white tape, as had each doorway to the buildings which flanked the grassy field. One such tape came loose of its moorings and flapped in the autumn breeze, coming to a gentle rest on the rubber-soled shoe of Aberdeen Police Inspector Robert Cameron.

The shoe led up to a suit in an unremarkable shade of gray, under which was tucked a rather ugly mustard colored tie, and over which rested a slightly worn tan overcoat. Inspector Cameron's white hair was cut very short so as to minimize the visual effect of his receding hairline which retreated sharply on either side, leaving a small snowy peninsula over the middle of his forehead. However, despite the haircut, whenever he looked down, as he was doing just then to gaze at the police tape wrapping itself around his shin, not only was the receding hairline in full view, but one could also see the bald spot starting on the back of his head.

"Thompson!" he barked.

A slightly built officer sprang from where he had been crouching by some bushes next to the J-shaped Edward Wright Building. "Yessir?"

"Tie this back up," the inspector lifted the ribbon with his foot. "And see that it's done right this time."

"Yessir!" and the young officer was quickly at his task.

Inspector Cameron turned, hands in the pockets of his trench coat, and surveyed the crime scene. On the stone path only a few feet before him chalk outlines marked where the victim had been found near eleven o'clock the night before last. The stones of the pathway were still stained with blood. A lot of it. The students who had found her body while on the way home from whatever it was students did nowadays had assured the police that they had not moved the body an inch. The police had had no difficulty believing that. The victim's body—and body parts—had been arranged meticulously in a pattern whose significance could only be guessed at. When he himself arrived at the scene, only a few minutes after the first constables, the Inspector had been struck at once by both the brutality and the familiarity of the scene.

The young woman's body, or what was left of it, had been laid at an angle across the pathway. Her arms had been placed at her sides and her legs pushed together. Her shirt had been cut away and her pants pushed down, but rather than exposing evidence of sexual abuse, the peeled back garments revealed the open, bloody and all but empty abdominal cavity of the victim. The killer had cut her stomach open like a cereal box, folding the flaps of skin and muscle to either side. Then each and every internal organ, from her lungs to her intestines, had been carefully and skillfully removed. Most of the organs would be found hidden under a nearby bush, all except five of them which lay in a bloody circle around the corpse. About three feet directly below her toes had been a pile of intestines sitting in a pool of blood and waste. To her left, the right as Cameron looked down, had been the stomach, a good five feet from the girl's left wrist. On the other side, the same distance away, a pile of reddish-gray goo the coroner had assured Cameron had once been the girl's bladder stuck evilly to the stone path. And above her head, again three feet or so away, was a combination of organs. Three for one, one might say. Centered directly above the girl's head, on line with the centerline of the prone body, sat the red, deflated remains of the girl's heart, flanked on either side by one of two gray, bloody lungs. Finally, the killer had placed on the bridge of the victim's nose, between two carefully closed eyelids, a single flat stone, approximately two inches wide.

It had taken almost twenty minutes before they had been able to find the rest of the girl's internal organs, hidden in a bloody, gory heap behind some bushes on the other side of the courtyard. The precision and meticulousness of the killer extended also to his desire to leave as few clues as possible to his identity. No murder weapons were anywhere to be found, and every finger-, palm- and footprint had been deliberately smeared into uselessness. The fact that the killer had kept the knife worried Cameron. It suggested he intended to kill again. The fact that the killer had succeeded in obliterating any decent clue as to his identity frightened the Inspector. It suggested he might get his chance. They needed to act quickly to catch this madman.

Cameron looked out over the dozen or so officers scouring the scene for additional clues, some piece of physical evidence which might shed some light on who had done this. And why.

"Warwick!" He yelled out to one of his sergeants. He was careful to pronounce it 'Warrick,' not 'War-wick' as he had done years ago when he had first met the rookie officer. 'It's pronounced "Warrick,"' she had explained, 'like the castle.' She had then launched into a rather long-winded, and utterly uninteresting, soliloquy on the proper pronunciation of the English name.

"Yes, sir." Sgt. Elizabeth Warwick stepped quickly from where she had been crouched inspecting cracks in the stone pathway. She was in her thirties, with soft features and short blond hair; and although she was tall for a woman, she had to tilt her head back significantly to look up at the solid 6'3" frame of Inspector Cameron.

"Tell me what we know so far about our victim's identity," Cameron instructed.

"Right," Warwick responded sharply. Most other officers would have reached for their notepads at this point, but Elizabeth Warwick's mind was a steel trap. No wonder she had made sergeant so quickly. "Name is—Name *was* Annette Graham. Canadian. Visiting student from MacGill University in Montreal. She lived at the Don Street flats up the way."

She pointed through the parking lot toward St. Machar Drive.

"That's all we know so far," she continued. "I've sent Richards over to the University Office to find out more."

"Good." Cameron rubbed his chin. "Cause of death? I mean besides being deprived of every one of her vital organs?"

"Cause of death still undetermined," Warwick frowned slightly. "We still haven't got the official word from Dr. W—"

"Cause of death: strangulation."

Both officers turned to see Dr. Andrew Wood, the coroner, walk up casually.

"Although it was bloody hard to tell," he added. "Here."

The slightly built, 70-year old Dr. Wood, with his light blue sweater and shock of white curls, handed the inspector a manila envelope marked simply, 'Graham, Annette Camille.'

"With all that trauma," he went on, "it was hard to see at first exactly what took her life. But the lacerations to the abdomen are post-mortem. You can tell by the bleeding pattern. Only the wound to the throat occurred while her heart was still beating."

Warwick suppressed a wince. Cameron just listened with no expression, save perhaps fatigue.

"That wound," Dr. Wood continued, "was caused by a rather thick wire—metal most likely, although it could have been nylon, I suppose, or something similar. The wire cut rather deeply into the outer layers of flesh, but not as quickly as a thinner wire would have done. Her hands had blood smeared on them, although I suspect it was her own blood. Most likely she clawed at the wire while she was still conscious."

The three just stared at the chalk markings on the path. After a moment, Inspector Cameron said, "Thanks for bringing this out, Andy. You could've just left it at my office."

"Oh, no trouble," the coroner said as if he'd just dropped off a cake for the local charity bake-sale. "I was on my way to the college anyway. I," he drew himself up importantly, "am a lecturer at the medical school. I need to speak with administration regarding the schedule. They've put my lectures on Wednesday evenings. That simply won't do. It conflicts," he explained earnestly, "with my jazz band rehearsals."

Warwick looked up at Cameron, but he had not reacted to Dr. Wood's conundrum.

"Good to see you, Andy," was all he said.

"Good to see you, too, Robert. Elizabeth." He nodded to Warwick, then turned and departed.

Cameron looked down at the manila envelope, then handed it to Warwick. "Add this to the file, Sergeant."

The inspector extracted his pipe from his coat pocket and began fishing for something else, presumably his lighter, in the other. "Now we need to find out more about our victim. Have we searched her flat yet?"

"Sergeant Willis took some officers over there just this morning," was Warwick's reply.

"Willis," the word oozed from the inspector's lips like poison.

He found his lighter and lit his pipe.

"Sergeant," he said, exhaling the first breath of sweet-smelling pipe smoke.

"Yes, sir?"

"Why don't you head over to the victim's flat? Check up on Willis." He smacked contemplatively on his pipestem. "I just don't trust that man sometimes."

Warwick's expression didn't change.

"Nice enough fellow," Cameron went on. "Just incompetent."

"Yes, sir," and she turned on her heels and headed directly toward the Don Street flats to the north.

Inspector Cameron watched the sergeant turn the corner around the Edward Wright building, and then let his thoughts return to the murder. He considered the positioning of the organs around young Annette Graham's body, then gazed down again at the white markings on the path and hoped to God he was wrong.

6. Friendly People

The registrar's office was located on the second floor of the University Office building, a modern structure with a distinctive entryway that reminded Maggie of both the Parthenon and a bus shelter. Her first order of business was to make sure that she was properly enrolled in the university. Heading inside, she quickly found the office and in no time was being told that she couldn't study there.

"I'm sorry. We're not expecting any more visiting scholars this semester," the remarkably average-looking, middle-aged woman behind the counter was saying. "I'm afraid you'll have to reapply next semester."

"But I'm *already* enrolled." Maggie cursed herself for having left her acceptance letter at the MacTary's.

"I really don't think so, miss," the bureaucrat said politely. "We don't have a file on you." It did not escape Maggie's notice that the woman had not actually looked for any file.

Maggie exhaled audibly. "Will you *please* just check the enrollment list for the Celtic Department?"

The woman didn't move at all, but instead just raised a

suspicious eyebrow. "What did you say was the name of the grant you claim you received?"

Maggie closed her eyes. This would likely not help matters. "The Ladies Albannach," she said through clenched teeth, "but—"

"No. I'm afraid I've never heard of them." The woman crossed her arms as if that were that. "Sorry."

Maggie was trying not to lose her temper. "Look," she started, leaning onto the counter and into the woman's comfort zone. "My name is Margaret Devereaux. I am a visiting student from the United States. I have already been accepted into post-graduate study in the Celtic Department. I am not here to get your approval. I am here to do nothing more than to confirm that you are aware of my presence on campus, and to find out whom I should contact in the Celtic Department to make arrangements for my studies."

The woman opened her mouth to respond, but Maggie cut her off.

"Check the enrollment list. Please."

After another moment's hesitation, the woman shrugged, said something under her breath, then turned and disappeared into a maze of wooden file cabinets. After a minute or so, she returned with a few sheets of paper and a file in her hand.

"Yes. Well. It appears," she stammered, "that you are correct, miss." She sounded almost disappointed. "You are enrolled in the Department of Celtic. And apparently we do have a file on you, although I usually create all the files and I don't recall seeing your name before."

The woman smiled weakly at Maggie. "In any event, you are classified as a post-graduate visiting scholar. As such, you are not eligible to receive credit for any undergraduate classes. Essentially you are expected to do your own research and you can audit any courses you feel might be relevant, after you obtain permission from the instructor, of course."

"Of course," Maggie replied dryly. "Does it indicate there who my faculty advisor will be or do I need to go over to the department to find that out?"

"Let me see," the woman opened the file she had sworn didn't exist. "Yes, right here. Professor Craig Macintyre. With a small 'i.' Oh, he's a very nice man."

Maggie thought the woman might be blushing.

"He's one of our newest—and youngest—professors," the woman continued. "Studied at Oxford, I think. Or Cambridge. Or some such. In any event, he's quite a charming young fellow. You'll like him."

"I'm sure."

"Oh, but you should head over to his office right now. It's in the Taylor Building. Do you know where that is?"

Maggie nodded.

"Good. If I didn't know you were enrolled, he might not know either. Yes, he should be in his office right now. I believe he's back from the Continent by now."

Maggie thanked the woman out of habit and left to go visit the charming young Prof. Craig Macintyre of the Department of Celtic. As she doubled back toward Taylor, passing the sadly modern boxiness of the Regent Building, she looked to her left to see the gothic splendor of Elphinstone Hall and the King's Tower behind it. She would have to check that out next.

Maggie pushed open the door to the Taylor Building and stepped inside. Taylor housed all of the professors and classrooms for all of the modern language departments. She was not thrilled at the idea of knocking on each office door in turn and so set out first to find a directory. In short order she found herself standing in front of a black reader board which detailed, in white plastic letters, the location of each professor's office. Under the heading 'Mac,' which preceded 'M,' she quickly found the entry: 'MAC NTYRE CRA G 213.'

As she searched for the stairs, Maggie wondered whether the 'I' in 'Macintyre' had not perhaps followed its brother from the forename off on some whimsical reader-board letter adventure. Arriving quickly, if not a little out of breath, on the *third* floor by American standards, Maggie set out to find room 213. Her scan of the room numbers painted in black numerals on the wooden doors led her to turn down a hallway marked with an arrow and the words, 'ROOMS 205-220.' As she passed 207, 209 and drew even with 211, she could hear voices coming out of the office ahead of her. Not just voices—an argument. Not sure what to do, she took a tentative step toward 213. The door was ajar. A quick glance confirmed no one else was in the hallway that Monday morning.

"—n't you threaten me!" a woman was yelling. Maggie instantly recognized the distinctive accent. Southern. The woman, whoever she was, was an American. "I'll go to the police with what I know!"

"You bloody well won't!" roared back the man's voice, a light Scottish burr rolling over each word. "If you know what's good for you!"

This threat was followed by a loud crash of something breakable and a high-pitched but unintelligible response from the woman.

Uncertain what to do, Maggie just stood frozen in the hallway. Maybe she should come back later? Her thoughts were scattered however by the very sudden and very unexpected impact of the woman who had just run out of 213. Maggie was sent reeling backwards, off balance and thoroughly embarrassed. She managed to keep herself from falling, albeit just barely, and looked up at the woman who was picking herself up off the floor. She was about Maggie's age, maybe a year or two older, with long thick banana-yellow hair ending halfway down her back. She seemed to have a pretty face, although Maggie thought it was hidden behind rather a lot of make-up. Her clothes were stylish and looked expensive, especially her shoes.

"Gosh, sorry about that," Maggie said in her own obviously American accent. "Guess you didn't see me standing there."

The blond woman ignored her while she fixed her attire.

"Um, my name's Maggie Devereaux," she extended her hand.

The woman, apparently satisfied with her appearance, looked at Maggie's hand, winced, and walked past her without a word.

Nice, Maggie thought, lowering her hand again.

Then from inside 213 she heard the Scottish voice again. "Get back here! Who the bloody hell do you think you are anyway?!" He finished this last sentence just as he emerged into the hallway to find, to his complete surprise, this pretty young brunette he had never seen before.

"Maggie Devereaux," she replied to his question with a smile. Then, cocking her head to one side, "Professor Macintyre, I presume?"

* * *

"Not that I wouldn't relish the opportunity to look over you," Craig Macintyre was saying from behind the officious little nameplate on his desk, his eyes resting somewhere well below Maggie's face, "but I've already more than enough to do. Besides, I was never notified of having to supervise another student."

The woman at the registrar's office had been right. Craig

Macintyre was young. As he sat before Maggie, leaning back in his leather desk chair in his cramped little university professor office, bookshelves bulging behind him, he could not have been more that 35, 37 at the oldest. His straight brown hair fell stylishly over his clean-shaven baby-face. And although dressed in typical professorial wools and tweeds, he looked more the fashion model than the absent-minded academic. Still, something about him had rubbed Maggie the wrong way immediately. It might have been the argument she had overheard. It might have been his wandering gaze. Or it might just have been her aggravation at the fact that everyone at the entire college seemed to be ignorant of her presence. In any case, assuming she won the impending argument, she would only succeed in securing Prof. Macintyre as her advisor. It would probably not be prudent to start off their relationship by throttling him.

"I'm sure if you check your records again—"

"No. No good, lass," he interrupted. "I was never notified and they can't expect me to just drop everything to supervise yet another student."

"You know, I had the same problem with the registr—"

"I mean, what am I? The expert on North American schoolgirls?"

Maggie's eyes narrowed. She had ceased being a girl some time ago. As she looked away from Macintyre's face, which continued to complain about the injustice of a professor being forced to actually teach students, Maggie's gaze landed on a letter sticking out from under some other papers in an overly full 'IN' box on the desk. The words 'Margaret C. Devereaux' jumped out at her from the stationery.

Laying her finger on the University of Aberdeen crest on the letterhead, she asked sweetly, "What's this?"

Macintyre stopped his soliloquy long enough to make a noise of surprise in the back of his throat and look at the letter. He pulled it out from under the pile and read it quickly. Maggie couldn't read the words from where she was sitting, but she did notice that it had once been folded in thirds, suggesting it had been mailed—and opened. She also noticed a small brown ringed coffee stain on one corner of the document.

"Mmphm," Macintyre grunted, not looking up. "I guess I spoke too soon. It appears I was given notice of your arrival."

He pushed the letter back down the desk roughly. "Damned if I remember ever reading that," he said, as if to himself. "Well, then, I suppose I've had a lot on my mind. I've just returned this morning from the Continent. Amsterdam. Promoting my new article." He smiled.

Unimpressed, Maggie nodded and glanced down at the letter. She wondered if it was from the same woman who had earlier that morning told her she couldn't study there. It was unsigned.

"But damn it all!" Maggie's thoughts were interrupted by Macintyre's hand slapping down on the desktop as he shot up from his chair. "How the bloody hell am I supposed to supervise yet another American student on her year abroad in Scotland?"

He was clearly not really talking to her, but she didn't like being ignored either.

"I've got my own bleeding research to do and I can hardly get that done if I'm expected to hold the hands of now three schoolgirls."

Again with the schoolgirls, she thought. *This is not going well.*

"First, it was just Kelly. But then they added Annette—" He stopped. His face went ashen and he turned to look at Maggie. "Oh. That's right." He retook his seat. "I'd forgotten about Annette."

Maggie looked at the professor blankly.

"Terrible business, that," he continued solemnly. Then a half-smile returned to his face. "Oh well. I suppose that opens a position for you. Lucky you."

"Lucky me," she repeated back as if to convince herself. She really didn't like this guy.

"So what will you be studying then, Miss, ah," he looked down at the letter, "Devereaux?"

"Well, in my grant proposal," she started, thinking that he ought to have read that too since it had been included in her application materials to the university, "I mentioned the article Professor Robert Hamilton published last year about—"

"Hamilton?" Macintyre interrupted. "Isn't he at Edinburgh?"

"Er, yes." Maggie understood the question behind the question, namely 'Why aren't you studying at Edinburgh?' She decided not to answer that one. She expected that Prof. Macintyre had neither the time nor the desire to hear about her familial connections to the area and the other influences which had conspired to bring her to the Highlands. She sufficed it to say, "But the Elphinstone Institute is here."

Macintyre nodded. He apparently accepted this explanation.

"In any event," she continued, "Professor Hamilton published an article last year which theorized the existence of a lost dialect of Old Gaelic—one used primarily in religious ceremonies. He had found some references—"

"Right," Macintyre interrupted again. "I think I remember reading that. So much rot, I thought. Load of rubbish, really."

Oh great. Who assigned me to this guy?

"I mean," he continued, more to himself than to Maggie. "What an utterly cheap way to be published. Theorize something the existence of which can never be proved or disproved. If no one ever actually confirms the existence of it, well that's just because it's old and mysterious," he wiggled his fingers in front of his lowered face. "But if by some miracle someone actually finds something even closely related, well then you can claim credit for everyone else's hard work."

Maggie said nothing, uncertain how to respond.

"Of course," he added, "that's how it works in the academic publishing world. I should give him credit for the idea really. Maybe I'll publish something next year claiming that both Gaelic and—oh I don't know, French—are descended from an ancient dialect of Martian. I bet I could find some pathetic little publishing house to print that, eh?"

He had at last returned his attention to Maggie.

"Sure," she replied blandly. *Time to go.*

"So what is it you'd like to do with Prof. Robert Hamilton?" He raised an indecent eyebrow.

Ignoring this, she replied simply, "I'm not sure yet, but I found the article interesting."

She elected not to tell him that her intent was to confirm the existence of the dialect. She expected he would only have laughed.

"Nice to have met you, Professor Macintyre." She stood up and offered her hand to shake.

"Charmed, Margaret," he said, taking her hand. Then, not releasing it quite soon enough, he added, "Call me Craig."

"Sure, Professor Macintyre." She extracted her hand and walked out of the office. She could feel his stare on her back and once in the hallway she shuddered slightly in an effort to shake it off.

She quickly descended the stairs, thankful that she would be conducting her research largely independently. As she approached the door to outside, another student entered into the building, thereby inadvertently blocking Maggie's path. Maggie stepped to her right, just as the other woman stepped to her own left, mirroring Maggie's move. Then, as if on cue, both women stepped in the other direction, again blocking each other's path. As they tentatively leaned in varying directions, both women laughed.

"Care to dance?" Maggie quipped.

The embarrassed grin of the other woman blossomed into full smile at the sound of Maggie's voice. Large, strong teeth beamed at Maggie beneath blue eyes and curly straw-colored hair.

"Are you an American?" the woman asked, her own Scottish accent unmistakable.

"Er, yes," Maggie replied. "My name's Maggie. Maggie Devereaux."

"Delighted to meet you, Maggie," the woman beamed. "I'm Ellen." Maggie smiled at the name. "Ellen Walker. Are you studying here this semester, then?"

"Yes. I'm studying here in the Celtic Department. Old Gaelic dialects and such."

"Oh, brilliant!" Ellen exclaimed. "I'm in the comparative literature program. Working on my doctoral thesis. I'm focusing on Middle Gaelic and Middle French, comparing similarities in oral narration during the twelfth century."

"Wow, that sounds interesting," Maggie said earnestly. "I don't know as much Middle French as I should—only those words that worked their way into Middle English, or are just like the Latin."

It was nice to talk shop.

"Well, then, I'll have to teach you sometime," Ellen offered. "Are you here just for a semester then?"

"No," Maggie replied. "The whole year. Then I'll see where my research is at. I'll probably head back to finish up my degree, although I suppose I could stay here, too." Her inheritance had given her far more flexibility in her future plans.

"Brilliant!" Ellen enthused. "It really is wonderful to have international students here at the college. Just makes it so much more well rounded, eh? The university's made a real commitment to it."

Then Ellen looked at her watch. "Oh dear, look at the time. I'm late for my seminar. I better run." She frowned at Maggie. "Are you living here on campus then, Maggie?"

"Eh, no. I'm staying with my aunt and uncle, not too far away from campus."

"Oh? You've got Scottish blood, do you? It's always hard to tell with Americans. 'Devereaux' hardly sounds Scottish. Well, look, we should get together sometime. I know how difficult it is to get used to a new country. Say," she paused. "Are you free tonight?"

Maggie had assumed she would be spending the evening with her aunt and uncle, but she supposed there was no reason why she had to. "I think so."

"Splendid. Look, do you know where 'The Boar and Thistle' is?"

"Erm, no. 'Fraid not. Is that a pub?" It sounded like a pub.

"Aye. Right over on University Road, just off High Street. You can't really miss it. Anyway, I'm meeting a couple of friends—other students—for a pint and some dinner around six tonight. Why don't you join us? Everyone's very friendly, one of the girls is even an American, so you two should hit it right off. What do you say?"

What should *I say?* thought Maggie. She had just met this woman. For whatever reason her initial reaction was to decline the offer politely and maybe she'd run into her some time again. But then she thought, *I came here to meet people and experience the culture, too. Not just to sit in a library and read musty old books. I can do that at home. What the hell. Why not?*

"Sure. I'd love to come. Six o'clock, did you say?"

"Right. Six o'clock. But I won't hold it against you if you're late." Again Ellen flashed a toothy grin. "But I really must be off now. See you tonight, Maggie Devereaux."

"See you tonight, Ellen," and Ellen's back disappeared up the stairwell.

Well, Maggie thought as she emerged from Taylor into the warm autumn mid-morning, *she was certainly friendly. I think I'm going to like Scotland.*

Looking down at her watch, Maggie could see that it was ten minutes after eleven already. Too soon to head straight for the MacTary's store, but too late to really do anything else of substance. She looked across at Elphinstone Hall, its gothic turrets rising to the cloud patched sky. Just enough time to scope out the area, she decided.

Her leisurely gait took her around Elphinstone Hall, to where it connected to another, smaller gothic building tucked away between Elphinstone and the King's College building. As she walked by the outside of this smaller hall, she noticed the plaque on the wall beside the door. Among other useful information stood the words:

'HISTORIC COLLECTIONS. MANUSCRIPTS AND ARCHIVES.'

Maggie smiled broadly. Just enough time to poke her head in and see what it looked like. Maybe she could even get her library card before lunch. She turned from the path and pulled open the door.

Inside she was greeted by the delightful sight of full bookshelf after full bookshelf, all resting confidently beneath the vaulted stone ceiling of the reading room. Long wooden tables filled the stone-floored hall and the walls were filled with beautiful stained glass portraits of people whose significance Maggie could only guess at. The light from the glass fell across the room in a gentle rainbow, careful not to disturb the dozens of students who were camped out studying. To her immediate left was a desk, staffed by two gray-haired ladies standing under a sign that read, 'INFORMATION.'

"Hello," Maggie said to one of the women. Maggie couldn't suppress her smile.

"May I help you, miss?" The heavier of the two women stepped forward, her black-framed glasses set firmly on the bridge of her nose.

"Yes, I'm a new student here. A visiting student, actually. From the United States."

The woman smiled politely. She had already noticed the accent, of course.

"I'll be studying Gaelic," Maggie continued. "Both modern and old. Do you have any resources which would be particularly useful? I noticed the sign outside said 'Historic Collections?'"

The librarian's face showed surprise. Maggie knew that Americans were not generally known for their foreign language skills. Of course, someone from Seattle would have to travel some two thousand miles before she got to anyplace where English wasn't the day-to-day language. However, the old woman's face also showed approval.

"Gaelic, then?" she confirmed. "Yes, of course, miss. As far as modern Gaelic, the university actually has one of the largest collections of Scottish Gaelic literature in the world. We also boast a rather healthy selection of Irish Gaelic literature as well. And of course, linguistic reference materials—grammars and the like—are also kept by the library. Most of that is housed at the Queen Mother

Library across campus."

Maggie nodded.

"As far as Old Gaelic—or 'Old Irish' or whatever you like to call it—we have a large collection of historic texts and documents right here in the Historic Collections. We also have several particularly old volumes in an ancient book collection which is housed in the subbasement."

Maggie's head jerked back, her eyes wide with academic excitement. "Ancient book collection?" she repeated.

"Aye, miss," the woman was clearly pleased by the reaction, but then added, "although it's of little use unless one happens to know Middle or Old Gaelic. Or at least Scots."

"How," Maggie began, trying to suppress her excitement, "do I go about looking at the collection? I assume it's not open to the general public?"

"Right enough," the librarian nodded officially. "Although anyone who really wanted to see it would be allowed to do. But we do keep the door to the subbasement locked. Only faculty and doctoral students—and the library staff, of course—may have a key. They may check out any items they wish, except for a few of the books which are simply too old and too fragile to be removed."

"I'm a doctoral student," Maggie enthused. "Would I be able to get a key if I could show some proof of that?"

"Well, let's see," said the woman pulling a large register from a shelf under the counter. "What's your name, love?"

"Er, Margaret Devereaux, but—"

"Are you already enrolled this semester?"

"I'm supposed to be—"

"And you said you're a doctoral student?"

"Yes."

"What department?"

"Celtic."

"Of course. Celtic." She slid a finger down the handwritten entries of the book. "Yes, here you are. Studying under Prof. Macintyre, correct?"

"Er, right." Maggie was stunned. Obviously this woman should be running the university.

"Yes, we have you right here. Would you like to sign out your key now?"

A smile unfolded across Maggie's face.

"Absolutely," she replied, and inside of three minutes she had provided proof of her identity, signed the check-out card, and looked down in her hand to see the key to the library's ancient book collection.

"Is there anything else I can help you with?" the librarian asked with a friendly smile.

Maggie did have one more question.

"What are the library hours?"

"Ah, good question. The reading room is open Monday through Friday from 9:30 until 4:30. We ask you to sign the register," she pointed at a book on the counter near the door, "on each visit. And of course there are certain simple rules we ask you to follow for the preservation of the books. The subbasement is available any time the reading room is open."

"It closes at 4:30?" That seemed a bit early.

"Aye. The Queen Mother Library has longer hours."

"But no ancient book collection?"

"But no ancient book collection," the librarian smiled. "But it's just as well. The sun sets rather early here in the winter. And it's best not to be out after dark. Especially—"

She stopped.

"Especially what?" Maggie asked.

"Well, it's just—" The woman was clearly debating whether to give voice to her thoughts. "Well, that awful business Saturday night. Ghastly. And right here on campus, too. That poor girl."

Maggie nodded as sympathetically as she could.

"It's just terrible." The librarian leaned forward and lowered her voice. "I read what they did to her body—all cut up like that. They say it's devil-worshippers. Or worse. So don't you be staying out late studying and walking home alone. It gets dark quickly here. Either get home while it's still light out or have a companion to walk you home. At least until the police catch whoever did it."

Maggie nodded again. "Thanks for the advice. And the key. And don't worry, I'll be careful. I'm sure the police are hard at work right now trying to catch her killer."

The librarian regained herself a bit and stood up straight.

"I'm sure you're right," she agreed.

7. Hard at Work

"The lass sure liked 'er lacy panties, eh?" Officer MacGregor pulled a black thong from the top drawer of the late Annette Graham's dresser. "I wish I could get me wife to wear things like this."

"Don't worry, lad," came the shouted reply of another officer. "She wears 'em for me often enough!"

"All right!" Sgt. Michael Willis interjected over the hooting and laughter of his patrolmen. "Have some respect for the dead. We're here to look for clues to her murder, not rifle through her unmentionables."

The word 'unmentionables' caused even greater laughter. Until Sgt. Warwick entered the flat.

"Where's Sgt. Willis?" she demanded of the officer nearest the door.

"In the bathroom," was the reply. Then, as Warwick shot a glance back at him, he added, "Sergeant."

"Warwick, is that you?" Willis stepped out from the bathroom, the end of his sleeve wet and dripping. Looking around Willis and into the bathroom, Warwick could see the lid to the toilet tank had been removed and set precipitously on the edge of the bathtub. She decided not to ask.

"Find anything yet?" Warwick inquired instead.

"Nothing worth reporting." Willis shot a glance at MacGregor in the bedroom. "Although," he added, leading her back into the living room, "the drawers to the desk are locked. There might be something in there, do you think? But I didn't know if we needed a warrant."

Sgt. Warwick looked expressionlessly at Willis. He really was a nice enough fellow, just not the sharpest knife in the drawer.

"She's dead, Willis," Warwick explained. "I hardly think she'll file a citizen's complaint with the local magistrate."

Warwick tilted her head and examined the writing desk critically. It was wooden, but most likely wood veneer over particle board, not solid wood. There was a thin top drawer centered just under the desktop and to either side was one slightly larger drawer. Each had a metal lock embedded just above the handle. Warwick grabbed the top drawer and gave it a respectable but controlled tug. The entire desk jerked lightly forward, confirming it was not solid wood, but the drawer remained steadfast. Looking around she caught glimpse of MacGregor's 6'1", 240 pound frame.

"Officer MacGregor." MacGregor looked at the sergeant to confirm it was he she meant. "Come over here and give us a hand."

As he stepped into the front room, Warwick asked, "Can you open the top drawer? It's locked."

MacGregor looked at the desk, then at the tall but slight figure of Sgt. Warwick. "What's the matter, Sergeant? Can't you open it yourself?"

Warwick could hear the chorus of gasps and stifled laughter behind her. Willis' face went white.

"MacGregor—" Willis started, but a sharp wave of

Warwick's hand stopped him. She locked eyes with MacGregor for a moment, then resolutely crossed to the kitchen, where she pulled from a wooden block a 10"-long butcher knife. Then, holding the knife at her hip, point up, she returned just as quickly to her previous position next to the desk. Without warning, she thrust the knife forward—causing MacGregor to jump back startled—and plunged the blade three inches deep between the desk top and the top of the center drawer. Pulling the knife handle firmly up, the metal lock was forced through the flimsy pressed board of the desktop. The drawer popped open.

Warwick pulled the drawer the rest of the way open and handed the bent knife to MacGregor without looking at him. "Put this back, Eric," she commanded, "or consider yourself on report for disobeying the order of a superior."

MacGregor looked around sheepishly, then took the knife and shrugged over to the kitchen to the friendly jeers of his compatriots.

"Get back to work, you lot!" Willis tried to sound forceful, but his men just looked at each other and shook their heads before returning to their tasks of their own accord.

"Look here." Warwick's words pulled Willis' attention back from his disrespectful patrolmen. In the top drawer were several sheets of stationery, both thin blue airmail paper and standard-weight white, some envelopes and stamps, a journal, various ballpoint pens, and an old photograph. On top of the stack of standard stationery was a half-written letter. Warwick pulled the letter out to examine it as Willis picked up the photograph for a closer look.

"What does the letter say?" Willis inquired. He turned the photograph over, looking in vain for some identifying inscription.

"It's only half-finished," explained Warwick, her forehead

creased in contemplation. "It's a rough draft by the looks of it. It says: 'Dear 'Mother''—the word 'mother' is in quotations—'Dear "Mother," While still pained by the vast distance which once separated us, my anguish has been alleviated in some small part by your wise decision to own up to your obligations of years past.'"

"Then the next paragraph starts, 'Unfortunately' but then the word 'unfortunately' has been crossed out, replaced with 'However, as you can well imagine, the cost of child support rises with each passing day and I am unable to extend my generous offer of previous letters. Although I understand this may present some hardship for you and your husband, it will pale, I dare say, in comparison to what might befall your reputation and status should—"

"Should what?" Willis inquired, the photograph still clasped between thumb and forefinger.

"Well, she's crossed a bit out. Looks like she wrote, 'should I be forced to,' then crossed it out and wrote, 'should our family secret see daylight.' Then the rest of the letter is 'I therefore must require—" and then it stops and she's written, 'Cold Blood' seven times down the remainder of the page."

"Hmm," Willis said.

"Damn odd, that," Warwick said, only half to Willis.

"Sure is," Willis agreed immediately. Then, after a few moments, he asked, "What is?"

"Several things," Warwick replied. "First off, this Annette Graham girl was Canadian, right?"

"Sure." Willis' tone betrayed his ignorance.

Warwick looked at her colleague impatiently. "She was. She was studying at MacGill University in Montreal. But this letter is written on regular stationery, not the airmail sheets she also had. And the only stamps in the drawer are for domestic postage."

Willis looked in the drawer to confirm this observation.

"And the business about 'mother' in quotation marks. And she wrote 'you and your husband.'"

Willis craned his neck to look at the letter. "So what?"

"What do you call your mother's husband?"

Willis pursed his lips and looked to the ground, his chin supported by his fist. After a moment he looked up and replied, "'Dad.'"

"Mm-hmm," Warwick confirmed, then she picked up the journal.

"What's it say?" Willis asked.

"I'm not sure," Warwick had to admit. "It's all in French." Her two years of secondary school French enabled her to do no more than recognize the language. "But this is interesting."

"What then?" Willis tried to see into the journal.

Warwick held it over for him to see. "Every page she's written on has the initials 'S.F.' scrawled on it somewhere." She flipped ahead until the pages turned blank again. "Every one."

"Who's S.F.?" Willis asked.

Warwick shut her eyes to keep from rolling them. "Well, that's the question, isn't it?"

She thought for several moment, checking off possibilities. Then she stated more than asked, "That photograph—It's of two young women, taken probably twenty-five years ago?"

Willis looked down at the photograph in his hand. "Dead on!" he exclaimed. "But how—?"

Pointing at Willis in a friendly but forceful way, she instructed, "Confirm she was Canadian. Then call and get a copy of her birth certificate. Call the university or the Provincial vital records or the R.C.M.P. for all I care, but get it. Then bring it to me."

With that Sgt. Elizabeth Warwick walked out of the flat. Sgt.

Willis looked after her in sincere admiration, and said more to himself than aloud, "Yes, ma'am."

* * *

The walk from the campus to the MacTary's store had been quite pleasant. The nice weather was holding out and Maggie had taken a route which allowed her to admire some more of the local architecture. She now found herself admiring the wooden sign above her. In the shape of an overly wide shield, it was painted a beautiful red tartan, with white, yellow and light blue lines threaded through it. Atop the tartan, white letters with gold trim boasted 'MACTARY'S WOOLENS—EST. 1897.' As Maggie grabbed onto the door handle she found herself looking squarely at the brass door knocker. It was a clan badge, a boar's head surrounded by a circular strap containing the words 'BE TRAIST.' The badge of the Clan Innes. She grinned at the familiar symbol and pulled the door open.

Upon entering the store, she was impressed by the combination of order and comfort she felt as she surveyed her surroundings. The three walls ahead of her were actually dark wood shelves stuffed floor to ceiling with bolts of fabric. Several tables in the center of the shop held piles of finished products: sweaters, coats, and, of course, kilts. To her right was the counter with its cash register and jars of last minute impulse buys such as miniature bagpiper dolls, tourist maps of Aberdeen, and clan badge refrigerator magnets. Behind the counter, carved out of the shelving, was a door covered by a red tartan curtain. On the front of the counter was a full sized shield, white with three blue stars. Again a symbol of the Clan Innes.

There were several customers in the store. A middle-aged woman with graying hair was thumbing through the sweaters on the table nearest the windows. A young couple was admiring pants folded in the back right corner. And in the back left corner stood Iain Grant, speaking earnestly with a couple who were probably in their late 50s. Judging by their brightly colored windbreakers, white tennis shoes, and the camera slung over the man's shoulder, Maggie guessed they were American tourists. Iain was holding a bolt of green and blue tartan.

"Now, ye say you've Campbell blood in ye?" Iain was speaking with a decidedly heavier accent than he had displayed that morning at breakfast.

"Well, my father's grandmother was named Agnes Campbell," the man replied in a flat, yet nasally voice.

Yup, they're American.

"Then she married Thomas Meckel," the man went on. "And their daughter, Alice Meckel, married my grandfather, Peter Wisniewski."

"Well, then, Mr. Wisniewski," the Scots brogue was getting thicker. "You've a claim tae clanship in th' Clan Campbell, one o' th' greatest an' most powerful clans in Scottish 'istory. Och, I could tell ye legend after legend of th' Clan Campbell. But, if I might say so, sir, it would be a shame fer a grandson of Scotland such as yerself to come all th' way back to th' motherland an' not claim yer bloodright tae wear th' tartan of your ancestors."

The man smiled. "Well..." he started. He was obviously interested, but also not completely ignorant of Iain's salesmanship.

"Oh, go on, Stan," his plump, dark-haired wife twanged out. "Everyone back in Libertyville would think it's so cute!"

Iain just smiled and raised an encouraging eyebrow.

"Well," Stan Wisniewski said as forcefully as he could muster, "we'll think about it." Then he added, "What time do you close?"

"Six o'clock, sir," Iain said, trilling the 'r' in 'sir' for all it was worth. "But we'll glad stay late tae take your measurements fer the kilt. An' the plaid as well, should ye so decide."

"Okay, thank you," and they turned to leave. As the couple passed Maggie on their way to the door she could hear them debating the novelty of an authentic Scottish kilt against the fashion impracticality inherent in kilt ownership. As they closed the door behind them, Iain crossed over to Maggie.

"The Clan Wisniewski?" she asked, arms crossed.

Iain laughed. "Aye, well, 'Devereaux' is hardly a sept of the Stuarts, now is it?"

Maggie narrowed her eyes at this barb. "My mother was a hundred percent Scottish."

"Aye?" Iain asked. "Was she clanned?"

"I think so. 'Ingram.' I think that's clanned. But I can also trace back along her mother to the Clan Innes," she pointed at the shield affixed to the counter.

"Aye, then?" Iain nodded approvingly. "Well, then you truly are come home. MacTary's a sept of Innes as well."

Maggie recalled the clan crest door knocker and considered the heraldic shield. "So I gathered." Then, returning the conversation to its original subject, she said, "But still, selling a kilt to that nice old man? You're quiet the salesman." Her voice gave no clue as to whether this was a compliment.

Iain appeared to take it as one just the same. "Och, no," he protested. "The kilts sell themselves. Either you've Scottish blood or you don't. If you do, why not get a kilt and plaid while you're here? They'll be back after lunch to order the kilt. If we're lucky, they might order a great plaid as well and maybe even a neck-tie."

Just then a large stack of seven or so bolts of fabric came walking through the curtain to Maggie's right. Behind it was Aunt Lucy.

"Let me help you there, Lucy," Iain offered, seeing her teeter her way toward a shelf in the back.

"Nonsense," Lucy shot back. "I've these. You help the customers." She then spotted Maggie from behind a bolt of Harris tweed. "Ah, there you are, lass. Just let me put these away, and we'll be ready in a minute." With that she dropped the bolts on the floor and quickly stacked them onto a half-empty shelf. A moment later she had disappeared again behind the curtain.

"So Lucy works at the shop too, then?" Maggie inquired of Iain.

"Aye, they both own it and they both work it every day. Lucy'd taken the day off to spend with you, but when you decided to nose about the college, she came into work straight away."

As Maggie considered this, Iain made sure the remaining customers did not desire any immediate assistance. Then he returned his attention to Maggie.

"So, how'd you like the college?"

"Oh, it's wonderful," Maggie enthused. "Just what a Scottish college should feel like." Then, recalling her difficulties with the registrar, she added, "And I'm properly enrolled and all that. I'll be doing independent study, not regular class work."

"Independent study?" Iain cocked his head to one side.

"Yeah, I'm here on a fellowship grant. I'm basically working on one big project all year. So I do my own research and meet with one of the professors periodically to check my progress. I can sit in on classes if I think it'll help, but I don't have to."

"So you don't have any classes tomorrow then?"

"No," Maggie replied cautiously. She wondered where this was going.

"Well, then, I was thinking, if you'd like, I know of this really rather good restaurant down on Crown Street. Serves traditional

Scottish fare, but a very nice atmosphere. Would you like to go tonight?"

"Tonight?" she repeated to buy herself a moment to think. *Is he asking me out on a date? It couldn't be. He's just met me. He's just being nice to his employers' niece. That must be it. Besides I've already agreed to dinner with Ellen Walker.* "Sorry. I can't. I've—Well, I've actually already got plans tonight."

Iain's brows arched incredulously at this assertion. Maggie realized how it sounded; she'd only been there one day.

"Oh," he started, but before he could utter another word, or Maggie offer an explanation, Lucy appeared through the curtain with Alex right behind.

"Okay, then, Maggie," she called out. "Are you ready for some authentic Scottish cuisine?"

Looking weakly from Iain to her aunt and uncle, she replied quietly, "Sure."

"Excuse me, sir, could you reach that tweed on the top shelf?" The young couple needed assistance.

"Of course," Iain replied, then bid his employers and their niece *bon appetit*.

Uncle Alex smiled as they stepped out into the street.

"Good man, that Iain," he remarked.

"Aye," agreed Aunt Lucy.

Aye, thought Maggie to herself.

8. Dinner with Friends

Maggie arrived at The Boar and Thistle at five after six.

Fashionably late, she thought as she pulled open the door.

If the outside of the pub had been a bit drab, this was more than made up for by the vibrant scene contained within. A bar against one wall was packed cheek-by-jowl with patrons. Around the remaining walls lay a string of booths, each of which seemed to house at least four people. In between were tables, again each occupied by several people. In a back room, patrons were playing pool and darts, and from where she stood by the entrance Maggie could see three television sets, each showing a different soccer match.

Maggie scanned the crowd for Ellen. She hoped Ellen had seen her enter because she wasn't at all confident that she would be able to locate the friendly Scot among the crowd. As her gaze continued to her left, approaching the booths by the windows, Maggie's eye caught an outstretched hand waving to her from a table just shy of the booths. Connected to the hand was the arm and in turn the face of Ellen Walker.

"Maggie!" Ellen called out over the buzz of activity inside the pub. "Over here!"

Relieved, Maggie walked over to the large round table nearest the wall. Ellen, smile beaming, sat facing the door. To her right sat a raven-haired woman who had looked up to greet Maggie, her encouraging smile peering out from beneath black curls. She was holding the hand of a young man with wavy brown hair and glasses, also smiling and wearing a gray sweater with an open V-neck collar. Next to him, Maggie could see only the long banana-yellow hair of a woman who had not turned around to look at her. Between the blond woman and Ellen were two empty chairs.

"Maggie!" Ellen exclaimed as she reached the table. "I'm so glad you made it!"

Then starting with the black haired woman, Ellen began the introductions. "Maggie, er—Devereaux, right?"

"Right," Maggie confirmed with a smile.

"Maggie Devereaux, this is Fionna FitzSimmons. She's studying comparative literature as well. Celtic and Romance."

"Hello, Maggie," greeted Fionna warmly.

Her accent seemed just a bit different from Ellen's somehow.

Ellen pointed to the man holding Fionna's hand. "And this is Will Hopkins. He's studying medicine."

"Pleased to meet you," he said in a decidedly English accent.

"And this," Ellen indicated the blond woman next to Will, "is Kelly Anderson. She's studying Gaelic too, like you and me, and she's also an American."

The woman had finally turned to look at Maggie, and Maggie immediately recognized her from the hallway outside Macintyre's office.

"We've met already, actually." Maggie grinned as Kelly Anderson looked away again to her drink. "We ran into each other over at the Taylor Building. I believe we're both studying under

Prof. Macintyre?"

Kelly just rolled her eyes and let a short derisive laugh escape her lips.

Given this response, Maggie opted to take the seat next to Ellen, leaving the sixth and empty chair between herself and Kelly.

"So where are you from in the States?" Will pushed his glasses back up his nose as he asked the question. Somehow, Maggie always felt more at ease when someone else besides her was wearing glasses.

"Seattle," Maggie replied, wondering whether anyone other than Kelly would know where that was.

"That's in the so-called Pacific Northwest, isn't it?" Will asked again.

"Yup," Maggie smiled. "Near Portland and Vancouver, Canada."

"Right. It's supposed to be beautiful there," Will observed.

"So what brings you to Aberdeen?" Fionna asked.

"Well," Maggie wished she had a glass of something to fiddle with nervously as she discussed herself. She settled for a cardboard coaster. "I'm getting a Ph.D. in Celtic Literature back in the States. I'm here for a year to do some research on Old Gaelic, like from the tenth century and earlier."

"Gaelic, eh?" Will replied over a sip of his chocolate brown beer. "Why Gaelic? Is there a lot of interest in it in the States?"

"Will," Fionna tugged at his hand. "Don't interrogate the girl."

"No, I'm serious," he insisted. "I mean, Kelly, you're studying it, too, right?"

Kelly gave a barely affirmative grunt and lifted her beer.

"I think it may be a function of where we are, too," Fionna theorized. "Most of the American students you'd meet in Paris are probably studying French."

"Granted," Will set his beer down. "But still, why Scotland? Are you of Scottish descent too?"

"Yes," Maggie replied. "On my mother's side." She decided not to enumerate her entire pedigree, but did add, "I'm actually staying with my aunt and uncle while I'm here. I think they might technically be cousins or something, but 'aunt' and 'uncle' is a lot easier. Anyway they live not too far from campus."

"Hmm. That's interesting." Will picked up the beer again. "Are there a lot of Scots in Seattle then?"

Maggie laughed lightly, recalling the Scandinavian flags which permeated Seattle's neighborhoods, but unable to think of any easily identifiable Scottish district. "I guess there could be. I don't know. There's actually a city called 'Aberdeen' about a hundred miles or so southwest of Seattle, toward the coast, so I suppose there must have been some Scots around at some time. Probably because of the Hudson Bay Trading Company. But I think there are a lot of Americans everywhere who have some Scottish background."

"Is that so?" This thought seemed to intrigue Will Hopkins. "Are there a lot of Scots in North Carolina, Kelly?"

"I guess. Sure," was the unenthusiastic reply.

"Wasn't Thomas Jefferson Scottish?" Ellen decided to join in the conversation.

Kelly didn't seem interested in fielding the question, so Maggie thought for a moment, then answered, "I think I learned in school that he was 'Scots-Irish.'"

"Scots-Irish?" Will echoed, squeezing Fionna's hand and grinning to her.

"Yeah," Maggie started, trying to remember her history lessons and hoping that she would not be conveying inaccurate information to her European friends. "I think that's a term they used in the seventeen-hundreds to describe people who came from Ireland, but were ethnically Scottish. Like from Northern Ireland, I guess."

"I'm familiar with the term," Will replied pleasantly. "In fact Fionna's from Northern Ireland," he explained. Fionna gave a pained smile.

Ah-ha, Maggie thought. *That's where that accent's from.*

Will continued, "She's from a town called Dungiven near—"

"If you say 'Londonderry,' Hopkins, I'll knock your bloody teeth down your bloody throat."

Maggie looked quickly over her left shoulder to see a rather large man looming over the table. His hair was thick and red and he sported a neatly trimmed red beard. He was about their age, maybe a little older, and wore work pants and a shirt which Maggie thought looked like a soccer or rugby jersey. Several tattoos disappeared under the pushed up green and white striped sleeves.

Will met the man's gaze and squeezed Fionna's hand once again. "Derry," he finished.

"Sean!" Fionna lashed out. "Mind your manners! You can leave your bloody nationalism at home. Will was just—" Then Fionna's face twisted up into tired embarrassment. She looked at Maggie and pointed to the man looming over her.

"Maggie, this is my brother, Sean."

Before Maggie could say anything, Sean FitzSimmons had already sat down next to her and taken her hand in his.

"Charmed," he said with a delightful Irish lilt. She half expected him to kiss her hand. Thankfully, he didn't.

"I'm sure," Maggie replied. She considered Iain Grant and Craig Macintyre. Apparently it was her day to be hit on.

"Please allow me to explain my confrontational arrival,"

Sean said directly to Maggie, ignoring the exasperated sounds of his sister. "You see, 'Londonderry' is the name the English colonists tried to hang around the neck of our lovely Irish city of Derry. As if there were actually some historical connection between England and Ireland other than wave after wave of English attempts to conquer our fair island. And so no self-respecting Irishman can stand by while some English bastard demeans our country with imperialistic place names."

"Sean!" Fionna screamed at her brother. "You apologize right now!"

"To whom?" he asked, his English surprisingly accurate.

"To Will!"

"For what?"

"For calling him a bastard."

Sean considered this for a moment, then rejected it. "I didn't call him a bastard," he explained with a cocky smile.

Somehow, Maggie found this exchange highly entertaining. Ellen seemed to as well. Kelly was looking in the general direction of the bar.

"You did too!" Fionna countered. Her white cheeks had turned a deep pink. Will knew better than to get in the middle. "You said he was a bastard for saying 'Londonderry.'"

"What I said," Sean corrected, one hand raised for emphasis, "was that he *would* have been a bastard, *if* he'd said 'Londonderry.' But he didn't. He said, 'Derry.' So I don't think any apology is owing."

Fionna's face grew even redder, but she had no reply. Will actually couldn't help smiling at the turn in the conversation.

"Is that how you remember it, love?" Sean turned to Maggie.

"As I remember it," she replied, "you didn't give him much of a choice. I believe you threatened to knock his teeth out if he chose the bastard option."

Sean laughed. "That I did. But Will there knows I'm only fooling, right, Will?"

Will didn't reply, just smiled again coolly.

"Just as well not to say 'Londonderry' though, eh?" Sean went on.

"If I say 'Derry,'" Will responded in his best English accent, "it's out of respect for Fionna, not out of fear of you."

Sean just smiled and looked away.

"Now, if you'll excuse me, ladies," Will stood up. "I really should be going."

"What?" Fionna was obviously upset. "We haven't even ordered yet."

"Yes, come on, Will," Ellen encouraged. "Stay a bit."

Maggie too wished he would stay, but elected to remain on the sidelines. Sean too remained silent.

"No, really. I do have to go," Will insisted. "I've class first thing tomorrow and I've still a lot of notes to review. But you stay, Fionna. Ellen, can you give Fionna a lift home?"

"Of course," Ellen agreed.

"Well, nice to meet you, Maggie," Will said. "I'm sure we'll see each other again soon." He looked at Fionna's brother. "Sorry I can't say the same for you, Sean. You're heading back to Belfast on Saturday, aren't you?"

Sean smiled again, leaning back in his chair. "I was gonna do, but now I'm not so sure. There's good work down at the docks. Good pay and few questions." He looked at Maggie and added, "I must confess I keep finding things in Aberdeen which interest me greatly."

Visibly unhappy with this bit of news, Will made his final good-byes and headed out into the cool Aberdeen evening.

"God, Sean." Fionna let out in full exasperation. "Why do you always have to be such a clod?"

"First off," Sean leaned forward, wagging his finger at his sister, "don't use the Lord's name in vain. Second, I'm not a clod just because I defend my country."

"Don't lecture *me* on the ten commandments," Fionna shot back. "You'd do well to remember the seventh. And there's a difference between defending your own country and attacking someone else's."

"Not when that someone else's is England," was Sean's angry reply.

"Sean, you're an idiot," Fionna growled. "It's not even like we're pure Irish. Mom's Scottish."

"Right, and Dad's Irish," Sean spat back. "So you and I are pure Celt. Half FitzSimmons and half MacKay."

Fionna huffed and shook her head.

"That's actually quite amazing when you think of it," Sean went on, expanding his attention to the others at the table. "Devereaux, was it?" he asked Maggie.

Maggie nodded.

"So you're French, then?" He looked to his left. "And Kelly, I'd wager you've more than Scottish bloods in your veins."

Kelly looked up from her beer. "My mother's maiden name was Schumacher."

"Right. See, Fionna? All watered down. And now you want to go ruin our line by carrying on with some Englishman."

"Will isn't just 'some Englishman!'" Fionna yelled, the flush returning to her face. "Why can't you just be happy for me?!"

Sean just sighed and looked away. Fionna did the same.

"Welcome to Scotland," Ellen whispered to Maggie with a sarcastic smile. "Sorry about this."

Maggie laughed lightly. "Don't worry about it."

Then becoming aware of her empty stomach, Maggie added, "But what about dinner? I'm starving."

Soon Ellen had flagged down a waitress and each of the four women ordered dinner. Sort of. Kelly just ordered a bowl of soup and another beer. When it came Sean's turn to order he declined, saying, "I have to shove off too, ladies, I'm afraid. I've other plans for the evening. Good to see you again, Ellen. Nice to meet you, Maggie." Then turning to Kelly, Sean put his hand lightly to her chin and said, "Always good to see you, Kelly."

Kelly pushed his hand away roughly and stated matter-of-factly, "You're not to touch me, Sean FitzSimmons."

Sean grinned as he rose. "The woman's prerogative." Then he turned to the waitress, pointed at Maggie and dropped a banknote on the waitress' tray. "Give this fine young lady a good *Irish* beer. Not that English piss."

And with this last jab he too was off into the Aberdeen dark.

"Wow," Maggie observed after a moment.

"Don't mind my brother, Maggie," Fionna practically pleaded. "He's a bit of a wind-bag, but not too bad all in all. He's just overprotective of his little sister."

"Don't worry," Maggie assured Fionna. "No skin off my nose. I'm here to meet interesting people, and your brother certainly qualifies."

Dying of curiosity, Maggie turned to Kelly and for the first time engaged her directly. "Do you know Sean, too?"

Kelly looked at Maggie through narrowed eyes. "I've known Fionna a lot longer than you, so yes, I know Sean." She stood up and dropped her napkin on the table. "I'm going home," she announced. "I have a headache."

"Kelly!" Ellen stood up too. "Your soup's not even here yet.

C'mon and stay a bit longer. You've only just met Maggie."

Kelly looked at the auburn-tressed, bespectacled woman next to Ellen. "Right," she replied through a scornful smile and turned to go, pulling her jacket over her shoulders.

The three remaining women sat at the table in silence for a moment.

"I don't usually have this effect on people," Maggie assured the other two.

"Don't worry yourself, Maggie," Fionna replied. "None of what happened has the slightest bit to do with you." She raised her glass. "*Slàinte.*"

"*Slàinte,*" Ellen raised her glass as well.

And Maggie hers. "*Slàinte.*"

* * *

"Wow, so you actually knew her?" Maggie asked Fionna.

They had finished their dinners some time ago and were now just enjoying each other's company over their last drinks. Ellen had switched to coffee once the food arrived.

Fionna smiled weakly and looked down. "Yes. Well, sort of. We had a summer seminar course together." Then turning to Ellen. "You were both studying Gaelic and French, right? Comparative literature? So you knew her too, didn't you?"

"Annette? No, not really. I'd seen her about, over the summer at Taylor and at the library, you know, things like that, but I never really spoke with her." Then, after perhaps considering the propriety of her next thought, went ahead and added, "She seemed to keep to herself a bit, I think."

Fionna nodded gently. "Yes, I think she did." She sighed. "I suppose I wish I'd got to know her a bit better. You know, her French was really excellent. I think she was from Quebec. She spoke that odd Canadian French—*Québecois* it's called—so every now and again she would say something the professor couldn't understand. Apparently it can be quite different from the Parisian we learn over here."

This succeeded in turning the conversation from Annette Graham's shyness to the more comfortable realm of an academic discussion on the linguistic differences between various dialects of a given language. The conversation milled about between *Québecois*, Parisian, Irish Gaelic, Scottish Gaelic, Scots English, the Queen's English, American English, and for some time the participants were able to avoid speaking about the murdered woman.

Finally, as the conversation wound its way to the subject of different professors, Maggie ventured, "Annette was studying with Prof. Macintyre too, right?"

Fionna looked at Ellen, and she at her. Then Ellen turned to Maggie as Fionna began staring intently at a beer stain on her cardboard coaster.

"Yes," was all Ellen said.

Surprised, and a bit dismayed, by this reaction to her question, Maggie followed up. "Is there something I should know here? I'm studying under him too now."

Ellen and Fionna both shook their heads.

"No," Ellen assured. "I mean, I've never really dealt with the man. I'm working primarily with Professor Rhys, who does modern Gaelic and Scots literature. And with Professor Duverney in the Romance Department."

Fionna agreed. "I've never even spoken with the man directly."

Maggie wasn't entirely satisfied. "But, I mean—"

"No," Fionna interrupted. "You should probably talk with Kelly about him. I know she's studied under him for, what, two years now?"

"This is the start of her third year," Ellen agreed quickly. "She knows Macintyre the best. You should talk with her."

Maggie shook her head slightly. "I don't know that Kelly is very interested in talking to me. She barely gave me the time of day just now."

Fionna and Ellen looked at each other. "Don't be too hard on her, Maggie," Fionna counseled. "She's been under, well, under a lot of strain lately. She's just got quite a bit on her mind."

"Sure," Maggie replied, unconvinced.

The three sat in uncomfortable silence for a few moments until Fionna asked, "So do the police have any suspects yet?"

Ellen shrugged, "Not according to the papers. It's just a lot of speculation is all."

Maggie looked out at the cold, dark Aberdeen night.

"Ellen, you drove, right?" she asked. "Can I get a ride home?"

"Absolutely," Ellen replied, a sympathetic smile exposing her large teeth. "You too, Fionna," she added—it was a statement, not a question.

Fionna looked out at the dark as well, a shiver running up her spine. "Absolutely."

9. Slow Progress

Inspector Cameron sat at his desk in the Aberdeen police station. It was actually a rather nice desk, for government-issue. Nothing special, but nice enough, with a wood veneer top and sturdy metal drawers. Better than most of the lads got, but then, he was an inspector. In addition to the desk, several metal file cabinets occupied the small office, together with the obligatory two guest chairs and half-dead potted plant in the corner. And of course, as an inspector, he had been provided with a large window overlooking Queen Street. One of the file cabinets was open, the keys still dangling from its lock, and the bottom drawer ajar. Strewn across the rather nice desk were an assortment of manila folders, carbon copy reports and yellowed newspaper clippings. Crouched over this clutter, his elbows rooted firmly to the desk and his hands grasping at the too short white hair on his head, Inspector Robert Cameron sat lost in thought.

There was a knock on his closed door. Looking up he could see Sgt. Willis through the glass. Although Willis could also undoubtedly see the Inspector—the only obstruction was the room number painted in three inch high black letters at the bottom of the two foot by two foot pane—he nevertheless looked away politely as

Cameron pushed the various papers loosely into one of the file folders before calling out, "Come in."

"Sorry to disturb you, sir," Willis started.

"What is it?" Willis, a nice enough fellow, still wore on Cameron's nerves. Best to cut to the chase.

"It's the Graham case, sir." Willis stood unnecessarily still. He didn't say anything else, although the Inspector could of course see the document Willis held preciously at his side.

"Yes? What is it?"

"We've got the girl's certificate of adoption." Again, however, Willis made no effort to hand the document over to Cameron. "We're still waiting for the birth certificate."

"Adoption certificate, eh?" Cameron rubbed his chin. "Well, it's a start."

Then after a moment he added, "Sergeant?"

"Yes, sir?"

"Is that it in your hand?"

Willis looked down proudly. "Yes, sir!"

"Sergeant?" Cameron really didn't have the patience for this.

"Yes, sir?"

"May I see it?"

"Oh!" Thoroughly flustered now, Willis thrust it forward to his superior. "Yes, sir. Here it is, sir. Sorry, sir."

With a gentle wave of his hand, Cameron both dismissed the apology and quieted his subordinate. Then, looking over the adoption certificate, Montgomery read aloud, "'City of Halifax, County of Halifax, Province of Nova Scotia. Certificate of Adoption. Adoptive Mother: Jacqueline Edith Graham. Adoptive Father: Donald Graham. Natural Mother: Destitute.'"

Willis started to offer another 'Yes, sir,' but stopped himself.

After a moment of thought, the Inspector looked up from the

document.

"Good work, Willis," he said simply. It was a dismissal as much as a compliment.

"Thank you, sir," Willis actually bowed slightly before turning toward the door.

As Willis stepped into the hallway, Cameron called out, "Willis?"

"Yes, sir?"

"Send Warwick over."

Cameron didn't look up from the document he had returned his attention to, but he could hear the disappointment in Willis' voice. "Yes, sir."

A few minutes later, Elizabeth Warwick stood in the doorway.

"You wanted to see me, Inspector?"

Cameron held up the adoption certificate. "You've seen this." It was a statement.

"Yes, sir," she confirmed.

"How soon?"

"I'm working on it. There's a lot of red tape. I'm hoping a week. Two at the most."

"Good," the Inspector looked down at the document again. "You'll let me know?"

"Of course."

"Good," he repeated. "Good work."

He looked up. Sgt. Warwick was still in the doorway.

"That'll be all, Sergeant," he said in as friendly a tone as the words would allow. "And close the door behind you."

With that, Inspector Cameron ran a hand over his head and once again spread out the reports and photographs and news clippings across his rather nice, government-issue desk.

10. The Book

Two weeks passed and Maggie still had not returned to the historic collections reading room or in any meaningful way begun her research. She had spent the first week unpacking and getting familiar with Aberdeen, touring the city with her Aunt Lucy or strolling through the streets and quays on her own. She also had lunch once with Ellen at another pub near campus, but that was as close as she had come to setting foot on the college grounds.

The second week was The Royal National Mod, or *Am Mòd Nàiseanta*. This annual festival of Gaelic language and culture was held annually during the entire second week of October, regardless of the academic responsibilities of visiting American students. As luck would have it, the festivities, held in a different Highland city each year, were taking place that year in the nearby city of Ballater. Having missed September's Highland Games in Braemar, there was no way Maggie could pass up the *Mòd*. Besides, the *Mòd*'s week long celebration of dancing and singing, poetry and prose, games and drama—all intended to showcase the vibrancy of Gaelic culture and language—was not entirely unrelated to her studies. She and Aunt Lucy had driven to Ballater and spent three days attending presentations, visiting booths and generally enjoying themselves.

And although she had not brought any real work with her, Maggie did thumb through a different one of her grandmother's books each night in bed by the light of the nearly full moon.

Maggie had hoped that at least one of the books might hold a reference to, or even an actual quote from her mystery dialect, but despite several passing references to the religious ceremonies of ancient Celtic-speaking druids, not one excerpt from their rites was secreted between the covers of any of the texts. The only lead she did find was the fact that all five books made reference to a sixth one whenever they discussed the subject of ancient Celtic religious practices. This sixth book was entitled, simply enough, 'The Religious Practices of the Ancient Peoples of Scotland.' According to the references, it was published in 1689 by Seumas MacAuliffe, and while Maggie had never heard of the volume before, its title held definite promise. As she closed her book and turned out the light next to her hotel bed on her last night in Ballater, Maggie resolved to go to the university library that weekend and see what she could dig up.

Of course, the reading room wasn't open on the weekend. So, by the time Monday rolled around, Maggie had again succeeded in filling her weekend with more sight-seeing and general acclimating, but no research. With the exception of having run across the title of Mr. MacAuliffe's book, Maggie was no further along than she had been when she arrived in Scotland.

And today was her first progress meeting with Prof. Macintyre.

Maggie of course was keenly aware of the impending conference. She had scheduled it herself after receiving a call from Prof. Macintyre suggesting they meet every other Monday to chart her progress. The fear of looking a complete idiot was the only thing that led her even to drag her grandmother's books to the *Mòd*.

Waking late that Monday, Maggie planned to spend the remainder of the morning rummaging around the ancient book collection, then spend the lunch hour organizing her thoughts into an outline to present to Prof. Macintyre at their two o'clock meeting. This plan lasted exactly halfway through her first piece of toast.

"I thought we could take a walk down by the waterfront this morning," Aunt Lucy suggested, spreading orange marmalade over an oatcake. "It's nice weather for it, and besides," she glanced over her shoulder even though Alex and Iain had left for the store over an hour earlier, "the young men working there are often quite robust. Good scenery down at the docks, eh?"

Maggie laughed warmly at this unexpected display of prurience by her otherwise matronly aunt. 'I'm afraid I'll have to take a rain-check. I really have to get some studying done before my meeting with my professor,' is what she should have said.

"Sure," is what came out of her mouth before the toast went back in. "Sounds like fun."

Lucy let out an approving "Good" as Maggie tried to convince herself she'd have enough time to at least think of something to tell Macintyre between the inevitable lunch with Lucy and her two o'clock appointment.

Not surprisingly, she was wrong. After a pleasant morning of stevedore-watching and a hearty lunch at yet another pub tucked away on some Aberdeen quay, Maggie had had only enough time to swing by the house to grab her backpack before her aunt dropped her off near the Taylor Building. But Maggie wasn't too worried. Macintyre couldn't be expecting that much from her so early in the semester.

"I expected more from you, Margaret," Macintyre leaned back in his leather chair. "Even this early in the semester."

Damn.

"Have you done *any* research at all?" The afternoon sun slashed across his face, adding somehow to the expression of tired disappointment.

"Well," she ventured with a smile. "I went to the *Mòd*."

Macintyre's expression didn't change.

"And my grandmother left me some old books in her will which—"

"Your ... grandmother?" Macintyre interrupted, eyebrows raised, "left you some old books?"

He seemed to be trying the idea on for size, but Maggie didn't like his tone. She felt like she was being teased.

"Tell me again," he said at last, raising his hands and clasping them behind his head, "what it is you're researching?"

Maggie could feel her face flush with both embarrassment and anger. Embarrassment because she had not done any work for two weeks. Anger because he knew damn well what she was researching. It was in her application and they had discussed it at their first meeting.

"Something to do with Old Gaelic, wasn't it?"

"Something like that."

"Well, look," he leaned forward. "We do things a bit differently from what you're used to in America. We don't coddle our students. You have to do your own work. And if you persist in lolly-gagging your way through the year, well then, that's your business—but don't waste my time with pointless progress meetings if you've nothing to report."

Maggie bit her tongue.

"On the other hand," he smiled broadly and locked his eyes with Maggie's. "If you *do* come up with something—something really good—well, then I may be in a position to help you get it published." He raised an eyebrow self-importantly. "Go think it over, perhaps over a hamburger and a Coca-Cola. And when your little mind has settled on an actual topic, maybe then we can have a productive conversation."

"Sure," Maggie replied, trying to control her temper. She stood up. "I guess I'll go. Get thinking and all that."

"Right-o," Macintyre agreed, also standing up. "That's the spirit. Oh, and Margaret?"

She turned from the doorway.

"Don't feel too bad. Most American students don't have any self-discipline. You'll learn it soon enough." He smiled again.

Having succeeded in not giving him the finger, Maggie made her way down the corridor to the stairs.

Well, it's official, she thought, *I do not like Craig Macintyre.*

Outside she was greeted by the growing chill of the mid-October afternoon. The sun was already approaching the tops of the buildings, beginning to cast a pink glow on the underside of some rather ominous clouds approaching from the east. Although she had not enjoyed her meeting with Macintyre, Maggie had to admit to herself that he had a point: she did need to get moving on her research. She looked from the clouds to her watch. Twenty after two. Elphinstone Hall stood before her, the reading room behind it.

Time to get to work.

* * *

The reading room was as beautiful as she had remembered it. Maggie could feel her heart slow as she glanced around. The two dozen or so wooden tables were covered in a variety of books and lap-top computers over which crouched a wide selection of students. Maggie walked slowly and quietly up to the information desk she had gone to a fortnight earlier. To her pleasant surprise, the same woman who had been there before was again working.

"Hello, Miss Devereaux." The librarian's smile revealed her

obvious pleasure with herself at having remembered Maggie's name.

"Hello." Maggie reflected the pleasant smile.

"Have you come to look at the Collection, then?"

"Yes, I have," Maggie glanced around quickly and displayed a slightly distressed expression for the librarian. "How do I get there?"

The woman's smile broadened. "Well, love," she leaned forward slightly and pointed toward a doorway in the far right corner of the reading room. "Do you see that archway there?"

Maggie nodded.

"Right, then. That'll be the stairs. Down to the stacks. There are three floors of bookshelves beneath the reading room. That's where we keep the regular part of the collection."

Maggie nodded again. Nodding seemed the appropriate thing to do.

"Take the steps all the way down to the bottom. You'll be on floor B-3. That's the bottom of the stacks."

"And that's the sub-basement?" Maggie ventured.

"No, child. That's floor B-3."

Oh, of course.

"You'll need to cross over to the other side of B-3 and in about the middle of the opposite wall you'll find a door marked 'Sub-Basement – Ancient Book Collection.' You've still the key I gave you last time?"

Maggie smiled and pulled the key from her pants pocket. "Right here."

"Good. That key will open the door. Then you'll be in the ancient book collection."

"Wonderful." Maggie was excited. The two weeks of frivolity had been nice, but there was a certain pleasurable satisfaction in returning to her studies. "Can I check out a book from there if I find a good one?" No reason to have to keep visiting a volume if she could just as easily take it home with her.

"Aye, lass, some of them, but not all." She eyed Maggie. "You're a doctoral student, in the Celtic Department, correct?"

Maggie nodded yet again.

"Good. Aye, you can check out books. But some of them are just too old and too fragile to allow them to be removed. Those ones we've marked with a small red sticker on the spine. If it has a red sticker, it can't be checked out. But if you find another book you'd like to check out, just bring it upstairs to me. We use a handwritten log, not a magnetic scanner like with newer books. We don't want to damage the books with the new technology."

"Makes sense," Maggie agreed. The clock on the wall showed 2:30. "What time does the reading room close?"

"Half past four," was the reply, as the librarian turned to look at the clock. "You've two hours still. As long as you bring the book to me by four twenty-five, I'll have time to sign it out to you."

"Great. Thank you." And with that Maggie strode across the reading room to the indicated archway, stopping only twice to inspect interesting-looking books on the way.

The stairs were made of the same stone as the walls, with worn foot grooves in each step, making use of the cast iron handrail mandatory. To Maggie's disappointment, however, after the first landing the weighty character of the stone gave way to a rather ordinary tile floor and white-washed cinder block walls, so that the remainder of the descent to B-3 felt little different than any other stairwell one might find anywhere in Britain, or the United States for that matter. Obviously, the lower floors had either been added later or else remodeled at a time of unfortunate trends in interior decorating. Perhaps they had been secreted away from the general public and only recently unsealed and refurbished. Although unlikely, this latter scenario helped to restore at least some of the academic weightiness which the florescent lights and linoleum tiles of B-3 seemed so intent on extinguishing.

No one had passed her on the stairs, so she was a little surprised to see other students among the bookshelves of B-3. As she stepped from the stairwell, she could see a line of study-carrels extending down the wall to her right. There was a young man curled over a book at the carrel nearest her, and she could see the head of at least one other student a few carrels down the row. Blanketed by the silence which filled the room, she could understand why some people might like to study down there. In addition to utter silence, there were no windows to distract one with such things as other students walking by, birds landing on window ledges, changes in the weather, or even the passage of time.

Parallel to the row of carrels were several floor-to-ceiling bookcases, each of which extended the complete width of the room, save for a narrow walkway at either end. As Maggie walked slowly by the rows of books she encountered only one other student, sitting on the ground looking for some volume on the bottom shelf. As Maggie walked by, the young woman looked up at her sharply, obviously startled by Maggie's presence in the otherwise still room. Maggie continued on and, upon reaching the last bookshelf, turned right and walked uneasily down the too-narrow aisle looking for the door the librarian had described.

Maggie spied an opening in the cinderblock wall ahead on her left. Reaching that spot she could see that the white-washed blocks gave way to the original gray stone wall behind it, even if only long enough to reveal a stone doorframe with its heavy wooden door. The door itself was solid wood, with no window and a very odd looking brass doorknob. Painted on the door in simple black letters, the paint cracked and peeling, stood the words: 'SUB-BASEMENT.' The phrase 'Ancient Book Collection' was nowhere to be seen.

Maggie pulled the key out of her pocket. It was a newer key judging by the shininess of the metal, but it was an older style, reminiscent of a skeleton key without actually being one. Glancing around, Maggie saw no other students at this far end of B-3. She could sense no activity at all. She slid the key all the way into the keyhole and twisted it hard until she could feel and hear the heavy trips of the old lock turn. Maggie turned the brass knob and the latch gave way with a loud 'clack' that echoed through the floor. She pushed the door open and was greeted with a blast of very stale air and a thick, pungent aroma.

Ah, she thought, breathing in the tangy air, *the scent of knowledge.* Then, as she fought to control her sudden coughing attack, she added, *and mold.*

Peering into the dark room, Maggie could see a stone landing directly in front of her. It was approximately three feet by three feet square, and was cracked and worn at the edges. The light from the room behind her fell down the first few of several stone steps which were then swallowed by the darkness below. Not eager to traverse a rutted stone stairway in the dark, Maggie groped on the inside wall for a light switch. Eventually her hand found a rather large electrical box with a plastic knob protruding. Twisting the knob as hard as she could, it finally gave way with a reluctant click. At first the room was still engulfed in blackness, but Maggie could hear the buzz of electrical circuitry overhead. Then a single light flickered on dimly, casting a faint yellow glow over a large wooden table on the stone floor far below. A second, and then a third light came on, illuminating a second table below her and the near ends of four wooden bookcases, not unlike those directly behind her, except that they seemed considerably older—and considerably better made. The bookshelves on either side were actually pushed flush against the outside walls, creating between the bookcases a total of three narrow aisleways which disappeared into the blackness beyond. Suddenly, the remainder of the lights popped on, both the one over the landing and also a row of lights meant to illuminate the recesses of the bookshelves. However, these had been placed directly over and only inches above the second bookcase from the left, which therefore succeeded in blocking most of the light and casting the far right aisle into almost complete darkness.

Inspecting the staircase, Maggie was excited to see that it was in fact the same worn stone she had encountered at the beginning of her descent from the reading room. She was less excited, however, by the fact that there was no handrail. Indeed, the right side of the staircase was completely open, no guardrail to speak of. Placing her hand against the cool, dirty stone wall to her left, Maggie carefully descended the rutted stone steps.

All in all the room was small. Probably not more that ten feet across and only twenty or thirty feet deep. It was hard to tell exactly how far the bookshelves receded because the light was so dim through there. In addition to the two wooden tables to the right of the stairs, there was also a large wooden card catalog pushed up against the side of the stone staircase, so that were one to fall off the stairs for the lack of guardrail, one would land squarely, and painfully no doubt, onto the card catalog. The stone floor was dirty and made of blocks shoved together far less evenly than those of the reading room four floors above. The table tops were also dirty. Maggie walked over the uneven stones to the nearest table and ran a finger over it. This revealed a rich amber wood beneath the thick green dust which stuck to Maggie's fingertip like glue.

Wiping her finger on her jeans, Maggie crossed over to the other table where someone had left a book. The book too was covered in the sticky greenish-gray dust, albeit a thinner layer of it. *'Ars Magica inter Celtas Antiquos'* was its Latin title. Maggie picked it up to look at it, but quickly dropped it as her hand was attacked by the slimy, sticky dust. The impact of the book on the table scattered some more recent dry dust, but the green-gray residue remained on the book and the table and Maggie's palm. The muffled thump of the book hitting the table did not echo, but rather seemed to be swallowed by the very age and stillness of the chamber.

Extracting several tissues from her backpack, Maggie smeared away the dust on the table to form a work area and set her backpack down on the now semi-clean wood. She then silently placed her books onto the table. It might be dusty, but she would never find a quieter place to study.

She stood her two dictionaries, Gaelic-English and Modern Gaelic-Old Gaelic, upright about two feet in front of the chair she planned to sit in. A yellow notepad filled the space between the dictionaries and the chairs, and ended up underneath one of her grandmother's books. After removing two pens, one pencil and both a yellow and a green highlighter, she placed her backpack on the floor next to the chair. Finally, she fished out the bottle of spring water she had brought and placed it north by northeast of the notepad.

After wiping off the chair, she sat down at the table and opened her grandmother's book to the bookmarked page—the one with the author and title of the book alluded to in each of the texts her grandmother had left her. 'The Religious Practices of the Ancient Peoples of Scotland,' by Seumas MacAuliffe. Published by Royal Press in 1689. This would be her first task. The title seemed exceedingly relevant to her research and the fact that not one, but all

five of the books had cited to it spoke to its academic value. It
would be wonderful to find the book, although she wasn't sure it
would be located in this particular room. It wasn't necessarily that
old, relatively speaking, so it might just as likely be shelved
somewhere above her. If so, she could still bring it down to her
quiet, if not a little dusty, work space.

She stood up and crossed to the card catalog, notepad in
hand with title, author, publisher and publication date all printed
neatly thereon. As she walked over, she glanced at the several
shelves of books to her right. Regardless of whether Mr.
MacAuliffe's book was to be found that day, Maggie would enjoy
sifting through the volumes in the subbasement. She hoped they
were arranged by subject, rather than by author—or as a friend of
hers who had studied in Germany had described with horror, by
date of arrival at the library regardless of topic or scribe.

There were no directions or instructions posted near the card
catalog explaining the system which had been used to organize the
titles, but there were only twelve drawers, each labeled with the
letters contained within. Most drawers had two or more letters
listed, but 'M' commanded its own drawer. Deciding to start with
the theory that they were arranged by author, she tugged open the
'M' drawer.

The first card was for a book written by a 'Mabury, Colum,'
published in 1582. The next card was by an author known only as
'Maoilios Ruadh'—Gaelic for 'Miles the Red.' This jump from 'Mab-'
to 'Mao-' with no 'MacAuliffe' in between concerned Maggie and
she flipped quickly through several more typed and handwritten
cards. The other cards confirmed that they were in alphabetical
order by author, and that Seumas MacAuliffe was not among them.
However, all hope was not lost. There was not one single 'Mac-'
until a 'MacManus' filed directly after a 'Mansfield.' Maggie smiled

at herself and shook her head lightly as she pushed the drawer back in with a soft thud and just a bit of dust. She had forgotten that many older alphabetizing systems in Scotland, and Ireland for that matter, routinely ignored the 'Mac' or 'Mc' or 'O' ' when alphabetizing names, instead ordering such entries by the root word; hence '(Mac)Manus' after 'Mansfield.' Really, she should have anticipated this and was slightly disappointed in herself that she had not outthought the ancient librarian, whoever he or she might have been, who had organized this particular card catalog.

Pulling open the 'A-B' drawer and standing on her toes to peer at the cards, she flipped through them quickly, searching impatiently for 'MacAuliffe, Seumas.'

'MacAdaidh.'

'Adamson.'

'MacAlaisdair.'

'MacAmhlaigh.'

'Armstrong.'

Then the name she had hoped for: 'MacAuliffe, Seumas,' written in that sure, well-taught handwriting of last century, the 'l' and 'f's rising threefold over their neighboring letters. But unlike the other cards, this one listed neither title nor publication date. On the stiff yellowed paper stood simply the name of the author and what was presumably some form of call number: 'Rel.Gael.-7.'

Intrigued, Maggie copied down the number on her scratchpad, again in neatly printed letters, and closed the drawer gently even as she turned her head toward the bookshelves to her right. Although no title was listed, 'Rel.Gael.-7' certainly suggested 'Religion, Gaelic,' the exact subject the book was supposed to have dealt with. She walked over to the first of the bookshelves, pressed up against the far left wall, and in the dim light could see that the books had all been affixed with small labels at the bottoms of their spines. The first five books had the call numbers, 'Arch.-1' through 'Arch.-5.' on their labels. Each dealt with some form of architecture and each looked several centuries old. The next book was entitled in Gaelic, '*Deailbh ann an Alba anns a' Seachdamh Linn Deug,*'—'Painting in Seventeenth Century Scotland.' Its call number was 'Art.-1.' and on a whim Maggie pulled it from the shelf and opened its brittle pages carefully.

It was completely in Gaelic, and although Maggie could have read it had she chosen to, she elected instead simply to flip through the pages to get the general feel of the book. Every thirty pages or so the text was interrupted by a half-dozen color plate reproductions of various paintings of the period. There were several landscapes and one or two still-lifes, but the majority were portraits. Maggie supposed the portrait subjects were probably nobles or aristocracy, although few of the plates identified much more than the year painted. Perusing the plates, Maggie was reminded of hearing somewhere that the most successful painters of royalty—at least financially successful—were those who were able to combine the realism needed for quality portraiture with an artist's eye for covering flaws, highlighting strengths and generally improving upon nature, lest a powerful, but perhaps unattractive, client be displeased with his likeness. Many of the noses and mouths and ears and even foreheads seemed to repeat themselves in the faces of apparently otherwise unrelated noblemen, and all of the noblewomen seemed to bear a striking resemblance to contemporary paintings of the Virgin Mary which Maggie was sure she'd seen in one of her college courses. All except for one painting of a young blond beauty dressed in luxurious red velvet, her hair done up in strands of pearls. Whoever the artist was who had painted this portrait had obviously found his subject too beautiful to render anything but the most realistic visage. What struck

Maggie the most were the woman's upturned eyes, bright blue and shining cat-like through the centuries. The only notation on the page was in Gaelic, its translation: 'A Healer. 1621.'

Maggie looked for an index to the plates in the back, but finding none, reluctantly closed the book and inspected the spine. There she found the small red dot sticker which indicated that the book could not be checked out. *Pity.* Frowning, she stole one last glance at the beautiful blond healer, then replaced the book onto the shelf.

As she walked silently to the back wall, she watched as the call numbers progressed from 'Arch.-1' to 'Cult.Gael.-3.' Turning around she followed them back to the tables as they rose from 'Cult.Gael.-4' to 'Hist.-16.' She then followed the same path down the middle aisle, even successfully resisting the urge to stop in the 'Liter.' section and pull from the shelf every book marked 'Liter.Gael.' Returning again to the open table area she had reached 'Mil.Hist.-3.' Then, with a purpose, she turned down the last aisle, closing in on 'Rel.Gael.-7.'

This last aisle was very dark, the overhead lights being two bookshelves away and succeeding really only in casting shadows into the book-lined recess. Maggie had to squint to be able to see the call numbers. 'Mil.Hist.-12,' 'Natur.-4,' 'Pol.Hist.-6.' By now she had noticed that, like the art books, most of the titles were in Gaelic, with a few in Latin and even less in English. This trend continued in the last aisle as well. Although she knew Gaelic and Latin well enough, she found herself having to concentrate intently to read the titles, the dim light preventing quick recognition of the foreign words. As she approached the end of the bookshelf, almost all light was blocked and she put out her hand to ensure she didn't walk into the wall. Assuming she did find Mr. MacAuliffe's work, and assuming it could be checked out, she really didn't want to have to explain to the nice librarian how she had skinned her knee, broken her glasses, cut her forehead open, and bled all over the university's valuable book. Unfortunately, with her focus solidly on preventing a collision with the impending wall, she didn't pay enough attention to the uneven floor beneath her. A jagged stone block jutted up and grabbed her foot, sending her tumbling off balance and crashing into the very wall she had wanted to avoid. She fell indelicately into a dusty, dirty, and thoroughly embarrassed heap at the darkened end of this last aisle of ancient books.

The brief shriek which had escaped her lips as her foot was caught by the stone was followed by a sincere "Ouch," as her shoulder hit the wall, and an even more sincere "Damn it," as her butt landed on the hard, filthy floor. At least her glasses hadn't been broken after all. She pushed them back up her face. She looked at her hands; although there wasn't enough light to see color, she was fairly certain she had skinned her palms enough that they were bleeding.

Great. I'm sure this centuries old filth won't infect these cuts in a matter of seconds, she thought, the sarcasm an effort to deflect some small part of the utter indignity she felt lying in a twisted dirty heap on the twisted dirty floor. Looking to her left, however, her heart lifted. On the bottom shelf immediately to her left the call number 'Rel.Gael.-2' could just be made out in the dim light. Her stinging hands temporarily forgotten, she leaned forward onto them and scanned the volumes: 'Rel.Gael.-2' ... 'Rel.Gael.-3' ... 'Rel.Gael.-4' ... 'Rel.Gael.-5' ... 'Rel.Gael.-6' ... 'Rel.Gael.-8'

"Damn it!" Maggie yelled again, slapping a palm against the cold stone floor. This, however, only served to remind her of the injury to her hands and she fell back again against the hard stone wall, smacking her spine painfully against it.

"Damn it! Damn it! Damn it!"

After a moment the pain subsided and she opened her eyes again. A strained scan of the nearby shelves confirmed no 'Rel.Gael.-7' to be seen.

"Damn it," she said softly, and leaned back gingerly against the wall, dirty and defeated.

After several more moments, she opened her eyes and looked back over to where 'Rel.Gael.-7' should have been. It still wasn't there, but at least she was in the right section. She reached out and pulled 'Rel.Gael.-6' from the shelf.

Maybe, she admitted to herself as she wiped her dirty, bloodied hands on her now completely filthy jeans, *this won't be a total loss.*

'Rel.Gael.-6' was actually one of the few volumes in English. Entitled 'Superstitions of the Highland Scot,' it held some promise. She opened it to the introduction and began reading:

Following the Battle of Culloden, wherein His Majesty's troops so gloriously crushed the Papist Pretender Charles Stuart and his traitorous Jacobite supporters, much speculation has arisen attempting to explain how the Gaels might have reached such a depth of depravity as to attempt to overthrow their lawful King. This monograph shall reveal that the Gaels' superstitious devotion to both Charles Stuart and the Roman Papacy finds its roots in the superstitious fears and backwards beliefs held by the ancient Celts before the arrival of the civilizing influence of the Angles, Saxons, and Normans.

"Uh, nope," Maggie said simply, closing the cover. "Don't think so."

Setting this text on the stone floor, Maggie pulled 'Rel.Gael.-8' from the shelf. It was entitled, '*Cumhachdan Diadhaidh Luath air a' Chrìosdaichd na h-Alba*'—'Early Religious Influences on Scottish Christianity.' Unfortunately, the 'early' influences discussed included Presbyterian firebrand John Knox who preached in the middle part of the 1500s.

Maggie then pulled 'Rel.Gael.-5' from its shelf. She read the spine—or rather tried to. Although she had never formally studied Greek, she was able to recognize its alphabet.

Okay, she leaned back against the wall, *maybe this* will *be a total loss.*

Tired, uncomfortable and frustrated, Maggie scooped up the three books she had removed and decided to just shove them back onto the shelf and call it a day. She could always return tomorrow. With a flashlight. But as she went to push the books back into place, they stopped short, blocked by something in the black recesses of the shelf.

Maggie's first instinct was to just leave the damned books on the floor and leave, but this idea was shouted down by two subsequent thoughts. First, no matter how frustrated she was, she needed to treat these library books with care and respect. And second, maybe—just maybe—the thing blocking the books was itself another book. And maybe—just maybe—it was 'Rel.Gael.7,' Seumas MacAuliffe's book, fallen behind its brethren. And maybe— just maybe—this would in fact not be a total loss.

Reaching quickly into the blackness of the shelf, Maggie felt a sudden flash of fear as she realized she had no idea what was under there. She could impale her hand on a rusty spike for all she knew. But before she could pull her hand back, her fingers brushed up against the leathery spine of yet another book.

Maggie stopped for a second, her hopeful heart racing. She took a deep breath. Then she grabbed the book and pulled.

If the other books she had encountered in this vault had been dirty, the one in her hand was beyond filthy. It was so covered with sticky, smelly dust and grime that Maggie couldn't even find the title on the binding, let alone read it. The sludge stuck to her scraped hands like so must paste. If this was MacAuliffe's work, it had been trapped behind these other books for some incalculable amount of time. Strangely, there was a metal clasp holding the covers together so she couldn't just open it and read the cover page. She would have to take it back to the table and the light to see if she could scrape off enough grime to read the title, and maybe jimmy the clasp open.

After carefully replacing the other books on the lightless shelf, Maggie walked with the filthy tome quickly, but carefully, back to her table. The yellow light over the table confirmed that there was too much slime to read either the cover or the spine. As if reminded by the filth on the book, Maggie looked down at her own very dirty hands, the scrapes on her palms covered in sticky grayish-green dirt. Setting the book on the table, she picked up her water bottle and twisted off the cap, trying to leave as little grime as possible on the neck. After removing some tissues from her backpack, she looked up at the light from the half-open door at the top of the stairs. No one was coming.

"I wonder if anyone *ever* comes down here," she muttered, surveying the dusty, dirty room.

She crossed over to the corner farthest from the stairs and bookshelves and poured water over her hands. Wiping strenuously with the tissue she was able to remove most of the sticky dirt from her hands. She was then able to confirm that she had in fact drawn blood. The bleeding had all but stopped though, due in part perhaps to the covering of gray-green dust. Maggie wasn't sure that was necessarily a good thing. In any event, the water had run off her hands and splattered and pooled on the stone floor by her feet. One brave band of water was setting out for a nearby crack, creating a small brook heading harmlessly toward the wall. Looking down,

Maggie felt some small regret about pouring the water right there in the room, but then she noted with some approval that this particular corner now looked measurably cleaner than the remainder of the floor.

Drying her hands on the remaining tissue, she returned to the book she had found. Fetching additional tissues from her backpack, she tried to wipe off the spine of the book to reveal a title. Smearing the thick green dust away revealed a deep black leather spine, raised in an intricate and attractive pattern, but no title to speak of. There was also no call number, nor a red dot sticker affixed. Repeating the process with the front cover proved more difficult as the raised leather pattern was even more intricate there. She turned the book 90 degrees so the spine was nearest her, and held the clasp firmly in her left hand as she smeared the grime off the cover with her right, pulling the tissue straight down toward her body. This extra leverage allowed the tearing tissue to smear off most of the filth, but again revealed no title. Then, with horror, Maggie looked down to see that her left palm had once again begun to ooze blood. In fact, she had bled onto both the clasp and the cover of this undoubtedly priceless book.

With another loud "Damn it!" she frantically dabbed at the clasp with the clean side of an otherwise grime-covered tissue. As she did so, the ancient metal of the clasp rattled quietly and fell open with a faint clink.

Surprised, but undeniably pleased by this turn of events, Maggie grabbed the last tissue in her back pack and finished wiping her blood off the dark tome. She then carefully pulled open the front cover, grimacing at the painful crackling of the ancient spine. Unlike modern books, the first page of this text was not blank, but held words, more or less centered on the page. This suggested to Maggie some sort of cover page or similar function. What Maggie found most interesting about the words, however, was the very obvious fact that they had been written by hand, not printed on a press. Either this was a personal journal of some sort or it predated the advent of Herr Gutenburg's 1451 invention. In either case, Maggie felt confident in her conclusion that this was not Mr. MacAuliffe's treatise on 'The Religious Practices of the Ancient Peoples of Scotland.' Rather than this English title, stood six words Maggie couldn't read:

'Inh Liabhor Dhurgha Dhiassiain Ochus Dhamnothadh'

Below the words were three symbols. In the middle was a large circle with two lines inside it intersecting like a plus sign, to the left was a smaller circle with a single dot in the center, and to the right was something that looked exactly like a crescent moon facing back toward its companions.

Maggie looked down at the words, reading them again and again, waiting for her brain to finally kick in and recognize the phrase—or at least a word or two. But this recognition never came. The only word she thought she might recognize was the *'inh'* at the beginning. This looked an awful lot like *'in,'* the Old Gaelic word for 'the.' Assuming that was the case, then the fifth word could be related to the Old Gaelic word, *'ocus,'* which came into modern Gaelic as *'agus,'* meaning 'and.' But the rest of the words were unfamiliar, although the general orthography was clearly reminiscent of Old Gaelic. Reaching for her dictionaries and smiling at the challenge, Maggie sat herself down in the half-clean chair and set out to translate the cryptic phrase.

* * *

Maggie leaned back in her chair and let out a deep, slow sigh. She had confirmed that the language was Celtic in origin, but she had only succeeded in translating two of the remaining four words. Ordinarily such slow progress would have led to a palpable frustration and an acidic burn in her stomach. However, rather than acid in her stomach, she had butterflies. Although the entire phrase still remained untranslated, the ancient words filled her language-loving, dialect-researching heart with cautious glee. As it stood now, the translation of the title appeared to be:

'The (something) Book of Rites and (something)'

And it was written in a dialect of Old Gaelic which Maggie had never encountered before.

"This book," Maggie whispered to herself, barely able to contain her excitement, "may actually be written in the Hamilton dialect."

She thought for a long second, then corrected herself: "The Hamilton-Devereaux dialect."

Rather than have to piece together bits and pieces of a dialect some scholars doubted even existed, she might just have stumbled across actual source material. The Rosetta Stone of her dialect—if she could succeed in translating it. It had taken her forever to translate just four of the first six words. What time was it anyway?

Maggie bent down and looked at the watch still looped to her backpack. It was ten after five.

Her heart dropped. The front desk closed at 4:30.

Quickly, she shoved her things helter-skelter back into her bag. The newly found book was still too dirty to put in there, but that was just as well. If she was lucky, the nice librarian had stayed late and would let her check it out. She double checked the spine: no red dot. She was good to go. In no time she was up the stone steps, had turned off the lights and was locking the heavy wooden door. She sprinted across Floor B-3 and up the steps. When she reached the top floor her heart dropped again.

The reading room was deserted.

Maggie found herself faced with two dilemmas. First, what to do with this wondrous book she had found. Second, what to do if she found herself locked inside the reading room. She liked books well enough, but she was not eager to spend the night in a cold library. Not to mention the fact that Aunt Lucy and Uncle Alex would be worried sick. Especially with a killer on the loose.

Maggie looked down at the book in her hand. There was just no way she was leaving it behind. The librarian had said that any book without a red sticker could be checked out. She had also said that there were no computer anti-theft devices on the books; no alarm would sound if she exited the reading room with it. She nodded her head in decision, tucked the dirty book under her arm and strode to the nearest exit. The door opened easily enough and no emergency alarm sounded. Both dilemmas solved. She checked to make sure the door latched behind her, then looked around to get her bearings.

The sun had already set. She was still amazed that Aberdeen, being so far north, had such short days in the fall and winter. The fog had also rolled in, but it wasn't so thick that she couldn't see Regent Walk to her left. The street lights were on and she knew her way to The Boar and Thistle. They would still be open and she could call home for a ride.

Maggie looked around. A shiver ran up her spine, but not from the damp chill. She was stupid to have stayed out past sunset all by herself. She would feel a lot better once she'd made it to the pub and was safely inside. Pulling her backpack over both shoulders, and clutching her newly found text close to her chest, she half-ran toward the lighted safety of Regent Walk and High Street beyond.

And from the darkness behind her, a pair of eyes watched. And waited. And wondered.

11. Offerings

It had ended up being rather a late night. Lucy and Alex had not been upset that she had called for a ride. Although the sun had set, five-thirty really wasn't that late and Alex had been happy to swing by the Boar and Thistle to pick her up after he closed up the shop at six. Maggie bided her time with a root beer, eschewing dinner at the pub in favor of Lucy's home cooking. After dinner and some light conversation over the dishes, Maggie had excused herself to her room where she immediately began further investigation of the black book. Although she had not cracked the dialect—not yet anyway—she nevertheless enjoyed looking at the handwritten pages with their various diagrams and illustrations. Any doubts she might have had that this was some sort of religious text were dispelled by the sketches of what very much appeared to be human sacrifices.

Just gimme that ol' time religion, she had thought sarcastically.

By the time she had finally set the book aside and fallen asleep it was after one o'clock in the morning.

When she woke up it was late—after ten o'clock. She felt a

bit groggy and stumbled from the bed. As she passed the still dirty leather-bound volume lying attentively on her writing desk, she couldn't help but smile at her good fortune.

"You and me, book," she said aloud. "We're partners."

Then she dragged herself to the shower to start her day.

* * *

Having eaten breakfast by herself—both Lucy and Alex had already gone in to the shop—Maggie was ready to head into campus. Although what she really wanted to do was to spend her entire day locked in her room translating her book, she knew the first order of business had to be going back to the reading room and properly checking out the text. Still, she felt a bit uneasy about it. She was afraid that the librarian might require that the book be returned to the sub-basement and she would therefore lose her exclusive access to it. Even though there was no red dot sticker on the spine, the librarian had said that some of the books were 'simply too old and too fragile to be removed.' The black leather book was definitely old, although it seemed less fragile that she might have expected. Nevertheless, Maggie was afraid the red sticker had perhaps fallen off, or just as bad, the librarian would take one look at the old tome and slap a sticker on it.

"Well, nothing to be done about it," Maggie sighed as she climbed the stairs to fetch her things from her bedroom. "It has to be checked out properly."

She sighed again. "If it even *can* be checked out."

* * *

Soon Maggie was strolling along Mounthooly Street on her way to the Old Campus, dark book tucked away in the backpack strapped securely to her back. With any luck she would be there by 12:30 or so. It was a nice day again so she had decided to forego the bicycle she had bought just after the *Mòd* in favor of the more mundane use of foot power. Indeed, she had intentionally walked several blocks out of her way so as to combine the march into campus with a bit of exploring. The fact that she was in no hurry to surrender the book to the sticker-toting librarian may have contributed somewhat to this decision. In any event, when she had walked far enough out of her usual path, Maggie turned north again to see where she would end up.

About halfway down one of the city blocks Maggie spotted a white cat sitting by the entrance of an alleyway, casually bathing its front paw. The cat looked exactly like her cat, Bàn, back home. She had two cats, an all black one named Dubh and an all white one named Bàn—'*dubh*' meaning 'black' in Gaelic, '*bàn*' meaning 'white' or 'fair.' Although Maggie felt reasonably certain that Bàn had not followed her from Seattle—white cats were not exactly rare, and Bàn didn't have any way to pay for an airline ticket—still she liked cats and crouched down to coo at him, hoping he might come over to be pet. The cat looked up at Maggie, then stood up and rubbed against the corner of the building next to him, his tail curling over his back. Then he let out the smallest "mew" and rolled over on his back, exposing his tummy for petting and locking his gaze expectantly on Maggie.

Maggie stepped over to the cat, saying, "Hello, kitten," as she bent down to pet him. But as if he'd never expected any such reaction to his display, the cat sprang up and bounded about three feet away, into the alley.

Following the cat with her eyes, Maggie could see that the alleyway was more of a pedestrian arcade really than any dirty back alley. Stone arches spanned over a cobblestone walkway and small doors lined the brick walls on either side, some obviously back doors to businesses facing the other direction, others appearing to be proper entrances themselves. The midday sun shone down on the wide walkway bringing out the rich red tones of the cobblestones. After about 50 feet, the arcade crooked to the right and she couldn't see past the bend. Meanwhile the cat had doubled back and stood about two feet from Maggie, rubbing against the side of the buildings again and purring loudly enough for her to hear.

Maggie took another step toward him and he waited until the last possible second before scurrying away again, deeper into the arcade.

He even acts like Bàn, she thought.

She took another two steps toward the snowy feline, but again he avoided her touch just enough to turn around and start purring again.

Maggie stood up and crossed her arms. She was not going to play this game. But then she remembered that she had taken this route specifically to explore interesting new areas—a category to which the arcade definitely belonged. And anyway, she was in no hurry to get to the reading room.

Fine, cat, let's see where you're headed. Maggie set out, intent on both petting the damned cat one way or another, and also seeing what lay down the walkway regardless. She half-hoped the arcade came to a dead end, just so the cat would have nowhere to scurry away from her. The animal, however, succeeded in avoiding her poisonous touch and soon they had reached the other end of the arcade, not a *cul-de-sac*, but an opening onto another cobblestone street and whatever businesses or residences it might hold. The cat stopped at the mouth of the arcade and waited for Maggie to catch up. This time he sat stock still while he finally let Maggie scratch his furry white head. Then he looked up at Maggie, let out a terribly loud "Meow!" and bolted out of the alleyway and down the street.

Maggie stepped around the corner to see where the cat had

gone, but there was no sign of him. What she did see, however, was the absolutely most adorable street café she had ever seen. It was tucked away from all the traffic and boasted an enormous—by European standards anyway—outdoor seating area surrounding the trunk of a mammoth oak which Maggie guessed was probably older than her home country. As if on cue, her stomach let out a small rumble and Maggie had no difficulty deciding it was time for lunch.

In short order, Maggie found herself seated outside at a small table, her lunch ordered and a pint of amber stout resting companionably before her. There were a few other patrons at various stages of their own lunches and/or drinks, but Maggie paid little attention to them, deciding instead to do a little reading while she waited for her ploughman's lunch. Delving into her backpack, which she'd removed and set on the ground, she pulled out the black leather book, followed by her grandmother's book and her Modern Gaelic-Old Gaelic dictionary. Then, thinking better of beginning any serious translating just before the waitress would be bringing her lunch out, she returned the dark tome and the dictionary to the backpack and instead cracked open her grandmother's book. Time to see whatever became of Diarmit and Catrìona. But as she set her beer back down on the table top, a cold shadow fell across the page. Maggie looked up, a bit surprised that her lunch was ready so quickly. However, when she turned to face the source of the shadow, she saw not the short twiggy figure of her waitress but the tall silhouette of a man, outlined by the sun directly behind his head.

Maggie squinted as the man stepped around to the other side of the table. The sun no longer backlighting him, she could finally get a good look. He was tall—at least 6'2"—and appeared to be about 40 years old, or close to it. He was also impeccably dressed. A dark gray vest and slacks combined with a crisp white shirt to frame an absolutely gorgeous golden necktie. Over this he wore an overcoat of just the right shade of camel. Each garment appeared to be of the highest quality. Atop this ensemble rested a not altogether unattractive face, with thick strawberry blond hair combed straight back and a blond goatee hanging stubbornly from his chin. There was no mustache. Black eyes shone out from deeply recessed sockets, and a long mottled scar traveled elegantly from the corner of his left eye down the side of his left cheek to just below his ear. The overall impression was of a man who was very much in control of himself.

"Can I help you?" Maggie asked. This seemed the appropriate thing to say when a strange man elected to hover over one's pint of stout.

"I hope so, Miss Devereaux," the stranger replied.

This had the desired effect of startling her. At least she assumed that was the desired effect. In truth, his face betrayed no emotion or thought, but clearly he was waiting for some type of reaction. What does one say to a stranger who already knows one's name?

"You have me at an advantage, sir." Maggie liked that. It had a certain 1930s Hollywood charm to it.

The stranger smiled ever so slightly. "That remains to be seen. May I sit down?"

"Um. Sure." What else could she say?

The tall man sat down opposite her. The waitress started to approach to take his order but he dismissed her with a commanding glance.

"You are Margaret Devereaux?"

"Yes. And—" She didn't get to the 'and you are?'

"You're an American."

"Yes, but—"

"And you're studying at the university, correct? In the Department of Celtic."

"Yes." This time she didn't try to interject her own question. He was speaking too quickly.

"In fact you're studying Old Gaelic, are you not?"

"Why, yes." Maggie was surprised, almost pleasantly so. Why had no one at the college had any idea who she was, but this well-dressed stranger seemed to be perfectly aware of almost everything she was doing?

"In fact, you're searching for a lost dialect of Old Gaelic, correct?"

Okay, forget the 'almost.' This guy knows everything. But this is too much.

"Alright, Spanky. Just hold it right there." She extended a still scraped palm to emphasize the point. She wasn't sure where the 'Spanky' had come from, but she liked it and it seemed to have thrown him off his game, at least momentarily. She pressed her advantage. "Before I endure any more of your cross-examination, why don't you answer a couple of my questions?"

"Devan Sinclair."

This anticipation of her first question startled her for a moment. *Not too hard to guess I'd ask his name,* she assured herself.

"I own a bookshop down on Mearns Street."

Maggie wasn't convinced that this was going to be her next question, but she accepted the information. She wasn't sure where Mearns Street was. Her face must have betrayed her.

"It's a bit off the beaten path still," he smiled. "Down near the docks. Off Regent Quay."

With that added information she was able to approximate where it was, based on her previous stroll with her aunt. If she recalled correctly, that was on the edge of the more dangerous part of the waterfront.

"I specialize in unique and difficult to find volumes."

Maggie's face greeted this information with a blank stare.

"Specifically, I deal in books on the occult."

Now Maggie's face showed a reaction. Her eyebrows raised significantly and before she could stop herself her eyes darted instinctively to her backpack, then back at this Devan Sinclair person.

"Miss Devereaux," he leaned delicately onto the table. "It is my understanding that you have come into the possession of a certain text."

Her eyes widened the slightest bit before she could control it. She was certain he had noticed.

"I think you know the one I mean," he went on. "The one with the interesting black leather cover. I would like to purchase this book from you."

Now that surprised Maggie. Whatever she had been expecting, it wasn't that. Her surprise must once again have shown on her face.

"I will pay very generously for it," he added simply. Maggie had no doubt he would.

He awaited her reply. She didn't know what to say. As she tried to recall the specifics of their whirlwind conversation, she was fairly certain she had not actually admitted to having any such book. Clearly he was referring to the library book she had in her backpack, but how could he know about that? She'd only had it for less than a day. Maybe he didn't really *know*, but was just guessing.

Pretty damn good guess, she thought.

Still, if this Sinclair guy had the brashness to accost her in this café—this café which she had only stumbled upon by chance?

Okay, this is getting too weird. This guy doesn't get any more info from me. And he certainly doesn't get the book.

"Well, here's how I see it," she began. "You're looking for a book you think I have, right?"

Devan Sinclair nodded patiently.

"And I'm a student here at the university, right?"

Again a silent nod.

"Well, then," she leaned back confidently. "It would stand to reason that any such book—and I'm not saying I have it—but if I did, any such book would most likely have come from the university library. And if that's the case, I wouldn't have the right to sell it to you anyway."

She crossed her arms triumphantly.

He looked at her for a moment, clearly puzzled. There were obvious faults in her logic, but when his lips parted, he said simply, "Maggie, it is *not* a library book."

Her shoulders dropped but she didn't say anything. Sinclair also didn't say anything for a moment as thoughts raced hidden behind his dark eyes.

"I admit I'm disappointed," he said finally, rising from his chair. "But not surprised."

Maggie guessed that he was rarely surprised by anything.

"But please consider my offer," he encouraged. "It will remain open indefinitely."

He reached into his inside coat pocket. "My card."

Maggie took the black business card with the silver lettering. 'Tales of the Occult Bookshop. Devan Sinclair, Proprietor.'

"Do stop by the shop sometime," he urged as he gathered himself up to leave. "We have many interesting old texts. I'm sure you'll find some pertaining to your studies." Then with the slightest of bows, "Good day."

He walked quickly past her chair but as she turned to look after him she was blinded again by the afternoon sun, this time reflecting off the café windows. When she looked again he was gone.

Wow, she thought. *What just happened?*

She wondered why he had been so eager to get his hands on the book. In truth, she didn't know more about it than four of the title's six words. But this Sinclair fellow certainly seemed to think it was important, whatever secrets it held. And what did he mean it wasn't a library book? How would he know? She had found it in the library. Of course it was a library book.

Wasn't it?

As she pondered these questions and more, she found herself becoming quite irritated at the man's intrusion into her peaceful afternoon. Just then, the waitress brought her plate of breads and cheeses.

"Oh, thank you." Then embarrassed, she asked in her American accent, "I can't remember, do I pay now or after I'm finished?"

"Don't worry about it, love," the waitress replied. "Your gentleman friend already took care of it. Said he'd see you at the bookshop."

Maggie's eyes narrowed. *I'll be damned if he will.*

"Anything else then?"

Maggie nodded and pointed at her half empty beer glass. "I think I'll be needing another one of those."

* * *

Maggie had finished her meal and was nursing the last half of her second pint, lost in thought. The sun had hidden itself behind some newly arrived clouds and a cool breeze played with her auburn hair. She paid little attention to the wind however. Her concentration was so focused on dissecting the conversation with Devan Sinclair that she at first didn't even notice the sound of her own name being called.

"—gie! Maggie!"

Maggie turned with a start to see Ellen Walker standing by the railing which separated the seating area from the street. She was smiling and waving. Behind her was Kelly Anderson who was doing neither.

"I see you've discovered The Duff Street Cafe," Ellen observed.

"Oh, is that what this is called?" Maggie replied. "I hadn't even thought to notice." Then a little belatedly, added, "Care to join me?"

"We would be delighted," Ellen enthused, although Kelly's face displayed anything but delight.

In no time, Ellen and Kelly had pulled up to the small table and had each ordered a pint to go along with Maggie's half-full glass.

"So how did you find the café?" Ellen asked. "This is a favorite spot for locals, but it's hard to find unless you know where it is."

Maggie decided not to relate the story of the mysterious feline tour guide and instead settled for, "I was just walking around, exploring, and stumbled across it."

Noticing that Kelly was looking around impatiently at nothing in particular, Maggie tried to include her in the conversation as well.

"Did you know about this café too, Kelly?"

Kelly turned, almost startled at actually being addressed. "Well, yes. But then I've been her longer than you, haven't I?"

"I suppose so," Maggie replied simply, wondering why it

was that Kelly seemed to dislike her so much.

"So have you got to see much of Aberdeen yet?" Ellen asked as the waitress set down their drinks.

"A fair amount," Maggie nodded as she set her own beer aside for a moment. A pint and a half of Scottish beer was not without its effects. Best to let the others catch up. "I'm staying with my aunt and uncle, you know, and so I've kind of been sightseeing with my aunt. And shopping."

"Ah, the best kind of sightseeing," Ellen agreed. Kelly made a sound somewhere between a grunt and a sigh.

"Oh!" Maggie slapped the table. "And we went to the *Mòd* last week in Ballater!"

Ellen's eyes widened in appreciation. Even Kelly seemed to show some interest.

"Oh, how was it?" Ellen asked. "What did you see? Anything good? I usually go, but wasn't able to make it this year."

So Maggie described the various language and music and art and sport competitions she and her aunt had seen, from the poetry recitations to the shinty matches.

"Oh, the *Mòd* is so much fun," Ellen said wistfully. She bumped Kelly's arm. "We should have gone this year."

"Well, we went to Braemar," Kelly offered. She seemed to be warming up a bit, perhaps due to the already half-finished pint of bitter. "That was fun."

"Yes, that's true," Ellen agreed. "Did you go to that, Maggie?"

"Um, no. No, I didn't"

"Oh, see," Ellen grabbed Maggie's forearm gently. "Now that you really should have gone to. It's not as high-brow as the *Mòd* maybe, but there's quite a few burly lads in short kilts, eh, Kelly?"

"Uh, right," Kelly agreed reluctantly to the nudge in her ribs.

"How come you didn't go, Maggie?" Ellen asked raising her

beer to her lips. "I'd have expected you to."

"Actually, I hadn't gotten to Scotland yet." Then after a moment she decided to just go ahead and explain. "My grandmother was pretty sick. I—um—well, actually, she passed away. The funeral was the same day I flew out."

"Oh," Kelly said.

"Oh," Ellen agreed. "Sorry. I didn't mean—"

"Oh gosh, don't worry about it." Maggie dismissed their concern with a wave of one hand as her other reached again for her glass. "You didn't know. And it's not like you killed her. She had a long, rich life. I miss her, but I can talk about it."

Nobody said anything for a minute or two, the Ellen blurted out, "Have you been to Inverness yet?"

Kelly leveled a glare at Ellen which combined disbelief with disapproval. Ellen ignored it.

"No, not yet," Maggie said. "But I plan to. 'Capital of the Highlands' and all that."

Ellen smiled weakly. "Something like that. Look, I'm actually from Inverness and a small group of us are heading up there for a long weekend. We're going to stay with a friend of mine from school." Ellen continued to ignore Kelly's glare and asked Maggie, "Would you like to come along too?"

"Sure." Maggie's reply was immediate. "Sounds like fun. When is it?"

Kelly began moping into her beer.

"Two weeks from this Friday. The first weekend in November. Nothing special, just visiting the home town. Maybe we'll do some sight-seeing. Clava Cairns and such. Things like that."

"Sounds great," Maggie beamed. "Who else is going?"

"Right now, just you, me and Kelly," Ellen replied. "Fionna may come too. She's not sure yet. And a friend named Sarah Bell may come along as well."

"Oh, well, I hope Fionna can come," Maggie said. She didn't know Sarah Bell, but figured she was probably nice too.

"Me too," agreed Ellen. "It's kind of a girls only trip. She and Will already had plans, but she's going to see if she can move those."

Kelly rolled her eyes. "She worries about him too much."

"Well, anyway, I hope she can come," Maggie ignored Kelly's comment.

"Aye," Ellen replied as she finished off the last of her pint. "It'd be a real shame if she couldn't make it."

Looking down at her empty glass and confirming that Kelly's was empty too, Ellen stood up. "Well, we'd better get going. We've got a seminar at two o'clock. Don't want to be late."

"No," Kelly agreed, obviously pleased at the prospect of leaving.

"Are you heading into campus too?" Ellen asked, looking at Maggie's backpack.

Maggie looked down at it as well. She thought about what it contained and her conversation with Devan Sinclair.

"No, I just came from there," she lied. "I'm on my way home now. I've—I've got some reading to do. Sometimes I can concentrate better at home."

"All right then." Ellen dropped a few banknotes on the table. "I'll call you about Inverness if I don't see you."

"Great." Maggie waved as they exited the café and turned toward campus. She too left some money for her second beer, then headed back the way she had come. Her thoughts returned to the dark book and the mysterious Devan Sinclair. She needed to find out more about this book before she did anything else. It would be a long night of translating.

The wind blew cold across the back of her neck and she hugged herself against the chill. She looked up at the sky. The dark clouds were rolling by fast. She'd be lucky to make it home before the rain started.

12. Confirmation

By the next morning, Maggie had enjoyed only three hours of fitful sleep, filled with restless dreams of Old Gaelic words and phrases. Nevertheless, the studying had borne fruit. If she had not completely cracked the dialect, she had at least made a few hairline fractures in it, and she was confident, as she rode her bike into campus that morning, that it was just a matter of time before she would be able to start translating the book wholesale.

Sitting upright on the old-fashioned, European-style red and white bicycle, complete with white book basket on the rear fender, she reflected on what she had accomplished. She had remembered from her high school German classes that there were often patterns which repeated themselves as words traveled from one language to the next. German words which started with 't' often had English cognates with 'd' as their initial letter. Similarly, the English letter combination '-ght,' as in 'right' and 'might' and 'night,' was found in German as '-cht.' Knowing this, and building on the few mutations she had hypothesized when encountered by the book's title page, she had been able to make at least some small inroads into the dialect, beginning to recognize at least a few words which had mutated in a predictable pattern from the standard Old Gaelic.

She had then been able to return to the title and finish its translation. The last word had continued to give her trouble until she had been able to step back and realize that its root was not Gaelic, but Latin. It was a borrowed word. This accomplished she had looked down at the handwritten title page and understood its words for the first time:

'THE DARK BOOK OF RITES AND DAMNATION'

It sounded ominous enough that Maggie was willing to believe that maybe it wasn't a library book after all.

Maggie was so lost in thought that she almost didn't realize she'd arrived at the college. Locking her bike at the large bicycle lot at the edge of campus, she headed directly for the historic collections reading room, the Dark Book hidden safely in her backpack. Once she reached the building, she hurried inside and walked straight to the information desk. It was time to clear up all this nonsense. As she reached the desk, however, she was surprised and disappointed to be greeted by someone other than the nice old librarian who had helped her twice before.

"Oh, you're not—" she started, then caught herself.

The woman looked at her expectantly. She was approximately the same age as the other woman, but several inches shorter and thin as a rail.

"I mean: Hello," she tried again.

"Hello," the woman replied, cocking an amused eye at Maggie.

"I was wondering," Maggie continued, "if you could tell me whether a particular book is in the university's library collections?"

"Of course," was the reply. "Do you have the title and author?"

Maggie winced. "I have the title, but I'm afraid I don't know the author."

"Well," the woman stepped over to a waiting computer terminal. "We may still be able to find it if the title is unique enough. What's the title?"

Oh, it's unique, Maggie thought.

"Uh, well," she felt a trifle silly. "It's actually called 'The Dark Book of Rites and Damnation.'"

The petite librarian looked up from her screen, eyebrow raised. "That *is* unique," she laughed. "Let's see what we can find."

"It's for some research I'm doing," Maggie felt compelled to explain.

The librarian just nodded and offered a friendly, "Mm-hmm."

After a few moments, the librarian reported, "Sorry, miss. It's not in the library's holdings."

"Does that include the ancient book collection?"

"Yes," she replied. "Every last volume the university has, no matter where it's housed."

Maggie frowned and thought for a moment. "The title's actually originally in Gaelic—well, Old Gaelic really. Would that matter?"

"It might," the woman admitted. "Do you have the Gaelic title?"

"Yes, it's—"

"Write it down, please," the woman smiled. "I don't speak Gaelic."

Maggie smiled, too, slightly embarrassed, and complied with the request. She actually wrote three titles: first, the letter by letter title she'd found on the first page; second, a translation into standard Old Gaelic; and third, a translation into Modern Scottish Gaelic. She did her best with the word for 'damnation.' "Here you go. Can you try all three?"

The woman let out that little sigh people let out when they don't really want to do something but then remember it's their job. "Of course."

A few minutes later, the librarian confirmed that no such titles existed anywhere in the university's holdings, regardless of who the author might be.

"Would you like me to check with another university? Perhaps Edinburgh or Glasgow?"

"Oh. No. That's all right," Maggie replied, somewhat distracted by this turn of events. "And you're certain that it's not a part of any of the university's collections?"

The librarian patted her computer monitor affectionately and smiled. "Quite certain, miss. Your 'Dark Book' is not a library book."

Maggie thanked the woman and walked back outside into the cool autumn morning. Somehow the fact that Sinclair had been right about the book didn't surprise her. And as she walked back to her bicycle she felt in turn confused, intrigued, excited—and worried.

13. Plans for the Week-End

Maggie spent the next several days feverishly at work on her translation. Aside from meals and about an hour or so Saturday night spent chatting pleasantly with her aunt and uncle while they all half-watched some strange British television comedy, Maggie was a hermit in her room, crouched incessantly over the dark tome while scribbling notes and translations in notebook after notebook. By the time Monday rolled around, Maggie felt confident that she had fully cracked the fundamentals of the dialect and all that remained was the mundane task of translating the book word by word and cover to cover, first to Old Gaelic, then to Modern Gaelic, then finally to English. She hoped to have the translations done by early December—six weeks—so she could then spend the second semester writing her academia-shattering article not only verifying Prof. Hamilton's theorized dialect, but providing a complete translation of an entire text written in it. She might even throw the slightest bit of cultural analysis into the article, just to put everything in its proper perspective.

Along these last lines of thought, it was becoming increasingly clear that an intelligent translation of the book was going to require at least some basic understanding of ancient Celtic religious rituals. The tome appeared to be a collections of rites, prayers, spells, and the like, but some of the words obviously possessed very specific meanings which would be difficult, if not impossible, to understand without knowing the cultural context. Sort of like someone who's never heard of baseball trying to figure out what 'sacrifice fly' means. With all this in mind, Maggie awoke early that Monday morning intent on getting to the reading room bright and early to comb through whatever books they might have on ancient religious practices in Scotland. But she would not expect to find Seumas MacAuliffe's work.

Aunt Lucy was clearly glad to see Maggie's face as she walked into the kitchen before breakfast.

"Well good morning, lass," she rang out. "It's grand to see you walking about like normal people again. Your studying's going well, I take it?"

"Yes, quite well, thanks." Maggie smiled at the find sitting upstairs on her writing desk. "But I think I need to adjust my studying schedule. I'm not getting quite enough sleep." She rubbed her neck. "Do we have any coffee?"

Her aunt laughed. "Aye, lass, we do. It's already on the table. I haven't set you a place yet—didn't know whether you'd be joining us—but just grab the nearest cup and I'll bring out another."

Maggie quickly found both the coffee pot and a suitable cup. After a full drink of the still-too-hot liquid, she called back to her aunt, "Is Iain coming over for breakfast again?" Three places had already been set and there appeared to be more oatcakes than usual.

"Aye, he is." Lucy walked into the dining room, a steaming platter of sausages in one hand, a new cup and saucer in the other. "'Tis Monday but again."

Maggie found herself pleased by this. And also by the fact

that she had taken the time to shower and put on make-up before coming down for breakfast. Soon the doorbell rang and Iain Grant stepped into the dining room where Maggie was nursing her coffee.

"Morning, Maggie." He seemed taller than before.

"Morning, Iain," she answered over her cup. "Good to see you again."

"Aye," he agreed, and then, after a moment's awkward hesitation, took the seat opposite her.

"Good morning, Iain." Aunt Lucy had returned again, this time with Maggie's plate and silverware. "Alex'll be down any moment."

"Alright then," Iain smiled back and Lucy disappeared again into the kitchen.

"So," Iain ventured with a smile.

"So," Maggie responded, adding a nod to her own smile.

After a moment, Iain tried, "So, what made you decide to study in Scotland? Was it Alex and Lucy?"

"Er, no, not exactly," Maggie replied, trying to figure out how she could explain her decision in fifty words or less. "I've always been interested in Scotland. I guess that would be my grandmother's influence. My mother's entire family was Scottish. In fact, my full name in Margaret NicInnes Devereaux. The 'NicInnes' is Gaelic for—"

"Daughter of Innes," Iain finished her sentence.

"Do you speak Gaelic?" Maggie asked, clearly surprised. Although she supposed shouldn't be that surprised at a Scot speaking Gaelic.

"No, but I do sell kilts to tourists," he laughed. "It's helpful to know the Gaelic names for the clans. Makes it seem even more authentic."

Maggie laughed too, in spite of herself.

"Besides you already told me you could trace back to the Clan Innes. Interesting clan, that."

Maggie narrowed her eyes behind her glasses. "You're not going to try and sell me a kilt, are you?"

"No, ma'am." She could see a faint blush dab at his cheek. "I don't think a kilt would suit you overmuch."

Maggie laughed, her cheeks reddening too.

"Did I already tell you," Iain decided to move the conversation along a bit, "that MacTary's a sept of Innes?"

"Yes, you did. I think my grandmother's mother was a MacTary. That's how I'm related to Alex and Lucy. I guess the clans kinda stick together a bit, huh?"

"Well, yes and no," Iain said thoughtfully. "It's not like two people from the same clan are automatically cousins. In fact, they might not be related at all. Any given clan might have a dozen or more septs. Sometimes those are just smaller families that sought the protection of the stronger clan. If you're both an Innes and a MacTary, it doesn't necessarily mean that your family tree hasn't any branches, if you know what I'm saying."

Maggie laughed. "I do."

"So why exactly is it you have the name 'NicInnes' in there again?"

"Well," Maggie started, trying to picture the family tree she and her grandmother had assembled. "Every first daughter of every first daughter for thirteen generations has had that name stuck in there somewhere. So it's my middle name. My mother's name was Ellen NicInnes. Her mother was named Catherine NicInnes. And so on. All the way back to a woman named Brìghde Innes, who was born in 1600. She married a man named, er, something Gordon, I think. She gave her first daughter the middle name 'NicInnes' so that the Innes family name wouldn't be lost. And it's made its way all the way down to lil' ol' me. It's actually pretty cool when you think about it."

"Aye," Iain had to agree. "That it is."

They both smiled in silence for a bit, then Iain spoke up again, "Ye know, the Innes' ancestral lands are not very far from here. And the Castle of Park, one of the Gordons' castles, is close by as well."

"Really?" This interested her.

"Aye, you ought to go and visit. I think you'd enjoy it. And you know, I could—"

"Iain!" Alex belted out his employee's name as he burst into the dining room and slapped him on the shoulder. "Sorry I'm late down. How are you today, lad?"

"Quite well, Alex. Thank you." Iain turned his attention momentarily to his employer. "And how are you this morning?"

"Also quite well." Alex took his seat at the table. "Thank you for asking. And a good morning to you too, Maggie."

"Morning, Uncle Alex," she replied. "Iain was just telling me that the Innes lands aren't too far from here?"

"Aye." Alex raised his eyes to the ceiling in thought. "I suppose that's true."

"What's true?" Lucy had returned with the last of the breakfast trays and was finally ready to sit down herself.

"The Innes lands are nearby," Alex explained. "Sounds like our Maggie here might like to visit them."

"What a wonderful idea," Lucy beamed.

"And apparently," Iain rejoined the conversation, "one of her ancestors married a Gordon. I was just telling her that the Castle of Park is not too far away either."

"That's true as well," Alex confirmed, as he pulled a piece of toast onto his plate. "You know, Lucy," he turned to his spouse, "we should take our guest out to see her ancestral lands. And we could overnight at Park on the way back."

"A splendid idea," Lucy clasped her hands together in excitement. "It's a plan then. When shall we go?"

Maggie looked at Iain for his input but his countenance had dropped somewhat and he avoided her gaze.

"Why not this week-end?" Alex offered. "We could get up early Saturday and be to Elgin by mid-morning. Spend the day there and in the area. Then make it to Park by nightfall and spend Sunday nosing about there. How's that sound, Maggie?"

"Um, fine," she turned to her uncle, then quickly back to Iain. "Can you come too, Iain? It was sort of your idea."

Iain forced a smile. "Och no. I'm afraid not. Someone'll have to mind the store if both Alex and Lucy are away."

"Oh," Maggie was sincerely disappointed. "That's too bad."

"Ah, well, it's all right, Maggie," Iain said, his smile returning. "It's probably just as well. Remember, I'm no Innes. I'm a Grant. And anyway the Grants have not always got along very well with the Gordons."

Alex and Lucy both laughed.

"Now that," Alex pointed at his manager but looked at his niece, "is a true statement. Although," he looked again at Iain, "I doubt they'd bar you from the castle, lad."

"Well, you never know." He turned a sly smile to Maggie. "And I'd hate to be put in a position of having to defend the honor of my clan against the wee schoolgirl selling the tickets at the front gate."

"That would be awkward," Maggie agreed. "You having to explain to the constable how she'd forcibly removed you from the premises and all."

"Aye," Iain laughed. "That would be awkward indeed."

"Well, all right," Alex took back control of the conversation. "This week-end then. We'll leave bright and early Saturday morn. So don't you stay up too late studying Friday night, eh, Maggie? The books can survive two days without you, can't they?"

"Yes," Maggie conceded. "They can."

Then, as Alex turned to asked his wife to pass him the plate of oatcakes, Maggie looked up at Iain and offered quietly, "Some other time?"

Iain smiled. "Definitely."

14. The Bookshop

Maggie closed the cover to Mr. Andrew Chisholm's 'A Survey of the Religious Practices of the Ancient Celtic Peoples,' and set her glasses down on the cover. Running her fingers through her thick brown hair, she let out a low sigh which signaled that emotion somewhere between the intensity of frustration and the melancholy of disappointment. She leaned back in the hard, wooden reading room chair and looked over at the stained glass window nearest her. She considered her progress of the past week.

She had spent the last four days examining every book she could find in three different university libraries concerning the topic of ancient Scottish religious practices, her aim to understand the context in which the Dark Book had been written. Her days thus spent in university reading rooms, her evenings had been filled with continued translation of the leather-bound text, becoming more familiar with the various rites and spells contained between its covers. Now it was Friday afternoon, she was leaving for Elgin first thing in the morning, and she felt that irritation which arises when progress has not stopped altogether, but is nevertheless slower than one had hoped.

To be sure, she knew far more about ancient Celtic religious rites than she had ever wanted to know. But she was finding, as she translated her black book, that it described realms of religious activity which most traditional books on the subject seemed to gloss over, if not outright ignore. For the leather text appeared to concern itself quite fully with the darker side of religion: the occult, the arcane, the demonic. Indeed, the pages seemed to hold a certain awe before the dark forces the rites and spells were meant to harness, one note explaining, '<Protection against evil forces comes best from mastery over them>.' And while it was certainly appropriate to refer to it as a religious text inasmuch as the author, or authors, had clearly believed in the gods and demons and magic they wrote of, there was nevertheless an obvious absence of the more polite aspects of religion: things such as morality, piety, and not sacrificing human beings to dark gods. Ultimately, Maggie's translating had confirmed that the book was dark not only in color, but in subject matter as well. A Dark Book of Dark Magic. And she could find no books in the university's libraries which were brave enough to deal with the subject, beyond the occasional vague reference to 'other more arcane practices.'

So she now knew a great deal about religious practices other than those contained in the book she was researching. And she was at a loss as to how to gain information about the practices she was encountering in the dark tome's pages. The simple answer, of course, was to find books from a different source. A source oriented toward the more arcane aspects of religious and spirituals rites. A source dealing in books on the occult. In short, an occult bookshop.

Maggie pulled Devan Sinclair's card from the backpack pocket she had shoved it into the afternoon at the café.

'*Tales of the Occult Bookshop. Devan Sinclair, Proprietor,*' she repeated in her head. *I wonder...*

As she debated this option, Maggie glanced pensively around the reading room. She was letting her gaze fall absently from student to student when she unexpectedly saw Fionna FitzSimmons standing near a bookshelf. As if feeling Maggie's gaze, Fionna turned and the two made eye contact. Maggie smiled and raised a hand in greeting. Fionna waved too and hurried over to Maggie's table.

"Why hello there, Maggie," she whispered in her light Irish brogue. "How are you? I haven't seen you since our dinner at the pub. That was, what, nearly three weeks ago, eh?"

"I'm fine thanks," Maggie replied in an equally low voice as Fionna sat down next to her. "And yes it's been three weeks already. Three and a half, I think."

"Three and a half weeks since my brother embarrassed me," Fionna said covering her face in half-faux mortification. "I really do apologize again."

"Oh, no need to apologize," Maggie pushed the very idea away. "I had a good time. It was interesting."

Fionna rolled her eyes at this characterization.

"Is your brother still in town?" This seemed a nicer way to discuss Sean.

"That he is. The work down on the docks pays quite well, and he's no wife or kids back in Ireland, so he's in no hurry to get back." She rolled her eyes again. "And besides that, I don't think he minds keeping a bit of a watch over his little sister. Particularly with that dashing young Englishman receiving so much of my attention." A smile exploded onto her face.

"That'd be Will, right?" Maggie was trying to remember everyone's name.

"Right. I'm afraid he and Sean don't get on too well. Sean doesn't care overmuch for the English, in case you hadn't gathered that already. But it's really just that he wants to watch out for me." She traded her tentative smile for a pensive frown. "Only I don't think he's given much thought to how I feel about Will."

"Yeah," Maggie agreed, not sure what else to say. Latching onto the memory of the dinner, she diverted the conversation slightly. "So have you seen Ellen or Kelly lately?"

"Well, I don't see Kelly much actually. She's more Ellen's friend. Ellen's very friendly."

Maggie had to agree with that.

"But I did see Ellen the other day. She mentioned you're going to Inverness with them?"

"Yes. Are you coming?"

Fionna frowned slightly. "I'm not sure yet. I was supposed to go away for the week-end with Will. Ordinarily I might move it, but—Well, we've got some important things to discuss, Will and I. So we'll see if I make it to Inverness."

Maggie wasn't sure where to go from there. Inquiring into what she and Will needed to discuss was obviously not appropriate. Her conversational dilemma was solved when Fionna changed the subject for her.

"So what are you reading?" Her voice was still hushed in the quiet of the reading room.

"Oh these?" Maggie put a casual hand on the several library books stacked before her. The book of true interest, the Dark Book, remained tucked safely out of view in her backpack. "Oh, I'm just trying to get familiar with the old religious customs of the Celts. It kind of pertains to where my research is going. Or at least where I think it's going."

"Really?" Fionna reached for Mr. Chisholm's book, showing the interest one student usually shows for another's work, sincere but not too probing. "How's it going so far?"

"Not bad. But slower that I'd anticipated."

Fionna laughed quietly. "That's always the way."

"Isn't it though?" Maggie let out a small laugh as well. "And my advisor is Prof. Macintyre. I met with him last week and let's just say he wasn't very impressed with my complete lack of progress then. I've got another status meeting with him on Monday and I'm hoping to have more I can tell him, but it's already almost four and I'm going away this weekend with my aunt and uncle, so I don't know how much I'll get done bef—"

Maggie noticed that Fionna's expression had changed, becoming rather serious. Maggie cocked her head and looked at Fionna questioningly.

After a moment Fionna whispered, "Oh, that's right. You're studying under Prof. Macintyre."

Maggie suddenly remembered the thinly veiled concern both Fionna and Ellen had shown at dinner that night when they first discovered who Maggie's advisor was. She was about to answer a cautious 'Yes,' when Fionna leaned in close.

"Look," she whispered especially softly so that even Maggie had trouble hearing her. The Irish woman glanced quickly around the reading room before saying, "You know Kelly's studying under him. Well, so did that poor dead girl, Annette. And Ellen and I have each had a class or two with him. If you're going to study under Craig Macintyre, there are some things you really need to know." Her tone, even in whispers, was deathly serious.

"Okay," Maggie invited her to say more.

"No." Another glance around the room. "Not here." Then, looking at her watch and frowning, Fionna said, "I've a seminar in five minutes, then I have to go to, well, to an appointment at five. Can you meet me at the King Street Pub at, say, six o'clock?"

"Yeah, sure," Maggie quickly agreed. Whatever it was, it

seemed important. Moreover, this display had validated her general dislike of Macintyre. She was eager to find out what Fionna had to say.

"All right then," Fionna whispered as she stood up. "I'll see you tonight a six." She smiled. "I'm really glad I ran into you."

"Me too," Maggie blinked. "See you later."

Well, Maggie thought as she watched Fionna head out into the already fading afternoon sunlight, *that was interesting.*

Maggie leaned back in her chair and considered the rest of her day. The rendezvous with Fionna set at six o'clock, that would give her just enough time.

* * *

Sinclair's bookshop was not as far away as Maggie had thought, but it was well hidden in the back streets extending away from the Aberdeen waterfront. His description of it being 'out of the way still' was dead on; a resurgent district of fashionable boutiques had sprouted up several blocks to the west but its impact had not yet reached Mearns Street. In any event, it was nearly five o'clock before Maggie had found the store. The sun had almost finished its descent into the western hills. As she stopped her bike in front of the shop, she looked up at the dark blue sky. She could see a handful of stars through the gathering clouds, but no moon.

Too bad, she thought. *Just the thing for a spooky old occult bookstore.*

The bells on the back of the solid wood door jingled thickly as she pushed it open on hinges that squeaked just the right amount. The shop was small, although not particularly smaller than she had expected. *After all*, she had thought, *how many books could there be on the occult?*

Quite a few apparently. Each wall was actually a recessed bookcase starting at the floor and rising at least ten feet to the vaulted ceiling. In turn, each mahogany shelf was crammed to capacity with books of every conceivable height, width and color. To complete the effect, each wall/bookcase was equipped with its own sliding ladder. A yellowed glass chandelier hung from the cream-colored moulded ceiling over an extraordinarily intricate blue, maroon, and ivory Persian rug which covered most, but not quite all, of the dark hardwood floor. A dark wooden table greeted Maggie from its spot directly beneath the chandelier. On it stood several volumes, each tilted back carefully on a pedestal to face entering clientele.

At the sound of the bells, Devan Sinclair, who was standing at the back of the store with the one other customer in the shop, turned to see who had entered his establishment late on a Friday afternoon. When he saw Maggie, he smiled in greeting, but then returned his attention to the rather disheveled young man next to him. Maggie was surprised to find that Sinclair's smile appeared quite genuine, even friendly, not the 'I knew you'd change your mind' smile she had expected. In any event, it was clear he intended to complete his business with Mr. Disheveled before coming to assist her, so she glanced down at the book on the table in front of her.

Obviously, she posited, *the occult equivalent to the bestsellers section. Or maybe the bargain table. The difference between which*, she considered, *is often more a function of time than quality.*

Picking up one volume, she read the title to herself: 'Satan and His Plan for You.'

Lovely, Maggie thought with a shudder and quickly set the book back down.

Content now simply to look and not touch, Maggie gravitated toward the bookshelf to her right. Further titles were equally uplifting.

'The Use of Human Blood in Druid Rites.'

'Human Sacrifices throughout the Ages.'

And of course: 'I'm Okay; You're a Sacrifice to Satan.'

Maggie was beginning to question the wisdom of having come here alone. She started to doubt whether the shop would have any books which might actually help her. She wondered where the history section was.

As if reading her thoughts, Sinclair looked past his customer to meet Maggie's gaze as it swept the shop. He quickly motioned to the other wall with his eyes, before returning his attention to the customer at hand.

Maggie turned around, carefully circumnavigated the bargain table and sidled up to the bookcase just next to the counter.

Ah, this is more like it.

'A History of the Occult Practices of the Ancient Celts.'

Bingo.

'Black Magic Among the Scots, Picts and Bretons.'

Score.

'Arcane Rituals of the Ancient Druids and Their Application Today.'

Why not?

Before she knew it, Maggie had selected six different books which appeared to hold the promise of shedding light, so to speak, on her Dark Book.

Okay, she told herself, *good start.* She should just buy these and get going. She didn't want to be late for her meeting with Fionna. She walked directly over to the counter to stand behind Mr. Disheveled, whose first name now appeared to be Fidgety. He was paying for several suspicious looking pamphlets with hand-drawn symbols on their covers. Maggie looked over to where he and Sinclair had been standing but was unable to make out what section the pamphlets had been selected from. Turning again to face forward, Maggie had to take a step back as Fidgety Disheveled hurried past her and toward the door, his evening's reading material tucked safely away in a plain brown paper bag.

"Thank you... sir," Sinclair called after him. "Come again."

The man turned and displayed a very unsettling grin among his black stubble, visibly pleased at this obvious omission of his name in front of another customer.

It's the little things that keep customers coming back, Maggie thought sardonically.

With a ring of the bells, the man exited out onto the street and scurried away into the twilight. Maggie noted with some annoyance that it appeared to have started raining.

"Miss Devereaux." The welcoming smile was back. "Good to see you again."

On the ride from campus, Maggie had been worried that Sinclair would pester her about reconsidering his offer to buy her book. Now that she was in his presence though, she felt sure somehow that he would not say word one about it unless she first broached the subject. He had made his offer. She could accept it or refuse it.

"Good to see you too, Mr. Sinclair." That was true enough, she supposed, if only because she had found her books. "I must say, I very much like your shop. The atmosphere is perfect. And your selection of titles in the particular area I'm interested in far surpasses that of the university's libraries."

"I thought you would approve." He reached for the books she had selected and began to inquire, "Were you able to find everything y—"

"Devan!" The woman's voice almost beat the sound of the bells as she threw open the shop door. "Devan! I need you!"

Maggie stared at the woman in stunned silence. She was six feet tall if she was an inch, but her cheeks were so gaunt that Maggie wondered whether she weighed even 100 pounds. Long, crazy red and brown and gray hair streamed from her head in frizzy curls and her neck held at least a half dozen different necklaces. Not to be outdone, each wrist boasted at least as many bracelets and, yes, bangles. She wore a long red overcoat, from whose sleeves her bony, silver-ringed hands were waving frantically. Under the red coat was an orange and gold dress which hung loosely over her scarecrow-like frame and ended at her ghostly white ankles, which in turn rested just above a pair of very nondescript black pumps. The heavy make-up she wore couldn't hide her age, which Maggie guessed was at least 50.

"Devan!" The raspy voice was quite insistent.

Sinclair looked calmly at Maggie, who had turned back to see what his reaction would be. "Will you excuse me for a moment, Miss Devereaux?" he asked.

"Of course," Maggie acquiesced. She doubted the willow woman would have accepted anything less.

"Ah, Madame D'Angelo." Sinclair glided around from behind the counter, gushing with the concern any wise small business owner shows for a regular customer. "What is it that troubles you, my dear?"

"Oh, Devan," she sighed and relaxed into his gentle concern. "It's horrible, truly horrible," and she proceeded to explain her dilemma. From what Maggie couldn't help but overhear, it seemed to involve a sick pet and some effort, apart of course from standard scientific veterinary medicine, to heal it. However, rather than attempt to eavesdrop, Maggie decided to return to the 'history' section and see if there might not be another interesting title.

Spaces had been left from the places Maggie had extracted

her soon (she hoped) to be purchased choices. Those left behind to mark the gaps did not appear to hold much promise, however. They appeared interesting enough, Maggie supposed, but were not terribly relevant to her studies. Several dealt with Eastern religious practices, including a surprising number with the word 'Byzantine' somewhere in their titles. And the general surveys of world-wide occult practices seemed a bit broad for her purposes. Good background perhaps, but she was hoping to avoid generalities and get right to the specifics of those beliefs which surrounded her Dark Book.

Just as she was about to turn back to the counter and wait, if not a little impatiently, for 'Devan' to finish dealing with Madame D'Angelo's crisis, a book caught her eye. Rather, its title did. This book was not standing on a shelf like all the others, but had been lain haphazardly on its side, resting atop several upright volumes. This position was enough to attract her attention; a quick glance around Sinclair's impeccably ordered shop would confirm no other book so stacked. But it was the title that compelled Maggie to lift it from the shelf with the intent of adding it to her purchase:

'Demonic Possession and Exorcism in Pre-Christian Scotland.'

Judging by what she had been able to translate so far of the Dark Book, this title was dead on target. She picked up the volume and examined it. It was older—not ancient by any means—but its proto-psychedelic soft-back cover suggested publication in the late 1950s. The cover's edges were bent and crumpled, an entire corner having been torn off the back, and it appeared that someone had spilled rather a large amount of coffee on it at some point, judging by the large brown stain rising from the bottom edge of the pages which still held a slight curl from immersion in the liquid. She opened the tattered cover and was greeted by a proud little sticker affixed inside, slightly askew but well above the highest reaches of the page-curling coffee stain. Its preprinted 'Ex Libris' was followed by a youthfully handwritten 'Jared B.' Maggie couldn't help but wonder who would let their children read something like this, or worse yet, what sort of child would want to. But those questions aside, the well-worn treatise would undoubtedly be of use to her. She stepped back to the counter and added it to her stack.

Sinclair seemed to be making at least some progress with Madame D'Angelo, but she was obviously high-maintenance. Maggie suspected she was looking for attention as much as for any book. Maggie gazed lazily around the counter area. Tucked under the counter, with its state of the art computer cash register, was a second shelf where the proprietor could stash away whatever items he might need handy when completing a transaction. In the darkened recesses of this second shelf, Maggie could see several pens, a notepad, two books whose titles were obscured by shadow, and a small silver photo frame, also half in shadow. Maggie could see that the frame held a photograph of a family: a man and woman with two children, one a teenage boy and the other a younger sister. Maggie would have thought it was Sinclair and his wife with their children, except that the man in the photograph had black hair while Sinclair's was a light strawberry blond.

This image of family bliss must have triggered thoughts of recently encountered pairs of brothers and sisters, because Maggie again remembered her six o'clock meeting with Sean FitzSimmons' sister, Fionna. Maggie slipped off her backpack and looked at her watch. It was already 5:30. It had taken her over 45 minutes to travel from campus and find the bookshop, but even discounting the time it had taken to locate the store once she'd reached the waterfront, she would still be hard pressed to make it back to the King's Street Pub in time. And it was uphill.

Come on, Sinclair, she thought. In another minute she might have to just abandon the titles and return after the weekend. She wondered if he might hold them until Monday.

As if in response to Maggie's rising stress level, Sinclair finally parted apologetically from the adhesive Madame D'Angelo and hurried back to the counter.

"My apologies, Miss Devereaux." Maggie thought he might have been just the slightest bit flustered, but she wasn't sure. "A small crisis. Now, where were we?"

"Oh, I just need to buy these," she pushed the now seven books in his direction. "Then I need to get going. I'm in a bit of a hurry actually."

"Of course. This won't take but a moment."

Maggie bent down to remove her wallet from her backpack. When she straightened up she found Sinclair frowning.

"I'm sorry, Miss Devereaux," he avoided her eyes, "but this volume is not for sale."

He held up the book she had just selected while he was busy with the great pet crisis.

"But—" That was as far as she got.

"I'm sorry." He raised his hand authoritatively and set the book on the shelf behind him, again sideways on top of some others. "It is simply not for sale. It should not have been on the shelves. I must have set it there inadvertently."

"But—"

"Miss Devereaux," Sinclair said somewhat severely. "We both know that you understand there are some books with which one simply cannot part."

This obvious reference to the black leather book in her backpack silenced her.

"However," a controlled smile returned to his face, "these

other titles you have selected are excellent. I'm sure you will find them useful."

Maggie decided not to take the time to argue about one book. She was already going to be late.

"What's the damage?" she asked, sounding quite American.

Sinclair looked at her, his expression a mix of puzzlement and caution. He was clearly trying to decipher Maggie's last question.

"How much do I owe you?" she translated, pulling several banknotes from her wallet.

"Oh, I see." Sinclair's visage relaxed. "An Americanism." And then the two proceeded to complete their transaction.

Maggie pulled her books to her, then looked down at her backpack on the floor. The Dark Book was in there, of course; she took it almost everywhere with her now, paranoid of losing this most vital resource. It was also the book, however, which she had pretended to Sinclair that she did not posses. She paused as she tried to think of some way of opening her backpack without letting him see inside.

Sinclair seemed to appreciate her dilemma, but made no effort to turn away.

Finally, Maggie pointed to the small silver frame behind him and asked, "Who's that?"

This had the desired effect. As Sinclair turned to look at the photograph, Maggie bent down and quickly shoved the newly purchased books into her backpack, then zipped it shut. As she pulled it to the counter in preparation of slinging the now quite heavy bag onto her back, Sinclair turned back from the photo and met Maggie's gaze with surprising force.

"My family," he answered almost angrily. "Good night, Miss Devereaux."

* * *

The rain was starting to let up a bit, but not enough to prevent Maggie from having to smear the raindrops off her glasses yet again. Between the precipitation and the extra weight on her back, she was compelled to ride slower than she would have liked. And it was uphill. She didn't take her hands from the handlbars to look at her watch, but as she pedaled up King Street, slicing a puddle into a razor sharp spray, she guessed it was already six o'clock. And she still had a ways to go.

* * *

"Way to go, Maggie," Fionna muttered as she looked at her watch. Almost 6:20. "Where are you?"

Fionna was already nervous about the meeting. Not always the smartest thing for one's academic career to be disseminating troubling information about one's professors. But if Maggie was going to be working closely with Craig Macintyre, then she had a right to know. And if she and Maggie were going to be friends, she'd better tell her now, lest she find out the hard way. Fionna knew she'd be wracked with guilt if she could have done something to stop it but instead had stood idly by.

She looked again at her watch. 6:21. *Damn rude Americans.*

"Are you sure I can't get you anything?" It was the waitress. Again. "Something to drink at least?"

They both knew Fionna was taking up valuable table space on a Friday night and still had not ordered anything.

"No, thanks." Fionna stood up, ignoring the curious glances that were beginning to fall from other patrons—any one of whom might be a friend of Macintyre's. "I think I'll just be going. It looks like my friend won't be showing up after all."

With that, she pulled on her coat, crossed the room under the inquisitive stares of the pub's *paying* customers, pulled up her hood, and headed out into the cold Aberdeen evening. The rain had all but stopped, but Fionna was still chilled by the damp air. She walked briskly toward her flat on Pittodrie Place, unaware that she had traded the stares of the anonymous patrons in the King Street Pub for the far more ominous surveillance of a shadow-darkened figure who waited across the street, just outside the reach of the streetlamp's glow.

* * *

Propping her bicycle haphazardly against a lightpole and not taking the time to lock it, Maggie dashed inside the King Street Pub. From where she stood, out of breath and dripping in the foyer, stone-heavy backpack still pulling her backwards, she could see the clock over the bar. 6:24. What she could not see was Fionna FitzSimmons.

"Party of one?" The hostess had approached, menu in hand. "Or will someone be joining you?"

"Actually," Maggie craned her neck to look around the twiggy blond in front of her, "I'm supposed to be meeting a friend here. But I'm a little late. Do you mind if I look around?"

"Of course not," replied the hostess and she stepped far aside to let Maggie pass without brushing the wet jacket against her.

The pub wasn't especially large so it only took a few moments to confirm that Fionna wasn't there. Maggie stood still, dripping on the floor, trying to decide what to do next.

"Are you looking for a friend, miss?" A waitress had walked over.

"Yes." *Maybe she's still here.*

"A young woman, long curly black hair and a pretty round face?"

"Yes, that's her. Is she still here?"

"No, I'm afraid you've just missed her. She left not more than five minutes ago."

Damn, Maggie thought. "Thanks anyway," she said.

She turned toward the door and headed back out into the night, the squeaks of her shoes on the wooden floor attracting the attention of more than one diner at the pub.

"Good job, Devereaux," she cursed herself. A long glance in either direction revealed no sign of Fionna. "Now what?"

She realized she didn't know where Fionna lived or even what her phone number was. Not eager to reenter—and remoisten—the pub, Maggie hopped back onto her bike and began the relatively short pedal to her aunt and uncle's woolens shop. They would probably still be there, cleaning up after hours.

Arriving at the shop a few minutes later, she was greeted heartily by her aunt who unlocked the door for her.

"Look at you," Lucy scolded. "You're soaked to the bone!"

"Aye," Alex added. "What brings you here on such a wet night?"

Maggie shook her head and laughed. "It's kind of a long story," she said as she pushed her thick, wet hair back away from her face. "But, um, do you have a phone book I could use?"

"Well, of course, lass," Alex replied, pulling the directory out from under the counter. Lucy took it from the counter and handed it to her still-dripping niece.

"Thanks," Maggie said as she took the book. "Can I use your phone, too?"

"Sure enough," Lucy replied, pointing to the red tartan curtain behind her husband. "There's a phone in the back room you can use."

Maggie quickly thanked her aunt and uncle and brushed damply past the tartan tapestry to the storeroom beyond. Flipping quickly to the F's, Maggie found first the Fitzes then the

FitzSimmonses. There was no 'Fionna' but there was a listing for a 'FitzSimmons, F.' on 'Pittodrie Place.' Maggie had no idea where that was, but figured, *What the heck. Might as well give it a try.*

What's the worst that can happen?

* * *

As Fionna approached the door to her flat, key at the ready, she heard her telephone start ringing inside.

"Oh, bloody hell." She fought briefly with the lock then flung the door open.

Throwing her purse down on the ground, she dashed inside to grab the phone only to hear the telltale click and hum of the caller hanging up before she'd even had the chance to say, 'Hello?'

The next sound she heard sent an involuntary chill through her veins.

It was the sound of someone closing her apartment door.

Stupidly, she had left it open when she had run inside. She didn't need to turn around to know that whoever it was that had closed her door was now standing inside her flat.

The adrenaline her heart was shooting into her bloodstream rooted her to the spot as she felt the intruder's gaze grab the back of her neck. Somehow though, she managed to turn her body enough to face her pursuer.

"Oh!" she said loudly, the terror falling from her like wet snow from a tree branch. "It's you."

Fionna FitzSimmons let out a loud sigh of relief. "You scared me half to death," she scolded as she turned again to hang up the phone. "What are you doing h—"

That was as much as she managed to say before the garroting wire seized her throat.

* * *

"C'mon, Fionna, pick up," Maggie urged as she counted the

rings. Three. Four. *Damn.*

"*Hello. This is Fionna. I'm not able to take your call right now so please leave a message after the tone. Thank you.*"

"Um, hi, Fionna." Maggie hated leaving messages on answering machines. She never knew what to say. "This is Maggie. Um, Devereaux. Uh, sorry I missed you at—er—I mean, sorry I was late tonight. At the King Street Pub, I mean. I, um, I got there about twenty after six, I guess. The waitress said you had just left. Sorry. I, uh, kinda lost track of time and, well, it's a long story. Yeah, uh, so anyway it's about six-thirty now, so maybe call me if you get in tonight, and um, otherwise I'll call tomorrow. Er, wait—no, I can't call tomorrow. I'll be out of town all weekend. Damn. I'm—okay, well—um, call me if you get in and if not I'll get a hold of you Monday. Okay? Okay. Um, bye."

Fionna FitzSimmons' murderer waited for the message to stop, and then drew the scalpel from a coat pocket and set to work, confident in the knowledge that the task at hand could proceed uninterrupted in the privacy of the victim's own flat.

15. Discoveries

The knock on the door startled Maggie awake.

"Maggie? Maggie, time to get up." Uncle Alex' voice at the door was kind but insistent. "We've a lot of ground to cover before tonight. Are you awake, lass?"

"Yes," Maggie groaned.

"Good. We'll see you downstairs in fifteen minutes for breakfast then."

"Twenty," she counter-offered. If she was going to spend the entire day driving around Northeast Scotland with her aunt and uncle, she was damn well going to shower first. Opening one eye tentatively as she sat slouched on the edge of the bed, she confirmed that the sun had not yet risen. Not terribly surprising for the end of October at the 57th Parallel, but slightly disheartening nonetheless. The bedside clock confirmed it was seven in the morning.

"There had better be coffee with breakfast," she muttered, and then she pulled herself to her feet and shuffled across the floor.

* * *

The hot shower having done the trick, Maggie stood before the mirror atop her dresser and inserted her earrings. She was more awake now and the residual heat from the shower was trapped nicely beneath wool slacks and the heavy wool sweater she had bought from her aunt and uncle's shop the week before—at discount of course. Looking to her jewelry box she noticed the silver Innes Clan crest pendant her grandmother had left her. Lifting it up, the light from a nearby lamp glinted off the letters which scrolled above the boar's head: 'BE TRAIST.' Be True.

Maggie hadn't worn the pendant she'd arrived in Scotland. It had seemed a bit contrived to wander around Aberdeen with her clan badge dangling around her neck. But it seemed more than appropriate to don the necklace now. After all, she was about to spend a day exploring the ancestral lands of the Clan Innes, followed by a night at the Clan Gordon's Castle of Park where her great-times-ten grandmother may have slept after marrying a son of the Gordon Chieftain. She fastened the clasp behind her neck and tucked the pendant securely inside her sweater.

She grabbed her two bags and headed downstairs for breakfast. In the small suitcase were her toiletries and a change of clothes. In her back pack were a couple of the books she had bought from Sinclair's shop and, of course, the Dark Book. She didn't really expect to have time to read anything, but she decided to bring the newer books along just in case. And the black leather tome would not be leaving her side again until the full translation was completed, published, and generally hailed by the relevant academic community.

* * *

"What a cute little town," Maggie opined as the MacTary's car approached the outskirts of city. "This is Elgin then?"

"Aye, the largest city in Morayshire," her uncle replied, "and the beginning of our tour. I believe Elgin boasts several monuments associated with the Clan Innes."

"Was Elgin," Maggie ventured as Uncle Alex turned the car

sharply into the parking lot which had suddenly emerged from behind a building to their left, "sort of the capital for the clan?"

"Not exactly," Alex answered as they rolled to a stop in a snug parking stall. "It's not as if the Inneses all lived inside some castle here and ruled the surrounding lands by proclamation. All the clans were different. The Inneses were more simply the landlords of the area than the government. And Elgin just happened to grow into the largest city on the Innes holdings. But there's plenty here to give you a taste of the importance the Clan has had in the everyday life of people here."

As they set out in search of such, Maggie looked up. It was a rare autumn day in the Highlands: not a cloud in the sky. She hoped she wouldn't end up being too warm in her wool sweater. Looking around the picturesque medieval town that was slowly passing by her on either side, she wondered whether it was this sunny back in Aberdeen.

* * *

The late morning sun shone down on the King's Tower, casting a short but distinct shadow on the grass below. Nearby, a group of students, enjoying their Saturday, avoided the cool shade under the red and golden trees and walked instead on the sunlit stone path toward King Street. The sidewalks of King Street in turn were bustling with students and shoppers and residents enjoying what threatened to be the last sunny Saturday for the foreseeable future. One young family, a husband and wife and their infant son, turned from King Street onto Pittodrie Place, heading for the park at the end of the quay. Just ahead of them, the warm sun radiated softly onto the cement sidewalk in front of the Pittodrie Flats, stretching up the building's facade and reflecting brilliantly off the apartment windows. And although it was still cool outside in the shade, the windows of all of the south facing flats had been opened in the hope that some fresh air might offset the oven-like effect of the sun beating down on their panes. The windows of all of the south facing flats, that is, except 3-E.

* * *

Lunch was had, of course, at a local pub in Elgin. By lunch time, they had visited several of Elgin's more popular attractions, including the ruins of the 13th century cathedral once called 'The Lantern of the North,' and the Elgin Museum, with its displays on life in the Highlands. In truth, however, there were few of the promised indications of the importance of the Innes Clan in the city's history, aside from the occasional name on the occasional plaque at the occasional historic venue. So over lunch it was decided to drive out to nearby Coxton Tower to view at least one monument clearly associated with the Clan.

The drive was short enough and soon Maggie found herself standing in a dirt path looking up at the Tower.

"So, this was the Innes castle then?" Maggie asked, her head tipped almost all the way back as she scanned the facade of the tower house. Four stories tall and not much wider than a large room, the tower's four small windows guided her eyes from the grass at its base to the blue sky at its top. The roof was pitched, with three parapets jutting from its corners, and a thin chimney completed the dimunitive tower's stretch toward the sky. She had tried to hide the disappointment in her voice at the sight of the small tower. She was pretty sure she'd failed.

"Well, no, not exactly," Alex replied. Lucy had elected to linger near the car. "This here isn't a full castle, it's just a tower house built for military fortification. I believe there may have once been an actual 'Innes Castle,' but it was destroyed during the Civil War—Cromwell and all that." He paused and stroked his chin. "But there is an 'Innes House' still in use not too far from here. It's really more of a residence than a castle, but it's impressive enough."

Maggie smiled at this bit of news. "Can we go there too?"

"Oh, aye, of course," Alex replied. Then he turned back toward his wife. "I think I'd best head back and see how Lucy's doing. But you stay here and poke around as long as you like. Then we can drive out to Innes House. It's close enough."

And with that, Alex began a leisurely stroll back to the car.

Maggie stared up again at the stone tower before her. She walked the perimeter of the structure, gazing up at the steep walls and high turrets, but she elected not to go inside save poking her head in quickly for a brief view of the abandoned first floor chamber. The afternoon sun was still high in the Highland sky, but she knew that it wouldn't be that long before it began its quick descent behind the horizon, and she wanted to see Innes House before dark.

* * *

Alasdair Baxter closed the door to his flat as he finished saying, "Thank you, Mrs. Davies. I'll look into it. Thank you."

"Who was that, love?" the rotund Mrs. Baxter asked from her comfortable wing-backed chair near the window. Afternoon tea was set out on the table next to her and she was awaiting her husband's return before pouring.

"Mrs. Davies from 3-F," Mr. Baxter responded as he lifted his keys from the hook by the door. "Says there's some kind of evil smell coming from 3-E."

"Oh," Mrs. Baxter replied. "Isn't that what the Hendersons said as well?"

"Aye," his voice held a slight weariness. "I imagine I ought to see what the girl's up to." He shook his head as his hand grasped the doorknob. "I wish they wouldn't rent to students."

"Aye, love," Mrs. Baxter smiled. "But if they didn't, then

they'd have not enough tenants and little need for a resident superintendent and his loving wife."

Alasdair smiled at his bride of thirty-four years. "I suppose you're right, of course." He opened the door. "I'll just go straighten this out and be right back. Keep the tea warm?"

"I'll not pour it 'til you return."

And as the door closed behind her husband, Emma Baxter felt a sudden chill despite the warmth of the day.

*   *   *

The car turned onto the long drive which led to Innes House, and Maggie got her first glimpse of the enormous stately stone mansion. It was all white and boasted an ornate facade, a stone perimeter wall, immaculately manicured lawns, and a large square tower crowned with a British flag waving in the afternoon breeze. To Maggie's eyes, Innes 'House' looked very much like a castle indeed. She was reminded of the French word *château*, with its combined meanings of house and castle.

They quickly motored to the end of the mile-long driveway which led to the majestic residence, and as they approached the front gate, Alex pulled the car onto the side of the road and turned off the engine. "The House is still inhabited by the descendants of Berowald, who was made First Earl of Innes back in the twelfth century," he explained. "So it isn't open to the public. However," he flashed a smile at his wife and niece, "there's no prohibition against admiring it from afar."

As they exited the car and walked toward the mansion, Maggie felt that contradiction of emotions inherent in being an American visiting a British castle. On the one hand, castles, being rather hard to find in the United States, cannot help but evoke romantic images of knights and chivalry and Camelot. On the other hand, the British flag flying atop the stronghold's square tower tended to remind Maggie of the war her country had fought to free itself from the oppression of the British system of royalty, hierarchy and privilege. She liked the castle, but she was glad she didn't have to be a citizen of a country where some people were accepted as being better simply because of who their parents were. And yet here she was touring the sites of her own ancestry. Her brow creased at the paradoxes. She decided not to think about it anymore.

"So how big did the Innes holdings get, Uncle Alex?" she was walking next to her uncle while Lucy trailed behind a ways. While pleasant enough company, Aunt Lucy had not shown a great interest in the sights they had visited so far.

"Fairly large, I'm sure, though I can't tell you exactly how big." Alex rubbed his chin as they stopped to gaze upon the intricate detailing of the House's windows. "Estate sizes would grow and shrink. The Highlands had a different way of owning land than the English system used in the Lowlands. In this particular area, there was likely a hybrid of both. In any event, land would move around from family to family and even clan to clan as people died or got married."

"Interesting connection you've drawn there," Lucy laughed. She had come up behind them. "Death and marriage."

Alex laughed too. "I didn't mean it that way. But I suppose they both could have a substantial effect on a family's holdings."

"What would happen if a daughter of the chieftain married into a different clan?" Maggie was thinking of her great-times-ten grandmother, Brìghde Innes. "Would she bring land to the new clan?"

"Well, that depends," Alex started.

"She might as part of her dowry," Lucy interjected. "But as a rule, women didn't own land."

"Now, that's not entirely true," Alex countered. "The clan

system allowed for a woman to own land." He raised a proud eyebrow at Maggie, "Unlike the English system."

"In theory," Lucy shot back. "But once she married, her husband would take over all administration of the lands. She might as well not own it."

Alex frowned over this for a moment. "Well, I suppose you're right. At least it's not worth arguing over. Things have changed for the better, I think, eh, Maggie?"

Maggie nodded in agreement, but before she could say anything Lucy jumped in again.

"Yes and no," she said with a cutting laugh. "We can own land and vote now, but we still have to take our husband's name."

Maggie had to nod at this too, although it was less true for her generation than perhaps it had been for her aunt's.

"Well, yes and no," Alex echoed back, obviously irritated that his wife seemed to want an argument. "You still wear your MacLeod badge to Braemar every year."

"Aye, but I'm a MacTary now, sept of the Clan Innes," she replied, not quite bitterly. "And if we'd have had children, they'd all be MacTary's too, not MacLeods."

"Aye, well," Alex looked away. "That's not a concern, is it?"

At this, Lucy's face turned a sick shade of white. She didn't say anything, just stared at her husband's turned away face. Then without a word, she whirled and started back toward the car.

Maggie looked after her, thoroughly puzzled.

After another few moments, Alex sighed and put his arm around his niece. "C'mon, Maggie. We'd best get going. We'll want to make it to Park before too late."

Maggie nodded a third time, still trying to figure out what had just happened.

* * *

"Oh, bloody hell!" Alasdair Baxter threw open the door to his flat. "I can't believe it! It can't be true!" He ran over to the telephone.

Emma Baxter pushed herself up from her seat by the window. "What is it, love?" She'd never seen him like this.

Ignoring his wife's question, Alasdair punched the wall as he waited for the call to go through. "Sweet bleeding hell! Hello? Police! Get me the police!"

"Alasdair, love," Emma put a hand on her husband's shoulder. "What's wrong?"

He turned to her and displayed the horror in his eyes. "3-E," he tried to explain, the receiver still to his ear. "The girl ... It's ... — Hello?"

Someone had picked up on the other end of the line.

"Yes. I need the police. Now!" His eyebrows knitted over the panicked sidelong glance he threw to his wife. "There's been a murder!"

Emma took a step back from her husband as her mind's eye filled with the sweet round face of their tenant in 3-E.

After giving the police the address and his name, Alasdair Baxter hung up the phone and turned to his wife, who had returned to her comfortable wing-backed chair. He walked over and touched her hand.

"Fionna?" she asked without looking up.

"Aye."

And they both looked out the window, there being really nothing more to say.

* * *

The drive from Innes House in Morayshire to the Castle of Park in neighboring Banffshire had taken a bit longer than expected, but that was fine with Maggie. It had given the tensions which had sprung up in front of Innes House the opportunity to slowly drain away over the course of the trip. They had stopped for dinner in the town of Buckie, so it was well after eight o'clock when they finally arrived at Park. The sandstone castle, again more *château* than fortress, was illuminated by floodlights, but Maggie had grown too tired to take notice of much more than the fact that she was almost to a bed. The long day of driving, sight-seeing, and fresh air had exhausted her. There would be time tomorrow to admire the castle's architecture and grounds.

Met at the front door by both a valet and a bell-hop, they were soon standing in the richly decorated lobby, Maggie and her aunt drowsily admiring the furnishings, Uncle Alex checking in at the front desk.

"All right then," Alex stepped over to his travelling companions. "We're all checked in. We have the 'Black Watch Suite' on the second floor. There are two bedrooms, plus a private bath and loo. Should be very nice."

Maggie grunted in tired agreement. The three headed up the stairs, and almost before she realized it, Maggie found herself tucked away in her bed, lavender pajamas on, and the door to her aunt and uncle's bedchamber safely closed. Reaching down to the backpack she had dragged to the side of the bed, she extracted the Dark Book.

Her body was tired enough, but her mind still needed a bit of quieting before she would be able to surrender to sleep. She had to admit that it had been quite enjoyable to see the various castles and houses and towers associated with her ancestry. She was still wearing her Innes pendant, the silver boar's head laying across her heart. It was pretty cool to be Scottish.

With that thought in her head, she pulled back the ancient leather cover of the book which predated even Berowald, First Earl of Innes. She carefully turned a few brittle sheets until she found an interesting-looking page. She was pretty sure she had previously translated the words she found there, so she concentrated and tried to remember what they said:

<Do not begin with too difficult a spell. Ability to use the magic comes from belief in it. Even the slimmest reed of belief can lead to small successes. Such successes lead in turn to greater belief and greater success. Start small. And believe.>

The Dark Book closed and slid from Maggie's limp hands. She was more tired than she'd thought. The soft cadence of her own voice over the ancient Celtic words had ushered her softly into the trance of dreams.

16. Mary Jane Kelly

Elizabeth Warwick looked up at the facade of the Pittodrie Flats. The street itself was rather dark, lit only by a pair of dim streetlamps and the glow from the occupied flats above. Her attention was therefore immediately drawn to the flood of light which spilled out of the door directly in front of her. In the doorway stood an older man in a light blue cardigan sweater, shivering against the cold and waving frantically to them.

"There he is," Willis announced unnecessarily. He had insisted on coming along.

"Thank you. I see him."

Although it had been surprisingly pleasant weather that day, the warmth had left with the setting sun, replaced by a typically cold, late-October Scottish night. The man at the door was likely freezing in his thin sweater, but he would just have to wait.

Warwick scanned the scene. She could feel the acid burning an ulcer into her stomach. The first murder, four weeks ago to the day, had been grisly enough. But ever since she first stood over the prone body of Annette Graham, Warwick had been waiting for the other shoe to drop. That murder had been so ritualistic, the methods of killing and dismemberment so exact, the positioning of the organs so precise, that it was obviously part of some larger plan, even if only the enigmatic machinations of a madman. It would have been an act of the purest optimism—and naïveté—to have believed that the killer would stop after only one victim. Warwick had therefore spent the ensuing days and weeks trying desperately to unearth the clue or clues which could point to the identity of the murderer, could lead to his arrest, could prevent the next killing. As the weeks dragged on, few leads turned up, but so too were there no more murders. And against her better judgment, Warwick had allowed herself to hope that perhaps she had been wrong, that perhaps there would be no more killings. But now she was on the brink of standing over the body of victim number two, her hopes dashed and her hard work inadequate to save the life of whoever this young woman used to be.

Warwick shook her head to clear her thoughts. She had been in the business long enough to know not to let her personal emotions interfere with the job at hand. It may have been too late for this victim, but she had to do whatever she could at this scene to prevent a third victim from falling at the murderer's hands. For this second murder, by initial accounts as violent as the first, had served to confirm her fear that they were in fact dealing with a serial killer. All the more reason to get on with the job and to do it right.

She walked over to the old man at the door. He was probably around 60, with an almost completely bald head framed in gray fuzz. His eyes betrayed his fear.

"Thank God you've come!" He didn't wait for her to say hello. "She's in 3-E. This way."

Following behind the old man, and Willis bringing up the rear, Warwick asked, "What's your name, sir?"

"Eh? Oh, Alasdair Baxter. I'm the superintendent for the

building." Then he added with obvious discomfort at the memory, "I'm the one who found her body."

Thankfully, there was a lift. Warwick really did not want to follow the aged Mr. Baxter up three flights of stairs. As they waited for the elevator, she could hear the approaching sirens of the other officers responding to the call. Inspector Cameron would most likely be among them.

After a brief but jerky elevator ride, Warwick, Willis and Alasdair Baxter walked down the narrow hallway to flat 3-E.

"All right then," Mr. Baxter said opening the door with his key. "Here it is."

An overwhelming stench of death and sorrow pounced on them from inside the flat. After an involuntary gag, Warwick drew herself up again and ventured into the room, hand over her nose. She could hear Willis still coughing in the hallway behind her.

"I'll just wait here with Mr. Baxter, shall I?" he called out between hacks. Warwick ignored him.

The only light was from the overhead fixture near the door. *Had the victim turned it on as she entered, or the killer as he left? Had he been waiting for her in the dark?* She would have to look closer for signs of forced entry. Turning the corner into the living room, Warwick suddenly stopped: the girl's lifeless foot was sticking out from behind the other side of the couch. She closed her eyes and steeled herself. This was not going to be pleasant. Taking as deep a breath as the pungent air would allow, she walked sharply around the couch and pulled up short in front of the bloody carnage she found there.

Sgt. Elizabeth Warwick had been an officer in the Aberdeen Police Department for five years, and had been in law enforcement in rural Northern England for two years prior to that. She had been to twenty-nine murder scenes that she could remember off the top of her head and had responded to an incalculable number of accident scenes where people had been burned alive in their automobiles or decapitated in some industrial accident. And of course, four weeks earlier she had stood over the butchered body of Annette Graham. She had known exactly what to expect when she came around that couch. She had known what to expect and she had been right. And still she turned away in horror, hand over her mouth, and hoped she wouldn't vomit.

After a few moments, she reluctantly returned her gaze to the bloody corpse at her feet. There was no doubt that it was the handiwork of the same evil soul. Indeed, at first glance the scene appeared identical to that of Annette Graham's murder. This woman had the same deep blood encrusted slice circling her throat. She too had had her arms placed at her sides and legs pushed together. She too had had her garments carefully pushed aside, her stomach carefully sliced open, and each and every one of her organs carefully extracted. And the killer had had the foresight to bring a two inch wide flat stone with him which he had once again balanced between the victim's closed, lifeless eyes. The only difference that Warwick could notice between this scene and the one on the stone pathway at the college was that the distinctive lung-heart-lung combination was now to the victim's right—Warwick's left as she looked down—rather than above the victim's head. Otherwise the same organs appeared to surround the body and Warwick didn't have to look far to spot the stinking brown pile of those remaining organs deemed unworthy of whatever ritual the killer had engaged in.

"Jack the Ripper he's not."

Warwick drew in a sharp breath despite herself. The voice itself was familiar but she had not been expecting it. Nor had she heard its owner walk into the flat while she was engrossed in thought.

"How's that, Inspector?" She waited to finish the question before she turned around.

"I said, he's no Jack the Ripper." Cameron stepped forward to stand next to the sergeant and pointed at the body. "You have heard of Jack the Ripper?"

"Of course," she replied, trying not to be offended at the question. "Whitechapel. 1888. But what makes you say our killer's not like the Ripper?"

"The Ripper killed five women, right? Do you recall when and where their bodies were found?"

"Not at the moment, no."

"Well, the murders took place over ten weeks. All the victims were prostitutes who worked outside the city gate to London. The first four victims were all found outside, strangled and butchered not unlike this poor girl here."

Warwick winced. "So how is our man not like Jack the Ripper then?"

"Ah well," Cameron turned away from the bloody corpse and looked about the room. "The fifth victim was a prostitute named Mary Jane Kelly. I only mention she was a prostitute because she must have been accustomed to taking strange men back to her flat. Her body was found inside, like this poor thing."

Warwick closed her eyes. She knew he hadn't meant what he'd just suggested, but she decided to clear it up anyway. "You're not saying the girl here was a prostitute?"

Cameron's face screwed up in embarrassment. "No, of course not. No, no. My point is this." He turned again to the dead girl's body. "All the Ripper's other victims—he killed them outside, and cut them up outside. He even killed two in one night, the first one just strangled, but the second one with her kidney cut out and taken from the scene. It was as if he'd been interrupted with the first girl so he found another victim as soon as he could. But with Mary Jane Kelly, he knew he'd have no interruptions. Just like here."

Warwick winced again at the thought of the killer taking his sweet time in his evil deed.

"But see, Mary Jane Kelly's body was different from the rest. He'd not stopped with just her kidney. He just kept cutting and cutting and cutting. Cut open every part of her you could think of. Her legs were sliced open to the bone from groin to ankle, and half her face was missing. He'd had all the time in the world and he didn't stop until there wasn't anything left to cut."

Warwick nodded. Now she remembered.

"And then," Cameron concluded, "the murders stopped. It was like he'd finally sated whatever demons had possessed him."

"But here," Warwick finished the logic, "our man had the same opportunity, but did no more and no less than he'd done outside where anyone could have run across him at any time."

"Which is not to belittle the severity of the butchery here," Cameron observed, "but he's not just a madman who wants to cut up women."

Warwick looked at the dead woman's body and frowned. She closed her eyes. "And he's not sated yet either."

Cameron sighed and nodded his head. "I'd wager you're right."

Then the two officers stepped back out into the hallway to give space to the forensics officers who were arriving. Neither had yet noticed the flashing light on Fionna FitzSimmons' answering machine.

17. A Healer

"Maggie Devereaux?" The voice was pleasant, with only the softest urgency. "Maggie, wake up, child."

Maggie rolled over and opened her eyes. She lay in a luxuriously decorated bedchamber and a woman's smiling face hovered before her. In her initial grogginess, Maggie let herself believe she was the lady of a medieval castle being awakened by her maid servant—before she then woke up enough to recognize her Aunt Lucy's smiling visage.

"Mmmhm," Maggie managed to say as she sat up in the surprisingly comfortable bed. The Dark Book lay to one side; She had to resist the urge to quickly shove it behind her lest she thereby actually attract her aunt's attention to it. She must have fallen asleep while reading. She had slept like a stone, and although she felt as if she'd dreamt the whole time, the night's visions were dancing just out of her memory's reach.

"What time is it?" she asked.

"A bit after eight. You were tired, weren't you? Alex and I have already cleaned up so the bath's free. You'll want to get up now. They stop serving breakfast at nine."

In short order, Maggie had risen, showered and dressed, once again stringing the Innes crest around her neck and under her sweater. Breakfast was a leisurely affair and although technically the kitchen stopped serving at nine, they had had no trouble allowing the MacTarys and their niece to linger over coffee to discuss the day's plans. The big event would be a tour of the castle's portrait gallery, but as that wouldn't open until noon on a Sunday, it was decided to spend the remainder of the morning strolling the grounds of the Park estate.

The grounds extended over sixty acres, an area far too great to cover in one morning, but there were several pleasant walking paths which led through various gardens and wooded areas on the property. After visiting two separate rose gardens and a shrubbery, Maggie and the MacTarys followed one of the paths to an old kirk nestled near the edge of the estate.

The kirk was made entirely of stone and stood no more than fifteen feet tall, save the steeple which jutted up proudly above the low front door. Old and somewhat in disrepair, the small church had been boarded off from entry, lest some curious hotel guest wander in and injure him- or herself. Luckily however, the kirkyard could not be so sealed off and soon Maggie found herself treading lightly through the smallish cemetery tucked behind the stone church.

"A lot of estates had their own kirks back in the late middle ages," Alex explained as he glanced back at the gray edifice casting a cool shadow over the graveyard. "It wasn't always convenient, or safe, to travel into town for mass."

Maggie was only half listening as she began to read the faded tombstones of the kirkyard.

"Most," Alex went on, "like this one, ended up being deconsecrated as it became easier to go into town, and too expensive to house a priest at the castle to administer mass to only one family and a few servants."

"Here it is!" Maggie shouted, entirely not in response to anything her uncle had been saying.

"What?" Lucy strode over quickly from where she had been examining the stones of the kirk wall. Alex followed close behind.

Maggie pointed triumphantly at a faded, weather-worn tombstone. She had been scanning the gravemarkers looking for a name she recognized from her grandmother's genealogy. She had succeeded.

"What does it say?" Her aunt squinted but couldn't make out the worn letters on the gravestone.

"It says: '*Brigia Innsia Gordonia*,'" Maggie read aloud, "'*Nata quartum decimum Aprilis A.D. 1600. Mortua septimum Augustus A.D. 1652. Uxor Alexanderi. Mater Margeritae. Sanatrix totus.*'"

Lucy smiled at her husband, then asked her niece, "And what does that mean? Our Latin's a bit rusty. That was Latin, right?"

"Uh, right. Sorry." Maggie grinned uncomfortably. "Let's see. It means: 'Brìghde Innes Gordon. Born the fourteenth of April, 1600. Died the seventh of August, 1652. Wife of Alexander. Mother of Margaret. Healer of All.'"

"Hm," Lucy observed.

"Margaret, huh?" Alex asked. "Like your name."

"Right," Maggie replied, her mind turning. "I think this is my great, great, great, and so on, grandmother."

"Really?" Lucy was surprised. "How do you know that?"

Maggie frowned in thought. "I did my genealogy once. We were able to trace one branch all the way back to a Brìghde Innes who was born in 1600. And I think her daughter was named Margaret."

"I wonder if she's buried here too?" Alex looked around the

small graveyard.

"Probably not," Lucy answered as Alex began to wander off. "She's likely buried with her husband at his family's cemetery."

"Yeah, you're probably right," Maggie answered dejectedly.

"Not necessarily," Alex called out from the kirkyard fence. "Take a look over here."

Maggie and her aunt scurried quickly over to Alex' position and peered down at two equally worn grave markers, one inside the fence and the other outside it. Maggie translated the names from their Latinized forms.

"'James Wilkie' and 'Margaret NicInnes Wilkie.' Yup, this is them." Maggie nodded her head authoritatively, then asked, "Is 'Wilkie' a clan name?"

Alex frowned for a moment. "Hmm. I don't believe so, although it may be a sept of a clan. If not, though, that may explain why they ended up here on her family's lands rather than his."

Maggie grunted in agreement, as she pondered why the fence would split the late couple.

"What else does is say?" Lucy encouraged.

Maggie looked to the stone outside the kirkyard. "Okay, um: 'Margaret NicInnes Wilkie. Wife and Mother. Born the eighteenth of January, 1620.'"

Maggie looked back to her aunt and uncle. "Hey, that's my birthday too," she shared. "Ooh, that's kinda spooky."

Shivering at this somewhat morbid coincidence, she turned again to the gravestone. "Anyway: 'Born the eighteenth of January, 1620...'" She paused, double checking her translation of the Latin.

"What is it?" Lucy asked.

"Um," Maggie's lips twisted into a crooked frown. "Well, I'm pretty sure it says: '*Burned* the twenty-second day of December, 1646.'"

"*Burned?*" Lucy and Alex asked in unison.

"Um, yeah." Maggie looked again at the iron rail separating her ancestor's grave from the churchyard. "That means she was a witch, right?"

"Well, they thought she was, anyway," Alex replied. "That might explain why they wouldn't bury her inside the kirkyard."

"Uh, yeah," Maggie agreed, peering back at the little Catholic church. "That it might."

Maggie considered this unexpected information. Grandma had conveniently failed to mention during any of their genealogy sessions that they had an ancestor who'd been burned as a witch.

"And she was only twenty-six when she died," Lucy observed. "What a shame."

Maggie and Alex both looked again at the gravestone. Maggie frowned again.

"Hey, you're twenty-six as well, aren't you, Maggie?" Alex asked.

Maggie paused and looked at the gravemarker. '<Burned the 22nd of December, 1646>.' "Um. Yeah," she replied quietly.

Then she gathered herself up. "Okay, I'm done," she announced. "We can go."

* * *

Following a light lunch—except for Alex who had enjoyed a hearty helping of beef and turnips—Maggie and the MacTarys made their way to the castle's portrait gallery, located conveniently on the third floor of the hotel. There was no lift.

Just before the entrance to the gallery was the castle's 'museum,' which looked to Maggie suspiciously like a gift shop. Her aunt and uncle had also noticed the museum and Lucy was already inside examining the crystal baubles for sale within.

"Did you want to look in the museum?" Alex asked Maggie

while keeping a watchful eye on his spouse.

"No, thanks. I'm really more interested in the portraits." She could tell where Alex wanted to be. "But you go ahead in there. I'll grab you guys on my way out."

"All right, then," Alex was quick to agree, and turned to join his wife, who had already selected two different crystal decanters. Although he knew better that to tell his wife what she could or couldn't buy, he at least wanted to be involved in the selection. "We'll see you in a bit."

The gallery proved to both fulfill expectations and disappoint hopes. It fulfilled expectations inasmuch as it looked exactly how Maggie would have expected a castle's portrait gallery to look. A long hallway stretched out before her, its butter colored wainscotting rising to hip level, giving way to a rich burgundy wallpaper which extended to the moulded ivory ceiling. A rich multi-colored Persian rug extended to a dark wooden table at the far end of the hallway, where the hall then extended to the right and left, forming a 'T' intersection. Overhead a series of small chandeliers hung every ten feet or so, casting a surprisingly dim light over the hallway. Mood lighting, Maggie assumed. The table at the end of the hallway held a display of cut crystal objects which collected what light was cast by the chandeliers and disbursed it into droplets of rainbow across the table and rug. The paintings which recessed down either side of the hallway were all housed in intricately carved gilded frames, each adorned with a small brass lamp throwing a strong, bright light onto the canvas below it, resulting in the obviously very intentional effect of placing great emphasis on the subjects of the portraits. Maggie stepped into the gallery and purveyed its offerings.

Which is when she confirmed that the gallery would disappoint as well. Although the collection boasted portraits from as early as the mid-1500s, there was absolutely no sign of Brìghde Innes Gordon. Indeed, with the exception of a rather harsh looking woman from the early 1900s and a pair of truly plain sisters from the 1800s, the remainder of the paintings were of the male leaders of the Clan Gordon. This included Brìghde's husband, Alexander Malcolm James Gordon, second son of the Gordon clan chieftain. In his portrait he was adorned in full Highland dress, green kilt and great plaid hanging aristocratically from his strong frame. He looked quite the chieftain—or at least chieftain's son. Maggie frowned at the likeness.

Behind every great man..., she thought. Then, she turned and exited the gallery.

Once outside she stepped into the 'museum,' where she found her aunt and uncle each with several items in their hands and an eye toward the salesclerk.

"Are we done already then?" Alex asked, suggesting he had little interest in looking at the portraits himself.

"Yeah. It was interesting, but I think I'm ready to go home."

"Well, we'll just be a few minutes more and then we can go." Alex looked to his wife for confirmation, who gave it in the form of a crisp nod.

"In that case," Maggie reflected on the long car ride home. "I think I'll go find the ladies' room. Then I'll just meet you downstairs in the lobby, okay?"

"The loo?" Alex translated. "Aye, good idea. Okay, we'll see you in the lobby in a few minutes."

That settled, Alex and Lucy returned to their appraisal of the various items they had selected, and Maggie set off in search of a bathroom. Her search appeared at first to be a short one; she immediately spotted a sign hanging over a door at the other end of the third floor landing. The sign had three of those international symbols which are always drawn inside boxes and are expected to be understood by all, regardless of language: the first box contained the letters 'WC'; the second a silhouette of a man, with his detached ball head; the third, a silhouette of Mrs. Detached-Ball-Head. Maggie hurried on and looked forward to getting home soon. This quick success proved to be a mirage, however, as she traversed the hallway only to find a paper sign taped to the women's restroom. 'Closed for Repairs,' it said, with an added notation underneath, in that small European handwriting: 'Ladies Toilet on 4th Floor.'

Great, Maggie thought. *Now I have to find the stairs* and *the bathroom.*

The stairwell they had ascended to the portrait gallery stopped at the third floor. So there had to be a separate staircase to the fourth floor. A castle safety precaution, Maggie presumed. She considered returning to the Black Watch Suite until she remembered that they had technically checked out at noon and put their luggage in the car, lest they be charged for another night's stay. Considering this, Maggie noticed for the first time that the castle was eerily quiet. It was that time in a hotel when the previous night's guests had already checked out, but the next night's had not yet arrived. As a result, Maggie was the only one around when she finally found the staircase to the fourth floor.

Apparently the management didn't expect guests to visit the fourth floor regularly. In addition to the fact that the only access appeared to be through a hidden stairwell that started on the *third* floor, the lofty stone corridors of this fourth *etage* were filled with legions of dusty furniture and boxes, some covered in tarps, others with dust and plaster chips adorning their exposed tops. The only light was from a series of small yellow paned windows set high in the stone walls. The light cascading in was filled with the swirling dust of this remote section of the fortress. Peering around, Maggie seriously doubted there was a usable ladies' room anywhere nearby. Nevertheless she set out cautiously down the hallway already planning her irritated demand of the front desk attendant to use the staff restroom.

Her irritation began to wane somewhat as she became interested in the items lining the walkway. Although no expert on antiques, still she appreciated their workmanship, not to mention their very existence, having survived perhaps centuries of political strife and household catastrophes. Her purview of the furnishings was cut short however, as she spied a recess in the hallway over which hung the same anachronistic 'WC' sign she had seen one floor below. Having thus found her quarry, and hopeful that this door would not bear the same paper-thin bar to entry as its third floor cousin, Maggie hurried past the remaining items and rejoiced at the absence of any 'do not enter' signs.

Exiting the ladies' room shortly thereafter noticeably more relaxed, Maggie lingered over the various items between herself and the stairs. In addition to furniture, there were also decorative items tilted against the wall. Here, a large carved coat of arms; there, a gilded framed mirror. Here, a tarnished shield; there, an oil-painting of a beautiful blond aristocratic lady.

Maggie stopped. She pushed her glasses back up her nose and stared in amazement at the portrait leaning against the wall to her right, a tarp lazily covering its upper left corner. It was a stare of recognition. And the woman inside the ornate frame seemed to return the look. Although Maggie couldn't read the tiny letters on the small brass name plate affixed to the bottom of the frame, she knew at least one word that appeared there. It was the same word that had appeared at the bottom of the page in the art book she had found in the subbasement. It was the same word she had read on the worn gravestone in the kirkyard. The beautiful blond noblewoman whose blue catlike eyes shone across the centuries, whose painted visage had been relegated to this forgotten hallway rather than being displayed with honor in the portrait gallery—even without reading the brass plaque, Maggie knew that this woman was her great-times-ten grandmother. Brìghde Innes Gordon. Healer.

Maggie crossed the room and read the plaque, confirming her beliefs. On it stood two lines: 'A Healer, 1620,' as she had read in the subbasement book, and 'Brìghde Innes Gordon, 1600 – 1652,' as she had read on the kirkyard gravestone. Despite her strong urge to do so, she knew she couldn't just up and appropriate the painting as she had been able to do with the Dark Book. But she felt just as strongly that she ought not to simply abandon ancestor's portrait to this dusty, unvisited corridor. The thought of her female Innes ancestor sitting neglected in this forgotten hallway while her husband stood so proudly below in his green Gordon plaid made Maggie's blood begin to boil. She seriously considered grabbing the portrait, marching back down to the portrait gallery and hanging it on the wall in the space where Alexander the Great's portrait had hung—before she'd flung it violently down the hallway, hopefully shattering a chandelier or two on its way. Or perhaps she should simply slam Brìghde's likeness down on the front desk and scream bloody murder at whichever poor soul happened to be unfortunate to be working there just now. Several more similarly violent and aggressive scenarios rushed through Maggie's mind until, stepping back from herself, she became conscious of just how angry she was. Not normally one quick to temper, she now found herself flushed and sweating, her hands clenched into fists, and her heart pounding in her ears. So thoroughly surprised was she by this, that she stepped away from the painting, took two very deep breaths, and then hurried back up the hallway and down the stairs, her fingers still tingling with adrenaline.

Perhaps, she considered as she descended the stairs, *a strongly worded letter.*

* * *

The ride home was quiet. Everyone was a bit tired and the beautiful rolling scenery of the Grampian Highlands made a welcome distraction. For her part, Maggie sat comfortably in the back seat and gazed contemplatively out the window. Across her glasses scrolled reflections of the Scottish hills, while before her mind's eye scrolled past a single word: 'Healer.' Among all the things she had seen in the weekend's whirlwind tour of her ancestral lands, it was this one word which had made the greatest impression. Printed in Gaelic in the black ink of the subbasement art book. Carved in Latin in the faded gray of the stone grave marker. Etched in English on the elegant brass plaque affixed to her ancestor's portrait.

Maggie wondered just what a 'healer' was exactly. But even more than that, the word had ignited a spark inside her that made her wonder what it had to do with herself, her studies, and her grandmother's insistence that she study at Aberdeen.

18. Twenty Questions

"Good morning, Mr. Hopkins."

Lt. Malcolm Russell's voice was calm and reassuring as he sat down casually on the corner of the table Will Hopkins was seated at. The policeman's relaxed demeanor contrasted sharply with the intimidating stone walls of the Aberdeen Police Department's interrogation room.

"G—Good morning," Will stammered, eyes wide behind his gold rimmed glasses.

"Thank you for meeting with us."

Will just nodded, his mouth slightly ajar. Russell stood up again. He was a strapping, heavy-set man in his early 50s. A balding head clung jealously to a small collection of black hairs atop a spotted scalp. His clean shaven face melted into a thick neck which stuck out of the unbuttoned collar of his light blue, underarm-stained dress shirt. A striped red and navy blue tie hung loosely over his sizeable paunch and his sleeves were rolled up, exposing large, hairy forearms and their blurry blue tattoos from his days in the British Navy.

"You and Miss FitzSimmons were in a relationship, is that correct?"

"Y—Yes. She," he paused at the tense of the verb, "*was* my girlfriend."

"All right then." Lt. Russell crossed over to the only window in the room—a small, depressing thing, its four panes had been frosted over to allow in light, but nothing more. "Boyfriend and girlfriend. Not engaged then?"

"No," was the simple reply.

"Any talk of it?" The lieutenant turned around casually, his tone conversational.

"What, marriage?" Will looked down at his hands, nervously rubbing each others' palms. "Well, I mean, it had come up. We'd discussed it, I suppose. But only generally."

Russell didn't say anything, just looked at him.

"Nothing specific," Will added, filling the silence.

"Okay." Russell walked back over and pulled out the chair opposite his subject, but didn't sit down. "And how long had you been boyfriend and girlfriend?"

Will looked toward the ceiling in thought. "Er, almost two years. We met during her first year here at Aberdeen. I was in my third year. We started dating in December."

Russell tuned the chair around and sat backwards on it, facing Will. "Your third year, eh? So you're in your fifth year now, then?"

"Right."

The lieutenant smiled, exposing large yellow teeth, stained by decades of coffee and cigarettes. "Just how many years does college take nowadays?"

Will smiled, despite the circumstances. "Yes, well, it depends on what one is studying," he explained. "A regular degree might take only four years, but I'm in the medical school, so it's usually five. Then residency."

"Oh, then you're almost done."

"Right," Will confirmed. "I'll be done in the spring."

"What's the plan then?" Russell raised his eyebrows in what appeared to be genuine interest.

"Well, then residency. Working at a hospital as a new doctor."

"And where will you do that?"

"I don't know for sure yet, but I'm hoping to get back to London."

"Are you from London, then?"

"Yes, Kensington," Will smiled.

Russell looked down at his thick fingers which had begun to drum the tabletop absently. "Medical residency. That's quite a bit of work, eh?"

Will gave out a nervous but proud little laugh. "Yes. Long hours and little money. But it's worth it in the end," he asserted.

"No time for a family really, then?" Russell looked up from the table to his subject's eyes.

"No, not—" Will stopped and met his questioner's gaze. "No. I don't know. Maybe."

The lieutenant stood up again and started to pace the room.

"All right then, Mr. Hopkins. Let's talk about Friday evening, shall we?"

Will sat forward and crossed his hands on the table. "All right."

"Let's start with the basics," Russell said. "Where were you that evening, say starting around six o'clock?"

Will loosened his hands and lowered his eyes in thought. "I, um, had an early dinner—around five thirty—and then spent the rest of the night studying."

"Where?"

"At my apartment."

"Alone?"

Will grimaced at this. "Yes," he sighed. "Alone."

"And at your apartment, not at the library?"

"No. I study best alone," Will defended. "Besides the medical campus is some distance away. I prefer to study at home when I can."

"Okay. If you say so." Russell clasped his hands behind his back, but continued to pace. "And you don't live out by the medical campus?"

"No."

"You live here near the Old Campus, then?"

"Right."

"Why's that?"

Will took in a deep breath. "Well part of it is that it's closer to Fionna." He grimaced again. "*Was* closer to Fionna."

"All right and where was Miss FitzSimmons while you were—what did you say?—while you were studying?"

Will thought for a moment, then answered, "I don't know. As I said, I was home studying. Alone."

"Aye, you did say that," Russell acknowledged, then stopped directly in front of Will and turned to look him in the eye. "So let me make sure I understand what you're telling me: On a Friday night, having chosen an apartment to be close to your girlfriend of two years, with whom you'd discussed getting married I might add, you elected to spend the entire evening home alone, studying, and you have absolutely no idea where she was. Is that what you're going to tell me?"

Will set his jaw. "Yes."

"And of course you have *no* witnesses to vouch for your whereabouts that night, I suppose?"

Will shoved himself back in his chair. "No. Look, Fionna knew how important my career is to me. It wasn't unusual for us to spend an evening apart—even a Friday evening. In fact it was rare that one of us wasn't studying either Friday or Saturday night. And as for witnesses, no, I don't have any. I didn't know I'd need any. In fact, it hadn't even occurred to me until just now that I was even considered a suspect and—"

"Calm yourself, Will." Lt. Russell's tone returned to its reassuring, conversational tenor and he held up a hand. "No one's accused you of anything. We're just trying to figure out what happened."

Russell sat down again on the backwards facing chair and lowered his chin onto his forearms which he had crossed atop the back. "Are you sure Fionna didn't say anything about what she was doing that night?"

Will took a deep breath, then let it out slowly. "I don't know. I—I saw her just before I went home to eat dinner and study. Sometimes we eat dinner together, sometimes we don't. We didn't that night. I think she had something to do, but honestly, I didn't ask. And that—" he paused, "that was the last time I saw her."

He took in a sharp breath and lowered his face to his hands. The lieutenant waited a few moments before reaching out and clasping Hopkins' shoulder.

"We're almost done, lad," he said soothingly. "I've only a few more questions."

Will raised his head and nodded. "Right," his voice cracked. "Go on."

"Did you see her at all on Saturday?"

Will cocked his head, a look of surprise on his face. "No. I— No."

"Okay. And did you make any attempt to contact her either

Friday evening or any time Saturday?"

Will's eyebrows knitted together. "No."

Russell leaned back and then stood up with a slap on the back of the chair. "All right then, Mr. Hopkins. You're free to go," he announced. "But, uh, don't leave Aberdeen without telling us first, all right?"

Will looked at the lieutenant, a puzzled expression on his face.

"If we need you to answer any more questions," Russell explained innocuously, "we'll not want to waste time trying to track you down in London. You were very close to Miss FitzSimmons. Hopefully you can help us catch her killer."

"All right," Will agreed as he stood up and walked to the door.

"Mr. Hopkins?" the lieutenant called out just as Will's hand touched the door handle.

"Yes?" Will turned back.

"Is there anything else we should know?" The conversational tone had once again drained away from Russell's voice, leaving behind the cold, serious inquiry of a police lieutenant. "About this weekend? About you? About Fionna? Anything *at all*?"

Will Hopkins turned back to the door and thought for a moment.

Finally, without turning around, he replied simply, "No," then pulled open the door with a metallic clank and walked out of the interrogation room.

* * *

"The wee bastard's lying." Russell exhaled the smoke through his nose and crushed the butt in the ashtray before reaching for another cigarette.

"Most likely," Inspector Cameron agreed. He peered through

the four small window panes that looked into the interrogation room. A two-way mirror would have been too obvious. "But that doesn't necessarily make him a killer."

Sgt. Willis chimed in from his seat in the back, near the door. "He seems the most likely suspect."

Cameron didn't even turn around, but Russell took the bait. "How do you figure, Mike?"

"Well, it could be a domestic violence situation."

Russell frowned at this suggestion. This time it was Cameron who responded, but still without turning around.

"Willis," he sighed, "have you ever heard of a domestic violence situation that involved a ritual killing?"

Sgt. Willis actually thought for a moment before answering, "No."

"And Willis," Cameron still faced the trick window. "Are you aware of any connection, domestic or otherwise, between William Hopkins and Annette Graham?"

"Well, no," Willis admitted. "But what about what Dr. Wood told us?"

"We don't even know," the inspector finally turned around, "if Hopkins knew about that."

Cameron was unable to continue, however, because just then a young female officer opened the door to the observation room.

"Lieutenant Russell, your next suspect is ready."

Cameron looked again through the window as a large man with thick red hair and a neatly trimmed red beard was escorted into the room. The man then lumbered over to the table and plopped down with an air of practiced boredom.

"And who is this?" Cameron inquired.

"That would be the deceased's brother, Sean Michael

FitzSimmons," Russell explained, extinguishing his cigarette in the ashtray.

Cameron frowned. "Seems an unlikely suspect," he opined.

"Perhaps," Russell acknowledged, "but he's got a criminal history as long as my arm. Ulster faxed it over this morning. Battery, assault, battery, arson, battery, battery, battery. The lad's got a right temper, he does."

"Hmmph," Cameron observed enigmatically.

"Well, in any event." Russell pulled the door to the hallway open. "It can't hurt to talk to him."

The door closed behind the lieutenant and Cameron repeated his "Hmmph," this time to himself. Sgt. Willis considered for a moment trying to make some sort of insightful comment, but thought better of it and instead returned to his perusal of the crime scene photos.

* * *

"Good morning, Mr. FitzSimmons."

Lt. Russell's voice hung on the word 'mister' just long enough to show he didn't mean it. The reassuring, conversational tone he had used with Will Hopkins was entirely absent.

Sean FitzSimmons looked up at the stocky old policeman who had just walked in, but he didn't reply. He appeared unimpressed.

"I suppose you know why you're here?" Russell went on.

Sean held the lieutenant's gaze for a moment, then looked away, arms crossed.

"C'mon now, lad," Russell coaxed. "Your sister was murdered. Don't you want to help us catch her killer?"

Sean continued to stare at the window to his left.

Russell stood up straight. "All right, mate, if that's the way you want to play it, so be it. Where were you the evening of Friday last?"

Still no reply.

"What about the evening of September twenty-seventh?"

Sean turned from the window and flashed a puzzled look at the policeman.

"That's the night the first girl was murdered," Russell explained. "Perhaps you can explain to me why your initials were found all through her diary?"

Sean FitzSimmons just shook his head as a bemused smile crossed his face. He turned away again.

"C'mon, FitzSimmons!" Russell slammed two practiced fists down on the table, inches from his subject. "You're making a mistake! Your sister's been murdered—butchered! We've got to eliminate everyone as a suspect. So just give me your damned alibis and help yourself out, lad!"

"Go to hell," Sean finally said, his temper evident just beneath his angry growl. "I'm not new to this. You bloody well know that. And I've done this enough to know that you don't drag people in here just to eliminate them as suspects. The only reason I'm here is because you think I had something to do with Fionna's murder. Well, thanks to your occupation of my island, I was born on British soil and I hold a British passport. So I think I'll just invoke my rights under 'Her Majesty's Royal Bleeding Government' and tell you to go to bloody hell."

Russell stood up slowly and smiled. "Aye, you're not new to this," he agreed. "And aye, I know it. But laddie, Her Majesty's Royal Government's done away with your right to remain silent. Silence in the face of questioning can now be used to infer guilt."

Sean's eyes narrowed at this new information.

"Aye, it's true," the lieutenant assured. "And you've your own bastard Fenian brothers to thank for it, too. Nothing like a few hundred I.R.A. bomb attacks to motivate Parliament to loosen up the restraints on the thin blue line."

Sean kept his narrowed gaze locked on the police officer.

"So if you insist on ignoring my inquiries, all I have to do is turn my questioning around a bit and you'll be signing your own arrest warrant."

Sean just stared at him.

"So then," the lieutenant started again. "Where were you Friday night starting at about six o'clock?"

Sean looked away to the window, then raised both hands, palm in, his index and middle fingers raised and separated—the British equivalent of the American middle finger. One hand was directed at Russell, the other at whoever was watching them through the window.

"All right then, mate," Russell's voice sounded tired, but betrayed just the slightest bit of anger. "Have it your way."

He pushed the second chair out of the way and leaned over the table, his meaty hands gripping either side and his face only inches from the obscene gesture still being raised to him.

"You were with your sister, Fionna FitzSimmons, the evening of Friday last, correct?"

Sean ignored him.

"Right," Russell continued, "and in fact you were the last person to see her alive, is that not so?"

Silence.

"I see. And it's true, is it not, that you bleeding killed her, didn't you, FitzSimmons? You garroted her then gutted her like a fish! Didn't you? Didn't you?!"

Sean exploded from his chair and grabbed the burly officer by the collar. "How the bloody hell can you say that?!" he screamed. "Some filthy bastard kills my sister—my bleeding *pregnant* sister—

and you accuse me?! *Me?!* How dare you? How dare you?!"

Russell didn't say or do anything; he just stared his quarry in the eye.

Sean stared right back, green eyes burning. Then he pushed the lieutenant away and let go. "Go to hell." He dropped again into his chair.

Russell sighed as he fixed his collar. "Now you've done it, lad. You lost your cool. And you up and said something you oughtn't have done."

Sean looked up at the policeman, puzzled.

"See, lad," Russell leaned in to explain. "You let out that you knew Fionna was pregnant. But I know I didn't tell you that. No one knew she was pregnant, 'cept the coroner—and whoever the bastard was who killed her and sliced her open to pull her bloody womb out."

Sean's eyes flashed. "*Fionna* bloody well knew it, you idiot! And she bloody well told *me* about it! Christ, man, think! And it was that English bastard, Hopkins!" Sean slammed a fist onto the table. "He wanted her to get a bleeding abortion! Said it would ruin his career! Just like a bloody Englishman. He wanted her to just up and murder my bleeding nephew!" He stopped and looked up at the ceiling, clearly pained by his next thought. "And she was bloody well considering it, too." He exhaled audibly, then looked the lieutenant in the eye. "Now they're both dead. So I guess he got his bleeding wish."

Russell stood silently for several moments, his eyes trained on Sean FitzSimmons. Finally he stuck a thumb toward the door.

"You can go, lad."

Sean pushed away from the table and crossed angrily to the door.

"But," Russell warned, "don't leave Aberdeen without our

permission."

Sean pulled open the heavy metal door. "Go to hell."

* * *

"That went well," Cameron observed wryly.

Russell had barely set foot back into the observation room before he lit up his cigarette. "Oh, aye? I hadn't noticed."

"He seems the most likely suspect," offered Willis.

Ignoring him, Cameron and Russell continued their conversation.

"Now what?" the lieutenant asked.

Cameron frowned slightly and pushed his hands into his pockets. "Now we talk to more witnesses. We hope the boys in forensics find something. We pound the pavement." He paused, as if uncertain himself. "Whatever it takes."

Just then the door to the observation room opened and in walked Elizabeth Warwick, a satisfied smile spread across her countenance.

"Got it," she announced simply and handed a document to the inspector. "Finally."

"What is it?" Russell asked. Willis too had risen from his seat.

"A birth certificate," Cameron explained slowly, not looking up from the paper.

"For a little girl," Warwick continued, "baptized 'Mary' but who ended up being adopted by Donald and Jacqueline Graham of Cape Breton, Nova Scotia, Canada."

Cameron read aloud from the document, "'Father: Unknown. Mother:'"

He stopped and looked at Warwick, confident that she had already made the arrangements for their imminent trip to the woman's home. "'Mother: Lucille MacLeod.'"

19. The Sins of the Parents

"Good show, Elizabeth," Cameron complimented from the passenger seat of the unmarked police car hurrying through the streets of Aberdeen. "It's good finally to be getting somewhere with this investigation."

Warwick smiled. Cameron only used her first name when he was particularly pleased with her. "Thank you, Inspector." She was savvy enough not to return the familiarity.

"Speaking of which," he went on. "Any luck tracking down that girl on the answering machine tape? Mavis Decocteau?"

"Maggie Devereaux," Warwick corrected as she turned onto a side street. "No, not yet. Based on her American or Canadian accent and the FitzSimmons woman being a student at the university I'd thought she was likely a student too. But the university office can't find any record of her."

"Well, keep looking," Cameron encouraged as Warwick pulled the car to a stop in front of a rather nice green house in the rather nice Aberdeen neighborhood. "I'm sure she'll turn up in no time."

* * *

Maggie picked up the platter with the two remaining oatcakes and carried it into the kitchen.

"So how come Iain didn't join us for breakfast?" she asked. "It is Monday, after all."

"Ah, well, Iain knew your uncle would be spending his weekend driving all over the Grampian Highlands," Aunt Lucy explained as she took the platter from Maggie. "So he and Alex agreed that Iain would go straight into the shop this morning while Alex got a wee bit extra sleep. Hence the late breakfast as well."

"Well, that was nice of Iain," Maggie observed.

"Aye, well, Iain's a good lad." Lucy slid the oatcakes onto a waiting plate and stuck the platter under the running water of the sink. "And it doesn't hurt that once Alex and I get to the store, Iain gets to leave for the day. We gave him tomorrow off, too, in exchange for having had to work all weekend alone."

"Well, then, that was awfully nice of you, too." Maggie looked back at the dining room. "I think that's all the dishes."

"Good. And I'm almost done here." Lucy placed the platter on the drying rack next to the sink. "Then we'll be heading into the store. Why don't we give you a ride?"

Maggie paused. "I'd planned on riding my bike..." she began.

"Nonsense," Lucy interjected. "It's almost November." She peered out the kitchen window as she wiped her hands on her apron. "And it looks like rain. Bad enough you got caught in that downpour Friday night, I don't want you coming down sick because you're bicycling this time a year. When is your meeting with Prof. Macintyre?"

"Uh, eleven." Maggie decided to just accept the ride. It was getting pretty cold for bike riding at that.

Her aunt looked at the clock in thought. "Why don't we try to leave in about fifteen minutes. That'll get you there a bit early, but we don't want to make Iain have to wait too long. Go get your things together and I'll rouse Alex from the couch."

"Sounds good," Maggie agreed and she turned toward the stairs.

Just then came a sharp knock on the front door.

"Do you want me to get that?" Maggie asked. The front door was right by the stairs she was about to climb.

"Eh, no, lass. That's all right." Lucy's face showed the cautious curiosity of one whose door has unexpectedly been knocked on. "You go and get your things. I'll see who it is."

So Maggie hurried past the front door with its unknown visitors and bounded up the stairs to pack her bag for a day's worth of studying.

Behind her and moving more slowly came Lucy MacTary, smoothing back her short black curls as she strode purposefully to the door. Upon opening it, her heart sank.

"Good morning, Mrs. MacTary." Inspector Cameron's voice was formal as he held up his badge and identification. "Inspector Robert Cameron, Aberdeen Police. This is Sergeant Elizabeth Warwick. May we come in?"

Lucy nodded slowly, her mouth twisted up into a tight, pained smile. "Aye," she said as she stepped to one side and motioned the police officers into her home. "I suppose I've been expecting you."

* * *

Maggie surveyed the books scattered across her bedroom. She was going to pursue an afternoon at the reading room after her not-much-progress meeting with Macintyre and a quick lunch at The Boar and Thistle. She began to gather up the books she would need: both dictionaries, the books she had bought at Sinclair's shop, and of course, the Dark Book. This last, but vital, volume had ended the previous day perched atop her dresser on the far side of the room. As she passed the vent in the floor, she couldn't help but overhear voices downstairs. And as her hand grasped the black leather spine of the book, her ear noted that the overheard conversation had an odd tone to it—one not caused by the metallic echo of the air duct, but rather one which betrayed a hint of fear. Maggie pulled the book to her and crouched down to listen.

"—ank you, Inspector," Maggie heard her aunt say.

Inspector? As in the police?

Lucy's voice continued.

"I'll save you the trouble of having to ask," she started, her hand held firmly by her husband seated next to her on the living room sofa. "Annette Graham was my daughter."

Inspector Cameron nodded across the table at Lucy and Alex MacTary. It was a practiced nod, one designed to impart both thanks for the information and encouragement to provide more.

"I'd expected," Lucy continued, "to receive a visit from the police sooner. Once—Once it happened. I suppose I should have come forward right away, but— And then, you didn't come by, and I thought—" She let out a frustrated sigh. "I didn't know what to do."

Alex put a reassuring arm around his wife, who lowered her head into his chest.

"Yes, well, it took some time to obtain Annette's birth certificate," Warwick explained. "She was adopted—well, you know that—and so it took a bit of work to get the Canadian authorities to release the records."

Lucy looked up. "Yes, of course," she squeaked, her dry voice barely audible.

Cameron leaned forward. "Why don't you tell us about it, Mrs. MacTary?"

Lucy glanced at her husband and squeezed his hand, both in thanks for his support and in apology for what would come next. "Right. Well, I was seventeen. He was twenty-two. His name's not important, but he was a student at the university. He seemed so worldly and mature. And I was so young. Well, things ... happened." She paused again and closed her eyes. "And I got pregnant. But he wanted nothing to do with the child. Or me anymore." She sighed at the painful memory and opened her eyes again. "There was never any question that I'd keep the child, but— well, my parents didn't want a scandal. So I contracted 'the nine month flu' and went to visit an aunt and uncle in Nova Scotia."

Lucy paused again as the memories washed over her. Cameron leaned forward ever so slightly, but said nothing. Alex squeezed his wife's hand.

"It," Lucy continued, "it was a difficult birth. I almost lost her." She grimaced. "They almost lost *me*. I— They christened her 'Mary.' I knew I wouldn't keep her, but she deserved a name. Even if they changed it, she deserved a name."

Lucy looked away, drawing her breath in sharply against the tears.

"They saved the baby," Alex stepped in, "but just barely. And they told Lucy she'd never be able to have any more children." He paused and smiled sardonically. "Of course they didn't tell her that until a few days later. After she'd signed the adoption papers."

"And that was the last you heard of her," Cameron confirmed.

"Aye," Alex replied.

"Yes," Lucy managed to say.

"Until when?" Cameron's voice, while still kind, displayed just the slightest edge to communicate the seriousness of the inquiry, and the expectation of a straight answer.

Lucy jerked slightly at the question, then looked at her husband. His helpless half-smile told her to go ahead and answer.

"About two months ago. Maybe a bit more." She lowered her eyes to avoid the inspector's gaze.

"How did she contact you?"

"A—A letter," Lucy looked sidelong at Alex who squeezed her shoulder in return.

"Did she say who she was?" Cameron probed. "That she was your daughter?"

"Not at first, no." Lucy looked at her husband, then the inspector, then down at the floor again. "I mean the letter didn't start out, 'Hello, I'm your long lost daughter.' But I knew it was her."

Cameron leaned back into the upholstered chair. "Were you glad to hear from her?"

Lucy's brows came together and she frowned slightly, but she did not look up from the floor. "Well, yes. Of course. But— Well, it was a bit of a shock. Twenty odd years later and all."

"Did she seem glad to have found you?" He fixed his gaze firmly on Lucy's countenance.

"Well, er, yes, of course." She turned to her husband, his face twisted into a pained expression.

"It was an awkward situation, Inspector." Once again Alex MacTary came to his wife's aid. "I'm sure you can imagine. We never actually met with her, face to face. Just letters. And then..." He trailed off. "Well, then, here we are."

Weak smiles emerged on both the MacTarys' faces as they looked at the police officers perched opposite them.

"Aye," Cameron didn't nod. "Here we are."

Several moments of awkward silence followed. Warwick, who had remained quiet since her initial explanation of the Canadian bureaucracy, was aware of her urge to blurt out something to fill the silence. She resisted it. The MacTarys too sat silently and uncomfortably in their seats across from the inspector. Finally, Inspector Cameron spoke, his tone as matter-of-fact as if asking the time of day, but as serious as if asking the time of death.

"When did the blackmail start?"

A dozen emotions flashed across Lucy MacTary's face. She turned quickly to her husband, whose expression had remained unaltered, save a slight raising of the eyebrows. Lucy returned her gaze to the inspector, but let it fall slightly below his eyes.

"Blackmail?"

"Aye," Cameron frowned. "She was blackmailing you, wasn't she?"

A long pause, then Lucy cocked her head to one side. "Annette, you mean?"

"Yes, Annette." If Cameron's voice did not yet display his impatience, it certainly hinted at it.

"Annette wasn't blackmailing us." Lucy looked to her husband for confirmation; he gave it in the form a single nod. "I'm not sure what you're talking about," Lucy continued. "Why on Earth would you think that?"

The inspector let out a long sigh. He knew better that to start answering *their* questions.

"Where were you, Mrs. MacTary, on the night of Annette's death?"

"Now wait just a second—" Alex started to object but a commanding gesture from Cameron quieted him.

The inspector turned back to Lucy MacTary. "Where were you?" he repeated.

"We were home," Alex explained. "Together. The entire night."

Cameron regarded Alex MacTary with a critical eye.

"We closed the shop at the usual time," Alex went on. "six o'clock. Then we came straight home. I believe we may have watched the tele a bit. Then we went to bed."

Cameron stared at Alex but still said nothing.

"I'm afraid," Alex concluded with a hug of his wife and a self-deprecating smile, "that we're rather a dull married couple sometimes."

"All right then," Cameron leaned back in his chair and nodded several slow nods. "Just a few more questions and we'll be on our way. Where were you this past Friday evening, starting at say six o'clock?"

"Uh, well," Alex looked to his wife trying both to remember his activities that night and to divine the relevance of the question. "I believe we were at home. Again."

"Yes, that's right," Lucy agreed. "We closed the shop at six and stayed a bit late to tidy up. We had to get ready for the weekend. We'd a trip planned." She nodded as the memory returned fully. "Yes, that's right. It was raining. Maggie came to the store absolutely drenched at about, what, half past six, would you say, Alex?"

"Aye, half past. Soaked to the bone she was."

Cameron looked at Warwick for the first time since they'd sat down. Her eyes reflected the inspector's thoughts.

"Maggie?" the inspector asked of the middle-aged couple. "Who's Maggie?"

"Maggie?" Alex repeated. "Oh, Maggie's our niece. From the States. She's staying with us this year while she studies at the college."

Cameron again looked to his sergeant. She nodded in encouragement.

"Maggie *Devereaux*?" Cameron asked.

Maggie, who had been listening at the vent the entire time, drew in a surprised breath at this mention of her name. Her uncle asked the question for her.

"Aye. How did you know that?"

Cameron exhaled slowly as he weighed how much information to divulge.

"There was another murder Friday night," he stated officially. "May we talk with Maggie? Is she home right now?"

Maggie stepped away from the vent, her legs a bit unsteady. An icy shiver slithered up her spine.

Another murder? she thought. *What could that possibly have to do with me?*

Quickly, she returned to the vent, but only in time to hear her aunt say, "We'll go fetch her."

The vent was silent for several moments, then, as Maggie heard two sets of footsteps come up the stairs, she heard the police officers again.

"So what do you think?" The man asked. *The inspector.*

"I'm not sure," the woman replied. "They seem nice enough. They've a nice home, nice things. They're not the sorts I'd expect to be involved in occult murders."

Occult murders? The selection of titles at Sinclair's bookshop raced through Maggie's head. And then the phrase, 'Dark Book of Rites and Damnation.'

"True enough," the man replied, "but we can't rule anything out yet. We know they have a direct connection to Annette Graham, and apparently they also have a connection, through their niece, to the second murder. It may not be a lot, but it's more than we have elsewhere at the moment. Let's see what this Maggie Devereaux has to say."

There was a knock on Maggie's door.

"Maggie?" her aunt slowly opened the door, Uncle Alex peering into the room from behind her.

"Yes?" Maggie heard herself answer, her voice dry and scratchy.

After a brief, halting and wholly inadequate explanation from her aunt and uncle—but one which did include their previously unmentioned connection to the woman who had been murdered just before Maggie's arrival—she followed them downstairs.

Why do the police want to talk to me? Maggie's mind raced as she proceeded to the living room. *What could I possibly know about the murder. Murders. Oh, God, there's been another murder! Who—?*

"Thank you for agreeing to meet with us," the woman police officer greeted Maggie as she entered the room. The man—the inspector—stood silently by the armchair across from the couch. Maggie just nodded weakly in response. The woman's voice seemed distant over the din of blood rushing in Maggie's ears.

"I'm Sgt. Warwick. Elizabeth," the woman said. "And this is Inspector Cameron."

"How do you do, miss?" Inspector Cameron nodded from across the room.

Maggie again nodded weakly, a faint smile pasted to her face. She was only vaguely aware that her aunt and uncle had left the room. At the request of the police, no doubt.

"I'm afraid," Sgt. Warwick began as she motioned Maggie toward the couch, "that we have some rather unpleasant news for you."

Maggie tried to make an expression of ignorance and concern. She wasn't sure she'd succeeded, but at least she didn't blurt out, 'Oh you mean the second murder? The one I was eavesdropping over? The sacrificial occult satanic black magic ritual killing? That one?'

Whatever Maggie may have expected them to say next, it wasn't what came out of Sgt. Elizabeth Warwick's mouth.

"Did you know Fionna FitzSimmons?"

'Did!' Maggie's head started to spin. *She said 'did.' Not 'Do you know Fionna FitzSimmons?' but 'Did you know Fionna FitzSimmons?'*

"Y—Yes," her voice seemed as distant as an echo across a canyon. "Is Fionna—?"

"Maggie," Sgt. Warwick leaned across and placed her hand on the American's ice cold fingers. "Fionna was murdered. Friday night, we think. And we need to ask you some questions so we can catch her killer."

"Okay," Maggie replied meekly. She was surprised to find that she was numb. She was glad to have the questioning to focus on, to keep her mind off of—

"You were supposed to meet with her Friday night, weren't you?" Warwick asked.

"Y—Yes. But how did you—?"

"You left a message on her answering machine," Inspector Cameron explained. "We listened to it while—while we investigated the scene."

"Oh, okay."

"But we need more details," Warwick explained. "It sounded from your message that you'd planned to meet that evening, but you arrived late?"

"Uh, yes," Maggie replied weakly, and then she proceeded to give the precise timetable of when she and Fionna had met that afternoon, when they were supposed to meet again at the King's Street Pub, and when she herself had finally arrived, only to be told by the waitress that Fionna had just left. The only thing she left out was exactly where she had been prior to arriving at the pub.

"Right," Warwick nodded as she listened. "And why exactly were you late?"

Maggie felt her stomach tie into a hundred queasy knots.

"Oh God," she replied, entirely unresponsive to the inquiry. "What time was she killed?"

Warwick was surprised by this question in response to a question. But Maggie's urgent visage seemed genuinely troubled.

"We're still establishing the exact time," Cameron interjected. "That's why we're talking with you. But we do believe it was sometime Friday evening."

"When she should have been at the pub with me." Maggie's eyes began to well.

"Ah well," Cameron raised a hand in caution, "we don't know that, Miss Devereaux. It may well have happened some time much later in the evening. It's always difficult to establish an exact time of death."

"No," Maggie said simply, a single tear breaking free and running down the outside of her right cheek. "She never called me back. She would've called me back."

"Okay, Maggie," Warwick soothed. "We've just a few more questions, and then we'll be finished."

Maggie nodded and wiped the tear from her jaw.

"Were you and Fionna very good friends?"

Maggie thought for a second. "No. Not really, I guess. Actually I'd just met her once before, a few weeks ago."

Warwick nodded. "So you were just meeting for dinner to get to know one another better?"

"Yes. Well, no actually." Maggie hesitated, but it was too late.

"Yes?" Warwick encouraged.

"Well, actually, I ran into her at the library like I told you and—oh jeez, this is going to sound bad." She frowned and looked for an escape, but there was none. "See, I'm studying at the university. And the professor I'm studying under is a man named Craig Macintyre. And well, Fionna said if I was going to study under him there were some things I should know."

Maggie regarded the stony countenances before her.

"That sounds pretty bad, doesn't it?" she asked with a sniffle and an embarrassed smile.

"No, Maggie," Warwick assured.

"No," Cameron added. "It sounds true." He turned to his sergeant. "Anything else?"

Warwick thought for a moment, then shook her head. "Not right now."

"Right. Well then," Cameron stood up and extended his hand. "Thank you for your time, Miss Devereaux. We won't detain you any longer."

"Okay," Maggie shook the inspector's large hand. "Let me know if there's anything else I can do to help."

Warwick smiled as warmly as she knew how. "We will, Maggie. Thank you." Then she reached into her coat pocket and produced a business card. "Here. If you remember anything else about that evening, please give me a call."

"Okay," Maggie repeated, and watched as the police officers walked out of the living room, informed the MacTarys, who were lurking in the foyer, that they would be in touch, and exited into the cool Aberdeen late morning.

When they had almost reached the car, Cameron turned to his sergeant. "Macintyre?"

Warwick nodded crisply. "Annette Graham's professor too."

* * *

The atmosphere inside the MacTary home had become understandably tense. Maggie just wanted to get out of there. Her repeated efforts to telephone Prof. Macintyre had resulted in several dozen rings but no answer. Ellen, however, had picked up. She too had heard of Fionna's murder. They agreed to meet at three that afternoon. For tea. For company. For support. It had been Ellen's idea, but Maggie was glad for it.

Maggie pulled her coat from its hanger in the front closet and slid it over her arms. Her backpack sat by the front door awaiting her departure. Aunt Lucy and Uncle Alex were in the kitchen. She'd just pop in and tell them she'd decided to ride her bicycle after all.

As she approached the door to the kitchen, however, the hushed tone of its occupants made her stop in her tracks. She didn't want to just barge in. However, as she stood there, uncertain what to do, she couldn't help but overhear their conversation.

"Why didn't you tell them she was blackmailing you?" Alex demanded.

"Oh, Alex. Let the poor lass rest in peace. She had a hard enough life, what with her mother abandoning her at birth and all, and Lord knows she had a hard enough death. Don't speak ill of the dead."

"Ach, well," Alex sputtered.

"And anyway," Lucy countered, "why did *you* tell them we were home together that night? You know that's not true."

"Well, it sounded better than saying you were home alone while I spent the evening drinking and watching football at the pub only to wake up on the couch the next morn, my clothes still on and a brick in my head. They obviously already know about the blackmail, and now we've lied to them. They suspect us of something. I didn't want you to have to admit you haven't any alibi."

"Alibi? Good Lord, Alex, what are you thinking?"

"It's not what I'm thinking, Lucy. It's what they're thinking."

"Mmm-Khhhnmm," Maggie cleared her throat and walked into the kitchen. "Aunt Lucy? Uncle Alex? Are you in here?"

They turned from their spot at the other end of the kitchen. "Aye, Maggie," her aunt responded, her face turning flush. "We're right here. Are you heading out then?" She'd spied Maggie's coat.

"Yeah, I, um, I decided to just ride my bike into campus after all. I'm going to apologize to Prof. Macintyre for missing our meeting, then meet Ellen for tea in the afternoon. I kinda want to be out and about right now."

"Understood, lass," Alex smiled a sad little smile. "But don't stay out too late. We don't want to have to worry about you."

"Fair enough," Maggie replied with the same sad smile. "I'll be home before dark."

And with that she exited the kitchen, grabbed her backpack and strode quickly out the front door.

20. Macintyre

The phone was ringing in Prof. Craig Macintyre's cramped university office. Again. He ignored it. Again. Without looking he knew it was almost noon. Maggie Devereaux had missed their meeting. It was most likely her calling. And if not, he could think of at least two other women who might be calling him just then and he had even less desire to speak with either of them. Closing his copy of John Barbour's *The Bruce,* Macintyre decided to stroll over to the refectory for lunch. As he stood up and stretched his back, two figures darkened his doorway. A man and a woman. Their expressions were deathly serious.

"Professor Craig Macintyre?" the man asked.

Macintyre finished his stretch before answering. "I see," he said, pointing casually to the nameplate on his desk, "that you can read. Is there anything more I can help you with? I'm just about to go to lunch."

"Prof. Macintyre," the man flashed a badge at the academic. "I'm Inspector Robert Cameron, Aberdeen Police. This is Sgt. Elizabeth Warwick. We need to speak with you."

"That is too bad," Macintyre stepped around his desk and

grabbed his coat off the hook on the back of the door. "As I said, I'm leaving just now."

"This is important, Prof. Macintyre," Cameron insisted.

"I'm sure it is. As is my lunch." Macintyre pulled the brown leather coat on. "I'm useless on an empty stomach."

He herded the two officers out into the hallway and closed his office door behind him with a decisive click.

"Besides," he added as he fumbled in his coat pocket, "I make it a habit never to speak to the police without my attorney present."

At the word 'attorney,' Cameron's expression shifted from one of growing irritation to one of grudging acceptance.

"I thought," Macintyre continued, "that I might have his card here somewhere, but apparently not. In any event, his name is Winfield Kirby. He has an office down near Provost Skene's House. If you'd like to schedule an interview, please contact him directly. Ta."

With that, Prof. Craig Macintyre scooted down the hallway, around the corner and out of sight.

"Well, that was bloody arrogant," Warwick observed.

"Aye," Cameron agreed with a scratch to his chin. "Interesting, too, though, don't you think?"

"What is?"

Cameron looked down the hall to where the professor had disappeared. "He wasn't at all surprised to see us. Not even curious. It was almost as if—" He stopped.

"As if he'd expected us," Warwick finished.

"Aye."

And one floor down, around the corner from the stairwell, Prof. Craig Macintyre stood silently, back pressed against the wall, his face flushed, his heart pounding, and his mind racing.

21. The Power of Suggestion

Maggie stood in the open doorway of Prof. Macintyre's office for several moments expecting that he would sense her presence and look up from his book and styrofoam-boxed take-out lunch. He didn't.

Finally, she knocked gently in the doorframe. "Prof. Macintyre?"

Macintyre dropped the pen from his left hand and drew in a startled gasp.

"Oh." He regained his composure. "Miss Devereaux." His voice dripped with disappointment. He returned his attention to his work without saying anything more.

"Hi," she started. "I, um, just wanted to stop by and apologize for missing our meeting this morning. And to explain."

"No need to apologize, Miss Devereaux." He did not raise his head from the book splayed out in front of him. "Or explain. You're a big girl. If you don't want to take your studies seriously, that's your business. But please, don't make it mine."

Maggie's eyes narrowed. "I was talking with the police."

Macintyre dropped his pen again. "The police?" Now he

looked up.

"Yes. There's been another murder."

At this news, Macintyre's expression changed ever so slightly, but Maggie couldn't quite read it.

"I think you knew her, too," she went on. "Fionna FitzSimmons? I think she may have taken a course or two from you."

Macintyre looked down again at his book and began fidgeting with his pen. "FitzSimmons, you say? No, I'm afraid the name doesn't ring any bells." He paused. "Why were they talking with you?"

Maggie shrugged. "I guess I was one of the last people to see her before—" She stopped. "Well, anyway, I'd seen her that afternoon."

This mention of her encounter with Fionna in the reading room suddenly reminded Maggie of the dead woman's cryptic warning about Macintyre.

"Uh, look. I have to go," she hurried to excuse herself. "You know, studying and stuff. I—I just wanted to stop by, you know, to explain."

Macintyre just nodded, his expression inscrutable.

"Okay, then." Maggie raised her hand in farewell. "I guess I'll see you again in two weeks. I'll—I'll study hard. I promise to have something ready by then."

"All right." Macintyre half-raised his own hand. "Good bye, Miss Devereaux." Then over her departing shoulder he called, "Miss Devereaux! Margaret!"

Maggie turned and looked back into the office.

Macintyre's face convulsed in obvious discomfort, but then he said, "Well, it's just— Well, be careful, Miss Devereaux. Apparently—at least until the police catch this killer—apparently no student is safe. Go ahead and study, but don't stay out too late on account of your research."

He tried a smile. "I doubt there's anything in those dusty old books that can protect you from the likes of this madman."

Maggie stared past him for a moment before answering, "Thank you, Prof. Macintyre." Then she walked quickly to the stairs with one thought ringing in her head.

* * *

It had started to rain slightly by the time Maggie arrived at the café.

How appropriate, she thought as she regarded the weather, and walked inside. The clock on the wall told her she was ten minutes early, but a quick scan of the interior revealed that Ellen had still beaten her there. She was crouched over a newspaper and had not noticed Maggie's arrival.

"Hey," Maggie said in subdued greeting as she approached the table.

"Oh, hello, Maggie." Ellen folded the paper and pushed it aside. "Good of you to come."

Maggie sat down. Even for a Scot, Ellen looked deathly pale.

"How are you doing?" Maggie asked.

"Not very well, I don't suppose." Ellen looked down again at her hands.

Maggie didn't say anything for a bit, then ventured, "When did you find out?"

"This morning," Ellen replied, looking up. "Will called me. He's in a right state."

Maggie closed her eyes in sympathetic pain. "Oh. I hadn't thought of Will."

"Aye. He's beside himself. The police questioned him early this morning. He called me right after."

"The police?" Maggie remembered the two officers who had sat in her aunt and uncle's living room that morning. "They don't think he's involved, do they?"

"I imagine not," Ellen replied. "He's probably just the last to see her alive. Still—" She trailed off.

Maggie cocked her head encouragingly.

"Well, I mean they don't really know, do they?" Ellen went on. "I mean, it *could* have been Will, couldn't it have been? I hate saying it, but it's true. That's what's so frightening."

Maggie frowned at this suggestion. "I suppose so, but," she felt the need to defend Will, "but did he even know the first victim, Annette Graham? I mean, what's the connection?"

"I don't know," Ellen admitted. Then pushing the newspaper toward Maggie, said, "Maybe they aren't connected at all. The police won't say anything."

Maggie picked up the paper and unfolded it to see the headline:

SECOND STUDENT FOUND SLAIN - Is Serial Killer
Loose at King's College?

"Don't bother," Ellen discouraged any further reading. "I'll tell you what it says: 'The police have declined to release details of this murder.' 'It is unclear whether this killing is related to last month's murder of another female university student.' 'The police have identified several persons of interest, but admit they have no suspects at the moment.'"

Maggie set the paper back down on the table.

"But you know it as well as I, Maggie," Ellen continued. "The murders are bloody well connected. Everybody knows it. And the police have no idea who the killer is."

Maggie wanted to tell her friend what she had learned that morning. That the killings were definitely related. That they both had been classified as 'occult' murders by the police. And she wanted to tell Ellen that Fionna's last words to her had been a cryptic warning abut Macintyre. But somehow, she couldn't bring herself to do so. Maybe she was getting paranoid too. Flailing desperately for some other topic, she latched onto one of the few things she realized she actually had in common with Ellen Walker.

"I suppose the trip to Inverness is off, then?"

Ellen laughed a bit. "Well, actually, I was thinking about that too. I haven't seen Jenny—my friend in Inverness—for, well, for too long." She paused, reflecting. "Definitely too long. But I don't know. I—"

"I was just wondering," Maggie tried to console her. "No big deal."

"No, it's all right, Maggie." Ellen sighed and ran her hands through her dark blond waves. "To be true, Maggie, I think I'd like to get away from Aberdeen for a bit. Maybe for good, I don't know. These murders—" Words failed her. Then she reached across the table and grabbed Maggie's hand. "None of us are safe. You know that, don't you? Something evil is stalking the women of King's College." She narrowed her eyes and set her jaw. "I'm going to do whatever I have to do to protect myself."

She looked earnestly at Maggie. "And you best do too."

Maggie just smiled weakly and nodded, but her mind was racing.

"Promise me, Maggie," Ellen implored. "I can't lose another friend. Promise me. Promise me you'll do whatever it takes to protect yourself."

The thought that had begun ringing in her head since she'd departed Macintyre's office now crescendoed. Maggie was looking at her friend, but all she could see was the black handwritten script, counseling her across the centuries:

<Protection *against evil forces comes best from mastery over them.*>

Maggie sat silently for a moment, her mind considering both the absurdity and the apparent necessity of what she was considering.

Then she refocused her gaze on Ellen.

"I promise."

22. Do You Believe in Magic?

It was still raining. Only harder. The thick drops threw themselves against the window panes, sliding earthward and tracing the paths of their predecessors. The droplets refracted the light from Maggie Devereaux's bedroom out into the black Aberdeen night. Inside, Maggie quietly closed her bedroom door and carefully turned the skeleton key in the lock, trying hard to muffle its dull metallic clack. Crossing to the windows over her bed, she pulled the curtains tight against the outside world. She repeated this with each window in the room and even closed the door to her private bath. Then, turning with her hands on her hips, she surveyed the room. Every window sealed, every shade drawn, the door locked. There was something she was forgetting.

She looked down at the floor. The vent.

The one that carries voices to all parts of the house. She quickly flipped the lever to close the vent's trap, cutting off both sound and air. She could feel the room begin to grow stuffy with seclusion and took comfort in knowing that the chamber was now sealed off from any who might detect her embarrassingly foolish endeavor.

She stepped up to her desk. The top was rolled back and the writing surface was empty save the black leather-bound spellbook, which sat closed and centered before the chair. Sitting down, she opened the fragile cover, the broken metal clasp jingling loudly in the otherwise silent room.

'<The Dark Book of Rites and Damnation.>'

She stared at the handwritten title page, remembering the first time she had gazed at it, uncomprehending, in the subbasement of the college's historical collection. Having since become familiar with the text's contents, she leafed quickly to one of the early pages, to reread the passage that had shot through her mind both outside Macintyre's office and sitting in the café with Ellen.

'<Protection against evil forces comes best from mastery over them.>'

Maggie squirmed slightly in her seat. The room was getting hot. She pulled off her wool sweater and threw it on the bed, exposing her silver clan badge dangling atop her red turtleneck. Flipping forward again, Maggie stopped at the advice section she had encountered as she had fallen asleep in the comfortable bed at the Castle of Park.

'<Do not begin with too difficult a spell. Ability to use the magic comes from belief in it. Even the slimmest reed of belief can lead to small successes. Such successes lead in turn to greater beliefs and greater success. Start small. And believe.>'

Believe.

The word, even in its strange Old Gaelic form, seemed to challenge Maggie.

She closed her eyes and tried to relax. Tried to believe. She thought of her great-times-ten grandmother, Brìghde Innes Gordon.

The healer. And Brìghde's daughter, Maggie's namesake, Margaret NicInnes Wilkie. The witch. The people back then had believed.

Maggie opened her eyes again and looked at the book. It seemed different. No longer an ancient linguistic relic, but now a living, breathing part of her present.

"Start small," she repeated aloud.

Flipping loosely through the tome, almost in a trance, she soon spotted her quarry. Before her, on the page she had remembered from her earliest efforts at translation, stood a small sentence in small handwriting. A small incantation. A small spell.

Her eyes absorbed the words:

'<Tear asunder the bonds which chain this object to the Earth. Deny Nature its order and raise this thing to the hated sky.>'

A smile played across Maggie's lips. A levitation spell. That was simple, and small. And damn it, despite herself, she thought maybe she did believe.

She quickly fetched a pen from her backpack and centered it on the desk, having slid the spellbook to one side. Silently, she read over the spell again, then she closed her eyes to confirm she had translated the words properly. She opened her eyes again and affixed her gaze on the pen which lay nervously in front of her, only inches from her outstretched hands.

"Tear asunder," she started in melodramatic English, "the bonds which chain this object to the Earth. Deny Nature its order and raise this thing to the hated sky!"

Nothing.

Maggie's face twisted into an expression somehow combining disappointment with fulfilled expectations. She pursed her lips and turned to the spellbook. She had translated the spell correctly. As correctly as she could given the centuries between the two languages. Then she had a thought and her expression melted into a smile. She double-checked the words on the page, then turned again to the pen.

"*Mhaidhid*," she had to guess at the accent, "*inh chuimriachan anh-í chonrig riátsha cho inh Thalum. Dha'shluindi ghrád ó nádhúr ochus ail riátsha chi inh niam dho'miecciathadh!*"

Nothing.

"Damn it." English this time. It was sincere, but quiet, lest she disturb her aunt and uncle. Then she realized again where was—and what she was doing.

Oh God, she thought, *what's wrong with me? Do I really think this will work?*

A hot blush seared her cheeks. She slumped back in her chair. Then she stood up and walked several brisk steps toward nowhere in particular, before stopping and staring at her shoes.

"Stupid," she murmured. "Silly. Dumb."

She sighed and looked at the clock. Ten minutes before midnight. Time for bed.

She kicked off her shoes and pulled off her hot wool clothes, changing into her far more comfortable lavender cotton pajamas. Soon she had washed up and was ready to climb into bed for the night. The spellbook still lay open on her desk and peered invitingly at her as she went to turn out the light.

"Okay," she said aloud. "One more try." She looked about the room. "But this time," she smiled, "let's have some atmosphere."

Crossing to one of the short bookcases behind the reading chair near the door, she grabbed two candles from its top and set them carefully at either back corner of the writing desk. Lighting them with the matches which had accompanied them atop the bookcase, Maggie turned off the rest of the lamps, leaving the room dark save a glowing tent of light cast by the candles over the desktop, the spellbook, the pen and Maggie's outstretched hands.

"<Tear asunder,>" Old Gaelic again, "<the bonds which chain this object to the Earth. Deny Nature its order and raise this thing to the hated sky.>"

Nothing. Still.

Maggie snatched up the pen and flung it across the room. Even the risk of her relatives hearing her couldn't stop the next words.

"Damn it!" Her fist crashed down on the desktop, threatening to topple the candles and succeeding in dislodging one from its brass base.

"Oops." Maggie quickly reached out and righted the teetering candle, pulling it toward her and shoving it securely back into its holder. The flame had not gone out, but rather had swelled, sending smoke billowing. After a moment, the flame shrank again and took its original shape, an orange droplet, floating strongly and unwavering above the wax of the candle, undisturbed by air currents in the sealed off room.

Staring at the almost hypnotizing flame, she was reminded of a trick she'd learned where one can light a candle without ever touching the match to the wick. The flame of a candle, she had learned, is actually fueled by flammable gas rising from the melting wax; the wick only holds the flame in place. Knowing this, one can have a lighted match at the ready when blowing out a candle, then, sticking the match into the smoke which billows from the wick, the gases are reignited. The flame will jump from the match to the untouched wick below.

Like magic.

The room was silent save the ring of nothingness in Maggie's ears. She closed her eyes, sore from staring at the flame.

Anyone who has studied languages can tell you that there comes a point in learning a new tongue when one suddenly begins forming ideas directly in the new language, rather than having to think first in one's native language and then translate. And anyone who was spent time with people who study languages can tell you that such people love to regale them with the stories of the first time this happened: the first time they dreamt in German; the first time they stopped translating Cyrillic letters into their Latin counterparts; or that time in France, when after only two weeks there, the street hot-dog vendor had asked, *'Voulez-vous moutarde?'* and without ever having taken a French course in their life, they responded without thinking, *'Oui, un peu.'*

The world exists independently of the words humans use to describe it, and every language has its own unique way of a categorizing the objects and events of life into its own system of words and phrases. The more languages one learns, the easier it becomes to accept this truth and thereby be able to shift among the various worldviews embodied in humankind's languages. Ways of expressing ideas which may have seemed ludicrous when learning the first language become expected when learning the third. Maggie Devereaux had spent her life learning languages. A semester of Spanish in middle school. Four years of German in high school. Latin and French. Modern Gaelic and Old Gaelic. And now Hamilton's dialect. Her brain was accustomed to this shifting of worldviews. She was a student of languages. And although it always took a while for the new language to be fully absorbed and its worldview accepted, so too did that moment always eventually come.

Maggie opened her eyes and looked at the candle before her. Almost without a conscious thought, she opened her mouth and spoke the spell—not again, but for the first time. She didn't worry about her accent. She didn't notice that the first noun was in the accusative case. She didn't follow along the English translation in her head. She just spoke the spell. Not the words, but the meaning behind the words.

"<Tear asunder the bonds which chain this object to the Earth. Deny Nature its order and raise this thing to the hated sky.>"

Her eyes widened. Her heart skipped a beat before then flooding her bloodstream with adrenaline. She couldn't have breathed if she'd wanted to. As soon as she had spoken the spell, the candle flame flickered violently and she froze in disbelief as she waited for the candle to rise into the air.

But then something happened which truly surprised her: Nothing.

The candle did not rise into the air. It sat, quite gravity-bound, in its brass holder on top of the heavy wooden desk.

Maggie stared at the candle for an eternity, but she knew it wouldn't move. The adrenaline dump was making her fingers tingle and she could hear the rush of blood in her ears. She had to remind herself to breathe again. Finally she shut her eyes against the candle's light and lowered her face into her heat-swollen hands.

"Damn," she whispered softly.

After several moments, Maggie stood up, placed her glasses carefully on the desk and unceremoniously blew out the two candles, leaving the room pitch black. She groped her way to the bed and climbed under the covers, entirely unable to sleep. It was still stuffy in the bedroom and she was beginning to sweat at the temples. She considered the rain beaten windows, but decided to forego the icy chill of a late October night and instead crossed over to the vent in the floor. She flipped the lever back and almost immediately the room began to cool as fresh air swirled into the chamber, chasing out the stagnant, uncirculated air.

She lay down again, the air from the vent blowing lightly across her face. She was tired and tried not to think about what had just transpired. She couldn't decide whether to be disappointed in the failure of the magic, or in herself for actually believing it would work.

The fresh, cool air was lulling her to sleep. She rolled onto her side and allowed her mind to replay the images of the day as she drifted off into dreams. Her last thought before succumbing to sleep—a thought she would not remember in the morning—was of the candle on the center of the desk and of hearing a voice, not her own, say, "It flickered."

23. Inverness

The next weeks passed by uneventfully, and torturously slow. Fionna's death had cast a pallor over not only Maggie's routine, but that of the entire university community. The police had been closed-lipped about the details of her murder but rumor and half-whispered opinions spread the conclusion fast enough among the halls and classrooms of the University of Aberdeen. The campus was in the clutches of a serial killer.

For those who actually knew Fionna, it was even more difficult to proceed with day-to-day life. Maggie had seen Ellen a few times over that period and each time it was clear Ellen had graduated to the next phase of grief. Maggie had also seen Will Hopkins once, but he had not seen her walking past him on the crowded sidewalk and had overlooked her wave. He had a lot on his mind, she supposed. As for Sean FitzSimmons, he was nowhere to be found. And Maggie—she had just fallen into a mundane lethargy. In mid-October, before Fionna's death, she had been thinking about organizing some type of party to commemorate American Halloween, so closely related to the Celtic festival of *Samhain,* with perhaps some ideas gleaned from the Dark Book. But the murders had made a Halloween party seem rather inappropriate, and she had not picked the book up in earnest since her embarrassing attempt at magickry. October 31st came and went with no more than Maggie noticing the date on the MacTarys' kitchen calendar.

The trip to Inverness had in fact not been cancelled, although it had been delayed until the second weekend of November for various reasons, not all of which pertained directly to Fionna's murder. Sarah Bell had elected not to come after all, and of course Fionna would not be joining them. So on that Thursday morning in mid-November, Maggie could look forward to a two hour drive with just Ellen and, for better or worse, Kelly Anderson.

Iain had joined the MacTarys and Maggie for breakfast that morning, despite it being Thursday, because apparently St. Andrew's Day was approaching. According to Lucy, a pair of kiltmakers and their store manager could ill afford to be unprepared for the increased tourist interest the celebration of Scotland's patron saint would hopefully create. And in November in Scotland, any increase in tourist interest was good news. When Maggie had inquired about the holiday, mostly out of politeness, Iain had explained that Scots usually celebrated in intimate family gatherings. She had thought he might invite her to spend the day with him, but her downcast mood and the presence of his employers had apparently discouraged him. It was probably just as well. In her current state, she had become exceedingly ambivalent about most things in her life just then, including Iain Grant.

Ellen arrived at 8:30. She had evidently graduated to the stuporous 'life's-too-short-*carpe-diem*' stage of mourning, as her face beamed with a smile unimaginable just two weeks earlier. In contrast, Kelly was her usual dour self. Lucy, Alex and Iain all came out to see Maggie off on her long weekend. As Maggie climbed into the back seat of Ellen's Ford Fiesta and pulled the door shut, Ellen kept her eyes trained on the waving well-wishers and purred, "Who's *that*?"

"Who?" Maggie replied. There were three people on the porch.

"That tall, dark, *gorgeous* man there. The young one, I mean. Please tell me he's not your boyfriend."

"That's just Iain," Maggie replied, expelling a nervous laugh. "And no, he's not my boyfriend."

"Good," Ellen cooed as she pulled away. "That'll give me something to do when we get back. Eh, Kelly?"

Kelly did not turn from the side window as she offered a disinterested "Whatever" in reply.

Maggie, for her part, crossed her arms and pushed herself back in her seat, her ambivalence over Iain Grant fading fast.

* * *

"*Inbhir Nis,*" Ellen announced in Gaelic as the car motored past the roadsign delineating the boundary of their destination.

"Cool," Maggie replied approvingly. Kelly said nothing.

"So how big is Inverness?" Maggie inquired as she appraised the surprisingly modern architecture which passed by her car window.

"Around sixty-thousand," Ellen answered. "Good sized, but not quite as big as Aberdeen. And nowhere near as large as Edinburgh or Glasgow."

Kelly hadn't said anything for the last hour or so; Maggie wondered whether she was asleep. Deciding that she didn't really care either way, Maggie turned and peered out the window again. Gazing at the bustle of the busy people on the sidewalks, she wondered absently whether Inverness didn't have a university.

"Here were are," Ellen announced as they rounded a turn

and pulled up to a rather average looking apartment building. "Jenny's flat is in this building."

Soon, the three of them had been warmly received by Ellen's school-days friend. Jenny MacPherson stood about one inch shorter than Maggie's 5'4" but otherwise seemed to sport the same medium-thin build. She too had brown hair, but darker and finer than Maggie's thick auburn locks. She wore brown plastic-rimmed glasses in front of her dull brown eyes and her skin was a pasty white, except for a rather large brown birthmark which bulged slightly from her left cheek. The end result was that Jenny MacPherson looked rather a lot like Maggie, yet at the same time entirely different.

After introductions and a tour of Jenny's flat, it was quickly decided to head downtown for a bit of sight-seeing and people-watching, followed by a spot of lunch at a place Ellen and Jenny had always gone to before Ellen had left for Aberdeen.

"So what's the plan for tonight then?" Ellen asked as she popped the last bite of battered cod in her mouth.

Jenny MacPherson looked at her friend in disbelief. "Thursday night?" she urged, hoping to jog her friend's memory.

An expectant and rather wicked smile crossed Ellen's lips. "You mean—? "

"Aye."

"The Digital Unicorn?"

"Still open," Jenny confirmed, hardly able to contain herself. "And," she passed a smile and nod around the table, "Thursday night is still ladies night!"

Maggie's heart sank. A nightclub? She was exhausted already. And hadn't there been some talk about some sort of day trip early tomorrow? And 'Ladies' Night?' She'd come to Scotland to study, not to meet boys. And, Good Lord: 'The Digital Unicorn'?!

Apparently her reaction was not overlooked.

"What's wrong then, Maggie?" Ellen jabbed. "Too tired already? Or is it that your Iain will be jealous?"

Before she could retort, 'He's not *my* Iain,' Jenny jumped in. "Oh, you've a boyfriend then, do you, Maggie? A Scot or a Yank?"

"A Scot," Maggie replied, trying not to be too irritated by the friendly teasing. "And he's not my boyfriend. He's just—" She wasn't sure what to say next. "He just works at my aunt and uncle's store."

"More's the pity," Ellen opined to Jenny.

"Really?" Jenny inquired.

"Oh, aye," Ellen enthused. "Handsome young lad. Tall. Strapping. Fine dark hair. And, as Maggie said, a Scot. All in all a good catch."

"Right then, Maggie," Jenny's voice had taken on the aura of cruise director. "You don't have to dance with any of the lads tonight. But you might as well let them buy you drinks. Cover is free on ladies night, so free drinks means a free evening."

"Well," Maggie had to admit, "that sounds pretty good."

"What about you then, Kelly?" Jenny turned her attention to the blond American sunk in the chair opposite her. "Have you any objections to the evening's planned activities."

"To free drinks," she raised an uncharacteristic smile, "I have no objection. To men, well, we'll just have to wait and see."

* * *

The Digital Unicorn turned out to be everything Ellen and Jenny had promised. With a dozen speakers blasting house-mix dance music, and with twice as many colored spot-lights flashing over a dance floor the size of a basketball court, the nightclub was packed with revelers. Ladies Night had succeeded in bringing out a large female crowd, but so too had it attracted a large number of young males with one thing on their minds. One such fellow was named Eric and had latched onto Maggie quite firmly once he'd heard her American accent. Maggie found Eric pleasant enough until his third pint, after which he became increasingly loud, incoherent and boring. After his fourth, Maggie found it easy enough to slip from his disappointing clutches and rejoin her friends who had staked out a table near the back of the club to use as a sort of home base. When she arrived, she found Jenny sitting alone at the table, sweaty from dancing and nursing some sort of clear, bubbly drink with a lime in it. A quick glance toward the flashing lights revealed Ellen and Kelly still on the dance floor.

"Hello, Maggie!" Jenny shouted over the music. "Having a good time then?!"

"Aye, to be sure," she mimicked the Scots burr she had been subjected to for the last bit of time. As she pulled out a chair and sat down again, she could feel the telltale dizziness that indicated she too had had enough to drink. "I have to admit," she continued, "this is a great place. I wasn't sure at first, but I'm having quite a good time."

"Aye," Jenny tried to nod as she sipped from her drink. "It's maybe a silly name, I suppose, but—"

Jenny's sentence was interrupted by the uncharacteristically boisterous entrance of Kelly Anderson.

"Hi, guys!" she yelled as she fell clumsily into the seat next to Maggie. "What are we talking about? Wow, cool place, Jenny. Is there a waitress around? My glass is empty. Hi, Maggie!"

"Hi," Maggie replied with a bemused smile. She always found it entertaining to see how other people acted when they got snockered. It also served as a gentle warning about her own condition, should she be tempted to have just one more.

"So who's that then?" Jenny pointed at the young man Kelly

had left on the dance floor. He was still watching after her but had apparently declined to stop dancing just yet.

"I think his name's Kyle," Kelly giggled through her empty glass as she turned it upside down to acquire its last precious drops. "Or Kevin. Or something."

As Kelly finished this minimal effort to remember the fellow's name, Ellen plodded over to the table as well, the song having, if not exactly ended, at least merged into the next song.

"He's cute," Jenny remarked approvingly about Kyle/Kevin/Something.

"Who's cute?" Ellen asked, sitting down rather ungracefully herself.

"Kevin," Maggie replied.

"Kyle," Kelly corrected with a frown.

"Right. Kyle. Kyle's cute."

"Who's Kyle?" Ellen looked around, becoming quickly confused.

"The cute bloke Kelly's been dancing with," Jenny explained, and pointed him out on the dance floor.

"Oh, aye," Ellen appraised. "He is cute enough. Are you keen on him then, Kelly?"

Kelly frowned again, this time into her now utterly empty glass. "Whatever," she pouted.

Jenny was a bit taken aback by the sudden glumness. Maggie wasn't.

"Come now, Kelly—" Jenny started.

"No, let her be," Ellen counseled. "Miss Anderson's a wee bit down on men just now."

Oh really? Maggie thought, her curiosity peaked.

"Oh really?" Jenny asked for her. "Why's that then?"

Kelly had not stopped frowning, but it now flared in

intensity. "Don't wanna talk about it."

Jenny smiled around the table. "Come on, then, Kell," she coaxed.

Kelly just looked away. Ellen, however, leaned forward onto the table. "Well..." she started.

Kelly's voice sliced through Ellen's sentence. "Don't!" Her pouty frown had hardened into an angry scowl.

Ellen sat back again, obviously deciding to heed her friend.

"Well, then," Jenny switched to a new topic. "Maggie had a cutie herself, didn't you, lass?"

Maggie smiled. "Not much to tell. We danced and talked a bit is all."

Ellen smiled playfully. "Iain'll be jealous," she teased.

At this Maggie could only smile as no words came to her, just emotions.

"Okay, now tell me again who this Iain is?" Jenny asked, her memory blurred by the clear bubbly lime drink.

Suddenly Kelly returned to the conversation.

"Let's talk about something else!" she commanded. "I don't want to talk about Maggie's boyfriend." She picked up her glass again. "Where is that damned waitress?"

So Ellen tried to change the subject. "How's your research coming then, Maggie?" It was the best she could do on short notice.

"Okay, I guess. I'm making some progress." Then she remembered her last 'progress' meeting and laughed at herself. "Although don't ask Craig Macintyre."

Kelly's fist crashed down on the table, jarring the glasses in a series of clanks and clinks.

"Damn it!" she yelled at no one in particular. "I said change the subject!"

Maggie looked at the other two, wondering what she had

said.

"No, Kelly," she said. "We were talking about Prof. Macintyre."

"Bastard," Kelly mumbled in reply. "Maggie?" Kelly leaned forward and draped an arm around Maggie's shoulder. "Maggie?"

Maggie smiled nervously. "Yes?"

"Maggie, don't—" Kelly stopped in mid-thought.

"Yes?"

"Don't—" She was having trouble tracking.

"Don't what, Kelly?"

"Don't—Don't let him read your notes!" At this Kelly broke out in drunken hysterics. She dropped her forehead onto the table and slapped at the tabletop with an open palm, all the while laughing uncontrollably.

Maggie and Jenny laughed too, but more out of discomfort than anything Kelly had said. Ellen giggled too, but she just sat back and shook her head.

"Get it?" Kelly asked, face still to the table. "He's the professor but you can't let him read your notes!"

Jenny laughed again, but this time sincerely. "I think she's had enough, eh?"

Maggie nodded as Ellen provided the formal concurrence, "Aye. I think it's time to go."

Ellen slipped an arm under her blond friend and helped her to her feet. Jenny opened her purse and extracted her car keys and several banknotes.

"Can you pay the tab, Maggie?" she asked, shoving the bills into Maggie's palm. "We'll put her in the car."

"Sure," Maggie replied. "Sounds like a plan."

Ellen and Jenny half-carried Kelly, who was still laughing at her own enigmatic humor, toward the exit as Maggie stood on her tip-toes and surveyed the room for some sign of a cashier or waiter. Their table had been, like all of them, set back a distance from the dance floor to give the club-goers a place to escape from both the pounding music and the prying eyes of other patrons. It was still an hour before closing time, but the crowd had started to thin a bit, so that just before spotting a queue of customers at a cash register at one of the several bars, Maggie again spotted Eric.

He was seated at one of the more secluded tables, only half lit by the flashing lights of the dance floor. Seated firmly on his lap, mouth attached securely to his, was a very thin, very petite brunette, with shoulder length brown curls and a blouse the same color blue as Maggie's, but three times tighter. Maggie couldn't help but watch this scene for several moments. Then she did the only thing she could do. She walked over to the bar, paid the tab, and left.

* * *

The next morning found Ellen still bubbly, Maggie a bit tired, and Kelly wickedly hung over. Luckily, the day trip had had to be postponed until Saturday. When they arrived home in the early hours of that morning, Jenny had had a message. Apparently her boss—she was an architect in a small three person firm in Inverness—had run afoul of some rather important government regulations. Her presence would be required at the office after all. So Jenny went into work and the field trip to Clava Cairns was reassigned to Saturday.

This was just as well, though, for it gave Maggie and Kelly the opportunity to take a more leisurely tour of Inverness with Ellen, whose frenetic energy was diminished somewhat by the absence of her school chum. When Jenny finally arrived home sometime after six, she was exhausted, and after the previous night at The Digital Unicorn, the evening consisted of a nice dinner at an

Indian restaurant near Jenny's flat and a subdued evening of wine and conversation.

"Three weeks," Ellen observed eventually.

"Three weeks 'til what?" Jenny asked, perplexed.

"Since," Maggie corrected.

"Since Fionna was murdered," Ellen explained.

"Oh." Jenny wasn't sure what else to say.

Ellen drank deeply from her wine glass. "I wonder how Will's doing?"

"I saw him the other day," Maggie offered, "just walking along. But I don't think he recognized me. I didn't stop him, though. I mean, what do you say?'

"There's nothing you can say," Kelly replied. Her glass was already empty.

They all nodded, and Maggie's thoughts returned to that dinner when she'd first met Fionna. "And Sean," she added. "It must be tough for him, too."

"I dare say he'll be all right," Ellen opined. "He's a tough skin."

"Yes and no," Kelly's face wore an expression Maggie had never seen on it before. "He puts on good show, but he's got a tender side too."

"Oh, that's right," Ellen nodded. "I'd forgotten."

"Forgotten what?" Maggie asked, justifiably.

Kelly smiled faintly. "I, well, I dated Sean a bit back when I first arrived from the States."

Maggie's mouth dropped open. Somehow, she couldn't imagine Kelly Anderson dating anyone. Although the gruff Sean FitzSimmons might have been a good match.

"Just a couple times," Kelly was quick to clarify. "That's his m.o. He says he lives in Belfast, but more often than not he's—he was—visiting his sister, meeting her girlfriends, chatting them up, asking them out for a pint. He can be quite the charmer."

He didn't ask me out for a pint, Maggie recalled. Not that she would've wanted to go, but she wouldn't have minded being asked.

"But he's basically a male chauvinist jerk," Kelly continued. "It took me three dates to figure that out. Besides he really wasn't my type. I prefer more ... educated men."

Maggie wasn't sure how they'd gotten from the anniversary of Fionna's death to Kelly's love life, but Kelly brought them back full circle.

"Even so, I'm sure he's shattered by this whole business. He adored Fionna. He was always so protective of her. That's why he disliked Will so much, I think."

The four women sat quietly for a moment.

"Poor Sean," Kelly said.

"Poor Will," Maggie echoed.

Then Ellen brought the true point home. "Poor Fionna."

* * *

Saturday morning arrived, and the four of them were soon tooling along Scotland's A9 highway toward Clava Cairns. 'Cairn' is a word borrowed from the Gaelic and is used to describe any number of above-ground gravesites which generally consist of piles of stones assembled to create small chambers for internment of bodies. The stones at Clava, probably the most famous of the Highland cairn sites, lie only a few miles south of Inverness. Maggie had heard of them, of course, but had only ever seen photographs of the stone piles among the thin trees which dotted the site. She was excited to the see the real thing.

Unfortunately, going on a Saturday—even early on a cold, misty, November Saturday—had meant a marked increase in tourists and to Maggie's disappointment they did not have the site to themselves. She could spot at least three other groups winding among the cairns, their brightly colored jackets standing out in sharp contrast to the gray stones, trees and sky. Nevertheless the site was more than large enough to allow them to explore mostly unmolested.

Maggie was surprised by the site's complexity. There were three large burial cairns, stretching in a line approximately northeast to southwest, with a smaller, less well preserved cairn also present. Each of the larger cairns was approximately 50-60 feet in diameter, its circumference being a ring of large 'kerb' stones, placed each next the other. Inside the kerb stones were piled the innumerable smaller stones of the cairn, under which the bodies had once been interred, although the burial chambers now lay exposed to the heavens. Then, each larger cairn was surrounded by its own rather stately ring of standing stones, several feet away and spaced far apart like the numbers on a clock face. Maggie didn't understand the exact significance of the placement of all these stones, but she had no doubt there was one.

"So when were these built?" she asked Ellen.

"Hmm, let's see." Ellen squished her face into a pensive expression. "I must have come here half a dozen times on school field trips. I remember the phrase 'Neolithic Period.' I think they date from around 3000 B.C."

"Wow," Maggie peered again at the ancient stones. "Does anyone know why they were built?"

"Religious reasons, I'd guess," Ellen replied. "I suppose you have to put your dead somewhere. This was probably where the most important members of the society ended up."

"Hmm," Maggie looked around. Jenny and Kelly had each separated off to examine the site individually. "What about these outer stones? They look kind of like Stonehenge."

Ellen laughed a little. "Aye, I suppose they do." Then she added, "I think I just read something about the alignment of these stones, actually."

She walked over to the nearest cairn, but pointed to the next one over as well. "See how each burial chamber lines up with the standing stone directly in front of it?"

Maggie confirmed that both cairns had a standing stone placed directly in line with the alignment of the exposed burial chamber. "Yup."

"And if you look, both of these burial chambers are parallel to each other," Ellen continued. "They're lined up the same on the compass."

A quick glance at the two large burial cairns and this too was confirmed.

"Well, anyway," Ellen continued, "I think people used to think this was just a burial site. But as you say, it looks a bit like Stonehenge, and they know Stonehenge was used as an observatory."

She paused, again trying to remember the details. She was taking her role as host and tourguide seriously.

"Okay, now I remember." A finger shot into the air. "They just ran an experiment a couple of years ago. Some people had noticed that the line from the burial chamber to the standing stone directly in front of it was roughly to the southwest of the center of the burial chamber. And in the winter, the sun sets in the southwest. So some archeologists wondered whether it wasn't lined up for the sunset on the winter solstice."

"Cool," Maggie observed. "And is it?"

"Aye, I believe so. They couldn't do it on the actual solstice because there are pagan ceremonies held here still, believe it or not." She shook her head at the thought. "But I think they laid down inside the burial chamber with a tarp over the top on the nights before and after the solstice, and they pretty much confirmed the light would shine directly into the chamber at sunset on the winter solstice."

Maggie shook her head. "Wow. How did the people back then know?" she asked admiringly.

Ellen mirrored her expression. "Aye, it is pretty amazing. But I think they probably understood the world a lot better than we want to give them credit for." She gazed approvingly around the site. "In fact, they probably understood things we can't even imagine anymore."

Maggie too looked around the site, and considered all the things she had seen and learned since she had arrived in Scotland some eleven weeks earlier. "You know," she replied, "I think you're probably right."

24. *Du Café*

The following Tuesday found Maggie at work diligently yet comfortably in an Aberdeen coffee shop rather far from the university. She had spotted it on one of her bike rides and had chosen it for her study location that day precisely because of its distance from the campus. Although it was populated with a steady stream of business people who regarded her entrenched presence in one of the café's corners with a mixture of curiosity and irritation, the café allowed Maggie to toil away in relative anonymity without locking herself away from all human contact.

The visit to Clava Cairns had rejuvenated her desire to proceed with her studies and translate the Dark Book. She had arrived home Sunday afternoon and visited pleasantly enough with her aunt and uncle, telling them all about her trip, before spending the remainder of the evening working on the translation of the dialect into standard Old Gaelic. But she had stayed up too late, and found herself genuinely disappointed when she woke up late and had missed breakfast. Monday morning breakfast with Iain.

In her disappointment, she had worked even harder that day on her translation and by Tuesday morning had almost completed the last of it. Although not quite finished, she had decided to heed the adage 'A change is as good as a rest,' and proceeded to the second stage of her project: translating from Old Gaelic to Modern Gaelic. She probably could have skipped this step on her way to an English translation, but she felt it would help deepen her understanding of the text, and she would end up doing it anyway, the Old Gaelic words evoking their Gaelic descendants in Maggie's mind well before the English counterparts could be located in her synapses. Another advantage of this subsequent stage was that she could work with the notebook full of the standard Old Gaelic translation on one side, a fresh notebook for the Modern Gaelic on the other, dictionaries in the middle—and the Dark Book tucked safely out of sight in her backpack.

This enabled her to pursue her work in more public settings such as the café, without risking the book being seen by anyone. She still did not want Macintyre to know of its existence. She had not yet divulged its existence to Ellen or Kelly. Even her aunt and uncle were ignorant of the treasure she kept hidden in their upstairs bedroom. And then there was that bookseller.

"Devan Sinclair."

Maggie looked up with a start at the dapper bookshop owner who had suddenly appeared over her table. As usual, he was dressed head and shoulders above his contemporaries in the coffee shop, not a blond hair out of place and mustache-less goatee perfectly trimmed. A regular Scottish GQ.

"Do you remember me, Miss Devereaux?"

His smile pulled pleasantly at his face, but also drew attention to the scar running down the length of the left cheek. Maggie had forgotten about the scar and peered at it with detached interest, noting that its broad, mottled path suggested a burn rather than a clean slice. Then, suddenly realizing how rude she was being, she fumbled for a reply, his sudden appearance reminding her of their first encounter when his shadow had darkened her book at the Duff Street Cafe.

"Of course. Have you—Have you come to buy some more imaginary books from me?"

She immediately regretted the quip. Their last conversation, at Sinclair's bookshop, had been quite pleasant and they seemed to have reached an unspoken agreement not to discuss the book they both knew she had, but which she refused to admit to.

Sinclair's smile remained but the warmth drained from it.

"No, actually. I hadn't. But since you mention it—"

He bathed Maggie in a penetratingly appraising gaze.

"I can see that your activities with the book have exceeded purely academic pursuits." He leaned forward onto the table, close enough for Maggie to smell his cologne, incongruously pleasant as he scolded her. "Do not continue down that path, Maggie. You don't understand what you're playing at."

He stood upright again and his hand went unconsciously to the scar she had been staring at. "It will consume you."

His eyes locked onto Maggie's for a moment. She could see some earnestly felt emotion hiding in them, but she couldn't identify it before he broke off the gaze and turned sharply toward the door, his impeccable overcoat swirling around his form.

As he exited into the cold November afternoon, Maggie had to ask herself, *What the hell was that all about?*

25. The Date

St. Andrew's Day, November 30th, was still over a week away. That meant two more Thursdays before the day honoring Scotland's patron saint. Two more Thursday mornings for a pair of woolens store owners to meet with their store manager to discuss preparations for the increased sales hoped to be realized from tourists who might celebrate the day with the purchase of a kilt or tam or shawl. Two more Thursday mornings Iain Grant might breakfast at the MacTary's home.

This had not escaped Maggie's notice.

So that Thursday, she did not sleep late. Rather, she awoke earlier than usual and took extra care with her morning toilette. Following a long, hot, relaxing shower, she broke out her seldom-used curling iron and gave her thick straight hair just the slightest wave and extra body—nothing too noticeable. She pulled on her favorite sweater and her most flattering jeans. Her make-up was just a little more prominent that its usual natural look. And most importantly, she had succeeded in locating, at the bottom of a still half-unpacked toiletries bag, the contact lenses she kept just in case, for such contingencies as swimming or lost glasses. And so when

Maggie Devereaux came down for breakfast that morning, the bookish school-girl had been ever so subtly replaced by a vision of a radiant young woman descending the staircase, wavy auburn tresses curling around her elegantly made up face, and nothing blocking the view of her big, beautiful caramel-colored eyes.

This did not escape Iain's notice.

"Good morning, Maggie," he said with as much enthusiasm as this standard greeting would allow. "You look... grand."

"Thanks, Iain," Maggie smiled. "How nice of you to say so." She decided to take the obvious surprise in Iain's voice as a compliment. Then waiting just the right amount of time, she added, "You look good, too."

Iain instinctively looked down at his nice enough but not particularly special ensemble. "Er, thanks."

Just then Lucy and Alex walked into the dining room, each with a tray of breakfast goodies.

"Good morning, Maggie." Aunt Lucy smiled approvingly at her niece. "You look nice this morning. Doesn't she, Alex?"

"Hmm? Oh yes, very nice." Alex barely looked at his niece, concentrating instead on finding space on the table for his tray of oatcakes and marmalade.

"Special occasion today?" Lucy cocked an eyebrow.

Maggie smiled. "Not really." She locked eyes with Iain. "It's Thursday."

Pulling out the chair directly opposite their guest, Maggie sat down without breaking her gaze. "You don't usually join us for breakfast on Thursdays, do you, Iain?"

"Er, no," Iain threw a hurried glance at Alex, "but St. Andrew's day is next Saturday, so we, you know, need to meet. And such. I was here last Thursday, too."

"Were you? Yes, that's right. I'd forgotten that," Maggie lied.

"So what's so special about St. Andrew's day?" Then before anyone could reply, she hurried to add, "I mean for business. I know why it would be important, you know generally. For Scots, I mean. I know he's the patron saint of Scotland. I'm not stupid, but, you know—"

She was losing it. She took a breath.

"But why the extra meetings, I guess I'm asking?"

Alex decided to field this one, after all it was his and Lucy's shop. "Well, for the tourists, they think it's like St. Patrick's Day back over in New York or such. So they want to buy all kinds of things they might not otherwise buy. Hats, scarves, ties, what have you. And for that gent who just isn't sure if he should spend that several hundred quid on that kilt, well, for him, the day might just be the nudge he needs to open his wallet. Especially if we can get him into the store with a few extra signs and half off any merchandise with the St. Andrew's cross on it."

Maggie nodded vigorously and made a pleasant "Hmm" noise as if interested in this discussion of marketing, which in truth she was not.

"So is it not like St. Patrick's Day, then?" She was more drawn to the social aspects of the explanation than the economic.

"No," Lucy was the one who replied this time. "It's mostly celebrated quietly enough at home. With friends and family. And a nice dinner."

"Kind of like Burns Night?" She remembered this uniquely Scottish January holiday from dinners of haggis prepared by her grandmother every year.

"Something like that," Lucy smiled.

Maggie turned to Iain. "Will you be having dinner with your family, Iain?"

He had better get this hint, she thought.

"Er, no. My family's all back in Glasgow mostly." He looked

to his employers. "And of course I have to work that day. I—I just planned to spend the evening alone."

Maggie waited a moment more, but then had to turn to her aunt. "We're not doing anything special, are we, Aunt Lucy?"

"No, child," she smiled knowingly. "We're not. Not anything special that you young folk would be interested in." Then, grabbing her husband under his arm, "Come now, Alex, I need your help in the kitchen."

"But," he protested, "I thought we'd already fetched all the food."

"Come along," and she pulled him from the room.

Maggie turned back to face Iain, who was still standing across the table. She held his gaze for a moment, then looked down at the table in a manner she really hoped was coquettish.

After a moment, Iain finally ventured, "If you'd like, I mean, if you're not busy—ah, of course you're not busy—Lucy just said so—oh, but maybe you are. I mean, you're a beautiful young wo— Oh, I didn't mean that. No, wait. I did. I mean, you are. I mean—" He stopped and took a deep breath. "Would you like to have dinner with me on St. Andrew's Day?"

She smiled broadly. "I'd love too."

Iain smiled back.

Lucy and Alex did not come back from the kitchen.

Iain kept smiling and let out a nervous little laugh.

Maggie smiled again. Then she looked away.

Still no Alex or Lucy.

The next nine days could be quite awkward, Maggie realized, as they waited for their date to come. Apparently also realizing this, Iain made a sound somewhere between a sigh and the word "Well" and then asked, "Have you been to see the amusement park yet?"

"Amusement park?" She was initially taken aback by the question, but then remembered reading something about an amusement park in one of the guidebooks about Aberdeen. She hadn't run across it yet though.

"Aye, Aberdeen's got it's very own amusement park. Like Copenhagen. Or Vienna."

"Okay," Maggie smiled. She elected not to add, 'Or Disneyland.'

"You've not been to see it then?"

"Er, no." It was a strange topic of conversation, but she liked it and couldn't help but giggle.

"Would you like to?" Iain gave an eager smile.

"Sure." *Why not?*

"Saturday then? I get off work at two. We could go have a look around. Most of the rides won't be running this time of year, but it's still worth a visit. And maybe afterwards, if you'd like," the smile faded slightly in uncertainty, "we could have a bite to eat?"

A soft smile played across Maggie's face. This had gone well. She smiled again at Iain, this time broadly, her caramel-colored eyes sparkling.

"Sounds wonderful."

* * *

Maggie was looking forward to the visit to Aberdeen's amusement park. There was just something interesting about an amusement park in the middle of a city, particularly a European city, rather than off on its own reserve with a 200-acre blacktop parking lot. Of course its real draw had been the excuse it had provided Maggie and Iain to spend an afternoon together, walking and talking and getting to know each other better.

The time between Thursday morning when the plans had been settled and Saturday afternoon when Iain picked Maggie up had not dragged as slowly as Maggie had feared. Indeed she had been surprised to find that the settled plans allowed her to relax and work on her continuing translation. And when she felt the occasional lingering sting of embarrassment at her attempt at the magic, she found some solace in the fact that someone, somewhere—even 1200 years earlier—*someone* had once believed in the magic.

Iain had picked her up at three thirty. The trip to and leisurely tour of the amusement park had taken just over an hour and a half. Although absolutely none of the rides were open, a few of the game booths were still open and Iain had wasted almost fifteen minutes and several pounds trying in vain to win Maggie a prize. Just when she was ready to be turned off by this seemingly excessive display of testosterone inspired machismo, Iain had given up with good humor and just the right mix of faux wounded pride and self deprecation.

By the time they'd finished doing everything there was to do at the park, it was a bit after five and just the right time for an early dinner. Dinner also seemed appropriate since the sun had set shortly after 4:30. November in the North Sea. The only saving grace had been the clear skies which had provided a rain-free walk through the amusement park and now offered a blue-ink canvass speckled with pin-pricks of starlight.

Dinner was at The Red House, a very nice restaurant on the edge of the Old Campus and one of Iain's favorites, he said. Maggie had been surprised. He seemed like a fish-and-chips kind of guy, but The Red House was more prime rib and steamed vegetables. Actually, prime rib, steamed vegetables and a side salad, with a glass of red wine. Maggie had the Atlantic salmon fillet with red potatoes, a salad, and a glass of white wine. But she made sure to save room for dessert. Iain ordered dessert as well. His own—it was far too soon to be sharing desserts.

"So after school," Iain had been saying as the waitress brought them their cheesecake and chocolate mousse. "I wasn't really certain what I wanted to do with myself. I worked a few odd jobs in Glasgow, then moved up here to work on an oil platform out off the coast. That was interesting enough, and the pay was excellent. But it's lonely work and not what I wanted to do. I looked for other work, but without a college degree it was hard to find good-paying work that didn't require me to break my back every day."

Maggie grunted in agreement as delicately as she could as she fed another bite of cheesecake into her mouth. It was really good.

"Eventually," Iain continued after a swallow of mousse, "I landed at Alex and Lucy's shop. I was sort of a stock boy, handyman, sales clerk, jack of all trades. Alex showed me the inner workings of the shop—you know, the business side of it: inventories, accounts receivable, thing like that. Well, that's when I knew what I wanted to do. But I only had a school diploma. And I didn't have the capital to start my own business."

He took another bite of mousse. Maggie's brown eyes remained attentively affixed to his face, at least between bites of her own dessert.

"So Alex offered to help me. He offered to pay for me to go to business college, so long as I was willing to come back and be his store manager. That way he could stop spending such long hours at the shop, and he could justify paying me a good salary. Your uncle Alex is a good man. Takes care of his own, he does. He'd do anything to help out someone he cares for."

Maggie smiled at this. He certainly had been generous and hospitable with her. Then, suddenly, a flash of angst burned through her stomach at some ignored memory. But it left as soon as it came and Maggie decided not to pursue it. She was enjoying herself too much just then.

"I spent two years at business college, earned my business degree. That's the same as a B.A. in the States."

Maggie couldn't help but roll her eyes at this, but she tried to keep her smile. It always irritated her when Europeans asserted that two years of their college was equal to four at an American institution. She'd been to both now and didn't find American college to be particularly easier than its European counterparts. In the event, however, she let the assertion pass without comment as she scooped up another bite of cheesecake. There would be time enough later to engage that argument.

"And when I finished up," Iain continued, his mousse almost gone, "true to his word, Alex hired me as the store manager. That was just over two years ago."

Maggie glanced upward as she did the calculations in her head.

"So let's see. You're how old now? Twenty—?"

"Five," he answered, mouth half full with the last bite of mousse. "I just turned twenty five this last September."

Maggie nodded thoughtfully. *A younger man. I like that.*

"I won't ask how old you are," Iain laughed.

Maggie smiled and raised her wine glass to her lips. "Good."

* * *

After Iain settled the check—he's asked her out after all—the two of them stepped out into the cold November evening. The sky was still clear but the growing breeze threatened to bring clouds soon enough, and with them rain. For the time being however, Maggie and Iain could enjoy an after dinner stroll beneath the stars.

"All we're missing," Maggie said, looking up at the sky as

Iain put his coat over her shoulders, "is a full moon."

Iain laughed lightly as they turned from University Road onto High Street. "Aye, well we've a bit of a wait for that. It'll be two weeks still. It's a new moon tonight."

"New moon?" Maggie was intelligent and educated, but astronomy had never really interested her. She'd heard the term before, of course, but that was all.

"Aye, the moon," Iain explained, "has four phases. It starts as a new moon, when there's no sunlight reflected at all, then as more sunlight is reflected it grows from a crescent to a half moon, waxing—which means its getting bigger. Then it grows to the full moon. Then back down to a half moon, waning, and then a crescent again before it's another new moon. Then it starts over. Takes about four weeks."

Then he added, "In fact, a lot of a calendars mark the moon phases, an open circle for the full moon and a black circle for the new moon. I suppose if you knew your moon cycle well enough, you could look at the moon and practically know the date."

"Well, that is interesting," Maggie admitted. "I never really knew all that. But why is it called a 'new' moon?"

"Hmm," Iain considered the question. He wasn't really more than an amateur stargazer himself. "I imagine it seems like it resets itself. Maybe they thought it took the night off to recharge."

Maggie laughed. "Doubtful," she opined. "So you can't see it all?"

"No, it's not even up there." Iain looked up at the sky. "It's on the other side of the planet right now."

By then they had reached the magnificent King's Tower, complete with stone imperial crown, and doubly impressive at night with flood lights shooting up its sides.

"But," Iain grabbed Maggie's arms gently to stop her gait.

They stepped off the sidewalk to allow any other pedestrians to pass, then Iain leaned his head over her shoulder and pointed up at the dark sky. "That just makes it easier to see the stars."

She could feel Iain next to her, his cheek against hers, his chest brushing against her back. His proximity distracted her from her efforts to see the stars. Trying to regain herself, she continued the conversation.

"You know, speaking of astronomy, I went to Clava Cairns last weekend and—"

Her thought was interrupted by the piercing scream of a woman on the other side of the King's Tower.

Maggie and Iain looked at each other, then at the few other nearby pedestrians, all of whom returned each other's gazes, as if to ask, 'Did you hear that too?'

In answer, a second, longer scream split the air and before its echo had died away, Iain was already sprinting around the far corner of the Tower. Maggie followed after him as quickly as she could, displaying both courage in seeking out the source of the scream and cowardice in not wanting to be left alone.

As she raced after Iain's retreating form, other passers by running beside her, she knew what all of them were thinking: 'Oh, no. Not another one.'

Maggie almost knocked Iain over as she pulled up behind him and slammed into his back. He had been the first from High Street to arrive at the scene, but he was not alone. Standing next to him was the source of the screams, a pair of young women whose eyes were streaming with tears and who must have been cutting through campus when they had stumbled across the grisly discovery which lay at their feet. Maggie stepped around Iain's large form and looked down at the blood soaked figure lying prone on the stone path before them. Before she knew it, she had turned her face into Iain's chest, a scream of horror having escaped her lips only to be followed by sobs of disbelief.

She had only glimpsed the carnage for a moment, but even as her chest expelled uncontrollable sobs into Iain's starched shirt, her brain held the vivid snapshot of the horrible scene relentlessly before her mind's eye.

The corpse was a woman. Her stomach had been cut open and left an empty, bloody husk. Fresh red blood pooled around the body and was soaking into the long banana-yellow hair of a woman Maggie might have called a friend, if only she'd had more time to get to know her better. But there was no more time.

Kelly Anderson was dead.

She lay murdered at Maggie's feet. And surrounding her body was a precisely placed ring of bloody dismembered organs—just like the standing stones which encircled the cairns near Inverness. And placed sickeningly on her forehead was a flat two inch wide stone—just like the small stones that centuries ago had covered the dead at Clava.

Eventually, the sobs subsided and Maggie took a deep breath. She wiped her nose on the sleeve of Iain's jacket and turned away from the emptied corpse. But she couldn't forget what she had seen.

And she found no solace in the fact that someone, somewhere—even 1200 years later—*someone* still believed in the magic.

26. Clues

"Too late. Too bloody late."

Sgt. Warwick stared down at the butchered carcass of victim number three, even as the popping flashbulbs of the police cameras lit the body in a morbid strobe. Warwick was trying hard to focus on the job at hand—collecting clues to the identity of the killer so they could stop him from claiming yet another victim—but all she could think of was how little progress she had made in the four weeks since the FitzSimmons woman's death. And how utterly she had failed in preventing this murder.

"Doesn't get any prettier, does it?" Inspector Cameron stepped up to her, his pipe bowl glowing slightly in the dark of the cold Scottish night.

"No, sir."

"Nor any more helpful." He leaned forward, puffing thoughtfully on his pipe. "Blood everywhere but forensics says still no usable prints—finger, palm or foot. Nothing. Just like the other two." He paused. "Still, it does look different somehow."

"It's the organs," Warwick frowned. "They're rotating."

"Are they?" Cameron squinted critically, his eyes tracing the circle of organs around the dead woman's body.

"Look at the heart-lung combination." Warwick pointed downward. "It was at the Graham woman's head, then at the second victim's side. Now it's at this one's feet. The other organs have followed suit."

Cameron smacked at his pipe. "Clear m.o. Well, that would seem to dispel any lingering doubts that it's the same killer."

"Or that he's not done yet," Warwick added through gritted teeth. "They're rotating a quarter turn each time. He's got one more quarter turn left."

"Or two," Cameron pointed to the bloody pile of intestines which occupied the space above the woman's head. "If he means to complete the circle."

Warwick sighed. "Or two," she had to agree.

The inspector looked again at the scene. "I'm still not clear on what the significance of those damned organs is, but the rotating is definitely something to consider. I wonder what else we've got." He smacked at his pipe again. "Richards!"

Over stepped a rather tall and extremely thin blond woman who bore the embroidered patch of the forensics division on her jacket sleeve. "Yes, sir?"

"Anything to report yet?"

"Not really, sir," Officer Richards replied. "We're just making initial observations. Wouldn't want to jump to any conclusions yet." She paused. "Although..."

Cameron raised an eyebrow. "Yes?"

"Well, I'm no expert," the forensics officer claimed. "Dr. Wood will be able to say for sure. But it looks to me that this one was a little messier. Just a bit."

Warwick looked down at the bloody carnage at her feet, so clearly reminiscent of the equally gory scenes of the weeks before.

"Messier?" her voice held a hint of disbelief. "How exactly? The others were rather bloody as well."

"Sorry," the woman offered. "I didn't mean the scene. I meant the cuts. We've had a chance to do a prelim inspection of the organs. They look to have been cut out the same way, but there's noticeably more trauma at the point of incision. The *cuts* are messier."

Cameron raised his other eyebrow, this time at Warwick. "What does that mean then?"

"Well, it could mean several things," Richards began. "Basically, it indicates some difficulty in executing the cut. It could mean a weaker hand, but everything else points rather clearly to it being the same killer. He may have suffered some injury which weakened his arm or hand. Or he may have switched to a different knife. Most likely, though, it's just that the blade's getting duller as he continues to use it."

Cameron sucked on his pipe stem. Warwick looked down at the body again.

"Thank you, Richards," Cameron dismissed her back to her work. Then he turned to Warwick. "Duller blade, eh?"

"Or weaker hand." She echoed his thoughts, "An injury?"

"Maybe. Something to consider anyway." He exhaled a puff of smoke into the dark air. "For now, let's see what else we've got. Do we know our victim's identity yet?"

"Yes. I found her wallet in her backpack." Warwick pointed at the rucksack resting a few feet away. "It was hidden—not very well—behind some bushes a few yards from here."

"And we know it's her backpack?"

"The photo ID matches," Warwick assured. "It's hers."

"So what was her name?"

"Kelly Marie Anderson."

"Scottish?"

"American.

"Student or tourist?"

"Both maybe. But definitely a student." Warwick fetched the backpack. "The ID was her university ID card."

Cameron took along drag on his pipe. "So three female students."

"Three foreign female students," Warwick added. "Not Scottish anyway. Graham was Canadian. FitzSimmons was from Northern Ireland. This one's American."

"Hmm." Cameron exhaled more smoke. "Well, it's something to consider," he said for the third time that night. "What else is in that backpack?"

"I haven't had the chance to look." She handed it to her superior's outstretched hands. "Here."

Cameron set the bag on the ground and carefully removed several books and papers from inside. Then he extracted what was obviously the woman's day-planner. He thumbed through the pages looking for some clue. At last he stood up with a groan, and handed the planner to his sergeant.

"Right then," he announced. "It looks like we'll be needing to have that chat after all."

27. Intentional Tourist

Maggie's hand skimmed the titles on the shelf, her finger extended like a divining rod.

'Aberdeen.'

'Aberdeen.'

'Aberdeen and Grampian Highlands.'

'Speyside Whiskey Trail.'

'Whiskey Trail.'

'Whiskey Trail.'

'Whiskey Trail.'

Man!

'Victorian Heritage Trail.'

'Balmoral Castle.'

'Castle Trail.'

Then her finger reached the next volume.

Aha. Here we go.

She pulled the book from the shelf and confirmed it contained the information and diagrams she would need. Then she walked to the counter, paid for her purchase and exited the store.

28. Twenty More Questions

"September twenty-seventh?" Craig Macintyre wiped the nervous sweat from his brow with the palm of his hand. "But that was two *months* ago."

"Fine. What about October twenty-fifth?"

"I—I don't know," Macintyre replied, looking down at the spartan desk in front of him. "I'd have to check my calendar."

"Right. Then what about last bloody night?"

Macintyre looked up, his eyes wide and his brow knitted. "Last night?"

"Aye, mate!" Lt. Russell's fist slammed down onto the table. "Where were you *last* night?!'

Macintyre's flinched at the strike against the table, and his eyes flitted nervously around the small, bare interrogation room. "Actually, I'm not exactly sure—"

Russell grabbed the table with both thick hands and sent it sliding wildly across the green linoleum.

"Look, *perfesser*," he intentionally mispronounced the word, "for someone who's supposed to be so bloody smart, you don't seem to know very much about your own activities. But wise up, mate.

Kelly Anderson is dead. And if you don't start remembering things straight away, then we'll be forced to draw some very unfavorable conclusions about your role in her untimely demise."

Craig Macintyre nodded weakly. "Okay."

"Let's start with the basics. Kelly was one of your students?"

"Yes."

"A bit more than just a student, eh, mate?"

Macintyre paused, then gave a defeated smile and looked down. "Yes."

"You were sleeping with her, right?"

Macintyre took a long deep breath then propped his elbows on his knees. "Yes," he admitted through the hands that covered his face.

"Right. But you're married, aren't you, perfesser?" Russell continued. "You've a wedding band on. Not that I can blame you really. She was a pretty bird—well, not when I saw her, not anymore, but—"

"Stop it!" Macintyre shrieked quite unforcefully. He looked up sharply, his eyes red. "Just stop it! Just tell me what you want to know."

Russell walked over and picked up the chair that had been knocked aside by the flying table. Setting it down backwards before his subject, he sat down firmly and leaned forward on the chair back. "Everything," he hissed.

And so it all came out. How Kelly Anderson had come to the University of Aberdeen two years before, pretty, exotic and eager. How she had latched onto him, showered him with attention and praise—something he couldn't get anymore from Mrs. Macintyre. How his meteoric rise to professor had been followed by a series of progressively more unimpressive articles published in progressively less prestigious journals. How his wife's interest in him had waned as his career had stalled but hers had begun to take off—and take her away, on 'business trips' to London and the Continent. And how this pretty young American, who was so taken with him, also just happened to have some of the most original ideas. Ideas well worth publishing, even in some of the most highly regarded journals. And she did so want to be published. Almost as much as Macintyre needed to be.

It wasn't long before the suppressed romantic tension flared into a full blown physical relationship. He used her youth and beauty to salve his wounded pride. She used his reputation and connections to get published. But he had had the better of the bargain. After assuring her that she would receive equal credit for the research they had conducted jointly between liaisons, he had gone and published their article under his name only. Not so much as a footnote mentioning any 'Kelly Anderson.'

After all, he was the professor. His status didn't lend itself to equal billing with a mere graduate student.

And after all, she was young still. She would get other chances to be published.

And after all, his wife, who by then earned the lion's share of their combined income, already suspected something. She would have interpreted the joint credit as confirmation of her suspicions and sent him packing.

And after all, he *needed* the recognition. His young career was slipping away from him, and that was threatening to send his wife packing, most likely to move in with some corporate vice president at the home office in London.

"And after all, I promised to give her equal credit on our next article."

Macintyre looked again at the police officer. "She wasn't very impressed," he admitted with a nervous laugh.

"No, mate," Russell spat. "Neither am I."

Macintyre frowned and looked down at the ground.

"What about last night?"

"Oh, right. Last night." Macintyre rubbed his hands nervously, but didn't look up. "Well, Kelly—she wasn't very happy with me. And that was difficult. Because, well, she had looked up to me so before. And that meant so much to me. But when she looked at me now, I saw that same scorn and disgust I saw in Janet's eyes."

Macintyre shook his head as he looked down, his hands clasped and extended below his knees.

"Go on."

"Well," he started tentatively, "she threatened to expose me. My plagiarism. To the dean, to the police, to anyone who would listen. And our affair as well, if she had to. She wanted me to admit she'd done half the work on the article."

"Half?" Russell had a hunch.

Macintyre looked up at the policeman for a moment, then dropped his head into his hands. "Oh God, I am pathetic, aren't I? All. All of it. It was almost completely her work and I stole it—entirely—because I was scared. Scared of losing my job, my status, my wife. I stole it all and published it under my own name and didn't give her any credit at all."

He hung his head in his hands and muttered something unintelligible.

"Why not just own up to it?"

"Oh no!" Macintyre's head shot back up and he looked at Russell wide-eyed. "I couldn't do that! I'd be ruined. If I admitted I'd plagiarized from a mere *student*? No, I'd have been fired on the spot. And no university would have touched me. I'd have been ruined. And Janet would have left me for sure—even without knowing about the affair."

"But you couldn't let Kelly expose you either, now could you?"

"No. No, I couldn't. That's what I'm telling you." His wide eyes twitched. "But wait, if you're suggesting—"

"I'm not suggesting anything," Russell interrupted, "yet. Let's stick with you and Kelly for now. You did see her last night, didn't you?"

Macintyre didn't respond.

"Don't screw with me, Macintyre," the lieutenant warned. "We've got her entire backpack, complete with her day-planner, her journal and her notebooks. I can probably tell you almost every word the two of you said to each other. So don't play games. You saw her, didn't you?"

"Yes," quivered Macintyre. "But not last night. It was more like late afternoon."

Russell narrowed his eyes, but didn't say anything.

"She came to my office. She knew I usually worked Saturdays when—when Janet and I weren't getting on."

"What time?"

"God, it must have been about four o'clock. Yes, just after four. She gave me an ultimatum. Either submit a formal acknowledgment of her work to the journal, or she'd tell the dean about the plagiarism—and Janet about the affair. She gave me until noon Sunday to agree to her demand, or she'd tell all."

"So what'd you do?"

Macintyre shrugged. "I threatened. I cajoled. I pleaded. But she wouldn't be swayed. I told her I'd have to think about it." He shook his head defeatedly. "She left in a huff."

"And what happened next?"

"Next?" Macintyre seemed perplexed. "Nothing happened next. She'd left. I never saw her again. I remember pulling a bottle of

Glenfiddich out of my cabinet. I was pretty upset. I drank the bottle. Then I fetched the other bottle and started drinking that one too. The next thing I remember I woke up this morning in my office with two empty whiskey bottles and a brick in my head."

The lieutenant considered this for several moments, then asked, "That wasn't the first time she'd threatened to expose you, right?"

"Oh no. It started much earlier, but she'd never been that serious."

"When was the article published?"

"Hmm. Let me think," Macintyre looked at his hands. "It was the summer volume. So July. Late July or early August."

"So before September twenty-seventh?"

Russell's question necessarily reminded Macintyre of how their conversation had started. "Now, wait a minute—"

"Annette Graham was one of your students." It was a statement.

"Yes, but—"

"Were you sleeping with her too?"

"No! How dare y—"

"Fionna FitzSimmons: one of your students, too?"

"No, I don't think s—"

"Our records show she took two courses from you." He recited them from memory, "'Survey of Gaelic Literature in English Translation' and 'Introduction to Comparative Literature.'"

"Ah well, those are large lecture courses. It's possible that—"

"Were you sleeping with her too?"

"No!"

Russell sprang up suddenly, knocking the chair aside quite loudly.

"Where *were* you last night?!"

"I told you! In my office—drinking myself to oblivion." He cowered beneath the large police officer.

"Where were you the night of October twenty-fifth?"

"I don't know!"

"Where were you the night of September twenty-seventh?"

"I don't— Wait!" Macintyre's eyes lit up. "Amsterdam! I was in Amsterdam!"

Russell's face had become beet red during his assault. He blinked slowly. "What?"

"Amsterdam! I was in Amsterdam! At a conference! From September twenty-fourth to October first. I must have over two-hundred witnesses!"

Macintyre's face had exploded into a giddy smile. "In fact, I led a discussion group the morning of September twenty-seventh. That was a Friday, wasn't it?"

The policeman put his hand to his head, covering his eyes. After a long silence, he admitted, "Yes."

"No, sorry," Macintyre beamed. "*I* was in Amsterdam."

Russell lowered his hand and turned away, taking a few absent steps toward the frosted window.

"Am I free to go now?" Macintyre's question held a nervous honesty rather than the relieved triumph it had displayed with the word 'Amsterdam.'

"Not quite, perfesser." The smile returned to Russell's still red face. "Take off your shirt."

Macintyre's mouth fell open. "Pardon?"

"We've reason to believe the murderer may have suffered an injury during the last attack," the lieutenant explained. "Now let's see your arms, mate."

Macintyre sat still for a moment, considering the request.

"Is this legal?" he asked at last. "I mean, do I have to?"

Russell sighed. "Do you want to talk to Mr. Kirby?"

"Who?"

"Your lawyer?"

Macintyre laughed nervously. "Oh," he recalled the conversation with the two police officers in the hallway of Taylor. "No, he's a copyright lawyer. He reads over my publishing contracts. No, he'll be of no help at all. I'm asking you."

"Well, I'm not your lawyer," Russell was sure to say, "so I can't give you legal advice. But I can tell you that's it's legal if you consent to it. And if you don't want to consent to it, then I'll have two choices. One is to let you go without having confirmed information I truly need to know for this investigation. The other is to arrest you on probable cause of murder and ask a magistrate to issue a warrant. Then it won't matter if you consent or not. Guess which I'll choose."

"Probable cause of murder?" Macintyre stammered the words back.

"Aye, mate. *Your* student and *your* lover is dead. She'd threatened to expose *your* plagiarism and *your* adultery. And I couldn't care less about Amsterdam—you've no bloody alibi for last night! So what'll be, perfesser?!"

Macintyre stared at Russell, eyes wide with shock. Then without a word, he slowly unbuttoned his light blue button-down dress shirt. He wiggled out of it without standing up and let out a small sigh.

Russell saw it immediately. A large yellow-purple bruise on the shoulder muscle of Macintyre's right arm.

"Well?" That was enough; the question was clear.

"Janet." Macintyre looked away.

"What?"

Macintyre pulled his shirt on again quickly. "Janet. My wife.

She wasn't happy I didn't come home last night, stumbling in this morning, hung over and with no real explanation. I could hardly tell her why I'd been drinking. She accused me of being with another woman, one of my students. She's pretty smart, Janet is. And she's a strong arm. She threw a lamp at me."

Russell didn't reply.

Macintyre laughed to himself—a pathetic, defeated laugh. "I've lost her anyway," he muttered. "Probably be gone by the time I get home."

"Okay, mate," Russell commanded his attention. "Here's the deal. You're not under arrest." He held up his hand, index finger and thumb only millimeters apart. "But you're this bloody close. We'll be watching you. If you so much as sneeze without covering your mouth, you'll be in a cell awaiting arraignment. Amsterdam or no. Do you understand?"

"Yes."

"And do *not* leave Aberdeen. For any reason. If you do, you'll be arrested. Do you understand?"

"Yes."

"Get out of here," Russell turned away and pointed to the door.

Without delay Macintyre stood up and scurried out of the room, his shirt still half unbuttoned.

* * *

"Well *that* went bloody well!" Russell's exclamation was punctuated by the crash of the observation room door smashing into the wall behind it and the ping of his cigarette lighter as it bounced off the wall behind Inspector Cameron, before hitting the ground and sliding to a stop at Sgt. Warwick's feet.

"Amsterdam, eh?" Cameron smiled.

"Can you believe that?'

"No, actually," Warwick replied as she kicked the lighter back to the lieutenant. "I probably would have arrested him."

"Aye, well don't think I wasn't sore tempted," Russell picked up the lighter and shoved it back into his pants pocket. "But if I do, then we've only seventy-two hours to arraign him on murder or we have to release him. And if he's telling the truth about being in Amsterdam when the Graham girl was murdered—well, then we'll just have to release him. *After* every news outlet in Scotland's reported we'd arrested the killer. We'd look like fools. And we'd damage our credibility when we do find the real killer."

He grabbed onto imaginary jacket lapels and began strutting like a penguin. "'And are you as sure about my client's guilt as you were about Mr. Macintyre's when you arrested him erroneously? Answer the question!'"

Warwick and Cameron couldn't help but laugh at this impression of a criminal defense attorney.

"We'll have him on a short leash," Cameron assured his officers. "We'll watch his every move, at least until we can verify that Amsterdam story. Sergeant?"

"I'm on it," Warwick replied. "I'll get it as soon as possible."

Cameron didn't bother saying, 'I know.'

"And we're sure it's the same killer?" Russell tried. "Any chance Macintyre did the Anderson girl, but somebody did the others?"

Cameron shook his head. "No, the details are too similar. And forensics is rather certain it's the same murder weapons—same wire and same blade, dulling or not."

Russell shook his head and punched weakly at the air in front of him. "Damn. I thought we had our man."

29. A Little Knowledge

Maggie sat on her bed, back against the headboard, knees pulled up, stocking feet shoved under the covers, and the spellbook propped open across her lap. She flipped absently through the pages as she recited, in a low, low voice, what she knew so far.

"There have been three murders." Her fingers turned to the page containing the unnamed author's introductory thought about the magic.

"Each about four weeks apart." A page with a crude rendering of a lunar clock passed before her half-focused eyes.

"Coinciding with the moon cycle?" She reached a page detailing the author's understanding of the bonds connecting the heavens and the Earth. "I'll have to confirm that."

"All the victims were women." Several more pages passed, including spells for healing and fertility.

"All were students." A drawing of a stone tablet reflected in Maggie's glasses as it passed.

"All were foreigners." Her hand reached the section on human sacrifices.

"All were butchered, with their organs laid out like a stone circle." A diagram of a similar sacrifice sat on the page before her. "Or wait— Were they?"

She flipped further ahead, almost to the last page. "The paper said Annette was 'butchered,' but no more details than that. And there was nothing helpful in the papers about Fionna." A spell on the transmutation of matter lay half-noticed on her lap.

"Were they killed the same way or not?" She began flipping back toward the beginning again. Notes about summoning demons passed under her fingertips.

"Is there really a pattern?" She flipped a few more pages, then slammed her hands down on the open book.

"I need to know more about the first two murders." Before she could ask, 'But how?' she looked down at the spellbook. Hiding beneath her now raised hands was some text she hadn't noticed before. She concentrated on the words, written in a dialect that only she understood, making sure she fully grasped their meaning. When she was finished, she set the book solemnly aside. If she had understood the writing correctly, she had stumbled across another magic spell. A spell designed to help those in need of more information. A spell which enabled its user to divine information about an unwitnessed event. From physical samples left behind.

The hair on the back of Maggie's smooth neck stood up on end as she considered the possibilities.

30. Unwitting Counsel

"Thank you," Ellen said in a soft voice to the waitress who brought them their coffees. She turned to her companion, "I love coffee. It warms me up." She paused. "It's been so cold recently."

Maggie nodded as she poured the cream into her cup. "Yeah, the weather's been awful lately."

Before, Maggie might have ventured a crack about the Scottish climate, but Ellen was in no condition for even such unoriginal ribbing. If Ellen had truly succeeded in coping with Fionna's death—a proposition Maggie had seriously doubted—then Kelly's murder had shattered any vestige of security in Ellen's psyche.

"Yes," Ellen replied to Maggie's all too obvious observation. "It has."

Ellen's tired blue eyes flittered around the coffee shop and landed on Maggie's light brown drink.

"Thanks for meeting for coffee, Maggie." A sad smile crept across Ellen's face. "I just don't like being alone right now."

"Me neither," Maggie lied. In truth, alone was the only way she could read the spellbook, and that had become her most urgent pastime. Even as they sat in strained conversation, the book sat silently in her backpack on the floor. "How are you doing?"

Ellen laughed coldly. "Not well, Maggie. I'm scared. I mean I'm really scared. Some madman has killed three girls here at the college. Two of them were good friends, and I'd met the third. Who's next, Maggie? You? Me?"

Maggie just nodded and sipped at her coffee. Still too hot.

"And God forgive me, Maggie, but better you than me. That's horrible, I know, but I can't help it."

"That's okay, Ellen," she assured her friend. "That's totally understandable. I'm scared too. And I know you don't mean it like that. Better no one at all, right?"

Ellen's eyes widened even as her brows knitted together. "Aye, but that's just it. *Somebody's* going to be next. He's *not* going to stop. And the police haven't any idea what they're doing."

"Come on, Ellen," Maggie tried to comfort her friend, but to no avail.

"And what if—" Ellen grimaced. "What if the killer's someone we know?"

Maggie cocked a skeptical eyebrow. "Like who?"

Ellen shook her head and looked down. "I don't know. Just someone." She looked around to ensure no one was listening, then in a low voice, "What about Prof. Macintyre?"

"Macintyre?" Maggie's voice was noticeably louder than her friend's and Ellen cringed slightly. But even as Maggie asked the question, her voice full of incredulity, she could hear Fionna's warning from their chance encounter in the reading room.

"I'm just saying, 'what if,'" Ellen protested. She looked around again, then decision hardened in her features. "You didn't know this, but Kelly and Macintyre were sleeping together."

Maggie's jaw dropped. She hadn't expected that little tidbit of information. But after a moment's consideration, she had to admit that it explained a lot about Kelly's opinion of men, and her demeanor in general. Maggie took a pensive sip from her coffee; it had cooled just enough to drink.

"And more importantly," Ellen again checked for eavesdroppers, "he stole her research."

The jaw dropped again. But then she could hear Kelly's drunken laughter. *'Don't let him read your notes.'*

Ellen went on. "Last year—almost the entire year—they were working together on some project. He kept promising her she'd get co-author credit when it was published. She was so excited. But she only told me and a couple of others. Macintyre had told her to stay quiet until the article was published. He said it was because of their affair. His wife would get angry that he was helping her. And the other students would be jealous. But then he just went and published under his own name. He took all the credit even though Kelly did almost all the work. He even got to give a lecture on it at some stupid conference in Amsterdam. Kelly was so angry!"

Maggie took the story in silently. She noted the feeling of satisfaction she was experiencing as this totally unexpected story filled in so many gaps of her appraisals of both Kelly Anderson and Craig Macintyre. It made sense. To a point.

"Wow. That's amazing," Maggie admitted. "I had no idea. — But murder?"

"Well, that's not all," Ellen continued in hushed tones. "Kelly wasn't going to put up with it. She'd threatened to tell the dean. Or his wife. Macintyre was worried. He knew his career was over if it got out that he'd stolen the article from a student he was sleeping with. He kept trying to sweet-talk Kelly. Kept making all kinds of promises. But Kelly told me last week that she was finally going to put her foot down. She was going to give him an ultimatum. And a deadline."

Maggie was still skeptical. "But what about Fionna? And the first girl, Annette? Was he sleeping with them too?"

"Of course not. At least not with Fionna." Ellen seemed offended by the suggestion. "But Fionna knew about the plagiarism too. I'm not saying I have all the answers. I'm just worried. If he killed Fionna because she knew too much, well, then..."

She didn't need to finish the sentence.

"I'm sure you'll be all right, Ellen," Maggie reassured. "The police will catch him soon enough—whoever he is."

"I know. I'm sorry." Ellen put her face in her hands. "It's just—It's just too much. I'm not handling it very well, I know." She sighed and looked up. "And exams are coming up soon. I just want to leave Aberdeen and go back to Inverness. But I have to finish the semester. I need these credits and they won't offer the same courses again until next fall. But right after exams I'm heading back to Inverness. Three weeks."

"Good idea." Maggie's coffee was almost gone.

"You should get away too," Ellen smiled weakly. "Go travel or something. Just get away."

"Maybe I will," Maggie smiled over her cup. "But what I really want to do is help the police catch this lunatic."

"Well, of course," Ellen swirled her coffee in her cup. "We all want to see him caught. But what can you do?

That's what I'm trying to figure out.

"Yeah, I don't know," Maggie said, looking down at the last of her coffee. "Nothing, I guess. "But I *want* to."

She paused and then finished her drink.

"Ellen, if you thought you might be able to do something that could help, would you? Even if it might be dangerous?"

Ellen paused and looked her friend over carefully, obviously trying to decide whether she was still speaking hypothetically, or actually had some half-baked plan in mind. Apparently deciding on the former, she replied, "I don't know. I'd like to think I would, but I can't say for sure. I scare rather easily, I'm afraid. I don't know that I'd be brave enough."

Maggie nodded thoughtfully.

"But we can't do anything," Ellen concluded. "So I'm just glad I don't have to face that decision."

Maggie smiled into the bottom of the bone-white porcelain cup. "Yeah."

* * *

After coffee with Ellen, Maggie spent the afternoon in a secluded study carrel on floor B-3, studying the divination spell she'd found until she could recite it by memory—in the Hamilton-Devereaux Old Gaelic. After studying, she met Iain for dinner. Following the disastrous ending of their first date, they had decided to get together for a quiet, and hopefully serial-killer-victim-free evening meal. The restaurant Iain had chosen, *Venezia*, was simple and pleasant and seemed to hold the promise of an uneventful evening.

"That's too bad about Ellen," Iain said as he passed Maggie the basket of dinner rolls. "I hope she feels better soon."

Maggie took a roll gladly. Having just coffee for lunch had not been a great idea. "Me, too. But I'm not too hopeful. She and Kelly were pretty good friends, I think. And she was friends with Fionna FitzSimmons, too."

"Mmphm," Iain agreed, swallowing a bite of roll. "I can't imagine what it must be like to lose two close friends. And in that way."

"Yeah, I know," Maggie replied. "I think she's just really

scared. I mean, the police don't seem to be getting anywhere. The whole thing is just so frustrating. You feel so helpless."

"Aye. But I'm sure," Iain tore off another piece of roll, "the police are doing all they can."

"I know," Maggie picked up her own roll, then set it down again, unbitten. "But it just seems like they can't figure out where to start. I mean, there must be someone who saw something. Someone who knows something."

Maggie paused while Iain chewed thoughtfully.

"If you know something," Maggie continued, her gaze relocating from Iain's face to somewhere in the middle of the table, "or even just might know something ... you should tell the police, right?"

Iain's eyes narrowed. "Maggie, do you know something about the murders? Something the police should know?"

"No," she insisted even as the images of Clava Cairns and Kelly's body overlapped in her mind. "It's just— I don't know. I just feel so vulnerable."

Iain greeted this shift in the conversation with some alarm.

"Surely you're not in danger?" His voice held genuine concern.

"Who knows," Maggie spun the roll absently around its small plate. "It hasn't escaped my notice that each of the victims so far has been a visiting female graduate student in languages. I knew the last two victims."

She stopped herself from saying, 'and I'm living with the blackmailed mother of the first victim.'

"I'm probably not really in any danger," she concluded, "but that doesn't mean I'm not worried."

Iain nodded and extended his hand across the table. "Well, don't worry overmuch. I'm here now. I'll watch over you."

Maggie frowned and shook her head. "It's not that," she said without taking his hand. "I just feel so helpless and so useless. I want to help catch this guy so it'll all be over. But—"

"Now, don't go doing anything rash," Iain admonished as he pulled his hand back, the concern again surfacing in his voice.

"No," Maggie looked up with a half-smile, "of course not."

"Besides," Iain picked up the last bite of his roll. "What can you do to help?"

That's the question, isn't it? Maybe nothing. Maybe something.

She didn't answer the question, but instead just sat quietly for several moments.

"Iain?"

"Yesff?" He swallowed the last of his roll.

"If you could help," Maggie asked earnestly. "If you thought there was something you could do to help catch the killer, would you do it? Even if it were dangerous?"

"Hmm," Iain exhaled audibly as he drummed his fingers on the table. "Even if it were dangerous, eh?"

He thought a bit more, then answered, "Well, I suppose you'd have to, wouldn't you? I mean, it's only the right thing to do. Some poor girl's going to be next if they don't catch this lunatic soon. I think maybe you'd have that girl's death on your head a bit if you could've helped, but didn't."

Maggie nodded, then picked up her dinner roll, bit off a sizeable piece, and chewed on that for a while too.

31. Do You Believe in Magic? (Reprise)

"Thanks for the ride home," Maggie opened the car door and climbed out. "And thanks for dinner."

"My pleasure," Iain replied with a smile. He leaned over to be able to see Maggie where she stood outside the car. "I had a very good time."

Maggie smiled, suddenly self-conscious. "Me too."

A moment of awkwardness followed as Maggie contemplated the obvious rudeness of just slamming the door in Iain's face. It seemed the only option, however, other than leaving the door ajar and walking away.

"Can I walk you to the door?" Iain asked at last.

"Oh no, that's all right," she protested. "I'll be fine."

"Are you sure?" Iain insisted, partially opening his own door.

"Yes, it's all right, really. Just wait for me to make it inside."

Iain closed his door again. "All right then," he said with a weak smile.

Maggie smiled again too, but her eyes were suddenly distant as she waved goodbye and took hold of the door to close it.

"Maggie—" Iain interrupted her movements.

"Yes?"

"Er, well," Iain stammered. "I—I just wanted to tell you that you look very pretty tonight. And I enjoyed spending the evening with you."

Maggie smiled broadly, her eyes no longer distant. "Thank you, Iain. I had a good time, too." And she closed the car door gently.

She walked up the dim walkway to the well-lit front door under the porch light. She unlocked the door and opened it just enough to let Iain see that she had indeed made it inside. Turning back to Iain, she waved one last time, watched him drive away, then pushed the door all the way open. As she walked inside, she could hear Iain's soft voice in her mind:

'Some poor girl's going to be next if they don't catch this lunatic soon. I think maybe you'd have that girl's death on your head a bit if you could've helped, but didn't.'

* * *

Maggie closed and locked her bedroom door behind her.

She closed and locked each window and drew the shades closed on each.

She closed the door to the adjoining bathroom.

And finally, she closed the trap on the vent in the floor, closing off the sounds of the television her aunt and uncle were watching in the living room, where just minutes before, upon her return from dinner, she had informed her relatives that it had been a lovely evening, assured them that she was doing fine despite the recent unpleasantness, and then excused herself to her room for an early bedtime.

Having thus sealed off the room to the best of her knowledge and ability, Maggie grabbed her large purse off the floor by the door and strode resolutely over to the desk. She quickly cleared the writing surface of its papers and books and set the purse on the desktop with a dull thud. She had bought a larger purse that afternoon before dinner with Iain. She knew she wouldn't be able to explain the need for a backpack at an Italian restaurant. But she knew just as well that she was not going to just leave it sitting at home where anyone could find it, or it might be damaged or destroyed. Maggie opened the choke-close neck of the purse and extracted from it the black leather-bound spellbook.

She set the book down on the desk and tossed her otherwise mostly empty purse onto the seat of the nearby reading chair. A smallish piece of paper stuck out from the pages of the Dark Book, tucked neatly between the pages, except for its top portion which had been crumpled and generally roughed up inside the depths of the handbag.

Maggie didn't have to open the book to know that the piece of paper was her crude attempt at a sketch of Kelly's murder scene, her lifeless body with its organs so carefully arranged around it. She also didn't need to open the book to know that the sketch marked the page of the divining spell. The spell that might enable her to learn the truth about her friends' murders.

* * *

Maggie sat quietly at her desk, the spell book before her open to the divining spell. Her eyes rested softly but unfocused on the black ink script of the pages as her brain tried to convince itself that what she was contemplating was not completely insane. In truth it didn't seem as ridiculous as it should have. The concreteness of her proposed course of action reminded her of the police psychics she had seen various times on television. Psychics who were used by the police to try to find the bodies of lost and murdered children. In fact, some departments even had psychics on the pay-roll year round, didn't they? And the levitation spell she had tried earlier—was that so different from the Japanese monorail trains which floated above their magnetic tracks? And the transmutation spell she had seen—wasn't that the dream of the ancient alchemists, the precursors to modern chemists? In fact, the atom bomb, wasn't that just changing uranium into a few new elements—and a whole lot of energy?

Maybe, Maggie let herself think, *there's something to this.*

* * *

Maggie paced back and forth across the hardwood floor by the foot of her bed. In front of her face she swung the silver clan crest her grandmother had left her. It was dark outside; she could tell that even with the shades pulled. She wasn't sure how long she'd been home and she didn't really care either. Her mind was occupied with other thoughts.

The crest filled her eyes. 'BE TRAIST,' it said.

"What is that supposed to mean anyway?" she asked aloud. "Be true to whom? Myself? My clan? My ancestors? What?"

Her thoughts traced her ancestry, the mothers upon mothers with the middle name of 'NicInnes.' The family tree her grandmother had taught her. The tree that ended with Brìghde Innes Gordon—the 'healer.' And Brìghde's daughter, Maggie's namesake, Margaret NicInnes Gordon Wilkie—burned as a witch and buried outside of the kirkyard's boundaries.

Maggie's eyes focused beyond the clan crest and rested on the books her grandmother had given her, lying haphazardly on the floor next to the desk. Those books with their Old Gaelic epics were filled with magic and wizardry. Indeed, the entire Celtic world seemed to have been filled with magic, from howling banshees to the little people. The world of the old Celts was permeated with magic the way other societies were preoccupied with trade, the sea, or invading hordes.

The ancient Celts had believed in magic.

Her ancestors had believed in magic.

Should she believe too?

Maybe, Maggie thought, *there's something to this.*

* * *

Maggie sat at her desk again. She wasn't sure what time it was, but she was sure her aunt and uncle were asleep by now. It must have been late. Looking down at the desk, her eyes were focused quite clearly on the papers before her. On the one side was her sketch of Kelly's body. On the other was the ancient diagram in the spell book of some poor victim of a fertility ritual. The arrangement of the bodies and the organs was not identical, but it was similar. Too similar. The conclusion was inescapable: Kelly's killer believed in the magic.

"*Believes* in the magic," Maggie corrected with a whisper.

There is *something to this*, she decided.

And Iain was right. If she didn't do something when she could have, she would be partially responsible for the next murder.

She knew she at least had to try.

'*<Ability to use the magic comes from belief in it. Even the slimmest reed of belief can lead to small successes. Such successes lead in turn to greater belief and greater success. Start small. And believe.>*'

Maggie turned to the levitation spell.

* * *

Maggie stood before her desk. The room was dark except for the light of the candle which stood by atop the desk, unsuspecting what Maggie hoped would befall it. The room held the same atmosphere as the last time she had attempted the magic. When she had failed. She had no intention of failing now, and a certain charge filled the room.

"<Tear asunder the bonds which chain this candle to the earth,>" she recited in the ancient Gaelic. "<Deny nature its order and raise this thing to the hated sky.>"

The candle did not move.

"<Tear asunder the bonds which chain this candle to the earth. Deny nature its order and raise this thing to the hated sky.>"

The candle did not budge.

Maggie closed her eyes. She was tired. She was frustrated. She was going to make this work, damn it.

One more try, she thought. But not one more try like last time. Not one more try before giving up. Not one more try just to confirm it wouldn't work. No, this was one more try, because it would only take one more try. This would work. She was sure of it.

She cleared her mind. She steeled her thoughts.

"<Tear asunder the bonds which chain this candle to the earth. Deny nature its order and raise this thing to the hated sky.>"

* * *

Maggie stood like a statue in the middle of her room. She had no idea what time it was. It didn't matter.

The room was dark except for the light of a single candle.

A candle which shone brightly on Maggie Devereaux's face.

As it floated silently in the air before her fully believing eyes.

32. Calling Dr. Freud

It had been a long night. Working the levitation spell was difficult. Like balancing warm butter on the edge of a razor-sharp knife. Or, as she had heard someone once say, like grabbing smoke. It was also tiring. Even though she hadn't been doing anything physically, by the time she got the spell down right, Maggie felt like she'd run a marathon. Every muscle ached and her heart and lungs felt spent. She had actually wanted to move on to the divining spell. That was her real goal. Levitating things wasn't going to help her solve the murders. Learning about what had happened those nights might. But by the time she felt confident with the levitation spell, she was so exhausted that even the thought of trying a different spell seemed just too much.

She had laid down on the bed, 'just to rest her eyes,' she'd told herself. She was asleep almost before her head hit the pillow.

* * *

The castle was familiar, although she knew she'd never been there before. The walls of gray stone enclosed a small but adequate courtyard. The courtyard was earthen and the ground held various stains of differing colors. Near the iron gate, wooden gallows stood ominously. Silence filled the courtyard as the prisoner was dragged to the center of the dirt field. There were no voices but she could feel the multitude of eyes focused on the young woman who cowered on the soil beneath them. A guard, his face and body obscured by armor, seized the woman and dragged her toward the gallows. Her face contorted in a scream but no sound could be heard. When they reached the wooden structure, rather than pull her up the steps to the hangman's noose, he quickly chained her arms and legs to the scaffolding. At her feet was a bed of steaming coals. The guard stood to the side of the white hot coals, ignoring their heat, and pulled a red hot blade from their depths. The prisoner continued to scream silently. Without ceremony, the guard plunged the blade into the woman's stomach and slit open her abdomen. Reaching inside, he pulled out a bloody bag of organs, some still connected to her insides, and threw them onto the fire. The organs exploded into a ball of gore and smoke that covered the courtyard with the color and stench of blood.

Maggie looked down at her hands. They were covered in blood. The blood of this young woman. She raised her left hand slowly to her face to inspect it. She turned the hand over and back, watching the thick red liquid drip from her wrist. Then she pulled her hand to her smiling mouth and slowly licked the blood from her fingertips.

"Aaaahhhh!" Maggie shot awake. She was sitting bolt upright in bed, covered in sweat and her heart beating a mile a minute. Her breath was short and labored as she recalled the grisly details of her dream.

She looked down at her hands. No blood. Good.

She lay down again, still breathing hard, her hair damp with sweat. She was scared. By the dream, to be sure. But she wasn't as scared as she thought she should have been. And that scared her even more.

33. Divine Right

Maggie stumbled down the stairs for breakfast. She was showered and dressed, but still shaken by the dream. She had overslept, so both Alex and Lucy were gone, at the store no doubt. She found some oatcakes in the cupboard and sat down at the table with these and a glass of orange juice. Alone with her thoughts, she reflected on her activities of the night before. She was chewing on a bite of oatcake when she finally woke up fully.

"Oh my God," she said aloud, as if she herself couldn't believe it. "It worked."

* * *

"<... raise this thing to the hated sky.>"

The pen rose from the desk, shaky at first, then relaxing onto a bed of air.

"<Tear asunder the bonds which chain this book to the earth. Deny nature its order and raise this thing to the hated sky.>"

The pen was joined by one of her grandmother's books, far heavier than the pen but equally suspended above the floor.

Maggie stared at the two objects, her hands raised into upturned claws, and a broad smile across her face. She had always loved language and in addition to the pure thrill of using the magic, she had a particular appreciation for the turn of phrase used in the spell. Not 'lift this object' but 'break the bonds with the earth.'

Gazing at the book, she envisioned bonds rising from the earth and surrounding the book to pull it down. The book faltered slightly in the air. Maggie then envisioned these same bonds breaking and falling aside. The book rose again, higher even than the pen which had preceded it into the air. She then imagined the bonds lurching upward from the floor and grabbing the book back. The book dropped to floor with a loud thud.

Maggie stared at the book for a long moment. Then she looked at the pen which still floated unmolested before her eyes.

Interesting, she thought.

Repeating the process, she imagined the bonds pulling the pen toward the center of the earth. The pen fell quickly back to the floor.

Cool.

Maggie picked the pen and the book up off the floor—with her hands—and set them back on the desktop. She grabbed the spell book from the same desktop and plopped herself down on the bed. Turning to the divining spell, still marked by the sketch of Kelly's body, Maggie studied the page. The divining spell was significantly longer than the levitation spell. And more complicated. But she understood it well enough and felt confident that, with some practice, she would be able to master it as she had the levitation spell.

She recalled the words of the book, '<*Even the slimmest reed of belief can lead to small successes. Such successes lead in turn to greater belief and greater success.*>'

Damn, she thought, *this is fun.*

Maggie scanned the room for a suitable object. She found

one. A small seashell sitting decoratively atop one of the short bookshelves behind the reading chair. Rising briefly to grab the shell from its perch, she sat down again at the desk, spellbook on her lap and seashell centered on the desktop, a few inches from the pen and book which had just moments earlier dangled across the room on invisible puppet strings. Rereading the spell to make sure she had it, Maggie then turned her attention to the seashell.

"<...Release the secrets hidden in this object's matter,>" the spell concluded. "<Dissolve the sheaths which silence its voice.>"

She waited for a moment until she was satisfied that nothing had happened. Then she refocused on the shell and went over the spell again in her mind.

"<Release the secrets hidden in this object's matter. Dissolve the sheaths which silence its voice.>"

A faint red glow spread across the seashell. Maggie hadn't really been sure what to expect, but this seemed to be a positive development. Still, it was hardly informative.

"<Release the secrets hidden in this objects matter,>" she encouraged.

The red glow coalesced into a brightly burning droplet on top of the shell, then a pink fog rose slowly from the center of the spot. The rosy smoke swelled then gave way to a vision which filled Maggie's amazed eyes. Looking into the mist, she could see a small scene of two people at the beach. A man and woman. They were walking along the beach, dressed in swimsuits only. Their lips would move occasionally, but Maggie could hear no sounds. They were young and Maggie could feel the love between them. And more than just love, Maggie could feel happiness, comfort, friendship—and just the faintest hint of anxiety. The image was small, and the memory old, but Maggie was fairly certain she could make out the younger faces of her aunt and uncle. She watched as they strolled along the beach, until the man—Uncle Alex—bent down and picked up a seashell and showed it to, well, to Aunt Lucy.

Cool, Maggie thought, and pulled away from the vision. Obviously they had found the shell on vacation some year when they were much younger. Maggie wondered whether the anxiety she sensed had anything to do with a baby girl named Annette an ocean away.

Maggie looked around for another object. One whose unveiled secrets she would recognize and could therefore confirm. Looking about the room for something small, but important, she remembered the clan crest hanging around her neck. Pulling the silver pendant out from under her sweater, she couldn't help but smile. Apart from being a gift from her grandmother, it was also a beautiful piece of jewelry—solid silver and shiny even in the artificial light Maggie was forced to rely upon with all of the shades drawn against the midmorning sun, and prying eyes. She set the pendant down carefully on the desk and closed her eyes for a moment.

She opened them again. "<Release the secrets hidden in this object's matter. Dissolve the sheaths which silence its voice.>"

The red glow wrapped itself across the pendant, then without further coaxing it coalesced into a small dot, the pink vapor rose and the vision appeared. She had expected to recognize the vision or at least the participants, but she found the faces unfamiliar. A woman sat in a chair, a young girl at her feet. The woman was saying something to the young girl and showing her the pendant, which dangled delicately at the end of a chain. The woman might have been her grandmother as a very young woman. Then again, the girl might have been her grandmother as well. Then Maggie noticed that the woman also had a book in her lap. She raised it to show the girl and pointed to something on the page. The book looked familiar and Maggie instinctively turned to see if it might be one of the same books her grandmother had left her. But when she turned her attention back to the vision, it had vanished.

Damn, Maggie thought.

She was just about to repeat the spell when she noticed a black smudge on the pendant. She snatched up the pendant to examine it, noting even as she did so that the smudge lay exactly where the red dot had been. Maggie rubbed at the black mark, but it would not be so easily dispatched. The metal looked stained. Even scraping with her fingernail proved to be fruitless. Turning her attention to the seashell, she observed the same black discoloration. She hadn't noticed it earlier. Aunt Lucy and Uncle Alex were not going to be happy.

Returning to the pendant, she noted that the smudge had partially obscured the motto written across its top. Rather than "BE TRAIST," the pendant now said "BE..AIST."

"Oh man," Maggie complained aloud. She was genuinely upset. "I've ruined it."

Further rubbing and scratching proved unsuccessful. Even dabbing it with water from the bathroom sink did nothing.

"Damn. Damn. Damn. Damn!" Maggie wanted to throw the blemished pendant across the room, but caught herself. That would hardly help the problem.

Maybe silver cleaner would help. Maybe it would fade with time. Maybe... Maybe the transmutation spell she had seen in the back of the book! If magic had caused the stain, maybe magic could undo it. All she would just have to do was change the surface back to silver. This thought buoyed her and she flipped the pages, a bit too roughly, to the transmutation spell.

"Oh," Maggie said.

The spell was very long. And very complicated. And she wasn't sure she even knew all the words, at least not without a dictionary.

She looked down at the discolored pendant. She looked again at the transmutation spell, its words filling the better part of a page. She looked at her pendant again.

"Okay," she said to no one in particular, "maybe later then?" There would always be time to get that spell down.

Maggie returned the seashell to the bookshelf, black stain turned discretely to the wall, and hung the pendant around her neck again, tucking it neatly beneath her sweater. After raising the shades, cracking open one window and opening the floor vent's trap, she returned her spellbook to her purse and headed to the door. Stopping in the doorframe she turned around and spied the pen, laying motionless on the desk.

"<Tear asunder the bonds which chain this pen to the earth.>"

The pen rose into the air. Then, with just a thought, she lowered it back onto the desktop.

"Cool." And she closed the door behind her.

* * *

Maggie stepped off the bus at the main King's College stop. It was too cold to ride her bike, and she was in too much of a hurry to walk. A fresh dusting of snow clung jealously to the grass, but had already melted from the wet concrete sidewalks. Maggie made a direct line to where she and Iain had found Kelly's butchered corpse.

Turning the corner of the King's Tower Building, she stopped dead in her tracks. She had been right about where the body had been. Unfortunately, she had forgotten that people other than her might be interested in what had happened that night. The entire scene was cordoned off with that blue and white British police tape. In addition, two police officers were still rummaging around the scene, one more interestedly than the other. Nevertheless, she knew she would have to wait to inspect the scene for artifacts for the divining spell.

She paused for moment, just standing there trying to figure out what to do next. Then she noticed out of the corner of her eye that one of the officers had turned from whatever business he had been conducting to look curiously in her general direction. Resolving to return to the scene as soon as she could safely procure some samples, she decided not to linger lest the police officer get a good look at her. No reason to draw attention to herself. She turned the corner and strolled as casually as she could back around the King's Tower.

Now what? she asked herself. Fionna's murder scene seemed the most obvious answer, but she suddenly realized she didn't know where that was. She had been away with Uncle Alex and Aunt Lucy that weekend. It could be anywhere.

Okay, next option? Of course, when there's only one option remaining, it's also the most obvious. So Maggie set out to retrace her steps from her first visit to the campus.

Ten minutes later found Maggie standing next to the Edward Wright Building looking across the courtyard where she had seen the same blue and white police tape so many weeks ago. At least she thought it was the same courtyard. It had actually been over two months since she had spied the police activity while searching for the university office upon her first visit to the Old Campus. She would have to rely on her memory in hopes of pinpointing the location where Annette Graham's body had been found.

Actually, once she thought about it, Maggie realized that she had no actual confirmation that what she had observed that day in early October had any relation to the first murder. She had later assumed that to be the case—and it probably was—but she now questioned her conclusion in light of the concrete consequences of her being wrong. If she was unable to locate any samples, she would be forced to put off her plans, at least until the police left Kelly's murder scene or she could learn where Fionna's murder had taken place.

Deciding that she didn't want to put off her plans at all, Maggie hurried across the courtyard to where she hoped, in a perverse kind of way, that Annette Graham's body had been butchered.

The courtyard showed no sign of having been the scene of a brutal and bloody murder. On the other hand, it had been two months since then. Two months of rain and wind and snow and general exposure to the elements. Maggie looked around for some clue, some confirmation that she was in the right place. A lot depended on her being right. Then she noticed a slight darkening of the pavement stones. The pattern of the dark spot crossed over several stones and seemed to be independent of their physical make up. Looking further up the path, she saw additional darkening, this time in the form of a thin line with one large splotch crossing it. While she was no Sherlock Holmes, Maggie deduced that the dark spots might just be half-bleached bloodstains. If so—if that splotch across the line marked where one of the organs of the circle had lain—then she was in business. Now, to find some artifact.

Maggie crouched down. *What in the world could have survived so long exposed to the elements?* she thought. *Maybe fabric from her clothes?*

Then she spotted it. A single hair barely visible between two stones, its length almost completely hidden under a small shelf of one of the granite blocks. Pulling it out carefully, Maggie was rewarded with a five inch long human hair, brown and curling, with a small piece of skin hanging from its end. *Yuck.* She didn't know what Annette had looked like, but the length certainly suggested a woman's hair. And Aunt Lucy had dark wavy hair. *Besides how else would a hair get jammed under some rock unless...*

Maggie let the unpleasant thought slip away. She had what she'd come for. Time to see what she could learn from it.

* * *

Maggie was hungry for lunch by the time she got back home, but elected to skip food just then, and instead hurried up to her room. She quickly cleared off her desk and extracted from her jacket pocket the folded tissue which housed Annette Graham's hair. Or at least, Maggie hoped it was Annette's hair. She really didn't want to have to settle for the vision of some young student falling and hitting her head on the pavement last week. Then, remembering the black stains from her previous attempts, Maggie fetched an old T-shirt from her dresser drawer. Placing this down on the desk first, she then laid the hair carefully across it. *Show time,* she thought.

Opening the spell book and placing it on the desk chair next to her, Maggie stood expectantly over the hair.

"<Release the secrets hidden in this object's matter. Dissolve the sheaths which silence its voice.>"

The vision rose quickly this time; Maggie didn't even notice whether the thin hair turned red first. She felt a sick combination of emotions as the vision satisfied her hopes that it had belonged to Annette Graham, but also turned her stomach as she was forced to watch its story play out. Annette was walking quickly down the path when a dark figure jumped her from behind, wrapping a cord around her neck. Within seconds, she had stopped struggling. Then the murderer had quickly extracted a knife from his coat pocket. Maggie watched in horror as he sliced open her abdomen and began extracting her organs with surgical precision. The red tint of the vision only made the scene bloodier. Eventually though, the killer had finished his work, and Maggie watched as he carefully placed a stone across Annette's eyes and methodically wiped down the scene with a cloth, smearing away any bloody finger or palm prints. The cloth, the knife, and the cord then were returned to his coat pocket and he pulled out a key of some sort. Then he stood up and Maggie was finally able to see his face—but she couldn't make out the visage. It looked familiar somehow, but she couldn't make out any specific features. It was like a double exposure on film, or ghosts on a television with poor reception. Just as her eyes would rest on a specific feature, it would seem to melt away to a different location. Then, suddenly, the entire vision faded as quickly as it had appeared.

Maggie looked down angrily. She had not disconnected from the vision. Why had it stopped? Then she saw the answer. On the T-shirt, where the hair had been, was only a long, thin black smear. She had used up the fuel for her spell. The hair was completely incinerated.

Moving past her immediate anger, Maggie reflected on her success. First, she had indeed found the right hair. Second, the spell had worked. Third, she knew how Annette had been killed, if not why or by whom. And the precision with which the killer had extracted and placed the organs was enough confirmation for Maggie that he was trying to accomplish something with the ritual.

A good start, she had to admit, and leaned back in her chair contemplatively.

* * *

The rain had come in about seven that evening, as Maggie

enjoyed a quiet but pleasant dinner with her aunt and uncle. Since all of her free time was being consumed by the spell book, Maggie had considerably less to talk about.

'Oh, the magic's going well,' she imagined herself saying. 'I'll be sneaking out tonight to find more samples for my divining spell.'

And indeed after dinner, and after she was sure her aunt and uncle had retired for the evening, Maggie did in fact sneak out of the MacTary's house and into the dark, rainy night.

This time she rode her bike despite the cold. There were few buses running after ten o'clock and riding her bicycle in the icy drizzle seemed preferable to walking in it. It was near eleven thirty when she arrived at the campus. Locking her bike to the nearest bike-rack, Maggie hurried to scene of Kelly's murder.

As she had hoped, the police were not terribly inclined to stand out in the cold and wet. The scene was abandoned save the official looking police tape. 'DO NOT CROSS,' it commanded. *I won't tell, if you wont*, Maggie thought as she ducked under the tape and pulled the flashlight out of her backpack pocket.

Be quick, Devereaux, she told herself. She knew it was stupid and dangerous to be out alone by herself, especially with a serial killer loose on campus. But she took some consolation in the fact that Kelly's murder had been recent. The killings all seemed to coincide with a new moon and it would be several weeks until the moon was new again. So she was safe, at least for now.

Or maybe not. With a flush of panic, she realized that the killer's requirement that he take a life on the new moon did not in any way preclude him from killing someone else in the meantime. Especially if that someone else were nosing around one of the murder scenes late at night. *Uh-oh.*

Maggie looked around frantically for some artifact as fear exploded from her stomach. The rain hiding the sounds of oncoming steps, Maggie tried to stay calm enough to find something of value. The scene was far better preserved than Annette's had been and she quickly located several bits of flesh stuck to the rock of the pathway. Then her flashlight caught glimpse of a thread of some sort. Maggie stood paralyzed between her instinct to flee and her memory of the all-too-short vision from Annette's single hair. Grabbing the thread roughly, she stood up, looked around, then ducked under the police tape and ran as fast as she could back to her bicycle.

* * *

Maggie turned the key as quietly as she could and opened the door equally so. No immediate sign of Aunt Lucy or Uncle Alex. Not that they owned her or could prevent her from going out whenever she wanted. But the niceties of living under the same roof with someone usually included explaining where you have been near midnight on a rainy December night. Luckily, it looked like she would be able to avoid that. Trying not to drip too much, she scurried up to her room and quickly locked the door.

In no time, Maggie was crouched over the bits of flesh she had collected. Repeating the spell, Maggie summoned a vision from the silent witnesses to Kelly's murder.

The vision was similar to the first one. A dark figure grabbed Kelly from behind and wrapped a cord around her neck. Strangulation was followed by dissection. The figure seemed to be wearing the same dark overcoat and gloves, but Maggie couldn't see his face as he crouched over the body. She got a few fleeting glimpses as he arranged the organs around the body, but again Maggie couldn't make out the details of the face. The features seemed to shift even as she looked at them. Then as abruptly as the first, the vision drained away.

Looking down at the black smudge on the T-shirt, Maggie

just gave out a resigned sigh and moved the thread into place. Again the divining spell passed her lips and again a vision arose.

This time, though, it was just of the killer. No murder victims to be seen. But Maggie recognized the coat, the gloves and the key from the first vision. She watched intently as the killer removed the coat and gloves and shoved them into a bag. The vision changed then, and the figure placed the bag inside a locker at what looked like the train station. Changing once more, the vision showed the killer walking up to a tree and placing a key into a knothole several feet up it. Maggie again could not make out the face, but she could see the number on the key clearly as it slid into the knothole: '99.' Then the vision gave out and Maggie was left alone in the room with what she had seen.

She doubted seriously that the police knew about any train station locker or tree knothole. And she was equally confident that they would be very interested in finding the murder weapons. But it was very late. That would have to wait until tomorrow.

For now the best thing to do was to get some sleep. She had developed a sort of post-magic routine and automatically began to follow it. Before going into the bathroom to wash up, she cracked one of the windows and went to open the trap to the vent. It was then that she realized that, in her haste, she had forgotten ever to close the trap. Maggie's mind raced as she tried to recall when she had last opened it and whether Alex or Lucy had been home during any of her other spell sessions that day. She wasn't sure about either.

She went to the vent and listened. No sound. That was good. Most likely they hadn't heard anything.

And if they had, so what? Maggie thought. *It wasn't as if either of them understood Old Gaelic.*

Right?

34. Missed Connections

This time the dream was different. She was roaming the hallways of the castle. It was the same castle, she knew that much. But the hallways were dark and she couldn't see more than a few feet in front of her face. She could hear screams and moans and wails clawing pitifully at the insides of the cold, stone walls. As she continued along the corridor, the cries intensified and seemed to bleed from the very walls themselves. Ahead of her shone a dim light, red as blood and flickering menacingly. She approached a sharp bend in the dank hallway and knew that the source of the flame was just around the corner. All around her, the screams had grown to a high pitched ring of despair and pain. She turned the corner quickly and looked into the heart of the red flame.

Then she woke up.

But she couldn't remember what she'd seen.

And that's what really bothered her. More than the obvious pain in the suffering voices. She wanted to know what that red flame was. But she didn't.

With a disgusted sigh, she pushed herself out of bed and shuffled toward the bathroom. Twenty minutes later she was dressed and walking down the stairs for breakfast. She had slept in late again; it had been another long night of magickry. She was sure Alex and Lucy were at the store by now and she would have the run of the house to herself. So she nearly fainted when she heard his voice.

"Mornin', Maggie."

After her heart started beating again, Maggie turned to see her Uncle Alex, dressed inelegantly in his bathrobe and holding a steaming teacup in both hands.

"Oh, geez," Maggie finally exhaled. "You scared me. I didn't think anyone else was home."

"Aye, well," Alex took a sip from his cup. "I'm not feeling very well today. Your aunt convinced me to stay home, at least for the morn."

"Oh, well, that's too bad," Maggie offered.

"Aye, I haven't felt right for a day or so."

Maggie nodded, unsure what else to say.

"Was up most of the night too," he raised an eyebrow as he sipped again from his cup.

"Oh?" This seemed noncommittal enough.

"Aye." He nodded thoughtfully. "You were up late yourself, no?"

"Er, yeah, I guess," Maggie wasn't sure where he was going with this, but no point in blazing the trail for him.

"Next time lock the door when you get back home, eh?" he smiled.

Maggie let out a sigh. "Oh, gosh. Sorry. I—"

"No need to apologize. I was up in the living room when you came home. I locked it right after you."

"Oh," this seemed to be a good word to repeat.

"What in blazes were you doing out so late on a night like

that, lass?" He sniffed deeply and wetly. "You'll catch a cold," he laughed.

"Er, yeah, I know." *Think, Devereaux. You can't rightly tell him what you were really doing.* "I was out late with Ellen. You know, girl stuff."

"Ah, I imagine I don't know." Another sip. "Not a girl, I."

Maggie laughed politely at this observation. But she was still quite uncomfortable.

Alex nodded again, sipped again, and looked at Maggie. A few awkward moments passed as the two stood uneasily in the hallway. Maggie suddenly realized that she hadn't spent much time alone with Alex since she'd arrived in the fall. Aunt Lucy had always been around. She didn't find this comforting.

"Gaelic was it?" He asked at last.

"Pardon?"

"Gaelic? I heard you in your room. Voices carry sometimes through the house. Especially when you're sitting in the dark trying to feel better. You're studying Gaelic, right?"

"Er, yes." At least now she knew whether she had been overheard.

"Funny, didn't sound like any Gaelic I've ever heard," he looked down as he sipped again from his anonymous drink. "I don't speak it myself, mind you, but I've heard it before. It didn't sound like what I've heard." He cast an inquisitive glance at his niece.

"Yeah, well," Maggie considered her several options, "I've got a pretty bad accent."

"Is that it?"

"Yup," Maggie decided. "That's it. Just practicing some Gaelic"

"Hmm."

Maggie looked at her uncle. *He doesn't believe me.*

"Well," she said at last, "I just came down to grab some food to take with me to campus."

"Oh, you're leaving?" Alex frowned.

"Yeah, I've got a lot of things to get done today."

"Well," Alex' disposition softened notably, "that's too bad. I'd hoped to spend some time with you this morning."

"Sorry, but, you know, duty calls."

"Aye. You do what you have to do." And he turned back toward the living room, hitching his robe tighter around him. "Have a good day."

"Thanks," Maggie suddenly felt bad about her suspicious disposition. After all, she was the one sneaking around at all hours of the night. "You too ... Uncle."

She couldn't see it, but she hoped he had smiled at this last word. She really hoped that.

* * *

"What?" Warwick's voice betrayed her irritation. "Are you sure? Damn it. Can you fax me some kind of confirmation? All right. You've got the number, right? Okay, yeah, I'll be here all day—all night too most likely. Okay, thanks again, Coles."

Warwick hung up the phone.

"Damn it," she murmured to herself. Staring at her desk, lost in possibilities and their elimination, she suddenly felt a presence in her doorway. Looking up she was greeted by the friendly faces of Inspector Cameron and Dr. Wood.

"Inspector. Dr. Wood." She greeted her visitors as she walked around her desk.

"Who was that, then?" Cameron asked his sergeant. "Something about the case?"

Warwick frowned. "Afraid so. That was the Royal Ulster Constabulary in Belfast. We can scratch Sean FitzSimmons off our list of suspects."

"Why's that?"

"Because he's spent the last week in the Belfast jail," she explained. "Apparently he got into a bar fight and tried to feed some bloke his beer bottle."

Cameron pursed his lips in disappointment, then nodded. "Well, we can't change that, I don't suppose."

"Suppose not," Warwick had to agree. Then, turning her attention to her other guest, "So, how are you, doctor?"

"Better," he answered, shaking the sergeant's hand weakly. "I'm afraid I ssuffered a mild sstroke the other week. Recovering sslowly, I'm afraid. A function of my age, I'm ssure. But it wassn't as sseriouss as it might have been. I'm a lucky man."

This news explained the slightly slack expression Warwick now noticed on the right side of the doctor's face, as well as his speech and weak handshake.

"Well, I'm glad you're—," Warwick started, but the phone rang again.

"Do you mind if I answer that?" she asked. "It could be Ulster again."

"By all means," the inspector replied with a smile. "Do your job."

Warwick smiled and grabbed the receiver.

"Warwick here. What? Uh-huh. Uh-huh. Okay. And you're sure? No chance of some sort of mistake? Yes, well, okay two-hundred witnesses... But they couldn't all have seen him ... yes, I know: he only needs one. Eh? Yes, can you fax it to me, or courier? No, don't worry. It's not your fault. Okay. All right. 'Bye."

The sergeant set the phone down on its cradle and let out a long exasperated sigh. "That," she pointed disgustedly at the phone as she turned again to face her guests, "was Professor Craig

Macintyre's alibi being confirmed."

Cameron's face again turned up into a disappointed pucker. "Was it then?"

"Yes." Warwick waved again at the phone. "Apparently he *was* in Amsterdam the night of Annette Graham's murder. And the days before and after, too. So, he's off the list as well."

"Today's not our day," the inspector observed dryly.

Warwick turned to Dr. Wood, hope glinting again in her eye. "Are we sure it's the same killer? Couldn't it be different people using the same method?"

"Well," Dr. Wood straightened up a bit. "We're as ssure as we can be. It'ss the ssame *moduss operandi*. The ssame cutss. The ssame preccission."

Warwick wouldn't be deterred. "What about what forensics said? That the killer may have suffered an injury to his arm? Macintyre had that huge bruise on his arm."

A puzzled look crossed Dr. Wood's still healing face. "I'm not ssure what you mean?"

"Forensics said," Warwick repeated, "that the cuts seemed less surgical, less sure. Weaker."

Dr. Wood's expression changed to one of sternness. "I've never ssuggested any ssuch thing," he assured.

"Well, they thought it might mean that the killer had suffered some kind of injury. That his arm was weaker—"

She stopped and couldn't help but look down at the doctor's stroke-stricken right side.

"—that is, er," she stumbled on, "maybe it was a different person?"

"No," Dr. Wood went to cross his arms, but couldn't quite. "That'ss not it at all. It iss the ssame killer. And although there iss ssome minimal trauma to the inccision ssites which wass not pressent in the other victims, I would chalk that up to a duller blade. The killer hass likely not taken hiss knife to the grocer to have it sharpened."

"Of course," Warwick answered carefully. "And the cuts are otherwise very exact, correct?"

Dr. Wood cocked his head. "Yes," his voice was guarded.

Cameron breathed in deeply, but didn't say anything just yet.

"Safe to say the killer knows his anatomy?" Warwick continued.

"He knowss it very well," was the doctor's reply.

"Like a doctor?"

After a moment, "Like a doctor."

Cameron couldn't hold his tongue any more. "All right, then. Is that all, sergeant?"

"Yes," she eyed the doctor critically. "Nothing else to report."

"Then we'll be going." The inspector led Dr. Wood back into the corridor. Then he turned back and stepped into Warwick's office as the doctor shuffled down the hallway.

"Sergeant." He would have her attention.

"Yes?"

"That was uncalled for." He looked down at the ground, obviously conflicted. "Look, Elizabeth, you're a good officer and a valuable part of this team. Hell, you'll have my job someday, but not if you start doing foolish things like that."

Warwick stood silent.

Cameron shook his head. "You're working too hard on this case, Elizabeth. You need to clear your thoughts. We'll crack this one, but not by working around the clock until our judgment becomes impaired. You need to get some rest."

"No," Warwick protested. "I'm fine."

"It's not a request, Sergeant," Cameron didn't like pulling rank, but it was one of the perks of his position. "I want you to take the next two days off."

"No, sir, really," she found herself actually frightened by the thought of wasting two valuable days on holiday—two days she could work on finding the killer.

"Two days, Sergeant. That's an order." Then he smiled. "You'll see. Your head will be much clearer after a bit of rest. Don't worry, we'll all still be working on it while you're out."

Warwick didn't respond. What could she say?

"I don't want to see you again until Thursday," the inspector concluded, and then disappeared into the corridor after the doctor.

Warwick stood still for several moments, staring after her supervisor, then turned back to her desk to grab some work to take home.

"Damn," she said softly.

* * *

She had procrastinated long enough. With a long, heavy sigh, Maggie looked up at the Aberdeen police station. She had to tell the police what she knew. But they didn't have to believe her. She wasn't happy about looking the fool. But what else could she do?

As she climbed the steps toward the front doors, Maggie reflected on how a police station is one of those places no one ever really wants to go to, kind of like the principal's office, arraignment court, or the morgue. The modern metal doors swung open begrudgingly at her heavy shove.

The lobby of the Aberdeen police station was surprisingly uninteresting. She had expected to see several colorful characters loitering about, drug addicts and prostitutes and lost children, together with tough looking police officers and maybe even a K-9 dog—all crossing the hallways in multiple directions. Instead she was greeted by a small empty room with a rather plain looking woman in a police uniform behind a bullet proof glass shield. There were three uncomfortable looking plastic chairs off to one side and what appeared to be dozens of different postings regarding the various regulations which apparently needed to be posted in police station lobbies. Since there wasn't anywhere else to go, she walked up to the window. She felt an urge to make a withdrawal.

"May I help you, ma'am?" the officer asked.

Maggie pulled Sgt. Warwick's card from her pocket. The sergeant had given it to her when they'd spoken so many weeks ago. Before the third murder. When Kelly was still alive.

"Um, is Sgt. Warwick available?" *Or does one need an appointment to speak with a police officer?*

"One moment, ma'am," was the reply. "Let me see if I can find her."

The policewoman picked up her phone and started pressing buttons. Maggie couldn't hear her voice through the glass and so she turned to glance around the lobby. It had not gotten any more interesting. The nearest posting explained that it was a felony to carry a firearm into a police station. Maggie supposed that if someone were actually bold enough to try that, they probably wouldn't be deterred by a piece of goldenrod photocopy paper. Oh well.

"Ma'am?"

Maggie wondered when she had turned from a 'miss' to a 'ma'am'—she was only 26. "Yes?"

"I'm afraid Sgt. Warwick is out today. She won't be available until Thursday."

Maggie's face must have shown her disappointment.

"Is there someone else you could talk to?"

Maggie thought for a moment. She didn't feel that comfortable with Inspector What's-his-name. And she didn't know any other Aberdeen police officers. A good thing, actually, she supposed. And this was too ... *strange* to speak with just anyone.

"No, thanks," she replied and started to try to think of her explanation for why she wouldn't talk to any other officer.

"All right, then," the officer accepted Maggie's reply without comment and quickly returned to some paperwork, turning her attention completely from Maggie.

Maggie smiled and nodded to herself, then turned toward the door.

"Damn," she said softly.

35. A Likely Story

Tuesday had proved unfruitful. Unable to speak with Sgt. Warwick, Maggie had instead resolved to find some samples from Fionna's murder scene. She didn't know where that was exactly, but it was small work to find a two week old newspaper in the college library. The paper said the murder had taken place 'at the victim's residence.' *How horrible*, Maggie had thought. Somehow being attacked out in the open seemed preferable to the same fate in one's own home. Maybe because a home is supposed to be a refuge. In any event, Maggie then had to look Fionna up in the college directory; she had never been to her apartment. All her work proved to be in vain, however. When she arrived at the apartment building, she found no ready access inside. And she couldn't think of any possible excuse she could give the landlord as to why she needed to be let into the dead girl's apartment, then left alone for a while. So after several minutes of discouraging thoughts, she shoved her hands into her pockets and walked away.

Wednesday wasn't much better. She had decided there wasn't any more to be done about the murders until she could talk to Sgt. Warwick. She knew she needed more information about the murders if the visions were to be helpful. Perhaps the police officer would allow her to help with the investigation and share information with her. Maybe even take her to Fionna's apartment? But in the meantime, she needed some distraction. So she spent the day at the library trying to think of a new research topic. Obviously the spell book was not going to be her thesis. If she ever chose to share its secrets it wouldn't be via some dry academic journal. But that didn't alleviate the need to produce some sort of tangible research for her thesis. She still had her day job.

With a lack of new samples and no one to talk to about what she had learned, Maggie passed the days without using the magic. She also slept soundly and peacefully for the first time since the candle had floated before her face. By the time Thursday rolled around, she felt rested and more than ready to get back in the hunt.

"Can I help you?" It was a different officer behind the teller glass. A man this time.

"Yes. I'd like to speak with Sgt. Warwick," Maggie replied. Then, just in time, she added, "Please."

"Do you have an appointment?"

Okay, maybe you do need an appointment to see a police officer.

"Er, no, but—" *But what? But I'm using magic to solve the recent serial killings?* "Could you tell her that Maggie Devereaux is here? Alex and Lucy MacTary's niece from America? It's about the murders."

The policeman looked Maggie over for a moment, then finally picked up the phone. After a moment, he hung up again and turned back to Maggie.

"Have a seat," he pointed to the plastic chairs.

"Thanks."

There were no magazines to read, and so Maggie's eyes fell onto the postings nearest her. She resisted the urge to pull the spell book out and practice her levitation spell. Within a few minutes, a large, ugly door on the other side of the lobby shook with a solid metallic thunk and creaked open on tired hinges. Pushing the door open was Sgt. Warwick. Somehow, she looked different than Maggie had remembered. Not as pretty.

"Maggie?" the policewoman said in the soft tone Maggie remembered.

"Sgt. Warwick?" Maggie gladly stood up from the uncomfortable chair.

The sergeant smiled, "It's pronounced 'Warrick.' Like the— Oh nevermind. Come on back." And the two of them disappeared behind the steel door.

The sergeant's office was smaller than Maggie had expected. But at least it had a window. Sort of. In the wall behind the desk chair was a frosted glass plane which let in light but permitted no actual view outside. Sgt. Warwick sat down at her desk and bid Maggie to sit in one of the two government-issue chairs opposite her. The walls were off-white and bare, save a large map of what Maggie assumed was Aberdeen. She thought that looked like the waterfront on the right. As Maggie returned her attention to Sgt. Warwick she noticed the officer discretely close the files on her desk and slide them to one side. 'King's College Murders,' read one label.

"You wanted to talk about the murders?" Warwick asked, getting right to the point.

That suited Maggie fine. She was anxious to proceed and wouldn't have suffered small talk well.

"Yes, I—" Maggie stopped. *I what? Oh God, what do I say? 'I have a magic spell book I found in the library?' 'It let's me see magical things?' I'll sound completely insane. But I can't just say nothing. I'm here now. Oops.* "Er, I'd like to help with the investigation."

A genuine smile crossed Warwick's face. "Well, that's

splendid. Do you have some additional information?"

"Well," Maggie grimaced. "Sort of."

Warwick's smile twisted away. "What do you mean? Either you do or you don't."

"Well, I—" *Oh God, you'd better think of something, Devereaux.*

"Come on, Maggie," Warwick leaned forward. "What is it, then?"

"Well, it's just, er—" *Maybe this will work:* "I—I can see things."

Warwick's expression was completely blank.

"Like a psychic," Maggie continued.

Warwick leaned back and crossed her arms. "You're a psychic?"

"Um. Sure."

Warwick rubbed her chin and mouth as she considered this information. Finally, she folded her hands on the desk before her.

"Miss Devereaux," she started, "I'm sure you can understand when I say—"

"I know things," Maggie interrupted. "About the murders. Things no one else knows." The sergeant eyed her critically. "They're related for one thing."

Warwick frowned. "Not a difficult surmise. Especially if you've been near a newspaper or television in the last few months."

"The victims were strangled first."

Warwick's eyes widened noticeably. Maggie had her attention.

"With a cord," Maggie added.

The sergeant's fingers drummed on the desk. Her eyes encouraged the young woman across it.

"Then their bodies were cut open, very carefully," Maggie continued. "Their organs were removed and placed around the bodies in a very specific pattern."

Sgt. Warwick leaned back in her chair again, hands folded together, fingertips to her lips. She was obviously considering this display. Maggie really wanted to help. She could hear Iain's words in her ears and she could almost taste the opportunity to do the right thing. But the sergeant's continued silence was making her nervous. Indeed, the silence in the room was becoming deafening. She was losing her. She could sense that the next words out of the officer's mouth would be, 'Thank you, but...'

"I know where the murder weapons are!" Maggie blurted out.

Warwick half stood, pushing her chair out behind her. "Where?" she demanded.

"Will you let me help?"

Warwick's eyes flared. "You're lucky I don't arrest you right now as an accessory to murder. And if you don't tell me where they are, I *will* arrest you for obstructing a police investigation. Now: Where are the murder weapons?"

Maggie swallowed hard. "Um—" she stammered. "They're in a tree."

Maggie wasn't sure what to expect. Warwick stared at her for a moment, then closed her eyes and raised her face to the ceiling. She took two steps toward the window then stopped and crossed her arms, her back turned to Maggie.

"What?" She didn't turn around.

"Um. In a tree," Maggie repeated. "Actually, they're not in the tree. The key is. The key's in the tree."

Warwick turned around slowly. She'd come this far. "How's that?"

Maggie took a deep breath. She knew she wasn't making a lot of sense. She calmed herself and explained as best she could.

"The murder weapons are a cord for strangling the victims and a large knife for the, well, the dissection. The killer, whoever he is, cleans them off, puts them in a black bag, together with a coat and gloves, and then puts the bag in a locker at the train station. I think it's locker number 99—that's what's on the key anyway. Then he hides the key in the knothole of a tree near the station." Maggie frowned. "At least it feels nearby."

"It *feels* nearby?" The sergeant didn't seem impressed by this level of certainty.

"I can find out more. If you let me help." Maggie's voice dripped with eagerness.

Warwick looked at Maggie for a long moment. Her face showed the conflict within her.

"Two of the girls who were murdered were my friends," Maggie said simply. "The third was a relative. Let me help."

Warwick paused. She knew the absolutely most important thing was to catch the killer. Standard police measures were not getting them very far. But she could hear Inspector Cameron's voice: 'You'll have my job someday, but not if you start doing foolish things.' This idea was definitely foolish. Still ...

"Wait here," she said at last and crossed to the door.

Maggie half-smiled. Maybe she would get to help after all.

Warwick turned back as she reached the door. "And don't touch anything."

Maggie looked at the file folders sitting so temptingly in front of her. She turned to the sergeant and smiled sweetly. "I promise."

Maggie listened as Sgt. Warwick's footsteps faded down the linoleum hallway.

"I promise," she repeated, "I won't *touch* anything."

She raised her right hand slightly as she spoke the spell. The top folder lifted gently off the desktop. Lowering her hand again, the folder came to a rest in front of her. With a wave of her wrist the folder opened and revealed the first of several photographs. It was Kelly's murder scene; Maggie recognized it. Quickly raising the photographs in turn, she scanned the photos of each of the three murder scenes, all taken from various angles. This confirmed what Maggie already had seen in her visions: each murder scene had been arranged as methodically as Kelly's, with a single stone on the woman's face, and the organs circling the body like the stones at Clava Cairns. Then Maggie noticed something else. The organs appeared to be rotating around the victims, like a clock face. The distinctive lung-heart-lung combination was at Kelly's feet, but to Fionna's side and above Annette's head. Then she noticed something even more interesting. The King's Tower was clearly visible over the buildings behind Annette Graham's head. But in the photographs of Kelly Anderson, whose body was also found north of the Tower, the distinctive stone crown was visible past her feet. Although she couldn't orient Fionna's body from the photographs inside her apartment, Maggie knew it wasn't the organs that were moving. The bodies were rotating in relation to the organs, the heart-lung combination always to the south.

Seeing the photographs of her friends, lifeless and gutted, evoked an unfamiliar emotion in Maggie. She couldn't name it. She had expected to feel shock, sadness, anger maybe. But the feeling in her stomach defied recognition. And Maggie wasn't sure she liked it.

Having looked at each photograph in this first file, she lowered the images again and closed the folder. She stopped for a moment and strained to hear, but there were no footsteps in the hall yet. So she repeated the spell in a low voice, and the second file folder opened. Maggie had expected to find typewritten reports, maybe more photographs, something like that. Instead she was surprised to find herself peering at yellowed newspaper clippings. They were upside down for her, but she could make out the headline:

OCCULT MURDER IN GLENNINVER

Occult murder? she thought. Weren't those the exact words she had overheard the police use to describe the current murders?

Deftly raising the article into the air revealed another newspaper clipping. This headline read:

THIRD MURDER SHOCKS GLENNINVER — POLICE BAFFLED

The print was a bit larger and Maggie could make out the first few words of the upside-down article:

GLENNINVER, ROSS-SHIRE — This small fishing town on the West Coast was rocked again by the news of yet another murder, this time a fourteen year old girl found strangled and butchered in the basement of her own home. Police have no immediate leads but believe this killing is related to two previous occult-like slayings....

Footsteps echoed down the hallway. She only had a few moments. Lifting the rest of the newspaper articles quickly to check for anything else helpful, she saw something that genuinely frightened her. A photograph. A mugshot. Even upside-down she could recognize the man in it, and seeing his face in these files, connected with the murders of her friends, chilled her blood.

No stylish goatee. Hair disheveled. But it was him.

Devan Sinclair.

The footsteps were just outside. *Damn,* she thought and quickly lowered the newspaper clippings back into their folder. As she did so she tried to see how old the articles were. Just as the folder closed on the clippings she caught a glimpse of the date of the article. With a final "<break the bonds,>" she maneuvered the first folder back on top of its partner right as Sgt. Warwick entered with Inspector Cameron.

"Hello, Miss Devereaux," he said, not extending a hand in greeting. She only half heard him, though, her mind processing the date she had seen. It was upside down, so maybe she read it wrong. But if not, those murders happened almost twenty years ago. Sinclair's mugshot was much more recent than that, though. *Wasn't it?*

"Um, hello," she replied at last. Hardly the way to instill confidence, not being able to respond promptly to a simple greeting. She wondered if the Scots used the word 'flake.'

"Miss Devereaux," the inspector repeated. "Sgt. Warwick tells me you may have information which could assist our investigation of the recent murders at the College?"

"Yes," Maggie replied eagerly. "Well, maybe. I think I can help. Like I told Sgt. Warwick, I can see things. If I could just have access to some of the evidence. I think I may be able to ... do a reading."

Cameron's eyebrows shot up at the phrase, 'access to some of the evidence.' He straightened up to his full height and sniffled thoughtfully. Turning to Warwick he stared at her silently for a long moment. Finally he turned back to Maggie.

"Miss Devereaux," he said for the third time. "The police in Scotland have not yet sunk to the level of desperation apparent in United States law enforcement. So despite your," he sought a polite phrase, "generous offer, we will *not* be needing your services."

"Good day." He added and turned to leave, but as he reached the doorframe Maggie could hear him whisper, "What were you thinking, Elizabeth?"

Warwick stood silently, arms crossed, as her supervisor left her office and walked down the corridor again. Finally she turned again to her guest.

"Sorry, Maggie," she offered. "I tried."

"Oh, I know," Maggie replied, forcing a smile. "I guess I shouldn't be surprised. It's okay. Really."

And actually maybe it was okay. She had at least learned a few things. She'd confirmed her visions were correct. She'd gotten to see photographs of each of the victims. And she had a new lead to follow: Glenninver. And Sinclair.

"I appreciate your trying," Maggie added standing up. "If you change your mind..."

Warwick just nodded and stepped aside to let Maggie walk out of the office. Then she escorted Maggie to the security door through which they had entered and opened it for her. As Maggie passed through into the lobby, Warwick called after her.

"Maggie, this gift you claim to have." Warwick frowned as she sought the right words. "For seeing things, I mean. Be careful. I think it might well end up consuming you. Maybe—"

Maggie cocked her head, listening.

"Maybe it might be better to turn away from it?" Warwick finished.

Maggie could feel the blood rush to her face.

"Why don't you—" The loudness of her voice surprised Maggie and she caught herself before she finished with the 'mind your own business!' She took a deep breath and let the anger subside.

"Thank you," she said in a controlled voice. "I'll consider that." And she strode resolutely to the doors.

Outside, still slightly irritated by this attack on her newly-found gift, Maggie practically ran down the steps to the sidewalk, not paying attention and almost running into a man walking by.

"Hello, Maggie," said the man.

Maggie looked up and her still half-boiling blood ran cold.

"Hello, Mr. Sinclair," she said as calmly as she could manage.

"Are you a suspect now?" He asked with an uncharacteristic grin and a nod toward the police station she had just exited.

Maggie resisted the urge to say, 'No, but you are,' and instead settled for a rueful smile.

Sinclair examined Maggie's face closely, a frown creeping across his own.

"I know I said I wouldn't renew my offer, but—"

"Good," Maggie barked. "Then don't." And she walked briskly away.

Sinclair looked after her for a few seconds before glancing back up at the door of the police station. There stood Elizabeth Warwick, also watching after young Maggie Devereaux.

Sinclair smiled and nodded to the policewoman, then continued on his way. Sgt. Warwick returned neither the smile nor the nod but ducked back into the precinct and closed the door behind her.

36. Glenninver

From Aberdeen, perched proudly on the easternmost shore of the Scottish Highlands, it's a long drive to the west coast of Scotland, the last land before the narrow body of water known as The Minch and the Hebrides beyond it. Luckily Iain's car was comfortable and there wasn't much traffic early on a Sunday morning.

"Remind me again where we're going?" he asked politely enough.

"Glenninver," Maggie replied simply.

"Och, aye," Iain nodded. "And remind me why?"

Maggie turned and smiled sweetly at her traveling companion. "Because I want to," she purred.

"Aye. That is the right answer, I think."

He paused for a moment as Maggie turned and looked back out the windshield.

"And, if I might ask," he ventured again. "Why is it that *I'm* coming along?"

"Oh, that," Maggie smiled again, but kept her gaze on the rolling blacktop road ahead of them. "Well, there are three reasons, actually."

"Three reasons?" Iain repeated grandly. "I'm sore honored. What might these reasons be then?"

"Well, first, you have a car."

"Och, I'm your chauffeur then, am I?"

Maggie ignored the jab and continued. "Second, you know the area."

"And your tourguide," he laughed. "Please, go on."

Maggie glanced up at him with a crooked smile. "Third, I don't want to go alone."

Iain looked over at her with a quizzical expression.

"I want you to be with me," she explained.

Iain looked back at the road and thought for a moment. Then a smile crossed his own face.

"Good enough for me," he said and pressed on the gas.

* * *

The drive took a bit longer than Maggie had anticipated. After all, they were essentially driving all the way across Scotland. Then again, Scotland is not the largest country in the world. So, sometime shortly after noon, the highway finally came to its end and the car rolled into a quaint village nestled on a small sea-worn peninsula. As they had approached the town, both of them had noticed that the road signs had changed to Gaelic-only; Iain with dismay, Maggie with excitement. They were in a *Gàidhealtachd*, one of the regions, mostly on the west coat and the islands, where Gaelic was still the primary language.

A large blue sign with white letters marked the entry to the village: "*Fàilte chun Gleainn Inbhir*," it read. 'Welcome to Glenninver.'

In short order, they found a parking spot on the street and were finally able to get out of the car and stretch their legs. After a quick stroll through what appeared to be the downtown, Maggie spotted a pub and grabbed Iain's arm.

"Come on," she pulled his arm.

"Where are we going?"

"*Tha sinn a' dol dhan taigh-seinnse,*" she explained.

"Come on, woman," Iain pleaded. "I'm from Glasgow. Speak English. Or at least Scots."

"We're going to the pub," she translated. "I'm thirsty."

Iain didn't really believe this last part but he let himself be tugged along just the same.

The pub was actually rather small, but very bright, with large windows lining one entire wall. Somehow Maggie had expected it to be dark. Bars were always dark. But then she reminded herself that this was a 'pub,' or '*taigh-seinnse*.' In English it was short for 'public house'; in Gaelic it meant 'house of singing.' And that was the reason she had come to Glenninver. She hoped to find some members of this town's public, singing or otherwise, who were old enough to remember a series of murders that had taken place almost twenty years ago.

She was not disappointed. There were several men in their late forties to early fifties sitting in the pub. Three sat at a table playing some game Maggie couldn't quite see. The other two were perched at the bar, their conversation with the bartender rolling along in the lilting and guttural contradiction that is Gaelic.

As they walked up to the bar, the bartender quickly looked them up and down, then asked, in English, "What can I get for you?"

Maggie was genuinely disappointed.

"Uh, just a pint of stout for me," Iain replied as he took a seat at the bar.

"Er, *bu toil leam uisge-beatha ri deigh, ma 's e ur toil e,*" she ventured, ordering a whiskey on the rocks. At least she hoped that's what she'd said. This was the first time she'd ever actually gotten to use her Gaelic in a real world setting. She hoped she hadn't just said something unpleasant about the man's mother.

The bartender just stared at Maggie. He was a large man, some six feet tall, well over 200 pounds, and bald as an eagle. Finally, he responded, in Gaelic, "<All right then. Coming right up,>" and he left to pour their drinks.

"What did he say?" Iain leaned over to where Maggie had sat down next to him.

"I think he said he was going to get us our drinks. Man, this is so cool." She could barely contain her excitement. "I'm actually speaking Gaelic."

The bartender returned with a pint of dark stout and a small glass of ice cubes with a bit of whiskey in it.

"Here you are," he said in English. "So where are you two from? Your Gaelic has a strange accent, lass."

"Aberdeen," Iain replied first.

"Aberdeen, too," Maggie started, then realized that when speaking English her accent quickly betrayed her true origins. "Well, the States actually, but I'm studying in Aberdeen this year."

The bartender nodded, bottom lip protruding slightly as he considered this information. Then a smile pushed onto his face.

"An American who speaks Gaelic, eh?" He laughed. "That's a first. Around here anyway. It's hard enough to find a Scot what speaks it."

Iain didn't have to look up from his stout to know the bartender was looking at him. He elected not to explain that, to the best of his knowledge, his ancestors had been speaking English since probably about 1300.

"So how do you like Scotland, miss?" The bartender smiled broadly.

"I like it a lot, thanks," she replied, sipping from her

whiskey. "Mm, this is good. Where's it from?"

"A local distillery nearby. They use a special peat to dry the barley."

Maggie took another sip and made an approving face.

"Better than the whiskey in Aberdeen?" the bartender asked, looking at Iain. Iain was starting to get a little irritated, but decided not speak up just yet.

"Oh no, Aberdeen does just fine with its whiskey," Maggie replied. "It's just so interesting how each town seems to have it's own blend. But no, I like Aberdeen very much. Well, all except—" She stopped.

"Except what?" the bartender asked.

Iain took another drink through his smile. He should have known she was up to something.

"Well," Maggie looked down at her drink, "except the murders, of course."

The bartender's brow creased above his frown. "What murders are those?" Maggie noticed that the two men next to her had stopped talking and were listening in.

"Well, there's some lunatic loose killing girls," Maggie explained with another sip of her ice and whiskey. "Cutting them open and drawing occult symbols in their blood and everything."

The bartender crossed his arms and stepped back. He slowly cocked his head to one side and looked at Maggie through narrowed eyes. Maggie guessed he was about 30 or so. He would have been about ten when the Glenninver murders had taken place; definitely old enough to remember. The ensuing tension caused Iain to look up.

"What are you up to, lass?" the bartender asked at last.

"What do you mean?" she asked sweetly. Iain set his beer down hard and squared his shoulders to the bartender.

"I've not heard of any such murders," the bartender said matter-of-factly, "so I want to know why you've come—"

"No, she's right," one of the older men at the bar came to Maggie's rescue. "I read about them in the paper this week. Three murders in two months."

"Right." Maggie turned to the man. He was probably 55, with a bright pink face and snow white hair that shot from his head in a collection of barely tamed waves.

"Hhmph," grunted the bartender and he walked away to find some glasses to clean.

"Hallo," said the man next to her. "My name's Tormod. This is Dòmhnall."

Tormod pointed to his friend seated next to him. Dòmhnall just grunted in greeting and returned to his drink.

"He doesn't like to speak English," Tormod explained.

Maggie smiled. "Well, then. *Feasgar math, a Dhòmhnaill.*" Dòmhnall looked up at the greeting with a smile.

"*Ciamar a tha sibh?*" Maggie asked in Gaelic, inquiring how he was doing that day.

"<I'm well, thank you,>" came Dòmhnall's Gaelic reply.

"<My name is Maggie,>" she began the introductions. "<And this is Iain. He doesn't speak Gaelic.>"

Iain looked up at the sound of his name among the otherwise unintelligible sounds.

"I just told them you didn't speak Gaelic," she explained out of the corner of her mouth.

"I figured as much," Iain smiled weakly. "Bartender?"

The large bald man returned to refill Iain's glass and Maggie continued her Gaelic conversation.

"*Hallo, a Mhagaidh,*" Tormod replied, translating Maggie's name into the Gaelic. Dòmhnall sat quietly, content for now to let his friend do the talking. The sun-tanned face with windswept wrinkles obviously belonged to a quiet man.

"<Those murders in Aberdeen,>" Tormod said, his hand resting leisurely at the base of his beer glass, "<those sound like what happened out here, eh, Seumas?>"

"Hmph," the bartender replied. Seumas the Bartender. Sounded like a medieval surname.

"<What happened here?>" Maggie asked innocently, cocking her head ever so slightly to one side.

"<We had our own set of demonic murders. Oh, must have been, what, twenty years ago?>"

"<Nineteen, I think,>" Dòmhnall piped in. "<Maybe eighteen. It's hard to remember exactly.>"

"<Really?>" Maggie sipped again from her drink, but kept her wide eyes fastened on Tormod's. "<Did they ever catch the killer?>"

"<No,>" Tormod shook his head. "<Never did.>"

"<Aye, never solved,>" agreed Seumas. He seemed to be willing to accept Maggie's curiosity as genuine now, even if only to placate Tormod, a customer and obviously a friend as well.

"<Huh. So what happened?>" Maggie glanced quickly at each of the three men. Iain looked on with interest. Although he couldn't understand word one, he could guess who was leading the conversation.

"<Well, then, it's been some time,>" Tormod started, looking up at the beamed ceiling of the pub.

"<Eighteen years,>" repeated Dòmhnall.

"<Aye, eighteen years,>" Tormod agreed with a sad smile. Maggie smiled too, in encouragement. Seumas didn't. "<It was a bunch of girls, wasn't it?>"

"<Aye, it was three lasses and a lad, I believe,>" the

bartender elaborated.

"<Four lasses,>" corrected Dòmhnall. "<Four lasses and a lad. Damn bloody business, that.>"

"<How were they killed?>" The concern shone plainly on Maggie's face.

"<Throats slit, was it?>" Tormod asked the other two men, almost casually.

"<Aye, I think so,>" Dòmhnall thought for a moment. "<Or strangled maybe?>"

"<Either way, they ended up with their guts cut open like a pig ready for the spit.>"

"<Aye, gutted like fish,>" Dòmhnall added. "<They found each of them sprawled out on the ground, their guts all around them like a fence around a pasture.>"

"<So they were each killed the same way?>" Maggie was so wrapped up in the information gathering that she barely noticed how fluently she was speaking the Gaelic.

"<Aye.>" This time Seumas the Bartender was the first to reply. "<I was rather young then, but I remember it fairly well. My parents were scared silly. Those girls all flayed and gutted like that. Horrible. My older sister was twelve years old at the time, the same age as the girls who were killed.>"

"<They were only twelve?>" Maggie's voice held genuine surprise. The victims in Aberdeen had all been in their mid-twenties.

"<No, no. Two of them were twelve, one was fourteen and one was eleven.>" Maggie wondered how Dòmhnall was able to store away all these details. "<The lad was fifteen.>"

"<So what happened?>" Maggie's drink was empty now, but she didn't care.

"<Well, that's just it,>" Tormod said disgustedly. "<They

never solved it.>"

"<Bloody incompetent cops,>" Dòmhnall grumbled and took a drink of his beer. "<They should've called in the Yard.>"

"<Aye, well,>" Seumas sneered derisively, "<Scotland Yard's too bloody good for Scotland, eh?>"

"<You'd think with five victims, the local police could've cracked the case,>" Tormod added with a grand wave of his hand. "<It wasn't just some isolated murder. They must have had plenty of clues to work with, leads to follow.>"

"<Aye, you'd think so,>" Dòmhnall frowned.

They all paused for a moment. Iain looked up again. He had been inspecting the grain pattern of the wooden bar. Maybe Maggie was done.

"<And that was it?>" she asked; Iain returned his attention to the countertop. "<The murders just stopped?>"

"<Aye,>" Tormod nodded.

"<Aye, they just stopped,>" Dòmhnall agreed. Seumas just nodded silently.

"<Wow,>" Maggie waited for just a second. She had to make this next question seem natural. "<Who were the victims then?>"

"<Och, it's been so long,>" Tormod started. Apparently her curiosity had been accepted as genuine. "<There was the MacKenzie's little girl.>"

"<Aye, and Iseabeil Matheson,>" Dòmhnall proffered.

Seumas the Bartender just shook his head. Maggie figured he must have been too young to remember any of the details. She was sure he was just glad that his sister wasn't among the victims.

"<I can't remember any of the others,>" Tormod said at last. "<That's sad, it is.>"

"<Aye, that's very sad,>" Dòmhnall took a long drink, emptying his pint of bitter.

Maggie looked at her own empty drink as a somber silence fell across the bar. Iain's drink was empty too.

"<Well,>" she said with a friendly nod. "<I suppose we should go. We came to see the ocean, not talk about sad memories.>"

"<Well, it was a pleasure meeting you, lass,>" Tormod stood and shook Maggie's hand. "Nice to meet you too, lad," he told Iain in English.

"<Good to meet you, Maggie>" Dòmhnall continued in Gaelic, adding, "<May the Lord keep you.>"

"<And you too, Dòmhnall,>" and Maggie couldn't help but smile at this man who clung so resolutely to his ancestors' language.

"Are we leaving then?" Iain asked, standing up.

"Yes, we are," Maggie explained in a sugar sweet voice. "Pay the man."

Iain looked up at Seumas the Bartender, who stood with a broad smile across his face and a thick palm extended.

"Here you go," Iain handed him a bank note. "Keep the change."

"All right then. Thank you, lad. Perhaps we'll see you again?"

"Perhaps," Maggie called back as she reached the door.

"Not likely," Iain muttered as he exited behind her.

The weather had worsened slightly while they were inside. Rather than cold and overcast, it was now cold and raining lightly. Iain pulled his collar up around his neck.

"Are you all right, Maggie?" he asked. "Do you need to fetch your umbrella from the car?"

"No, that's all right," Maggie smiled up at Iain. "I'm used to rain."

"So what did you all talk about with your 'achs' and your

'oots'?"

Maggie laughed despite herself. "That's not what it sounds like," she insisted. "Anyway, they said that there were murders here twenty years ago just like in Aberdeen now."

Iain stooped dead in his tracks. Maggie took two more steps before she realized it. She turned around.

"What?" she asked, palms turned toward the sky.

"That's reason number four, isn't it?" Iain's arms were crossed as he recalled their conversation on the drive over.

"Of course," Maggie smiled.

Iain wanted to be angry, and he did feel a bit used, but he couldn't help but be disarmed by her honesty. He fought it for a moment, but then smiled.

He shook his head. "I don't know about you, Maggie Devereaux."

"Well then, stick around," she grabbed his arm. "There's a lot to learn."

And they headed off toward the waterfront.

* * *

After a nice lunch at a small restaurant near the docks, Maggie and Iain took a stroll into the residential area of Glenninver. It was a relatively small town, and looked like it could probably be traversed on foot quickly enough. They walked past the rows of diminutive fishing shacks and through a small business district tucked away from the road and waterfront. They passed two parks and found the local school. Throughout their walk they maintained a pleasant conversation about nothing in particular, but Maggie was having a difficult time focusing on their discourse. Her mind kept searching for additional ways to find out more about what had happened in the quiet little village of Glenninver so many years ago.

Eventually, they came upon a small church—the village chapel, no doubt. It was only as tall as a two story house, with a short steeple rising from the pitched roof and its slate gray walls almost melting away against the thick, overcast, December sky. Maggie had first spied the church from down the street and had examined its outlines as they approached. When they finally came up to it, both she and Iain stopped and looked admiringly on the little house of worship, tucked so far away from the world on these rocky shores of the northwest Highlands. A small placard on the side of the church read, 'Noter Madre de la Mer.' Latin for 'Our Lady of the Sea.'

"Come on, let's go in," Maggie said grabbing a hold of Iain's elbow.

He hesitated. "Oh, are you Catholic?" he asked, surprise in his voice.

Maggie smiled a bemused smile. "No," she replied carefully. "Does that mean I can't go in?"

"No, I was just—" Iain paused, "—curious, I suppose."

"Well, stop being so curious," she chided sarcastically, "and let's see what it looks like inside."

The inside of the church was as rustically elegant as the outside. It was adorned with such beautiful statues, paintings and mouldings that one almost didn't notice that there was absolutely no stained glass. The sanctuary was decorated for Christmas and appeared empty except for a single nun, in full habit, busying herself with something near the altar. When the two visitors had entered, she had looked up, but then returned to her chore. Maggie and Iain stood and looked around the interior of the church, then took a seat in the last pew.

"Wow, this is really beautiful," Maggie whispered to Iain as she continued to gaze around the sanctuary.

"Aye, it is," Iain agreed, his eyes skimming the walls as well. "You should come to St. Machar's sometime. It's got a big old oak ceiling with the coats of arms of some 50 different popes, princes and the like."

"Is that in Aberdeen?" Maggie was still looking around.

"Aye, it's where I go."

"You're Catholic, then?" Maggie turned to look at his face.

Iain smiled but didn't look at Maggie. "Aye."

Maggie nodded and turned back to look around the chamber. To one side she observed a painted statue of the Virgin Mary, Christ Child in her arms, placed on a pedestal in an alcove. At the base of the pedestal was a table with what must have been two dozen small white candles, their flames flickering softly in the draft that circulated through the open room.

"What are all those?" she asked in a low voice.

Iain followed her pointing finger and spied the alcove. "Oh, those?" He looked at her, then nodded thoughtfully. "Those are candles."

"Thank you," Maggie whispered sarcastically. "I mean what are they for?"

"Oh, aye," Iain smiled. "Good question. Well, do you see underneath, on the second shelf of the table? There are some unlighted candles down there. If you want to pray that something might happen—a loved one recovering from an illness, say—then you can light one of the candles to symbolize the prayer."

"Wow," Maggie whispered. "I guess that's kind of cool."

"Aye, well, thank you," Iain's voice held friendly sarcasm.

"No, I mean," Maggie stammered. "We never did that growing up. I think it's kind of neat." Then after a moment's reflection, she added, "I like candles."

Unsure exactly how to respond, Iain ultimately decided that

no response was necessary just then and returned his attention to the altar. Two more nuns had joined the first.

Maggie stood up.

"Where are you going?" Iain asked in a hushed tone.

"The candles. I'm going to make a wish."

Iain rolled his eyes slightly. "You don't 'make a wish.' It's a prayer."

An embarrassed frown cramped Maggie's mouth. "Sorry," she winced, then stepped quietly toward the alcove.

Maggie looked up at the statue. It was old and the edges of the features had rounded with time. Still she found the experience strangely conflicting, unsure if she liked the way the figure watched her from its pedestal. Shaking her head to dislodge such thoughts, she bent down and retrieved a candle. Its wax was set directly into a glass cup about the size of her palm. There was a large candle at the feet of the Madonna, and Maggie concluded that this was where she was supposed to light her own candle from. Tipping her candle so that the wicks could meet, she lit hers then held it in front of her. She really wanted to speak the levitation spell, raising the candle into the air as she had done that night. But she resisted the urge. Iain would likely not have approved.

She closed her eyes and whispered, "I wish that I find out what happened here eighteen years ago." That didn't seem sacrilegious. After all, she was trying to help prevent another murder and that was a good thing. Still, she already felt strange making the wish—'prayer,' she corrected herself—and so was doubly startled when she heard the voice behind her.

"No need to use a candle for that, my child." Maggie spun around to see a nun staring her kindly in the eye. "I can tell you well enough."

"Oh!" Maggie's voice rang embarrassingly off the walls. She

lowered it again, "You startled me."

"I'm sorry," the nun's smile dispatched a series of deep wrinkles to envelope her face, adding to those which permanently hovered around her eyes and mouth. She must have been at least sixty years old. Her face was kind, with a wisened expression. The rest of her was covered by her black habit. "I'm Sister Màiri."

"I'm Maggie," she whispered in reply. "Er, Maggie Devereaux." Etiquette seemed to dictate that she divulge her last name as well. It was different for nuns somehow.

"You needn't whisper so low, Maggie," Sister Màiri smiled and pointed upwards. "He hears either way."

Maggie smiled. She liked Sister Màiri already.

"So what would you know?" The nun gestured toward the nearby pews. As they sat down, Maggie noticed Iain smiling at her. *He's getting used to this*, she thought.

"Well, I—" Maggie's mind started to reach for some sort of plausible cover story, but then she thought better of it. Catholic or no, it was probably not a good idea to lie to a nun. Still, she was *not* going to be mentioning anything about magic spell books. "I learned about the murders that happened here twenty years ago. Eighteen." She could hear Dòmhnall's voice as she corrected herself. "And I was talking earlier with two gentleman who were telling me about them. I—I just want to know what happened."

"Well," Sister Màiri smiled gently, "I've lived her my entire life. I remember those unfortunate murders. The devil can be found everywhere, even out here at the ends of the Earth. I'm not sure exactly why it's troubling you so, but if I can answer any of your questions, I certainly will do."

"Well, how many victims were there?"

"Five lost their lives. Four young girls and one young boy."

"Do you know who they were?" This seemed especially

important to Maggie for some reason.

Sister Màiri blew out a quiet sigh. "Well, now. It's been some time. But I think I remember. They were each buried here in the churchyard." The nun folded her hands and looked up in concentration. If Maggie hadn't known she was trying to remember the names of murder victims from two decades ago, she would have thought she was praying.

"There was Iseabeil Matheson," she started.

Maggie remembered the name from the conversation at the pub.

"Heather Drummond. And Muriel MacKenzie."

Another name from the pub: 'the MacKenzie's little girl.'

"And Heather Sinclair. And the young lad's name was Jared something—Jared Blake, I believe."

Maggie's mind screamed at the name. *Could it be?*

She wasn't sure how to ask the question though, so she asked another instead. "And it was never solved?"

"I'm afraid not. They just stopped. Eventually things returned to normal again." The sister paused, then added, "Except for the families, of course."

"Of course."

"I'm afraid that's all I really can tell you. Maybe I wasn't that helpful after all?"

"Oh, no," Maggie assured her. "You were very helpful." Maggie paused before venturing, "Is there anywhere else I could find out some information about this?"

"Well, let me think," Sister Màiri put a hand to her cheek. "The library might have old newspaper articles on file, I suppose." She looked Maggie in the eye. "Why is it you're so interested in those terrible murders?"

Maggie frowned. How could she explain? "Well, I'm living

in Aberdeen now. And we've had a series of similar murders. Two—" the sentence stuck in her throat, which actually surprised her. "—Two of my friends were killed. I thought, maybe, I don't know. Maybe there's some clue here that could help stop the murders in Aberdeen."

Sister Màiri nodded and smiled. "A noble purpose," she lauded, "but I think you may be doing this for other reasons as well. Even if you don't realize it yet. Be careful, my child."

And with this, the nun patted Maggie on the shoulder and took her leave, walking back toward the altar where her sisters still busied themselves.

Maggie watched after her, wondering over this cryptic warning. She didn't hear Iain step up behind her.

"Ready to go?" he whispered.

"Eh? Oh." Maggie turned and looked up at Iain. "Yeah, sure. Let's go."

Outside, Maggie squinted as her eyes readjusted to the daylight. The rain had turned again to mist, fogging up Maggie's glasses. She had long gotten used to seeing through wet lenses.

"Anyone else you'd like to interrogate today?" Iain asked with a warm smile.

"Yes," was Maggie's simple reply and she turned back toward the center of town.

"Where are we going?" Iain called after her.

"The library."

* * *

The sign was in both Gaelic and English:

LEABHARLANN GLEAINN INBHIR - GLENNINVER LIBRARY

DÙINTE NA DI-DÒMHNAICH – CLOSED SUNDAYS

"Damn," Maggie muttered.

"Oh, that's too bad." Iain's voice held no sarcasm; he was genuinely disappointed for her. "Maybe we can come back some time."

Maggie stared at the sign, deep in thought, her arms crossed and her toe tapping.

"Can you stay until tomorrow?" she asked at last.

Iain looked dumbstruck. "What? What are you talking about? No. I can't stay. I have to work. Tomorrow's Monday. We have to get back tonight."

Maggie didn't reply. Her brow was still creased in thought.

Finally she said, "Okay you go on ahead. But will you help me find a hotel room first?"

"What?!" Iain was incredulous. "You're not coming back with me?"

"Iain," she said in a tone that approached, but didn't quite reach, that reserved for explaining the painfully obvious to the painfully stupid. "I can't. But it's okay. I'll take a train back tomorrow afternoon."

"A train?" Iain looked around exaggeratedly. "What train? There's not even a train station in this village."

"Oh, of course there is," she dismissed the suggestion with an impatient wave of her hand. "And if not, I'm sure I can take a bus up to, uh, well, to whatever the nearest town with a train station is."

"Maggie," Iain's tone approached, but didn't quite reach, that reserved for coaxing the painfully stubborn from doing the painfully ill-advised.

"Iain, I'm staying," Maggie's voice was firm. "Now, are you going to help me find a hotel room or not?"

Iain crossed his arms and stared at her, weighing his options. He hadn't known her that long, but he was getting to know her pretty well.

"There's no use trying to talk you out of it, is there?"

Maggie smiled. "No."

"All right then. I'll help you find a room at an inn. But," he raised a finger in emphasis, "I'm staying with you 'til after dinner." He threw a glance across their surroundings. There must be a good restaurant in this town someplace."

Maggie's smile broadened. "Sounds good to me."

* * *

Dinner had been nice. Fresh fish with a view of the sea. By now Iain was on his way back to Aberdeen. It was a long drive and he had to be at the MacTary's early the next day for breakfast.

He had helped Maggie find a room at the local inn. Halfway between a bed and breakfast and a standard hotel, the Glenninver Inn (a.k.a., *An Taigh-Òsda Gleainn Inbhir*) boasted a total of four rooms, none of which were occupied on a Sunday night in December. The proprietor, a Mrs. Murdoch, had therefore only charged Maggie for the cheapest room while giving her the key to their best—a sort of penthouse tucked under the roof of the old building, complete with its own small bath. It was on the third floor.

The steps to the room hugged one side of the building, winding back and forth and creaking with each of Maggie's steps. She climbed valiantly up the narrow staircase, stopping at the second story landing long enough to look out a dusty, curtainless window into the black, rainy night. Having thus caught her wind, she continued upwards. After about five more steps, she passed a small door, built into the inside wall and leading seemingly to nowhere. She tried the small metal handle, but it was locked. With a puzzled "hmm," she climbed on, reminding herself to ask Mrs. Murdoch in the morning what it was that the miniature door hid.

At the top of the stairs she had expected to be greeted by a hallway or at least a small landing, however she was surprised to

find that the steps ended directly in front of a door—a door she
assumed must be to her room. With each creak of the wooden
boards she had realized just how tired she had become. The day
had been filled with fresh air and long drives, two things that
tended to make her very sleepy. So it was with relief that she turned
the rickety metal lock with the old-fashioned skeleton key Mrs.
Murdoch had provided, and tumbled into her room.

The chamber was rather large, with hardwood floors
covered by oriental rugs, and lace curtains in the paint-cracked
windows. A large, soft-looking bed occupied one wall, while two
overstuffed chairs in a bright green and blue tartan occupied the
opposite corner, next to the door to the bathroom. Several
houseplants in need of watering were also scattered about the room.
Safely inside, Maggie locked the door behind her. She was
unimpressed by the weak 'click' the latch offered as proof of its
security. Maggie thought the ancient lock might stop a stiff breeze,
maybe even a small bird, but probably little else.

She stripped down to her T-shirt and underwear and
climbed into bed. It was one of those hotel beds that would be too
soft to sleep on every night, but was kind of fun to sink into for just
one evening's rest. The spellbook accompanied her to the bed and
she rested it firmly on the covers bunched up over her lap. She
flipped through the pages, realizing absently that she had not used
the magic all day, despite her momentary temptation at the church.
She wondered what the nun would have done if she'd found
Maggie levitating candles in front of the Virgin Mary. She couldn't
help but laugh a little at the thought, but felt bad about it too.

Glancing over to the bedside table, she spied a small glass jar
filled with various dried leaves and the like. Some sort of pot
pourri. With a minimal raise of her left hand, she muttered the well
learned spell, "<Break the bonds...>" and the jar lifted slowly but

securely off of the table.

Soon a book, one of the houseplants, and Maggie's purse joined the jar as they danced on puppet strings around the room. Energized by the magic, she turned to the divining spell. Maybe she could find out something about the inn, or its previous guests. She wondered who had slept in the bed before her, who had sat in those chairs. But then she remembered her pendant, with the black stain blotting out the '..TR..' in 'BE TRAIST.' She knew she shouldn't risk damaging any of Mrs. Murdoch's things, at least not until she got that transmutation spell down. Reluctantly, like a school child setting down a comic book to pick up a math text, she flipped to the transmutation spell at the back of the spellbook.

It was even longer than she had remembered. But she was comfortable in bed, letting her sleepiness slowly build, and she didn't have anything else to do. Using the levitation spell again, she floated her backpack over to the bed and extracted her Old Gaelic-Modern Gaelic dictionary. Time to get busy.

Her efforts at remembering the proper translation for 'eòlas' were interrupted by a tapping at her window. Now, she knew she was on the third floor. She knew that no one was out there. She knew that people didn't just float in the air and knock on the windows of scared American students. But she also knew that houseplants and books and jars of pot pourri didn't float around rooms either. So she was open to any possibility. The tapping recurred.

Maggie felt a strange combination of emotions flood her veins. On the one hand, she was terrified at the thought of someone trying to get into her room late at night when she was all alone. On the other hand, the sense of impending—well, battle, for lack of a better word—gave her an unexpected rush.

Okay, she thought confidently, *let's see who's out there.*

She threw the covers back, shimmied off the bed and sidled up the window, her back to the wall.

Her right hand twitched in readiness at her side.

Then she jumped to the window, threw the curtains open and found herself staring face to face with—nothing. There was no one there. Just an oncoming storm that was hidden by her reflection in the glass. Then to her surprise, she heard the tapping again and saw as the tip of a tree branch emerged from the blackness to tap against the window, blown by the wind of the black storm.

Maggie smiled, just a little disappointed, and headed back to the warmth of the bed. On the way she pulled her lipstick out of her purse.

Sitting down again on the bed, this time cross-legged with the book off to one side, she twisted the burgundy lipstick all the way up and set it on the bed in front of her. She had wanted to set it standing up, but the soft bed wouldn't have it. She held her left hand out over the lipstick while she traced the letters of the transmutation spell with her right.

Her lips spoke the transmutation spell, clumsily at first but with increasing eloquence. It appeared to actually be a series of spells, each to be spoken in turn, as the 'evil forces' upon which so many of the spells called were to break down the bonds which held the object together. These bonds broken, the resultant scattering of particles then needed to be captured like loose cattle, and subjugated to the wishes of the spellcaster. This was the tricky part. Trying to put the square peg of the existing substance into the round hole of the desired substance. Not surprisingly, when Maggie finished, she still had a tube of burgundy lipstick.

"Hmm," she said aloud with a calm smile, "this one's going to take some time."

But she was proud of herself for trying and sat back, going

over the spell again in her mind. Her thoughts were interrupted by a new sound, directly above her. She looked up.

The ceiling was made of hard wood beams identical to those of the floor. Indeed, it looked like a hardwood floor hanging over the room. This was noteworthy for two reasons. One, the inn had a pitched roof, which meant some sort of attic or crawlspace existed between her ceiling and the actual roof. Two, the creaking above her head crossed the room in a pattern frighteningly similar to footsteps.

She listened as the creaks methodically made their way across the room, from over her head to the far corner. Then they faded away. Maggie's heart was beating a little faster, but she supposed there might be a storage area above her. Maybe Mrs. Murdoch was fetching fresh towels. But then the footsteps returned, this time in the hallway outside her door. Now she knew where that little door led to. And she could feel the dump of adrenaline into her blood as the footsteps made their way cautiously up the stairs, their only possible destination her door. What frightened her most was the fact that the owner of the creaking footsteps was trying so hard not to creak. Loud, boisterous stomping up and down the staircase wouldn't have bothered her because the rude, inconsiderate people who would have been keeping her awake obviously would not have been concerned with her. But the person creeping up the stairs just then was taking slow, light steps, pausing to let each faint creak and squeak fade before attempting another step. Whoever it was hoped not to be heard. Eventually, the slow, methodical, creaking footsteps stopped. Right outside her door.

Maggie had to force herself to look at the doorknob. The bravado she had exhibited before at the rain-spattered window had vanished and she watched the knob with wide eyes, her heart pounding, waiting to see it turn ever so slowly. She hoped the lock was sturdier than she had thought.

She watched and waited. And waited. And waited some more. Nothing.

The knob never turned.

And the feeling of having someone nearby—watching her, sensing her—slowly drained away. After several more minutes passed, Maggie let herself believe that maybe she had been hearing things. It all seemed like watching a movie. Her ears were still ringing from the blood which had been rushing, soaked with adrenaline, throughout her body. But the danger apparently past, fatigue shuddered through her limbs.

Wow, I am tired, she thought. She set the spellbook down to her side and leaned back on the bed for a moment. *I'll just rest my eyes for a sec.*

That's when she heard it. The sound of the doorknob's rusty scraping as it was turned first in one direction, then slowly to the other.

Paralyzed, Maggie could only look out of the corner of her now wide open eyes to see the knob turning slowly back and forth. To the right. To the left. To the right again. Then it stopped.

And Maggie could do nothing but wait.

She strained to hear some telltale noise out in the hallway.

The door burst open! Maggie's ears were filled with a horrible noise that seared into her very brain. A figure stood in the doorway, black as pitch and entirely undefined within the blinding red light flaring into the room past it. The only thing she could see was that it was large and it was coming at her.

Maggie grabbed the spellbook, not as a reference but as a blunt object. But the book dissolved in her hands, covering them with a sticky crimson blood. Looking down she realized it was her own. Her white T-shirt was soaked black with blood and she could see more oozing out from under her legs. Pulling up her shirt, she saw not the round little tummy she had gotten used to, but a bloody gutted carcass, empty but for the stained silver pendant that read "BEAIST." She screamed—

—And woke up.

Maggie took several deep, desperate breaths, like someone who's made it to surface of the pool just in time. Her lungs clutched at the air as she tried to calm down.

It was just a dream, she tried to convince herself. *Just a dream.*

But it was so real. She looked to her side. The book was still next to her. It had not dissolved to blood after all. *Good.*

Looking out the window, she confirmed it was still night. The clock by her bedside table said 12:01.

Maggie swung her legs off the bed and sat forward, still panting slightly. She was obviously not going to be sleeping that night.

"Okay," she pushed her fingers through her thick brown hair. "Now that one scared me."

* * *

Maggie had in fact been able to sleep restlessly a few times during the night, but only right at the surface and never long enough to dream. After a long night of tired wakefulness, she was grateful for the hearty breakfast Mrs. Murdoch had prepared. As she sat eating the bacon, eggs, toast and fruit, she wondered whether the locals had eaten this well when it was just crofters and fisherman and no tourists. In any event, she was glad for it and soon was out the door for her busy morning.

The first order of business was to buy a ticket back to Aberdeen. Iain had been right; there was no train station in Glenninver. There was, however, a short bus ride south to Kyle of Lochalsh where she could catch a train to Inverness, then transfer to

Aberdeen. She would need to be at the bus terminal by 1:15.

This left just the morning for the library and so once she had purchased the necessary tickets, she proceeded directly there. The library was small, as most of the buildings in Glenninver seemed to be, and appeared to be housed in what was once a home. The front entry felt just like walking up to a friend's house. Maybe the effect was intentional. Wondering over this, Maggie pushed open the doors and stepped inside.

She was greeted by the sight of dozens of bookshelves crammed one against the other, each filled to the brim with books. The foyer even had a built-in bookcase with paperback novels lining each shelf. Maggie stopped and pulled one off the shelf. It was in English. Somehow that disappointed her. Even out here in the *Gàidhealtachd*, the influence of English could not be avoided. She knew she shouldn't have been surprised. Even if every man woman and child who spoke Scottish Gaelic bought a copy of a new book, the publisher would still only sell around 75,000 copies. Compare that with the market available in London—and New York, and Los Angeles, and Toronto, and Sydney, etc. Maggie often wondered whether Gaelic might have fared better had its competitor not turned out to be the single most widespread and economically important language of the last 200 years.

Maggie replaced the book on the shelf and strolled into the main hall of the library. She seemed to have the place to herself. To her right was a small desk with a fashionably dressed middle aged woman sitting at a computer.

The woman looked up and smiled. "*Madainn mhath.* Good Morning."

She was giving Maggie the choice of which language to use. Maggie chickened out. She was tired.

"Good morning."

"How can I help you?" the librarian asked.

"I was wondering whether you have any old newspapers on file?"

"How old?

"Er, twenty years or so?" Maggie smiled apologetically.

"Hmm," the librarian didn't seem phased. "I believe we should have those on microfiche or microfilm. We don't have every newspaper of course. Which were you looking for?"

"Oh, I don't know," Maggie tried to think what paper people there probably read. "The Inverness Courier?"

The woman nodded.

"And is there any sort of local paper?" Maggie asked. "One that was publishing back then too?"

"Hmm," the librarian said again. "I believe so. But it's in Gaelic, I'm afraid."

Maggie smiled. She was being given a second chance. "Oh, that's all right. *Tha Gàidhlig agam.*"

"*A bheil?* <Really?>" the librarian smiled. "<Well, then, let's get you set up.>"

In short order, Maggie found herself sitting at the table that hosted the microfilm machine, several boxes of old microfilms stacked up to one side of it.

"<Let me know if there's anything else I can get for you,>" the librarian offered kindly, then returned to her desk.

It took a bit of hunting but eventually Maggie was able to find an article in the Inverness Courier about the murders. It was about the first murder. She recognized the headline from the clipping in Sgt. Warwick's file: OCCULT MURDER IN GLENNINVER. The article was easier to read right side up and Maggie quickly perused it in full. It told of the discovery of the body of young Muriel MacKenzie. The police vowed to catch her killer in short order.

A second article and then a third revealed the police's promise to be hollow as next Iseabeil Matheson, then Heather Drummond lost their lives. Then Maggie found the article she was really interested in. The one with the name she truly sought: 'Sinclair.' Heather Sinclair, thirteen years old, had been found butchered in the same way as the others, but with one difference: laying across her body was the lifeless corpse of Jared Blake, his neck snapped like a rag doll's. He had not been gutted or in any other way defiled—he was simply dead at the age of sixteen. The two were found in the basement of the Sinclair home on Mara Road. To the best of everyone's knowledge, Jared and Heather were not romantically involved. Jared, the newspaper explained, was simply a friend of Heather's older brother, Devan.

So it was *him.* But she wasn't sure what to make of this revelation.

Maggie searched for more information, but could find none. Assuming Dòmhnall and Sister Màiri were correct, there were no further murders, so it shouldn't have been surprising not to find anything else written about it. In fact, as regrettably happens, the murders seemed to have been getting commonplace, the first murder seizing a headline on the second front page, whereas the last double murder was lucky to gain 100 words on page B17. In any event, further skimming of the Courier proved fruitless.

Maggie then turned her attention to the *Tìm Gleainn Inbhir,* 'The Glenninver Times,' a weekly Gaelic language paper with a circulation no doubt approximately the same size as the number of households in the small town. The articles in the *Tìm* were different from those in the Courier, not just the language, but the focus. Glenninver was definitely a small community, and the reporting focused more on the families involved and the effect the murders were having on the little seaside village. Muriel MacKenzie's parents were too distraught to keep their store open. Heather Drummond's family decided to move to the Isle of Skye to try to forget. And the Sinclairs—they too were crushed by the death of their daughter. But they had decided to stay in Glenninver, for, after all, it was their home.

Another aspect of the weekly paper which was difficult to overlook was its caustic treatment of the local police working on the case. In truth, 'local' was probably not an accurate term. It appeared that Glenninver had a something like three police officers and two of them were part-time. When these murders occurred, Glenninver called in for help, and received it in the form of a young police lieutenant from Fort William named Robert Cameron.

Curiouser and curiouser, Maggie thought.

Apparently the *Tim* was not pleased with the general lack of progress in the investigation, a displeasure which flared with each subsequent killing. By the time of the fourth and fifth murders, Heather Sinclair and Jared Blake, Lt. Cameron was essentially run out of town. And then the murders stopped.

Maggie leaned back in her chair and smiled a satisfied little smile. She had learned more than she had expected on her trip. It was nearing noon already and she wanted to grab a bite to eat before her long trip home. She decided to fast-forward to the end of the microfilm reel but at a slow enough pace that she could see the headlines in case any interesting words should pop out at her.

Her eyes watched for telltale words: '*mort*,' meaning 'murder,' or '*poileas*,' meaning 'police.' But the text streamed by in an uninteresting pattern of Gaelic vocabulary.

Until she saw the word: '*Suinclair*.'

This was obviously an attempt to spell 'Sinclair' in Gaelic convention without translating it completely into its Gaelic equivalent. Sometimes such 'equivalents' looked nothing like their English counterparts, the meaning of the name having been translated rather than its sounds. For example, the Gaelic name for the Clan Sinclair was '*Mac ca Ceardadh.*'

She rewound to the article and started reading. It was dated roughly one year after Heather Sinclair's murder. The Sinclair residence had burned down. Trapped inside were the parents, James and Rebecca Sinclair. The only survivor was seventeen year old Devan, who had somehow made it out of the house unscathed. There was a photograph of him standing near the gutted remains of his home. He was looking at the camera and although he was almost twenty years younger than the man Maggie had come to know, there was no doubt this was the same Devan Sinclair who now owned an occult bookshop in Aberdeen. Even in this early picture, he already bore the same implacable expression she had become accustomed to seeing cloak his visage. The young face in the photograph appeared completely emotionless, despite the death of his parents only a year after the murder of his younger sister. Emotionless except for a single tear. Running down the outside of his left cheek. Exactly where the adult Devan Sinclair sported his untidy scar.

Maggie stared at the photo for quite some time, lost in examination of its subject. Finally she looked at the clock on the wall. She had just enough time to print out photocopies of the articles she had found before a quick lunch and the bus ride to Kyle of Lochalsh.

As she walked out of the library, photocopies tucked neatly away in her backpack, she felt confident that the question was no longer whether the two sets of murders were related, but how.

And she had a whole afternoon of travelling ahead of her to think of her next step.

37. The Men in Her Life

Iain had called Monday night to make sure she'd made it home safely. She had, of course, and they made general plans to 'do something' that coming weekend. For the next few days, Maggie wandered around Aberdeen, stopping at her usual spots, but her mind dwelled continually on the subject of the murders—and what she had learned in Glenninver. Obviously Sinclair was connected somehow to the current murders, but how? Was he the killer? She found that difficult to believe based on her contacts with him. He may have been a little reserved at times, but she couldn't believe she had looked into the eyes of a cool-blooded serial killer.

She knew she only had ten days before the next new moon. She was sure that was the cycle. She had checked the dates of the Glenninver murders against an old copy of a farmer's almanac in the college library. Those murders had also coincided with the new moon.

By Thursday, she had finally calmed herself enough to spend some time on her school work. Macintyre had not bothered calling her back about the missed appointments. They had not met for a month now, which was fine with Maggie. She didn't like the thought of being alone with him, even less sharing her research with him. Of course, that begged the question: What research? The spellbook would have been a wonderful research project—except that it actually worked, and there was no way she was sharing that knowledge with everyone and his brother. Unfortunately, this meant she had to find some other subject to delve into. The college expected it, her university back in the States expected it, her grandmother had expected it. But most importantly, Maggie expected it. She loved her studies and she didn't want the year to end up being a total waste. She spent therefore the better part of Thursday in and out of the library, toying around with different possible subjects. But it wasn't that easy to just dismiss thoughts of the murders, and her progress was slow and distracted. She went to bed Thursday night exhausted and little closer to a thesis topic then she had been when she'd arrived home from Glenninver.

Friday afternoon found Maggie back at her favorite pub, The Boar and Thistle, nursing a rootbeer and pouring over several texts containing ballads in Middle Gaelic. Maybe she could still finesse some connection to early non-Christian religious practices and their appearance, although masked, in later Christian-era sagas.

Maggie yawned.

She tipped her head side to side to work the kink out of her neck. She had slept well enough last night—no nightmares—but it had been several days of leaning over dusty old books in the library. She had finally come to The Boar and Thistle just for a change of scenery, finding a table in a back corner and instructing the waiter to keep the rootbeers coming. As she looked around the establishment, her eyes taking a break from the black and white of the printed text, she noticed a man who, from the back, looked remarkably like Iain. She found this irritating because one, Iain was supposed to be at work, and two, the man at the pub was with a rather striking blonde with long legs, too much make-up and no glasses. So it was with relief that the couple stood up and Maggie got a better look at the man's face. Unless he had grown a mustache in the last five days, that wasn't Iain. However as they walked away from their table, Maggie was able to see another couple sitting behind them, and this couple she knew she recognized.

It was Ellen. And Will Hopkins.

She hadn't seen Will since that one afternoon several days after Fionna's murder when he walked past her without greeting. She had chalked it up to the fact that they had only met once and he, understandably, had other things on his mind. Watching Ellen and Will from the corner, she wondered how he was doing now.

They were talking about something, but of course Maggie couldn't hear from the other side of the room. Will put his hand out on the table and Ellen took it in hers. She was looking into his eyes and saying something which was obviously important and heartfelt. After a few moments she reached out her other hand and stroked Will's cheek. He tipped his head into the stroke and closed his eyes. The conversation appeared to continue for a bit until Will finally looked at his watch and stood up to leave. Ellen stayed seated, but Will came around the table, embraced her, then turned to the door, a half-smile hanging on his face.

Maggie was getting ready to leave herself. While this was going on the waiter had stopped by and asked her if she wanted *another* rootbeer. She declined with an embarrassed smile and asked for the check. After paying, she was left with the dilemma of whether to stop by Ellen's table and say, 'Hi.' On the one hand, Ellen was a friend. On the other, she felt awkward having just spied on her. The first hand won out.

"Hi, Ellen."

Ellen looked up with a blank expression that quickly

changed to one of friendly recognition. "Oh, hi, Maggie! How are you? Did you just get here? Sit down."

"Oh, no, that's okay," Maggie waved her hand at the suggestion. She thought the waiter might still be watching her. "I've actually been here for a while, sitting in the back studying." She slapped gently at the book under her arm.

"Oh," was all Ellen replied.

"Was that Will?" Well, she had to ask eventually.

"Er, yes," Ellen decided to answer. "Yes, it was."

"How's he doing?"

Ellen frowned and shrugged. "Not good. He's really terribly sad. Can't blame him really, though, can you? And being here in Aberdeen all the time just reminds him."

"I bet," Maggie offered.

"Aye, so he's heading back to London tomorrow. He's actually been in London every weekend since—since Fionna was murdered. He was there when Kelly was killed, too. He's had most of his exams either waived or postponed. I don't—" She hesitated. "I don't know if he'll be coming back."

"That's too bad," Maggie nodded supportively. "It must be unbearable to lose someone you love." The sentence brought back faint stabs at the thought of her grandmother's death, and of her mother before.

"Aye," Ellen fiddled with her glass. "And it's all the worse. You didn't know this, but— Well, Fionna was pregnant."

Maggie was stunned. And then deeply saddened. "Oh dear..." she started.

"Aye," Ellen nodded, "and it was complicated. Will wasn't even sure if he was ready to be a father. They'd talked about— Well, they'd talked about other options, and I don't mean adoption. Fionna's brother was livid. But now, Will— Well, you can imagine the guilt." She shook her head sadly, then raised her gaze to Maggie. "I was trying to console him, you know?"

Maggie smiled at her friend. "I know."

The conversation paused then and the two women waited uncomfortably for several moments.

"Are you heading back into the college, then?" Ellen asked finally, standing up.

"No, actually. I'm heading home. It's getting late."

Ellen nodded and dropped a banknote on the table. "Aye, good idea. I'll walk out with you."

The two walked out into the dimming late afternoon. Ellen thinking about Lord knows what, and Maggie thinking about everything but her school work.

And only ten days left.

38. *Feasgar Math, a Shuinclair*

After another good night's rest, Maggie spent Saturday morning debating whether or not to proceed with the course of action she had thought of the evening before. She had concluded that her problem lay in the fact that she had learned the how and the what of the murders—both in Aberdeen and Glenninver—but not the why. Or the who. It was in search of the why that she had considered this option. It was because of the who that she hesitated.

Eventually, though, with a good lunch in her stomach and her nerves calmed by yet another rootbeer at The Boar and Thistle, Maggie elected to pursue the only option she knew of which might shed some light on the reasons behind the murders, on whatever it was the killer hoped to accomplish with his ritual.

The bus dropped her off only a few blocks away, and she only had to take one deep calming breath before pushing open the door, jingling the string of bell's which hung on its back.

The bookshop was just as she remembered it, except that a rather old looking man was walking straight at her.

"Excusse me misss," he said as he ducked around her to the door.

From behind his counter, Devan Sinclair called out, "See you again soon, Doctor."

Then Sinclair looked as his new arrival. A faint smile broached his lips.

"Good day, Miss Devereaux."

Okay, so what's the best way to play this? Maggie asked herself.

"No 'Maggie' today?" she asked.

"Ah, well, I'm working, aren't I?" Sinclair's smile deepened. "Sometimes it's best to stay professional." This last observation was accompanied by a curt and confident nod.

"Most likely," she agreed. "Well then, could you help me find some books, Mr. Sinclair?"

"I'll try to help. What are you looking for?"

"Do you have anything in Gaelic?"

Maggie wasn't sure but she thought she saw the slightest glint of surprise cross behind his eyes. "That's right, you speak Gaelic. For your studies, correct?"

"*Tha, tha Gàidhlig agam,*" Maggie smiled broadly. "*A bheil Gàidhlig agaibh?*"

Sinclair paused and stared at Maggie. Finally he answered, in English, "Yes, I can speak Gaelic. But I choose not to."

"Oh, that's too bad," Maggie flashed an enigmatic smile. "How is it that you know Gaelic? Most Scots don't."

Sinclair paused again. He appeared uncomfortable under his controlled facade. "I learned it when I was young."

"Oh," Maggie tipped her head in interest. "Are you from a *Gàidhealtachd?*"

Sinclair paused again. His longest pause yet. Finally he straightened himself up. "What kind of book are you looking for, Miss Devereaux?"

Maggie smiled again. "Well, putting aside the Gaelic books

for a moment, I was actually hoping that I could buy that book I saw the last time I was here."

Sinclair's brows lowered as he tried to recall what book she was referring to. "Which one was that again?"

"Er, the one that wasn't for sale then?" She opened her big brown eyes as wide as she could.

Sinclair frowned. "It's still not for sale, Miss Devereaux."

"Oh, come on, Devan," she leaned forward onto the counter. She hoped she was being flirty. "Won't you be nice to me?"

"Miss Devereaux," he looked at her, the way one might look at a younger sister. "Maggie. I *am* being nice to you. I won't help you in what you've been doing. I warned you against it, but you've obviously ignored me. I won't help you on this path. So don't ask me to."

Maggie was uncertain what to say. Finally she pulled her purse around and fished in it for her wallet. "Look. Fine. Whatever. Just sell me the stupid book. How much is it? I'll pay double."

"The book is not for sale."

"Come on—"

"No. It's impossible. The book is gone."

Maggie stopped, her wallet halfway out of her purse. "Gone?"

"Gone."

Well, great. Now what? "Well..."

"Actually, do you know what, Miss Devereaux?" Sinclair walked around the counter. "I think I'll close up the shop early today. Suddenly I'm not feeling so well. Thank you for coming, but if you'd be good enough to accompany me to the door?"

"Well, I—" Sinclair took her by the elbow and steered her to the exit.

"Thank you for coming. Good day."

He closed the door solidly behind her. She turned around just in time to see him flip the 'OPEN' sign to 'CLOSED.'

Maggie stood there for a moment in the cold December afternoon, disbelieving and unsure what to do next. An old lady walked up to the door as well, but then stopped and looked at the 'CLOSED' sign.

"Is the bookshop closed already?" she asked with obvious disappointment.

"Afraid so," Maggie replied. "Apparently Mr. Sinclair's not feeling himself today."

She was unaware of the truth hidden in her own words.

39. Open to Suggestion

Warwick walked slowly down Aberdeen Quay. She could see the train station two blocks away down Victoria Street. She was reviewing the case in her head. There were lots of numbers to remember: three victims, four weeks apart, five dead children a generation ago, six bloody organs around the corpses. And seven days until it would be four weeks since the third victim.

She glanced around the area. There were more trees here then she had ever realized or noticed before. She heard Maggie Devereaux's voice in her head: 'The key's in the tree' and 'It feels nearby.'

But she could also hear Cameron's voice: 'You'll have my job someday, but not if you start doing foolish things' and 'What were you thinking, Elizabeth?'

"Maybe..." she mused aloud. "But no, that wouldn't be prudent."

As she walked along she caught sight of a stout oak in a small park. The park had a view of the train station and the oak, its branches bare in the winter cold, had a large knothole about six feet off the ground.

Warwick stopped in the middle of the sidewalk and stared at the knothole. She stood there for a very long time, her hands on her hips and her mind debating fiercely with itself. Finally, she looked around, confirmed there was no one watching her, and stepped off the concrete path onto the frozen lawn of the park.

* * *

Maggie sat twisted up on the couch in her aunt and uncle's living room. Spread out on the cushions and the floor were several books, including a tour book of Aberdeen and the surrounding countryside. In her hand was her guidebook about Scotland's stone circles. As she had hoped, several of the better preserved circles were near Aberdeen.

Now she just needed a ride...

* * *

Warwick removed her empty hand from the knothole.

"Stupid, Elizabeth," she muttered, embarrassed. "Stupid to even try."

She hurried back to the sidewalk and walked quickly away from the small park, her head down and her hands shoved into her pockets.

What were you even thinking? she asked herself.

After a few more strides, she finally raised her head again. The flush of self-conscious failure had faded from her cheeks. She glanced around to make sure no one she knew had seen her walk up to a tree, stand on her tippy-toes and start fishing around inside some knothole. No one appeared to be looking at her. In fact there were very few people about at all on that particular Monday morning. Her scan of the horizon ended as it fell onto yet another nearby tree with yet another large knothole high, but not too high, off the ground. This one was in a yard in front of an old commercial building.

Warwick stopped again, her hands inside her pockets and her mind racing.

"Damn," and she walked over to the tree.

* * *

"I can't," Iain protested, his voice hushed. "I have to work."

He pointed through the curtain to the back room. "Your uncle expects me to be here all week. Can't it wait 'til Sunday? Or at least Thursday. I've the day off then."

Maggie crossed her arms. She felt a bit of anger rise in her throat. It's not like she had asked this sort of favor before. Well, Glenninver, but that had been his day off anyway. But this was important. And Sunday would be too late. Even Thursday would be pushing it. Every day counted. Still, anger and yelling was clearly not the way to go here.

"But Iain—" her voice was as sweet as honey and drew the words out slowly. "Are you sure? I really need your help. You know so much more about Scotland than I do. And it's so important for my studies."

"Maggie—" he protested again.

She grabbed his hand and held the length of her body against his arm.

"Please, Iain. I really need you." She looked him square in the eye, and lowered her voice just a notch. "I'd do anything, if you'd just help me out."

Iain looked into her soft caramel eyes. He could feel his will draining into them.

"Well..." he started.

Gotcha.

"... I do have some sick leave saved up."

Maggie's face exploded into a broad smile.

"And I do—cough, cough—feel a bit of a chill coming on."

He smiled weakly at her. "But I can't do it tomorrow. I only have so much sick leave, and knowing you, I'll end up having to spend the night or driving halfway across Scotland in the dark. We'll do it Wednesday. I'm off Thursday, and that way we'll have extra time in case you suddenly need me to drive you to London. All right?"

"Oh, thank you, Iain!" Maggie beamed. "Thank you. I'll meet you outside The Boar and Thistle at nine o'clock, okay?"

"All right," he said in a hushed voice, worried his employer might overhear.

"Thank you again, Iain!" She leaned up and kissed his cheek. "You're a dear. 'Bye!"

And she was out the door.

Iain stood for a moment, watching after her, his hand to his cheek. Then he laughed at himself and turned back to his work.

40. Stone Hinge

Iain's sporty sedan sped over the rolling highway.

"So what's with the sudden interest in stone circles?" he asked, justifiably.

"It's a part of my studies," Maggie explained, less than candidly.

"So you had me lie to my employer—and your uncle I might add—because of your studies?" His tone wasn't angry, just curious. "Why not wait until Sunday?"

"First," Maggie held up a finger. "He's not actually my uncle, he's my third cousin once removed or something. Second, there's a time pressure on this. And besides, they're probably closed on Sundays, at least in the winter."

"Well, I'm not sure stone circles close exactly," Iain let this thought trail off as craned his neck to look up at the sky through the windshield. "But it's a lovely day, no?"

A freezing rain was splattering across the windshield and it was still dark even at 9:15 in the morning.

"No," Maggie laughed. "Not really. You're not sorry you're

with me now are you?"

Iain took his eyes off the road for a moment to glance at her. "No, of course not." He smiled, half to himself. "Damn, you are clever, aren't you?"

Maggie just smiled back and turned to look out her window.

* * *

The stones at Mundurno lay just to the northwest of Aberdeen. They were the first set of stones one would encounter when leaving Aberdeen on the highway toward Elgin. Unfortunately, they had fallen into almost complete disrepair and consisted of little more than several small stones scattered seemingly at random across a grassy field. Someone with training in archeology generally, and Scottish stone circles in particular, could probably have looked at the few remaining stones and been able to visualize the circle as it had originally stood. Maggie had no such training.

"It's not very big, is it?" she asked Iain as they completed the short walk from the car park to the stones.

"Aye, well, size isn't important." He leered at her, a smile pasted across his face. "Sometimes."

Maggie could feel herself blush. "I mean," she forged ahead, "I expected it to be bigger. And more stones."

"Well, stones can be rather heavy, no?" He walked up to one of them and inspected it. "And they hadn't any lorries back then. I imagine I'd probably choose just a few small stones myself if I had to drag them across the countryside on my back."

Maggie ignored this comment and pulled out her guidebook. She had hoped there might be some sort of tourist information stand, but what was left of this circle was just sitting in the middle of somebody's field. No information stands, no gift shops, no nothing. Barely any stones, for that matter. She was beginning to wonder how helpful this field trip would turn out to be.

"What does your book say?" Iain walked back from the now fully inspected stone.

"Not much, I'm afraid," Maggie frowned. "I was kind of hoping to see more."

"More what?"

"More something."

"Oh, aye." Iain gave exaggerated nod. "I understand."

Maggie shot a sharp glance at him then walked over to the largest of the stones. It was still no more than two feet tall. She bent over to touch it, and as she did so, her clan crest pendant fell out of her sweater.

"What's that?" Iain asked. He had followed behind her.

"Oh, it's my clan crest." Maggie grabbed hold of it and looked down. "My grandmother gave it to me."

"Can I see?" and Iain carefully took hold of it. "It's smudged," he observed.

"Yeah," Maggie admitted. "I've tried to clean it off, but nothing seems to work."

Iain let go. "Aye, well, that's too bad. But it's pretty anyway. What's the motto again?"

"'Be Traist.'" Maggie shrugged. "But now it says 'Be Aist.'"

"Aye, well that probably means something too," Iain laughed, then he gestured at the field around them. "So what are we looking at?"

Maggie frowned again. "Good question."

There were only three stones of any size and she could not make out any top or bottom to the circle. The thick cloud cover made it impossible to figure out east from west.

Maggie flipped through her guidebook. "Come on," she said

at last.

"Where are we going?"

"To the next circle."

Iain decided not to make any disparaging comments about the length of the drive out there in comparison to the length of their visit. It could turn out to be a very long day, no need to make it feel any longer.

"And which would that be?" he jogged up next to her as they returned to the car.

Maggie frowned into her book. "Tyrebagger Hill," she replied at last, and opened the car door.

"Aye, well that does sound promising," and Iain hopped into the car himself.

* * *

Sgt. Warwick sat at her desk, the freezing rain beating against the translucent window behind her. Spread out on her desk was every last piece of documentation she could find on two sets of murders eighteen years apart. Directly in front of her she had the photographs of the three Aberdeen victims: Annette Graham, Fionna FitzSimmons and Kelly Anderson. Each body lay in the same peaceful position and the same gruesome condition. The organs were definitely rotating around the bodies: the heart/lungs combination was at Annette's head, to Fionna's right, and at Kelly's feet. What did it mean? And would she be able to stop the madman before some poor girl ended up with her heart and lungs a meter from her left hand?

* * *

Tyrebagger Hill commanded an excellent view over Aberdeen and the bay beyond. The stone circle there rested inside the gated entrance of a small field. According to the guidebook, it was a 'recumbant circle,' meaning that at the head of the circle lay a large horizontal stone—hence 'recumbant'—flanked on either side by two upright stones. The rest of the stones were smaller than the recumbant and decreased in size as they got farther away from the main stone. As a result, someone standing inside the circle would be left with the very distinct impression of standing on a clock-face with the recumbant stone sitting squarely at twelve o'clock.

"Is this better?" Iain asked as he strolled around the interior of the circle.

"Somewhat," Maggie replied. At least there were more than three stones. In truth, Maggie was quite happy with this circle, but she was also surprised. It looked quite different than Clava Cairns. To begin with, it was smaller, only about fifteen feet across. In addition, there were no stone burial mounds inside the circle as at Clava. Finally, and most obviously, Clava Cairns had not had the recumbant stone, which was so striking a feature of this circle as to command almost all of Maggie's attention

"So what was this used for?" Iain laid a hand on the recumbant stone.

"I'm not sure," Maggie peered into the guidebook. "Let me see what the book says."

After a moment she looked up, "Well, it doesn't really say what it's for, just that it's kind of the trademark feature of this type of circle."

"Aye, I can see why."

"And it's usually placed to the south," Maggie read.

"Really?" Iain looked to the sky for directional guidance but was given none. At least the rain had started to let up. "I'd have expected the north."

"Yeah, me too," Maggie said. "Although I'm not sure why."

Then she saw it. Not three stones, two upright and one flat, laying in a field of grass. But three organs, two lungs and one heart, laying in a pool of blood.

"So what else does it say?"

"Er," Iain's question jerked Maggie back to the present. She quickly skimmed the one page devoted to Tyrebagger Hill, half of which was filled with a rather poor photograph of the site. "Not much."

Maggie walked to the recumbant stone, where Iain still stood.

"What—?" but he was stopped by a raise of Maggie hand.

Iain held his tongue while Maggie faced the recumbant stone and closed her eyes. Silent for several seconds, she opened her eyes again and began walking, clockwise, around the circle stopping briefly at each stone on the outer circle. There were eight in all, one each at southwest, west, northwest, north, northeast, east and two sharing the duties for southeast. When she had completed the circuit, she closed her eyes again for several seconds.

Finally she opened them again.

"All right," she announced, "we can go."

"All right, then," Iain smiled incredulously; he was enjoying himself. "Where to?"

Maggie smiled, her face returning to a more normal expression. "Lunch, I think. I'm hungry."

Iain laughed at the unexpected answer.

"Do you know anywhere around here that's good to eat?" Maggie asked, heading back toward the car.

"No," Iain smiled, "but I'm sure we'll find something."

* * *

Salad dressing dripped from the lettuce leaf onto the newspaper clipping on Sgt. Warwick's desk.

"Damn," she muttered through her full mouth and hurried to wipe the oil and vinegar off the brittle paper before it stained. She had read and reread every last piece of paper in the files. Nothing new was jumping out at her. But after a day of sticking her hands in knotholes, she had decided to return to more traditional police methods. Still, it was leading nowhere.

There were no witnesses. No fingerprints. No murder weapons. No clues.

The only thing she knew for certain was that when the sun went down on Friday, another one of Aberdeen's young women would most likely die. And all the increased patrols in the world were unlikely to prevent it.

* * *

Lunch was pleasant enough. They had found a small pub in the town of Blackburn and enjoyed sandwiches and beer. Following their meal, they had driven to several nearby circles, but each appeared to be about as dilapidated as the one at Mundurno. Eventually, though, in the later afternoon, the rain finally stopped and they arrived at a stone circle called Easter at Aquhorthies.

Maggie's guidebook explained that the Easter at Aquhorthies circle was believed to be approximately 4000 years old, its stones having been erected some 1700-2000 years before Christ. Nevertheless it was also one of the best preserved sites in Scotland, or at least around Aberdeen. The crown feature of the circle was its recumbant stone, consisting not just of the expected upright-recumbant-upright combination, but also of two additional stones, placed against the inside of recumbant. The effect was of a very solid and very important keystone to the circle.

"This one's even more impressive than that Tire-bag Hill," Iain observed sincerely, if somewhat inartfully. He was enjoying the field trip. "I'm surprised I've not seen these before. You'd think my mum and da would've taken me out to see these when I was a lad."

"Ah, yes," Maggie replied, eyeing the recumbant stone

herself. "A tourist in your own city. I still don't think I've been to half the things every tourist does when they come to Seattle."

Iain just nodded silently. He was smart enough not to insult her by suggesting that tourist traps built in the 1970's were a bit different than structures erected four millennia ago.

"So what are we looking at then?" he asked instead.

Maggie pulled her book open and flipped through the pages. "Let's see here. Easter at Aquhorthies ... Okay, here it is. Hmm. Okay, it's another recumbant circle."

"'Recumbant'—that means this one laying down, right?"

"Right."

"So what's it for? Looks very important, this one."

Maggie frowned slightly as she read the description. "Apparently, this is a circle that has confirmed astronomical uses."

She squinted into the distance, not because it was bright out—it wasn't—but just out of habit. "See that stand of trees over there?"

Iain squinted too. "Yes."

"It says that those are new, but before they were put in, you could probably see to the horizon. That's where the sun rises on the equinox."

"Really?" Iain looked back at the stones, then again at the stand of conifers. "They knew that back then, eh?"

"Guess so," Maggie replied.

"I wonder how they knew that?"

Maggie thought for a second. "They probably watched it rise once."

Iain looked down at her smug smile. "Be careful, lass. Impertinence doesn't become you."

"'Impertinence'?" Maggie laughed. "That's a rather large word, don't you think?"

"Aye, it is," Iain agreed with a proud smile. "I read books too, you know. And I think I may have even used it correctly just then, eh?"

"Maybe," Maggie's eyes narrowed. "Although I think it suggests some sort of superior position for you."

"Well—" Iain started.

"So," Maggie continued over him, "maybe 'smart-ass' might have been better."

Iain seemed willing to accept this correction. "All right, then. Don't be such a smart-ass. It doesn't become you."

"Thank you," Maggie said with an approving nod.

"You're very welcome."

The two continued to walk around the circle as Maggie read out descriptions of the various astronomically significant configurations. When they reached the recumbant stone again, Iain inquired with true interest, "So what was this one for then?"

"Hold on," Maggie paused. "It's on the next page."

"'Twas fer the moonset," said the gravelly voice behind them.

Both spun around to see a very old man standing just inside the circle, at the northwest corner—assuming the recumbant stone was to the south as it should have been. The man was tall and thin, wearing heavy wool pants and large black shoes. A red wool jacket hung to his hip and covered a white wool sweater, from which protruded a thin, wrinkled neck. Upon this old neck sat a grizzled but kindly face. Large thick glasses hid his eyes and a tweed cap sat atop a head which showed absolutely no sign of hair.

"Hello?" Iain tested.

"'Ello, lad, miss," said the old man with a tip of his cap. Sure enough, no hair underneath. "I cooldna help but overhea' ye. That stine thare was ust tae watch th' moonset."

"Er, thanks," Maggie replied, unsure what else one says to a scary old man inside a 4000 year old circle of upright stones. "Thanks a lot."

The man smiled again and just looked at them for a few seconds. Maggie and Iain both smiled back, each uncertain what to do next. It was rather uncomfortable. Finally the old man spoke up.

"Name's Angus," he raised a bony hand in greeting. "Angus MacCadie."

"Iain. Iain Grant," Iain stepped forward to shake the old man's hand. "This is Maggie." He didn't offer her last name.

"Good tae meet ye, Iain, Maggie," the old man replied with the slightest wheeze. Maggie wondered just how old he was. Eighty if a day. "Int'rested in th' stines, are ye then?"

"Aye," Iain replied first. "They're quite interesting."

Maggie just smiled and nodded in agreement.

"Aye, tha' they are." Angus said with a grin. Maggie was surprised to see that he still had all his teeth, even if they were rather yellowed.

"Ye see tha' wee hoose o'er yonder?" Angus pointed to a small blue house not 500 yards away.

"Yes?" Maggie replied, joining Iain's "Aye?"

"Ah've lived me whole life in tha' hoose," Angus shook his aged head slightly, "an Ah thin' thare's nae been a day Ah'm nae come up to see th' stines."

"Really?" Maggie found this both interesting and unlikely.

"Weel. Mebbe a day or two," he smiled again. "But Ah do ken th' stines as well as anyone."

Oh really? Maggie thought.

"Why's that?" she asked. It seemed a fair question. She noticed Iain looking at her disapprovingly. He probably just wanted to get going now that strange old Angus had arrived. *Too bad.*

"Weel, Ah'll tell ye," Angus narrowed his eyes and he raised a thin finger in emphasis. "Ah groo up in tha' hoose. Me da groo up in tha' hoose. *His* da *bilt* tha' hoose. An' fer as long as anyone kin rem'mber, th' MacCadies ha' lived right aboot where tha' hoose stands."

"Okay..." Maggie was trying to see the relevance.

"Now, these stines 'ere, they've been 'ere fer quite a time as weel."

"True enough," Maggie encouraged.

"Sae it seems a fair conclusion tha' a MacCadie, or at least an ancestor of a MacCadie, most likely 'ad a hand in biltin' this 'ere circle. An' Ah've nae intent of breakin' 4000 years o' fam'ly tradition."

Maggie smiled warmly at this conclusion. She had gained a deep appreciation for family tradition in the recent weeks.

"So, tell me," she asked, "what do you know about this circle?"

Angus smiled broadly, his skin bunching up loosely at his eyes and cheeks. "What woold ye like tae ken?"

"How old is it, did you say?" A sort of test question. If she was going to rely on what this old man she'd never met before was about to tell her, she wanted to feel at least moderately comfortable with his qualifications.

"No one kens fer sure, mind ye," he stroked the short white whiskers just sprouting across his wrinkled face. "But the best guess is tha' it was bilt aboot 1700 or 1800 B.C."

Got that one right.

"And what's this larger stone here?" She pointed at the recumbant.

Meanwhile, Iain had gone from scowl to the bemused smile he wore whenever Maggie turned on her charms to obtain information from people she'd just met. He stood to the side, arms crossed and head cocked, and watched the show.

"Och, that's the recoomba' stine," Angus answered promptly. "Tha's th' main stine fer th' circle."

Not bad, she thought, *although it's pretty obvious that it's the main stine. Stone.*

"Th' signif'cance o' tha' stine," Angus went on, "'as tae doo wi' th' moon cycle."

* * *

Warwick looked up at the clock on the wall. Almost 3:00. It was starting to get dark already. And she hadn't made any appreciable progress. She wanted to run some ideas past Cameron, but she doubted he was around. He had started ducking out early last week—at a little before five o'clock—and had been pushing it back ever since. Probably just as well. He hadn't been terribly helpful lately anyway. Quick to dismiss her ideas, but not offering any himself.

She shook her head hard. No good in dwelling on that. She had a job in front of her.

She looked down at her desk. She had a mess in front of her too.

She glanced again at the clock. Okay, a quick walk around the block to clear her head, then back to work. She still had two days.

* * *

"The moon cycle?" Maggie felt her throat catch on the question.

"Aye, th' moon cycle," Angus answered. His raised his arm, the jacket hanging from it like a scarecrow's. His finger pointed out a large arc across the sky. "On th' major stan'still, the full moon sets right o'er tha' stine."

Maggie looked at Iain inquisitively, her brows drawn together. He shrugged helplessly.

"The major standstill?" Maggie asked the old man.

"Aye, tha's th' day when th' moon rises high'st in th' sky. High'r e'en than th' sun."

"Wow." She didn't even know they were competing.

"Aye, it rises more north'rly than th' sun, and gets high'r in th' sky." He traced the arc with his gnarled hand. "An' when it sets tha' morn, it sets right o'er th' recoomba' stine."

"Really?"

"Really."

Okay, this guy knows what he's talking about, eighty years old or not.

"Wow," Maggie wasn't sure what else to ask. "So this is just a big astronomical observatory?"

Angus' face twisted into disapproval. "Nae, lass. Nae 'juss.'"

Maggie smiled apologetically. "I didn't mean it that way, I just—" She better get this right. "I just thought that these circles were, I don't know—I thought they had some sort of religious significance or something?"

"Aye, lass, they doo."

"But you just said it was all set up for the moon and sun and stuff?"

"Aye. But tha' nae means it wasna ust fer cer'monies too."

"Oh, really?"

"Aye, it's all related. They mark'd th' moon an' sun a'cause they worsh'ped the moon an' sun."

Maggie considered this. "Well, I suppose that makes sense," she admitted.

"Weel, aye, lass, o' coorse it doo. You're nae likely tae bilt somethin' just to mark a moonset wha' comes 'roond ev'ry eighteen years or so."

"Eighteen years?" Maggie didn't understand.

"Aye, lass," Angus was just so obviously enjoying himself. He knew so much, and his wife, if she was still alive, was probably pretty tired of hearing it all again and again. He had a fresh audience. "Th' moon cycle's more than juss full moon to full moon."

Uh-oh. Did she have it all wrong?

"Full moon, haff moon, waxin', wanin'—them's th' *phases* o' th' moon. Th' *cycle* o' the moon, thare's much more to it than juss th' phases. Th' moon rises an' sets a wee bit later each night. Rises in diff'rent places, sets in diff'rent places. Arcs 'cross th' sky in diff'rent places. It's all part o' th' lunar cycle. It takes th' moon eighteen yeers tae get back up to th' same spot in th' sky relative to th' sun an' earth, what with th' earth spinnin' 'roond th' sun and th' moon spinnin' 'roond th' earth."

"Eighteen years?" The words hung on Maggie's lips.

"Aye. 'Tis a long time, nae? Lot kin happ'n in eighteen yeers."

Maggie just nodded, her jaw slightly slack. "And so what kind of ceremonies...?"

"Weel, tha' depends," Angus raised a thoughtful hand to his lips. "Thare were all kinds o' cer'monies. Moon an' sun watch'n o' coorse. In addition tae th' moon, th' sun's got its own cycle too. In fact the winter solstice is this Sunday. Juss afore Christmas. No coinc'dence that. Ah expect thare'll be plenty o' folks what'll come out tae th' circle here fer the solstice."

Sunday's the solstice? Maggie thought. *I thought Sunday was the new moon.*

Angus continued, "An' then thare's your ev'ry day sort o' cer'monies: sacr'fices fer th' harvest, most likely. Praying to gods. Mebbe e'en summon'n demons."

Maggie raised her hand at that one. "Wait. Summoning demons?"

"Och, aye, most likely. 'Coorse canna ken fer sure."

"Why would they ever want to summon a demon?" Her voice betrayed her eagerness for the answer. Iain sensed her agitation and walked back over.

"Weel, thin's were a wee bit diff'rent back then, wern't they? Evil an' sin an' demons—tha' was juss a part o' life, I think. An' o' coorse, your en'my was always more evil than ye are, ye ken?"

Maggie forced herself to smile as she waited for more information.

"So, th' old ones, they believ'd in demons th' way ye or Ah might believe in, och, television or th' Glasgow Rangers. Verra reel thin's. An' if your en'my—who was more evil than ye, remember— if your en'my is goin' tae take advantage of this resource—an' o' coorse he is—weel then, you'd better too. It was likely a sort of arms race."

"Makes sense," Iain conceded.

"So what would they do?" She needed specifics.

"Och, weel. I dinna ken th' specifics, but most likely they summoned th' demon to fight alon' side the chieftain. Or mebbe imbue th' chieftain wi' unholy pow'r by graftin' th' demon directly tae him."

"Wow," Iain beamed. He looked at Maggie. She did not return his gaze.

"Um-hmm?" she encouraged Angus to go on.

"O' coorse, th' problem lies in th' nature o' a demon, Ah'd imagine. As a gen'ral roole, Ah nae think they've much use fer humans. I canna imagine they'd take kindly tae being order'd 'roond by some chieftain in a kilt wi' blue paint on his face. More likely, if ye succeed'd in summonin' one, he'd kill ye on the spot as soon as look at ye."

"You're right," Maggie agreed a little too enthusiastically. "You're absolutely right."

Angus smiled broadly. "Weel, thank ye, miss. Is there anythin' else you'd like tae ken?"

Iain looked at Maggie. It was her show.

Maggie smiled as kindly as she knew how. "No. No, thank you, Mr. MacCadie. You've helped more than you can know," and she shook his hand warmly in departure.

"Glad tae have helped," he called after them. "God keep ye."

"God keep you too, Mr. MacCadie," and Maggie broke into a jog toward the car.

Iain picked up his feet as well and met her at the vehicle. "What's the rush all of a sudden?"

"Oh, I just want to get going," she explained. "It's getting dark and I want to get back to Aberdeen."

Iain opened the car up and climbed in next to Maggie. "Dinner first?"

Maggie closed her eyes so Iain couldn't see them rolling into her head. What should she do? She had new information. She wanted to hurry home and figure out how it all fit together. On the other hand, Iain had been such a dear all day. And she would have to eat dinner at some point anyway. She opened her eyes again.

"Okay. Sounds good."

After all she still had four days until Sunday.

* * *

The walk had done no good at all. Warwick felt like she was staring at a brick wall for all the good it was doing her to pour over the files again and again. The truth was they had no hard forensic evidence, and every suspect they had considered had some sort of alibi.

Annette Graham had been blackmailing her birth mother, Lucille MacTary, and her husband, Alex. But when Fionna FitzSimmons was murdered the MacTarys had been with their niece readying for their week-end.

Fionna FitzSimmons had a hot-headed brother, Sean, and an ambitious boyfriend, Will Hopkins. Her pregnancy could have cost Will Hopkins his professional goals, but the abortion she was considering had outraged Sean. But Sean FitzSimmons was in a Belfast jail the night of Kelly Anderson's murder, and Will Hopkins' parents and sister had confirmed that he had spent that weekend with them in London.

Kelly Anderson had been sleeping with Craig Macintyre, who had also plagiarized her work. She ended up dying the night after she'd given Macintyre an ultimatum: either he confess to stealing her work, or she'd broadcast his infidelity and plagiarism on every available channel. And Annette Graham had also been one of his students. But Macintyre was in Amsterdam when Annette Graham was murdered. Confirmed by 200 witnesses. And he only needed one.

So everyone who seemed to have a motive could be eliminated from being the single killer Dr. Wood was certain they were dealing with. That left only two alternatives. Desperately attaching guilt to every male she came into contact with. Or accepting the most frightening proposition of all: they were dealing with a madman, whose sick twisted mind they could never truly understand, and whose next move they could therefore not even hope to anticipate.

The only saving grace on that Wednesday evening was that Warwick had two more days to try to think of something. Anything.

Just then, she heard a knock at her door. She looked up to see Jenkins, one of her patrolmen, standing in the open doorway, his knuckles only millimeters away from the doorframe he had just knocked on.

"Sorry to bother you, Sergeant," he said, "but there's been another one."

41. Annie Gwyer

"What was her name?"

Cameron had finally arrived. Warwick was beginning to wonder where he'd been. Even Dr. Wood had been and gone by now.

"Annie Gwyer," she responded. Then anticipating the next question, went on, "She was a dancer at the club round front."

The two officers hunched their shoulders against the freezing rain as they stood in a dirty alleyway not four blocks from the shipping docks and directly behind a seedy nightclub frequented by longshoreman, transients, and people looking to avoid too much attention. The club had lost a lot of business that night. If there was one thing their clientele wanted to avoid it was police officers, and the area was lousy with them just then. A dozen officers if there was one, and all swarming over the several blocks surrounding the club. All because of a young woman named Annie Gwyer.

"Same killer, then?" Cameron lit his pipe.

"I'm not sure," Warwick titled her head and looked at the corpse lying in the oil streaked puddles which danced with each rain drop. "It's different."

"How so?" He leaned in to look as well.

"Well, to start off with, the abdominal cavity's not been emptied. The only things removed were some intestines and a couple of smaller organs. I think Dr. Wood said one of them was the gallbladder. So the organ arrangement's not the same."

"So, perhaps he's moved on to a new pattern?" Cameron smacked at his pipe stem. "You said you thought it was an evolving pattern."

"Well, yes, I did say that," the sergeant frowned. "But that's not all. Dr. Wood did a preliminary exam. He said the cause of death was a broken neck, not strangulation."

"Maybe she struggled?" Cameron countered.

"Maybe." She wanted to say, 'As if the others hadn't?' but she was done trying to convince him.

"So you think it's a different killer, then?" he prodded.

Maybe. Could be. Probably. "Yes."

Cameron nodded a few times and smacked again at the pipe. He turned away from the body. "Could it be that it's the same killer, but he's become more violent? Perhaps the methodical manner of killing had lost its thrill?"

"Possible," Warwick conceded.

"Or perhaps it's a simple matter of location. We're only feet away from a busy street, frequented at night by dozens and dozens of local revelers. Perhaps he was interrupted, or perhaps he simply wished to hurry so as to avoid detection. This would seem to be a more heavily trafficked area at night than a college campus."

"True enough," Warwick answered, "but that just begs the next question: Why choose your next victim from this area, when you just increase your chances of detection?"

"Does he though?" smoke wafted from the inspector's

mouth. "We've increased patrols, haven't we? And where? Why, in the college district. Not the docks. Detection by a random civilian is far preferable than detection by law enforcement, I should think."

Warwick pursed her lips and looked away. He was not to be persuaded. She decided not to mention her belief that the next murder should have happened Friday night, not Wednesday.

"Fine," she replied. "But I still think we should be open to at least the possibility of a copy-cat killer."

Cameron frowned deeply and tapped his pipe on his lip. "No. No, we don't need a copy-cat killer. That won't do at all."

Warwick found this reaction puzzling. *'We don't* need *a copy-cat killer'*?

"And in any event, it's unlikely," he went on. "That would require knowledge of details we've mostly kept out of the press."

Mostly, Warwick thought.

"Oy, right! To one side!" The voice came from the end of the alley. A man was trying to push past two officers who were restraining him from entering the alleyway. "I need to talk wi' the head copper!"

Cameron walked slowly up to the man, who was still struggling, and exhaled a rather large cloud of smoke in his general direction.

"I'm the head copper," he announced calmly.

"Right then!" The man shrugged off the two officers and straightened his shirt, stained at the bottom where it curved under his belly and back into his too tight blue pants. He wore no tie, and his sleeves were rolled up revealing thick forearms with black hair hiding several faded tattoos. What was left of his hair—his hairline had already retreated halfway across his scalp—was a reddish brown. A gold tooth shone as he spoke to the inspector. "Right, I need you blokes out of here. Now. I can't have coppers traipsing aroun' me nightclub. 'S not good fer business."

Cameron exhaled slowly. "And you are?"

"I'm Jamie Lancaster an' I own this nightclub," he pointed to the back of the building which abutted the alleyway. "And I need you coppers to leave."

"Sir," Cameron's voice was calm. "There's been a murder."

"Well, thank you very bloody much, Officer Obvious," Lancaster threw his hands in the air. "I bloody well know that. But I don't see why you need a bleeding battalion to investigate one bloody murder. You're scaring me customers away."

Cameron elected to ignore the 'Officer Obvious' comment. "Your customers don't like the police?"

Lancaster narrowed his eyes and met the inspector's gaze. "Me customers don't like questions. And coppers ask questions."

"You do understand that your yelling and interrupting will not speed things up any?"

Lancaster just glared at him.

"However," Cameron raised his pipe-stem to the black sky, "if you're willing to cooperate, things will go far more smoothly. And quickly."

"Cooperate how?" Jamie Lancaster crossed his arms.

"First, leave these officers to their work. They needn't waste time restraining the likes of you from contaminating a crime scene."

Lancaster just grunted.

"Second, I'll need to ask some of your customers if they recognize some photographs."

"Absolutely not," Lancaster stamped his foot and shook his head vigorously.

Cameron returned his pipe to his mouth. "I don't think you understand," he said through clenched teeth. "I'm not asking your permission. A woman—one of *your* employees—has been brutally murdered. Behind *your* bar. We intend to find her killer. We need to speak with your customers."

"But—"

"And we can do it one of two ways. The first way is that you cooperate. You let us approach a few select patrons as they sit in the bar and we quietly show them a few photographs."

Lancaster glared at the inspector. "And the second way?"

Cameron nodded slowly and exhaled more pipe smoke onto Jamie Lancaster. "The second way is that you don't cooperate. In which case, we will lock down your club. We will interview each and every customer until we've spoken to them all. And before which we will not open the doors again."

Lancaster's eyes widened and his mouth opened to respond.

Cameron beat him to it. "What do you think *that* would do to your business?"

Lancaster's face turned bright red, and his chest heaved in heavy breaths. "Fine," he said at last. "But hurry."

"I'll do my best," Cameron replied. "Now go inside and let us do our jobs."

Lancaster stared at the inspector one last time, then turned away and stormed off toward the front of the club, muttering several words far stronger than 'bloody.'

Cameron walked up to one of his patrolmen. "How much longer do you lads need?"

"We're almost done here, Inspector," was the reply. "Not much longer."

Cameron walked back over to where Sgt. Warwick stood. "Have them finish up, then get the body to the morgue for a full examination. I want confirmation that it's the same killer. If it's a copy-catter, then we've got serious trouble."

"Yes," Warwick replied. *Yes, we do.*

"I'll head inside," Cameron continued. "See if anyone recognizes any of the current suspects." He patted his coat pocket where the photographs of the suspects obviously were.

He walked toward the street, then turned back. "And stick around 'til I'm done. We can head over to the morgue together. See what Andy has to say before we start trying locate the girl's next of kin."

* * *

All in all it took Cameron just over forty minutes to make his rounds inside the club.

"Lovely establishment, that," he said sarcastically as he climbed into Warwick's patrol car. "It's a wonder we've not been called out here every night."

"Anyone recognize the photos?" Warwick asked, not hopeful, as she pulled the car into the roadway.

"Some of them," Cameron let out a grunt as he reached into his coat pocket for the envelope with the photographs.

He pulled out a few and held them up for Warwick to glance at as she drove.

"Several of them recognized Sean FitzSimmons. Knew him just as 'Sean.' Said he worked down on the docks and was a regular for a time. Haven't seen him for a while."

"Being in jail across the Irish Sea will do that," Warwick observed.

"No one recognized the others: Alex MacTary, Will Hopkins, Macintyre. I'd really hoped they'd recognize Macintyre, but it doesn't surprise me much that he's never been in that place. Not exactly his pot of tea, I'd wager."

"Most likely not," Warwick agreed.

"But they recognized this one," he held up another photograph. "He's a regular, they say."

Warwick glanced quickly at the photograph, but had trouble seeing it in the dark of the car while trying to stay on the slick, winding road leading up to the morgue.

"Who—?"

"Don't recognize him?"

"I can't really see it," Warwick explained, her attention was focused fully now on the quickly approaching morgue to their left.

"Devan Sinclair," Cameron said simply, and tucked the photograph away. Then pointing out the front windshield, said, "Right in front there. No one will give us a ticket."

Warwick pulled the car up into the no parking zone in front of the morgue. Before the car had even stopped rolling, the inspector opened his door and hopped out into the rain.

"Let's see what Andy has to say."

42. Information

Iain's silver car pulled slowly up to the MacTary's house, headlights dimmed.

"Thank you so much, Iain." Maggie smiled warmly at him.

"No problem at all, Maggie," Iain smiled back. "I'm starting to like these little excursions." He looked at her with narrowed eyes and raised brows. "You're very mysterious," he observed.

Maggie's smile broadened. "Well, I don't know." She wasn't sure what to say. "Thanks, I guess."

"Can I walk you to the door?"

"Oh no, that's all right," Maggie waved the suggestion away. "Just wait 'til I get inside again?"

Iain's smile faded a bit. "Sure."

Maggie cocked her head at him. "You don't want Alex and Lucy to know you were with me today, do you?"

Iain's face lit up in recognition. "Oh, right," he agreed. "I'd forgot about that."

Maggie smiled and nodded. She began to open the car door, then she realized what he had really meant when he'd asked if he could walk to the door.

"C'mere." She leaned over and pulled his face to hers, kissing him fully on the mouth.

After a moment she pulled away, her face and body flushed. "Good night, Iain. Thanks again. See you tomorrow?"

Iain grinned happily. "Aye. See you tomorrow, Maggie."

She stepped out of the car and quickly trotted up the walk to the waiting porch. Unlocking the door, she turned to wave at Iain as his darkened car pulled away, waiting until the next house before turning his lights back on. She had had a good day with Iain, in more ways than one. But returning her mind to business, she pictured the moon symbols on her calendar. Four days left. Time to get to work.

"Maggie, is that you?" It was Uncle Alex' voice.

"Yes," she replied cautiously.

"Come in here with us for sec, love." That was Aunt Lucy.

They were watching the television in the living room, lights off, the room illuminated only by the multicolored lights on the Christmas tree and the blue glow of the television. It looked like the evening news was about to start. Maggie was amused by the similarities the introduction had with local news shows back home.

"How was your day, dear?" her aunt asked.

"Well enough," Maggie replied. "Ellen and I visited some of the local stone circles. Very interesting. And helpful for my research."

"Oh really?" Alex asked, and followed it up with a more pointed question about her studies. But Maggie didn't hear him. Her attention was focused on the television anchorwoman.

"What did she say?" Maggie pointed to the screen, filled with the anchorwoman's face in front of an illustration of a chalk body-outline. "Turn it up."

Alex complied with a press of the remote control.

"... —lice aren't saying yet whether this murder is related to the others which have plagued Aberdeen in recent weeks. However, preliminary information from an unnamed source close to the investigation confirms that the woman's body was found in the same badly mutilated condition as the other three victims. Police are not yet releasing the name of this latest victim of the Aberdeen serial killer until they have notified her family ..."

Maggie stared at the television in disbelief.

It's too soon.

* * *

The Aberdeen City Morgue was housed in a rather old building not too far from the Old Campus. It was made of sandstone and brick and looked much like any other municipal building from last century, save the word 'MORGUE' carved somberly into a gray stone inserted above the front door. Walking along the street and looking up the seven cement stairs to the front door, one's perception of the entire structure would change once that word was encountered. The warm red bricks would become far less inviting and one would undoubtedly hasten to be out of the shadow of this depressing, yet necessary building. Every city needs a place to store its deceased while proper arrangements are made. This is especially true when the deceased has no family or friends to attend to such details, and even more so when the deceased was the victim of a crime. In such cases, a morgue becomes not only a storage facility, but an investigative resource, and the coroner a detective.

"Andy!" Inspector Cameron walked into the examination room where Dr. Wood and his assistant had just finished their work.

"Robert," came the friendly reply before the coroner turned to his young assistant. "David, go ahead and put her back into sstorage. The ssame place we got her from, okay? Then you can go home. There's no telling when we'll get the go ahead for the full autopsy. No need to wait around. It'll keep 'til tomorrow."

"All right then, Dr. Wood," replied David. "Thank you. G'night. G'night officers."

"'Night," responded Warwick, as the assistant rolled the gurney into the hallway.

Cameron just nodded.

"You're looking better, Andy," he remarked. And it was true. The doctor's face had lost its last hint of slackness.

"Thank you, Robert. It's sslow, but improving. One thing about this job," he waved around the room with his left hand, "you learn to appreciate every day you're alive."

"So what can you tell me?" Cameron quickly got down to business. "Is it the same killer?"

Dr. Wood pursed his lips and drew his left hand up to his chin. "It's hard to ssay of course. Always is. But I'd have to ssay, no. No, it's not."

Told you so, thought Warwick, but she knew better than to say anything, or even let the thought cross her face.

Cameron frowned. "Are you sure?'

"Ssure? No," Wood replied. "But you asked what I thought, and I think it's a different killer."

He raised his right hand slowly and pointed to its fingers with his left. "First, this girl ssuffered a broken neck; sshe wasn't sstrangled. In fact there are no indications of any true attempt at sstrangulation. There are bruises on the neck, but they are pre-death and I think relate to the breaking of the vertebrae, not any attempt to clamp the esophagus sshut. I think whoever did this sshook her until her neck broke. That's very different from the other killings.

"Ssecond, the organ removal was entirely different. Whoever

did the first three killings knew his anatomy." The doctor paused for a second and smiled at Warwick. She smiled back, a bit embarrassed. "But this bloke—assuming it was a bloke—he had no idea what he was doing. He cut her open and pulled out the first things he could find. Pulled 'em out like he was pulling taffy and then cut 'em off when they wouldn't budge anymore. He only got the sslightest part of the intestines out. Our other lad, he removed everything nice and clean. And of course with this one, most of the organs were sstill inside, whereas before we had to go looking behind bushes to find the rest of them.

"Third, there is absolutely no way it's the ssame murder weapon, unless he's sspent the last four weeks chopping wood with it. The incisions are rife with trauma—the blade was too dull to cut well. Most likely that's why he ssettled for the few organs nearest the incision.

"Sso, it would sseem," Dr. Wood lowered his right hand and balled his left into a loose fist, "that we have two different killers."

Cameron frowned.

"But I could be wrong," the doctor added. "Maybe it is the ssame killer, but he's sswitched to new methods. That wouldn't be unheard of. I wasn't there, sso I can't know for certain."

Cameron added a nod to his frown. Then he laughed quietly. "Not very helpful, Andy."

The doctor looked a little surprised. "Ssorry," he said with a glance to Warwick.

"No, it's not you," the inspector went on. "It's this damned case. It's getting to me. If you're wrong and it is the same killer, then we've missed him again. If you're right, then we've got two of them on the loose."

Warwick shrugged at the doctor, who shrugged in return.

"Any next of kin?" Dr. Wood asked, changing the subject.

Now it was his turn to worry about business.

Cameron shook his head and looked to his sergeant. "No word, right, Warwick?"

"Right," she replied. "I called it in to the station while you were inside the nightclub, but no reply yet."

"Well, then," Dr. Wood wiped his hands on his lab coat. "I'll sstart looking into arrangements for a pauper's funeral. Hopefully that won't be necessary, but just in case."

"And we'll confirm there's no other family," Warwick added.

Cameron looked over the doctor's shoulder toward the hallway David had disappeared down. "Are you going to wait to do the autopsy then?"

"Yes, if that's all right," Dr. Wood replied. "I'd prefer to wait until we have confirmation there's no next of kin. Is there any reason it can't wait until morning?"

Cameron frowned. "Well, it is a homicide."

"Oh, I know they couldn't refuse the autopsy," the coroner explained. "It'll be necessary for the inquest, if nothing else. But I've found it generally more considerate to explain the need for the autopsy in advance rather than afterward. Particularly if there are religious objections."

"You're a good man, Andy." Cameron put his hand on his friend's shoulder.

The doctor displayed a crooked smile. "If you ssay sso," he replied. He then turned to Sgt. Warwick. "Good night, Elizabeth."

"Good night, Dr. Wood."

The ice-cold rain hadn't let up any, but the two officers nevertheless walked slowly to their car. They were used to such rain.

"You were right," Warwick said, climbing behind the wheel. "That wasn't very helpful."

"No," Cameron laughed slightly. "No, it wasn't."

He stared out the windshield for a few moments, then said, "I wish I knew. I just—"

Warwick nodded in agreement, and empathy, as she pulled the car away from the curb.

"I really hope this isn't a copy-cat killer," Cameron went on. "We don't need two serial killers running loose."

Warwick frowned and looked out on the wet, shining road, considering whether to voice her own opinion. Finally she said, "I actually hope it *is* a copy-catter."

"You do?" Cameron seemed genuinely surprised. "You want two killers on the loose?"

"No, of course not," she chided. "What I mean is, I hope this one isn't related. That it's some sort of isolated incident and the killer tried to cover it up by making it look similar to what he'd read in the papers."

She paused, but Cameron didn't say anything.

"At least then," she continued, "we've still got some chance of catching the real killer before he kills again."

Cameron nodded weakly. "But how much of a chance?"

Warwick recalled what she had read from the eighteen year old newspaper clippings.

"A day and a half at least," she replied. "And every day counts. We do what we can."

* * *

Maggie sat on the floor of her aunt and uncle's living room. The news had long since moved on to other topics. Football scores seemed to be the current one. Alex and Lucy were still talking with her and each other, but Maggie gave only the most limited of responses. She sat transfixed on the floor, her mind numbed by the news of another murder.

This is wrong, she thought. *It's too soon. By three days at least.*

She looked around the room at the television, at her aunt and uncle and at her heavy, full purse lying to her side.

What can I do?

43. Consideration

"Aaaahhhh!!"

Maggie shot awake, her heart racing.

Another night of studying and practicing the magic. Another dream.

She wiped the sweat off her brow with her pajama sleeve. She looked down at her hands—no blood. Good.

In this one, she was back at the castle. But this time it was she who reached into the prisoner's stomach and ripped out the still beating heart. She had raised it to her mouth, salivating at the raw power she was about to taste.

Nice. She shuddered at the memory of the image.

Instinctively, Maggie dabbed at her mouth with her hand. No blood there either.

Good.

She swung her feet off the bed and took a long cleansing breath. Then up and across the room to the magic book. Back to business. She may have found the spell. The one the killer was using. Or similar to it anyway. The one in the book was for grafting a demon to a human host. It seemed to be a very powerful spell, but it was a long process. It required sacrificing four victims, one each on the vernal equinox, summer solstice, autumnal equinox and then finally on the winter solstice. So it would take approximately nine months to complete. And even then, the demon wouldn't appear until the next equinox. It actually seemed a bit of a waste to Maggie. That's a long time to wait to get help in a war. You'd probably lose well before then.

Of course, the spell in the Dark Book clearly wasn't the exact spell the murderer was using. The murderer was killing on the moon cycle. *Moon phases*, she corrected herself, Angus MacCadie's voice echoing in her head. The book did contain another spell having to do with sacrificing victims on the phases of the moon, but it involved killing pigs every full moon. Maggie did find one scrawled note interesting, however; it was a caveat that the sacrificer should take care to wait until the moon had actually risen. It wasn't enough to just do it the day of the event. It was the moonrise that controlled.

In any event, the spells she had encountered confirmed two things: First, the killer was definitely following, or attempting to follow, some sort of ancient sacrificial ritual. Second, it wasn't any spell she had in her book. So she couldn't know for sure what his next move would be. But the next new moon seemed the most likely bet.

That was Sunday, a small black circle on her calendar marking the day the moon phases started over.

And today was Thursday morning. Three and half days to solve the mystery.

And one person who might believe her.

* * *

There were so many trees near the train station. But Warwick had already checked them all. She was sure that Annie

Gwyer's death was not related to the others, except inasmuch as they had inspired her killer to hide his culpability behind a poor imitation of the college killings. But that meant there was only one more day before the next murder. And she had no clue of how to stop it.

Actually, she had one clue. A young woman named Maggie Devereaux—the American niece of one of the suspects no less—had told her that the murder weapons were in a locker at the train station. And that the key to the locker was hidden in the knothole of a 'nearby' tree. And Elizabeth Warwick was desperate.

But scanning the area, she could see no trees she hadn't already inspected.

She looked around again. Maybe it was farther away than Maggie had realized. Maybe over there. She spotted a line of trees across the street, but just as she fixed her gaze on them, a city bus pulled up and blocked her view.

Damn bus, she thought. *Move already.*

Then she paused.

Bus?

* * *

"All right then," Dr. Wood said wiping the blood off of one of the saws. "We can put her back now. We'll need her to keep 'til Ssunday."

"What's Sunday?" David asked as he pulled the sheet over the corpse's head.

"That's the funeral," Dr. Wood replied conversationally. "They can't find any family, sso the church is going to bury her remains on Ssunday."

David started to fill out the log they kept for removal and return of bodies from the storage area. "Why Sunday?"

Dr. Wood looked up from his gore-stained instruments, his

face awash in unchecked astonishment. "Why, lad," he explained, "that's the Ssabbath."

* * *

Iain knocked on the door.

Lucy MacTary opened it.

"Oh, hello, Iain," she said warmly. "How are you? What brings you by?"

"I'm fine thanks," Iain replied, trying to look past his employer. "Is Maggie ready?"

"Ready?" Lucy tilted her head.

"Aye," Iain raised an eyebrow. "We had plans for the day. It's my day off and all"

Lucy turned and looked back into the home, unease crossing her face. "Well, actually, Iain, she's left already."

Iain was taken aback. "Left?"

"Aye," Lucy turned back to face her visitor. "She left this morning. She didn't mention ... She's been a bit distracted lately."

Iain smiled and nodded. He'd noticed that too, but he kind of liked it somehow. "Aye, she's like that sometimes. Okay, well... Please tell her I stopped by then."

"I will, Iain," Lucy smiled softly. "And you're feeling better?"

"Eh?"

Lucy's eyes held her question still.

"Oh. Oh, aye. Much better," Iain remembered his fib. "Thanks for asking."

"All right then, Iain," Lucy's eyes sparkled with understanding. "I didn't think it was anything too serious. Neither did Alex. We'll tell Maggie you stopped by."

"Right. Thanks." And he scurried down the stairs and back to his car.

* * *

Aberdeen, being Scotland's third largest city and Britain's eighth, is connected with the other major cities of the island by airplane and by train. And by bus. The main bus terminal stood on Guild Street, quite near the train station in fact, its busses leaving the station several times a day to such destinations as Inverness, Glasgow and Edinburgh, with connections to England and Wales beyond. The bus station was actually rather large and held a similar feel to the nearby train station. There were schedule boards, and ticket booths, and long lines of passengers. And lockers.

Warwick stood in front of the main doors of the bus terminal and scanned the horizon for trees, or more correctly, for knotholes.

She started walking away from the bus station, along Guild Street. There was a row of medium sized oaks standing each approximately twenty feet apart, designed to cast shade and beauty across this stretch of the road. As she passed, she scanned each tree, looking for just the right sized knothole. One large enough to allow a human hand to reach inside and grasp a key, but not so large as to risk losing it within. The first tree she came across had no knothole at all. The second one also had no knothole. The third had a large decaying hole about three feet off the ground. A quick visual inspection confirmed no key inside. The next tree again had no knothole. The next two appeared previously to have had knotholes, but they had been filled in with some sort of tar-resin compound. Good for the tree; bad for the investigation.

Then she came to the seventh tree. She didn't see the knothole at first, because it was rather high off the ground and faced away from the direction from which she was approaching. But as she craned her neck to see the other side, and just before she pulled her eyes away to inspect the next tree, she saw it. Some nine inches across and more than six feet from the pavement. Warwick held her breath and looked at her watch. It was almost noon. She had thirty, maybe thirty-five hours left.

She strode over, stood on her tip-toes and reached up, sticking her hand inside the hole.

The inside of a tree knothole is not the most disgusting surface in the world, but after several months of Scottish rain, it is not the most pleasant either. And not being able to see inside it as one's hand traverses the slimy bark doesn't enhance the experience in any positive way. Neither does scraping one's wrist across the opening of the knothole because one is only 5'9" tall and has to stand on one's toes to be able to reach inside.

The only thing which could make such an endeavor worthwhile to Elizabeth Warwick was about to happen. Her hand hit something. Something hard. And small. And metal. She grasped at it as best she could, her fingertips slipping on the slick metal, but eventually she was able to wrap her hand around the object and pull it out.

When she opened her hand, what she saw made her not care one whit about the scratches on her wrist which had started to ooze the smallest amount of blood.

In her hand was a key.

The key.

With the number '99' etched into its side.

Elizabeth Warwick felt a flood of different emotions wash over her that moment, from relief to exhilaration. But one of the emotions, almost lost in the tempest, was admiration for young Maggie Devereaux. She had been right after all.

Warwick squeezed the key in her hand and reflected.

After a moment, she looked around to see if anyone had noticed her actions.

Then she stood back up on her toes and returned the key to the knothole.

* * *

"No, I'm sorry, miss," said the teller in the police officer's uniform. "I'm afraid Sgt. Warwick's not in her office just now. Would you like to leave her a message?"

"No, thank you," replied Maggie dejectedly.

She turned around, lowered her head, and crossed over to the door.

As she pushed the door open onto the gray Scottish afternoon, she asked herself, *Now what?*

44. Reflection

This time it wasn't just any bloody, mutilated carcass. It was Iain's.

Carved up and lying at Maggie's feet. She bent down to touch his lifeless form. At her touch he gasped and forced open one half-dead eye. He was still alive.

Maggie reached out and touched his face gently, tracing the curve of his cheek and jaw. Then she lowered her hand to his neck—and dug her fingers into the flesh, ripping out his windpipe in a single, life-ending flourish.

Looking up, Maggie could see the demon watching her. And although he'd never say so, she knew she had pleased him. He produced a golden jewel-encrusted chalice and held it under Iain's torn throat to catch the blood spurting down the crimson stained neck. Maggie too raised a goblet of Iain's blood. She interlaced arms with the demon and drank. Fully.

Maggie jerked awake. No scream, but she immediately spit onto the floor. No blood. And yet it had seemed so real. Had tasted so ... good.

Maggie looked over at the spell book she had left open last

night. Next to the spellbook was the T-shirt, four new black splotches added to its already stained fabric. Reminders of her failed attempts to divine more information from samples from the murder scenes. She had been unable to find any more good samples. The threads and the hair and the blackened blade of grass proved to be wholly unrelated to the murder of her friends. She stayed up until nearly midnight, the rising sliver of a moon her only companion, as she had learned where some the students at the college shopped for coats, got their hair cut, and so on.

Maggie looked down at her hands—the same ones that she had just watched rip out Iain Grant's esophagus. The dreams were so awful. But the magic was so useful. So powerful. So … addictive.

She sighed and shoved a hand through her thick hair. Then, reluctantly, she stood up. Time to shower.

* * *

Breakfast was somehow unappealing that morning. The tomato juice in the refrigerator had not helped. She grabbed a single scone from the bread basket and walked out into the misty, drizzly Friday morning.

She needed to clear her head.

* * *

The walk had led Maggie haphazardly through the MacTary's neighborhood. Earlier in the year she would likely have followed a direct path toward the college, but now—now she wanted to get away from things for a bit. And the college was smack in the middle of things.

She found herself adrift in a residential neighborhood filled with nice, middle-class townhomes. Aberdeen, like most European cities, was too crowded to afford every resident the luxury of a yard. Most had a small two foot strip between their building and the sidewalk, but nothing like the yards which were part and parcel of homeownership in the United States. Still, the streets were lined with trees, dark and leafless as they might be in late December, and traffic was light on the narrow streets. The sheltered calmness of the neighborhood gave Maggie the chance to clear her head a bit and let her brain concern itself with suppositions about the residents of some of the more interesting homes, and minding uneven blocks on the pavement.

Even still, it proved to be an effort to force out the thoughts about the evil that was happening all around her. And how she could possibly help put a stop to it. Whenever she entertained the idea of just forgetting about it, she could hear that stupid Iain saying, '*Some poor girl's going to be next if they don't catch this lunatic soon. I think maybe you'd have that girl's death on your head a bit if you could've helped, but didn't.*' A very real part of her wanted to just forget the whole thing. After all, she wasn't a policeman. It was their job, not hers.

She didn't know what to do.

She approached an intersection with what appeared to be a major road. More major anyway than the side-street she was on. She was uncertain how far she'd walked from her aunt and uncle's home as she'd mused over her plight, but she was certain she'd entered newly discovered territory—for her at least. The college should have been nearby, but she couldn't see the King's Tower over the rows of townhomes. Instead, Maggie found herself staring across the intersection at a rather impressive-looking church she'd never seen before. It was quite large, with an even larger cemetery extending behind it toward the next street over. It might have seemed out of place in the residential neighborhood had it not been for the fact that in its enormity it still held the same quiet dignity as its neighbors. This was a neighborhood of affluent, if not exactly wealthy Aberdeenians. Doctors, lawyers, professors—and small business owners like her aunt and uncle. Every neighborhood needed a place of worship, Maggie supposed. This was this neighborhood's.

She crossed the street and approached the path to the church's entryway. 'ST. CATHERINE'S.' Catholic. Maggie could again hear Iain's voice, *'Oh, are you Catholic?'* No. But somehow the sanctity of a church, whatever denomination, appealed to her just then. Maybe it was skipping breakfast, maybe it was the depressing drizzle, maybe it was the restless nights and tortured dreams. Whatever it was, she wanted someone to just wrap their arms around her and tell her it would all be all right. Somehow, this church seemed to offer that.

She turned up the path to the door.

The inside of the church was breathtaking. All stone and stained glass. Gilded statues filled a dozen alcoves circling the sanctuary. The pulpit was adorned in cloths of white and purple and gold, and a large gilded crucifix hung over the altar. And to the right was a table filled with small white candles twinkling at the feet of a statue of the Virgin Mary, her hands extended to her sides in invitation. Looking around at the beautiful interior of the church, Maggie's couldn't help but reflect that even her beautiful Episcopal church back home had not been so ornate. She suddenly became excruciatingly conscious of the fact that she was a non-Catholic seeking comfort in a Catholic church. Thus feeling the slightest bit ill at ease, she quickly grabbed a seat in the last pew and lowered her head.

Denominations aside, she had come in seeking comfort, and time to reflect on what she should do next. It was true that she was not the police, and that it was their job to catch the killer, not hers. But it was equally true that she had information which they did not. And despite her earlier rebuff by the police, she still felt she had some moral obligation to act on the knowledge she possessed.

'I think maybe you'd have that girl's death on your head a bit if you could've helped, but didn't.'

The safest thing to do was to just tell the police what more she had learned. But she had tried that yesterday and Sgt. Warwick had not been in. And there was no guarantee they would believe her anyway. They hadn't the first time. What had changed? She'd gotten better at the magic, but that hardly seemed likely to persuade them. No, they had their methods, and they weren't interested in some crack-pot from the States who claimed she could read the killer's identity at the bottom of a tea cup.

So what then? What was she to do? And who was this fourth victim? Had she been wrong about the fourth (and fifth, if Glenninver was the blueprint) murders happening on the new moon? That was still two days away. The news had said the girl's body had been found behind a nightclub down by the docks, not at the college. But where at the docks? And was she really the fourth victim or not? If so, had the demon already been summoned? Was it too late?

For a moment she considered how silly it was to believe that a demon could actually be summoned. Then she remembered the candle floating in front of her face, and thought again. And if a demon had already been summoned, already been grafted to its host, what would that mean? She tried to imagine what a demon would do in modern-day Aberdeen. She wasn't sure, but she knew it couldn't be good. But what if she was right and the murder was supposed to happen on the new moon? Was this latest murder unrelated or not? Was there still going to be a murder on Sunday? One that would complete the spell? One that would summon a demon to this plane to possess a human host and do God knows what unspeakable acts?

If she could prevent that, and didn't, she'd have a lot more than just one girls' death on her head.

Maggie looked up, a decision reflected in her eyes. She needed to find out whether that fourth victim was related to the other killings or not. And if not, then she had to find Sgt. Warwick and plead with her to let her help.

Just then, another parishioner entered the church from a side entrance toward the front of the sanctuary. Maggie noticed only because the church was so empty otherwise. The front pew was occupied by a very old woman praying the rosary, but she had been otherwise alone in the sanctuary. The man who had just entered walked directly over to the candles by the statue of Mary, and selected three unlit ones from below. Slowly lighting each in turn, he muttered a prayer, then crossed himself. When he turned to take a seat in a nearby pew, Maggie could finally see his face. And his scar.

Devan Sinclair. The man whose sister had been murdered eighteen years earlier in Glenninver—just like the girls in Aberdeen. The man whose parents died in a fire a year later. The man who spoke Gaelic as a native. The man who owned a bookstore on the occult. The man who refused to sell her the one book which could have helped her peg down the spell the murderer was using. She didn't think to question what he might be doing in this neighborhood. Instead her mind raced to more pressing questions.

Is he summoning the demon? she couldn't help but ask herself. *But if so, why would he be at a church?*

Maggie decided not to stick around for the answers. She got up as quietly as she could and made a bee-line for the door, hoping desperately that Sinclair had not seen her.

45. Frustration

Warwick waited in her car up the road from the tree. It was just after sundown and probably a bit too early for the killer to show up, but better to be early than late. She didn't dare go up to the tree to check if the key was still there. That would alert the killer that she had discovered his scheme; then she'd never catch him. No, the better way was to watch silently from up the road and wait. It was Friday night. He would come.

She had decided to do this stake-out alone. Cameron would likely not have believed her. She could always call for back-up once the killer came and fetched the key to unlock his garroting wire and dissecting knife. But if she was going to base her actions on the word of a twenty-something American college student, she didn't need to broadcast that to the entire department.

The minutes passed, but no one came. The minutes turned to hours, and still no one came. She was cold and hungry in her small car up the road from the bus station and she started to question her own judgment. A stake-out by one's self was starting to seem less of a good idea. She also remembered that Kelly Anderson's body had been found on a Saturday night. Perhaps she was a day early.

Well, there was no leaving now. She daren't risk the killer arriving just minutes after she'd left. She would stay the night, until dawn if necessary. But if no one came, then she would tell Cameron after all. She would just have to convince him. And they could have a whole undercover team out there the next night. Catch him red-handed. Or even better, not-yet-red handed, the fourth victim, whoever she might have been, safely making her way home unmolested by the killer Warwick had finally caught.

The night dragged on, and Warwick started trying to figure out the best way to convince the inspector.

* * *

Maggie had spent the rest of Friday trying to track down details as to where the latest murder had taken place. 'The docks' was both a rather large area and hardly the sort of place one would want to just go to and start asking questions. She had finally found some details in the afternoon papers—for example, the victim's name was 'Annie Gwyer'—but by the time she had done so, the sun had already begun setting. The solstice was two days away and a three o'clock sunset was one indication of that. Having discovered that the girl's body had been found behind a bar called 'The Rusty Spike' also did not encourage her to rush down there after dark. She could go again in the morning, discretely collect a few samples from the alleyway, and return home. Besides, the police were that much more likely to have left by tomorrow morning. There would still be plenty of time to contact Sgt. Warwick before the next murder Sunday night. Well, maybe not plenty of time, but enough time anyway.

She woke up early Saturday morning. She had deliberately avoided the magic and had enjoyed a peaceful night's rest. In short order, she was showered, dressed and ready for breakfast. Looking in the mirror, she fixed the clasp to her necklace behind her head and tucked her silver clan crest pendant into her sweater. 'BE..AIST,' she read. *'Be Traist,'* she thought.

* * *

The docks weren't as scary as she had imagined, but then it was early. Not that anyone was directly threatening her, but it was a little dirtier than she was used to, a little more industrial than she was used to, and a little more run-down than she was used to. Even in the early morning sunshine she felt out-of-place and vulnerable. So she lowered her head, kept her stride purposeful, and tried not to look anyone in the eye. Of course, there weren't really any eyes to look into, even if she'd wanted to. The few longshoreman she saw were busy loading freight onto ships, entirely oblivious to her presence. And the man she saw passed out in a doorway was, well, passed out in a doorway, and therefore appeared to be of minimal threat. She picked up her pace. She just had a short ways to go from the bus stop and she would be at where the paper had said the bar was.

Sure enough, she found the bar. And sure enough, she found the alley behind the bar. And sure enough, some worker in a greasy apron was washing the entire alleyway down with a hose.

"Stop!" Maggie yelled without thinking.

The worker turned and looked at her, but did not in fact stop.

"'Ow's that, love?" he asked, still spraying any hope of a divining sample down a nearby grating.

"What—" Maggie had to follow up now. "What are you doing?"

The man looked down at the hose for a second, wondering perhaps if it looked different somehow than he would have expected. Satisfied that it looked precisely as it ought to, he looked up again at Maggie. "I'm 'osing down the alley's what. What's it to you?"

A fair question, Maggie thought. "Isn't this were that girl was murdered?"

"Aye," he answered. "The police just okayed 'osing down the alley. Was starting to smell rather bad, it was. And Jamie—Mr. Lancaster—wanted it cleaned up as soon as possible. 'Bad fer business,' 'e said."

"I'd imagine so," Maggie replied, still watching the dirty water run down the grating. The man returned to the side to side sweeping motion she had first observed. Very effective is cleaning the street, she noticed.

"So who the 'ell are you, anyway?" he demanded.

"Er—" That was an even better question; one she had not anticipated. But she was getting pretty quick on her feet. "I'm Caroline. I'm a distant cousin of Annie's. From America."

The man narrowed his eyes and looked Maggie over with a scrutinizing glance. "Annie never mentioned no relatives in the States," he stated flatly.

"Well, like I said. We're distant cousins, me and Annie Gwyer," she felt the need to say the girl's full name to bolster her credibility. She wasn't sure it worked. "The, uh, police contacted me. About the body. Funeral arrangements and all that, you know."

Apparently he didn't. He just stared at her, the water from the hose falling to the pavement in a shimmering arc.

"Do you know where they took her body?" She asked. Maybe she could still get a sample...

He stared at her for a few more seconds. "No," he said finally.

Maggie frowned, half at the answer, half in thought. "Do you know anyone who would?"

The man joined her frown. "Maybe some of 'er friends from

the club. They should be in tonight, if you want to come back. Club opens at seven."

"Seven, huh?" Maggie was ready to get out of there. "Thanks. Maybe I'll be back tonight. Thanks."

"Uh-huh," the man replied and watched her walk the few steps back to the street and around the corner out of sight.

Seven o'clock, eh? Maggie walked quickly back toward the bus stop. Seven o'clock would be well after sunset. She wondered whether Sgt. Warwick would just take her word for it that this murder wasn't related to the others.

Probably not.

She had some thinking to do.

46. Decision

The police wouldn't believe her without proof of some sort, Maggie decided. So rather than marching into the police station and demanding to speak with Sgt. Warwick, she instead wandered around the college most of the rest of the morning, trying to figure out what to do. She was in a catch-22. She didn't feel she could approach the police without more information, but she didn't know how to get more information without approaching the police. The only solution seemed to be to get some access to the girl's body, or at least her belongings, and confirm whether or not this murder completed the spell. If it did, going to the police was probably moot. If it didn't, going to the police would be imperative. Tomorrow was Sunday.

The problem of course lay in returning to the docks after dark. She hadn't been comfortable there even in the day time. And so she spent the rest of the morning searching her imagination for alternatives. She could approach Warwick directly and ask for access to the body. That request seemed unlikely to be granted, however, since she had already been turned down once, and that had simply been an offer to help, not a request to be alone with a murder victim's corpse. She could ask Iain or Ellen to help, but they would think she was crazy. If only that worker hadn't washed everything down the drain.

After a sparse lunch at a café, Maggie went to the library and found a secluded study carrel in one of the lower levels. There she poured over the spellbook trying to find a spell she might have overlooked. One that would confirm whether the summoning spell could be completed early. Or one that would enable her to learn more about the murder without physical samples from the crime scene. But her efforts proved fruitless, and after several hours of frustrating search, she emerged, even less sure of what to do than before.

She found herself winding her way slowly toward the police station without even realizing it, becoming aware of her position only once the precinct came into view. She even paused for a moment at the front steps of the station, only to turn away again and continue walking down the street. She had nothing to offer but speculation, and she had not forgotten Sgt. Warwick's threat, however empty, to arrest her for interfering with a murder investigation. She walked away from the station and tried to remind herself that she still had one more day.

She looked at her watch. It was nearly 2:45 and the sky was already beginning to dim. She had two choices. Go home, knowing that she would likely not go out again that night. Or stay out, find someplace to sit for a few hours, and at least keep open the possibility of returning to the docks that evening after seven.

She looked up the street toward the bus stop for the ride back to the MacTary's. Then she looked down the street at the direction from whence she came, the direction back to the college. She thought for several moments, then sighed heavily, and decided.

Maggie turned back toward the college.

* * *

The Boar and Thistle was hopping. Maggie had found a table prior to the rush and had finally supplemented her rootbeer orders with fish and chips once it had become clear that she was wasting the establishment's money by just sitting there while perfectly good dinner patrons were waiting to be seated. By the time she had finished her dinner, it was after eight o'clock.

The Rusty Spike had been open for over an hour. And yet there she sat.

She was still waiting for some other alternative to present itself. The one that would enable her to convince the police that there would be another murder tomorrow night without requiring her to head into one of Aberdeen's seediest neighborhoods after dark. Not surprisingly, this option did not walk into the pub and pull up a chair next to her.

Iain, however, did.

"Hello, Maggie!" he beamed as he sat down at her table. "How are you then?"

"Oh, hi, Iain," Maggie replied lethargically. Her mind was definitely elsewhere. Ordinarily she would have loved to see Iain. Now he was just a distraction. "Fine thanks. And you?"

"Well enough," he replied with a smile. "What happened Thursday?"

Maggie turned to look at him. She wasn't exactly sure what he'd said. "Thursday?"

"Aye, Thursday," Iain smiled good-naturedly. "We had plans, I believe?"

Oh, that's right. She had completely forgotten.

"Oh, Iain, you're right," she touched his hand. "I'm sorry. I forgot. I—I've had a lot on my mind the last couple of days."

Weeks, Iain wanted to correct, but thought better of it.

"No harm done," he shook it off. "And let me know if I can help out any. I haven't had much on my mind at all lately. Except you, of course."

Maggie smiled. It was a smile mixed with irritation at the sickly sweet clinginess of that comment, appreciation that he was trying to be nice, pleasure at the thought of him thinking of her, and exasperation at him interrupting her at this precise moment.

"That's all right," she replied. "I think I'll manage."

She looked at her watch. It was approaching eight-thirty. A decision was about to be made, one way or the other. Either she got up soon and went out to the docks, or it would be entirely too late to do so and she would have missed her opportunity.

"So, have you eaten already?" Iain looked around for a waiter. "We could grab a bite here or—"

"Look," Maggie interrupted. "I can't really do this right now. I have to go."

Iain was surprised. "Go? Where?"

"Out," was the curt reply.

"Out?" Iain's brow creased as he looked out the darkened window. "But it's dark out now. You shouldn't be out alone in the dark. Not with that madman on the loose. Did you hear, another girl was killed Wednesday night?"

Maggie looked him right in the face and tried not to smack him across it. "Yes," she said flatly, "I know."

"Well, then," Iain stood up. "Let me come with you."

Maggie smiled. A weak, tired smile. "No. That's all right, Iain. Thanks anyway. I'll be all right."

It was one thing to drag Iain to Glenninver and the stone circles. A little local interest. Doing the tourist thing. Easy enough to explain.

"No, really. I'll come along."

"No, really, Iain. Thank you anyway."

It's entirely different to be slinking around back alleyways and seedy nightclubs looking for fragments of some dead girl's hair or clothes. And anyway, if I do find something, I'll need privacy to do the divining spell.

"I insist." Iain crossed his arms.

"No, Iain." Her tone was flat but firm. She was really just too stressed out for this. He need to back off.

"I'm coming with you." It was a challenge as much as a statement.

Maggie had had it. She had tried to be nice. She had tried to spare his feelings. But there was no way in hell Iain was coming along with her while she tried to track down the body and belongings of a girl murdered at the Aberdeen docks.

"No!" she barked back.

Iain's brows raised and his eyes shot around to see whether anyone else had noticed Maggie's shout. They had.

"Look, here, Iain Grant! You are *not* coming with me! I am my own person, and I don't need you to chaperone my every move!"

Iain raised his hands gently in an effort to get her to lower her voice, but it was too late.

"And you don't own me just because of one stupid kiss! Now, just back off, okay?!"

Iain just stared at her, dumbstruck.

"Okay?!" she demanded.

"Okay."

"Good!" She was angry, and now she was angry at herself for yelling like that. And angry at Iain again for making her have to. Why couldn't he have just left her alone that night? Why couldn't he have just taken no for an answer? She just needed to get out of there. Without a further word, she stormed out the door into the cold black Aberdeen night.

Iain Grant stared after her, wondering what exactly had just happened. Then he looked around the pub. He noticed some of the lads in the back pointing at him and having a good laugh. He could feel the blood rush to face in embarrassment. And anger. He hadn't deserved that. He was just trying to be nice. To protect her. And she went off and embarrassed him like that? She ought not to have done that.

"I could use a pint over here," he called out to the bartender.

"I expect you could, mate," chuckled the bartender and he turned to pour Iain his beer, stopping to say something to one of the busboys who then laughed and looked over at Iain.

She really ought not to have done that.

47. Action

"Are you sure this will work?" Willis' voice was hushed, but not quite enough so.

"Yes," was Warwick's one word reply.

They sat in an unmarked car just a few hundred feet up the road from the tree where she had found the key. The sun had set several hours ago but still no one had come by. Warwick was beginning to wonder whether maybe she had been wrong again about the day. Kelly Anderson's body had been discovered around seven o'clock. But it was already past 9:45 and no one—no one at all—had even so much as passed the tree. She was starting to get worried.

Willis, on the other hand, was clearly excited. The stake-out was an opportunity to do something other than the paperwork Cameron constantly shoveled his way. Willis was a nice enough fellow, just not terribly bright, and irritating in large doses. Warwick had often wondered how he'd made sergeant.

But at least Willis believed her that the killer would come soon to fetch the key. She hadn't told him the whole story of course—about Maggie Devereaux and her psychic visions. Warwick had a reputation in the office for cool-headedness and intelligence. Basing important investigatory decisions on the imagination of a young American college student would not help to perpetuate that reputation. But when her hand wrapped around that cold, slimy key in that knothole yesterday afternoon, she knew that Maggie Devereaux had been right. The key had to belong to the killer. There was no other reason a bus locker key—number '99' to boot—would be lying hidden away in a tree knothole just outside the bus station. Sherlock Homes had once told Dr. Watson, once you've eliminated the impossible, whatever remains, however improbable, must be true. And however improbable it was that Maggie Devereaux had really seen a vision of the killer tucking the key away in a tree knothole, Warwick was left with the truth of the key's presence there. So apart from Maggie's willfully misleading the police—a serious offense which Warwick didn't believe the girl would attempt—the only explanation that remained was that the killer had in fact hidden it there.

That was enough for Warwick. And ultimately it had been enough for Cameron.

Not that convincing him was easy. He had not liked Maggie Devereaux when the girl had first offered to help. He was even less impressed now that Warwick was asking for four men to help follow up on the girl's tip. But he too had had to concede that the coincidence was uncanny. In the end that was what had swayed him. That and the fact that despite all his feet-dragging and posturing to the contrary, he too was desperate to solve the killings. And he'd finally gotten desperate enough to take a chance.

But Maggie Devereaux had better hope she was right, otherwise she'd find herself in the precinct tomorrow morning answering questions about why she'd planted a key in a tree knothole and wasted the time of six of Aberdeen's finest.

'Tomorrow morning' because it was already getting dark and Cameron wasn't going to let another night pass without following up on the one lead they seemed to have found. And 'six' because Cameron was coming too.

"So explain to me again how this is going to work," Willis piped up. Ordinarily Warwick might have thought such a question betrayed either the speaker's lack of confidence in the plan, or his desire to engage in pedantic small talk while they waited with luke warm coffee and no food. But this was Willis—he really didn't understand.

"The Inspector," she sighed, "is inside the bus station, with a few of the boys, all in civilian clothes. Once the killer comes and fetches the key, we radio the Inspector inside with a description. We know it's locker number 99, so they'll wait for him to turn the key, then they'll grab him."

Willis frowned. "And the murder weapons are in the locker?"

"That's what we think."

Willis looked at his hands for a moment. "Why don't we just nab him out here once he's grabbed the key?" he asked.

Warwick rolled her eyes. "And charge him with what? Unlawful possession of a bus locker key? He'll just claim he was looking for acorns or something and found the key accidentally. And we'll have no proof to the contrary; nothing to connect him to the murders."

She paused and stared at the tree. "No, we need to wait until he opens that locker and has the murder weapons in his guilty little hand." She smiled. "Then, finally, we'll have him."

Just then a man walked into their view. Something about him made Warwick's hair stand up on end as he strolled up.

"Okay, but what—" Willis' mouth was suddenly clamped

shut by Warwick's hand. She pointed at the figure. Willis nodded silently.

The man walked past the bus station and slowed down as he approached the row of trees. He didn't appear to notice the officers in their darkened car. He looked over his shoulder, but only once. Once was all it would take. There was absolutely no one else about. Apparently inter-city buses were not terribly popular on Saturday nights. Unless you needed to be somewhere first thing on a Sunday morning. Or you wanted to fish a locker key out of a tree knothole.

The man stopped at the seventh tree. Warwick's heart pounded. She could see he was tall, but that was about it. Dark hair, she thought, but hard to tell in the night. Not surprisingly, the seventh tree was not well illuminated by the streetlamps— undoubtedly why it had been chosen. Warwick's eyes widened as the man quickly stepped over to the tree and in one swift motion reached up into the knothole then whirled and started back toward the bus station.

Warwick was on her radio immediately.

"Inspector, the suspect just grabbed the key and is heading your way. Description: he's tall, maybe 6'2", medium build, dark hair, wearing a long black or dark-colored overcoat."

She reflected on the inadequacy of the description. "Sorry. That's the best I can do. But he's got the key."

* * *

She had not expected a neon sign. She wasn't sure why, maybe because it was 'the docks,' but Maggie had imagined a weathered, old, painted wood sign, hung perpendicular to the building and swaying heavily in the breeze. Instead her eyes were filled with glowing purple letters that spelled, 'The Rusty Spike.'

It was late, after ten o'clock. Apparently the city busses switch to a reduced schedule on Saturday evenings. Once an hour.

And she had missed the 8:40 bus thanks to Iain. She considered going home to fetch her bike, but she doubted Alex and Lucy would have let her out again, not with the most recent murder so fresh in their memories. They didn't own her, but by the time she got home, spoke with them, waited for them to go to bed, and then sneaked out again, it would have been even later than it already was. This way, she could go ahead and be an idiot with Alex and Lucy tucked safely away in their beds, with no idea where she might be.

Maybe, Maggie thought as she gazed at the tavern across the street, *this isn't such a great idea after all.*

She had expected to be a little scared by the men hanging around a bar down by the docks on a Saturday night. It had not occurred to her that she would be frightened by the women as well. In front of the club's entrance stood four people: a rather large and hairy man dressed in a black leather motorcycle outfit, and three women any one of whom could easily have beaten up Maggie—and probably most of the men Maggie had ever dated. All at the same time. They sported long dirty-looking hair, various items of leather clothing and the tightest jeans Maggie had ever seen. She looked down at her own L.L. Bean *vêtements* and shook her head.

Well, I came to Scotland for new experiences, she thought. *And I've never been beat up before.*

She looked up at the sky. Not a cloud, and it was freezing cold as a result. The stars were pin-pricks in the blue ink sky, but she couldn't see as many stars as she'd have liked thanks to the light pollution from the city. She instinctively looked for the moon, but it wasn't risen yet. She was not yet an expert on the moon, but if it was going to be new tomorrow night then Maggie expected it would be the thinnest crescent of a waning moon tonight. That would be pretty. She wondered when it would rise.

She looked across the street again. One of the women had

left, only to be replaced by two tall men.

Okay, Devereaux, she swallowed hard. *Time to put up or shut up.* And she crossed the street.

She had expected some type of comments from the patrons hanging near the door, maybe even a confrontation, or, God forbid, something physical. But they let her pass unmolested, just staring at her like she was wearing nothing but a smile and a sombrero. This was a pleasant surprise. She could save her adrenaline for once she got inside. She might need it. She grabbed the ornate metal handle on the wooden door and pushed.

* * *

The Aberdeen bus station did in fact bear a striking similarity to a train station. It was large, institutional, and filled with people who wanted to be somewhere else. On one wall hung a mural painted by someone who obviously had not been willing to take the time to obtain any formal art training. Taupe splotches melted behind brightly colored slashes of oil paint. On the opposite wall were the lockers.

There was just the one wall of them, six lockers high and twenty rows across. 120 lockers total. Some, those not in use, still had their keys sticking out of the locks. Others, whose patrons had deposited the coins necessary to free the key, were locked shut, their contents hidden from prying eyes and dishonest hands. Locker 99 had no key in its lock.

Inspector Cameron sat on a bench under the mural. He was reading a worn copy of a paperback—he had always felt reading a newspaper was too obvious, particularly at night—and he had a small bag tucked against his side. He looked like any other traveler waiting for a bus at this late hour. In truth, there were not more than a dozen people in the station, not counting staff of course, and of those twelve, four of them were employed by the Aberdeen

Police Department. But they were undercover and indistinguishable from the other travelers, save the small radio receiver each wore in one ear. And it was through these radio receivers that each had heard Sgt. Warwick's description. She had been right, her description had been somewhat generic, but the added information that the key was for locker 99 would make it possible for the officers to effectuate an arrest.

Their quarry entered the station. Cameron looked up casually and saw a tall man, easily 6'4", with dark brown hair and a long black overcoat buttoned up against the cold. He just looked guilty. And Cameron allowed himself to become just the slightest bit excited at the prospect that maybe they had finally, finally caught up with the killer.

Quick glances shot discretely among the four officers and they watched as the man, carrying no luggage, walked slowly toward the lockers. He put one hand into a coat pocket and they waited for him to pull it out again, key glinting in his hand. He was walking toward the right half of the lockers, those from 61 to 120. Cameron stood up and tucked his book into a pocket on his bag. The bag was filled with rags and he wasn't even really reading the book. Let somebody steal it. He walked toward the lockers.

The man stopped before the lockers and looked around quickly. He couldn't see Cameron approaching from behind and the other officers had been smart enough to watch only with peripheral vision as other matters ostensibly held their attentions.

The man then shrugged slightly and walked straight to locker number 99. Cameron could feel his heart race as the man shoved the key into the lock and turned it. The locker opened. He reached in and pulled out a black leather bag.

"Stop!" Cameron yelled out. The man turned around, fear in his eyes. "Don't move!"

Cameron grabbed the man's arm and spun him around.

"You're under arrest for the murders of Annette Graham, Fionna FitzSimmons, Kelly Anderson and Annie Gwyer!"

* * *

The interior of 'The Rusty Spike' was closer to what Maggie had expected. It was loud, dirty and filed with the stench of cigarette smoke and beer. It was packed with all kinds of people, the likes of whom Maggie had hoped never to meet. The waitresses scooted between tables wearing little more than their underwear and an apron. In the back of the dim club was a small stage with three women wearing even less and dancing for the enjoyment of the patrons.

Maggie walked to the bar.

She could feel the stares of the customers on her back. She just wanted to get her information and get out of there. The return bus to the college wasn't until 10:45, but she was more than willing to wait at the bus stop if need be.

The bartender spied her from the other end of the bar and slowly pushed himself up off the counter he was leaning on and trudged his large frame over to her. He had long blond hair tied back in a ponytail, three earrings in his left ear and tattoos that disappeared up his dirty shirt sleeves. When he arrived, he didn't say anything. He just looked at her.

"A beer, please?" she squeaked. If she was going to pump them for information she could at least buy something. Besides, just then the thought of a beer had its appeal.

The bartender grunted and quickly returned with a pint of something darker than what she was used to drinking.

"Er, thanks," she stammered.

The bartender grunted.

"And, er," Maggie looked at the very drunk old man next to

her, then back to the bartender, "can I ask you a question?"

The bartender didn't respond verbally, but crossed his arms and raised an eyebrow. At least he didn't walk away.

"I was wondering if I could talk to somebody about Annie. Annie Gwyer."

The bartender's other eyebrow raised at the dead girl's name. He looked at Maggie through narrowed eyes. "Annie?"

"Yes."

"Annie Gwyer?"

Maggie's palms were starting to sweat. "Yes."

The bartender didn't move. Finally he uncrossed his arms and leaned onto the bar directly in front of Maggie. She leaned back instinctively.

"And you are?" he asked, his breath stale, from his wares no doubt.

"Um," Maggie knew enough to be consistent with her earlier story. "I'm a cousin. From America. Distant cousin. And, er, I was over here on holiday when, um, it happened. And the police called me. And told me."

That was almost coherent, Devereaux.

"Uh-huh," the bartender said noncommittally. He had very large forearms.

"And so I was wondering," Maggie continued, "if I could talk to someone who knew about the, um, funeral arrangements. I'd like to attend."

"Uh-huh."

"The, um, police said she worked here?" Maggie looked around in demonstration, but then caught view of the 'dancers' in the back and quickly spun back around.

The bartender rubbed his nose vigorously while he scrutinized the small little American in front of him. Finally he said,

"I 'magine you'd want to ask down at the morgue."

Maggie smiled. "The morgue?"

"Aye." He looked her right in the eye. "Annie never mentioned no family."

Gulp.

"So," he went on, "I 'magine she'll likely get a pauper's funeral at the church tomorrow morn, it being Sunday and all."

"Okay, the morgue, huh? And where's that?"

"Do you know where the police station is?" *An interesting point of reference*, Maggie thought. "Well, from there..." and he explained the quickest route from police station to morgue. She decided not to ask how he knew that.

Maggie let out a quick little sigh of relief. She had gotten what she'd come for. Time to go. "Well, okay then. Thank you so much."

She stood to leave, reaching into her purse, past the spellbook, for her wallet so she could pay for the untouched beer.

"Say, lass?" The bartender crossed his arms again.

"Yes?" Maggie's eyes widened. She could always just run for the door...

"You say the police contacted you?"

"Yes," it was almost a question.

"If that's so, then why did you no ask them where Annie was going to be buried?"

Uh-oh.

* * *

"What?!" yelled the priest.

Cameron had not seen the telltale white priest's collar when the man had walked in; he'd had his jacket pulled up around his neck. But now the collar and its owner stared at him in dumbfounded amazement.

"What did you say?" the priest asked again.

"Oh, dear God. Forgive me, Father." Cameron had said that before in his life. "I'm afraid we've made a terrible mistake."

He looked down at the bag the priest had in his hand.

"The bag—?" Cameron asked weakly. It wasn't completely outside the realm of possibility that the priest was the killer. Unlikely, but he did have to confirm it.

The priest looked down at the satchel in his hand. "This?" he asked.

"Yes, Father. May we look inside?"

The priest drew himself up. He was trying not to be insulted, but he had not gone to seminary to be accused of murder, particularly not late at night in bus stations.

"Of course," he replied and opened the bag himself. It was filled with several dozen small red books. "They're Bibles. I'm taking a bus to Glasgow tonight. I'm visiting an orphanage first thing tomorrow morning and these are for the children. I locked them away while I ran out for a bite to eat."

"Bibles?" He was going to kill Warwick. She and her damned American psychic. "Glasgow?"

The priest shrugged. "Yes. The diocese thought it would be more frugal if I took an overnight bus and slept on the way. With the money we saved, we were able to buy Bibles for all the children."

Cameron closed his eyes and took a deep cleansing breath. "Of course, Father. Quite good of you." He shook his head in mortification. "Sorry to have bothered you. Have a good trip."

The priest just smiled, bewildered. "Thank you."

"Come on, boys," Cameron announced with a wave of his upraised hand. "Let's go."

He and the other three officers gathered up and walked back

out into the cold clear moonless evening.

And in the corner of the bus station, in the shadows near the restrooms, stood a tall dark figure, who looked down into the palm of a wet hand, where sat the cold, slimy key to locker 66.

* * *

"The police?" Maggie hadn't anticipated that question. It was a good one. "Yeah, well, I talked to the police. But they weren't really very helpful."

That much was true. Sort of.

"Thanks anyway, though," and she pulled out her wallet. The bartender walked away and she finally found a banknote inside her pocketbook. Setting it under the still full beer glass she turned to leave.

"Hey!" she heard from behind her. "Hey you, lass!"

She stopped. *Probably better to see him coming.* She turned around.

She had expected to see either the large bald bartender or someone else equally mammoth. Instead, she was staring almost directly into the eyes of a very short, very angry, and most likely very drunk man. He had very short bleached blond hair, several rings in various parts of his face, and tattoos up and down his bare and very strong looking arms. He also had a two long red welts down the side of his neck from his right ear.

"Yes?" Maggie gulped.

"You're nosin' 'round 'bout Annie?" he demanded.

"I was just asking a couple of questions," she replied as calmly as the heart in her throat would allow. Surely he wouldn't punch a girl. *No, he's probably got girlfriends to do that for him.* She looked around his shoulder to see who might get the honor of beating her up, but saw no one who immediately fit the bill. She did notice however that most of the customers had turned to watch the excitement.

"Don't lie to me, lass!" barked the strong little man. "Annie ain't had no fam'ly. 'Specially not no Yanks. She was me girl, so she'd bloody well a' told me if she had." He narrowed his eyes and leaned into her face. "Who the bloody hell are you?"

"Er, Maggie Devereaux," she replied without really thinking. Her fear was actually fading. Somehow she almost liked the confrontation. So she added, "And you are?"

His eyes flared at this. "Look 'ere, lass. You don't want to start nosin' 'bout where you don't belong. It's a sure way o' endin' up hurt. Badly hurt." He cracked his knuckles.

Maggie imagined using the levitation spell to throw Mr. Annie's-Boyfriend across the room. It was a pleasant image, but she thought better of it.

"Fine," she said firmly. "I'll just be going then."

"You damn well better, you Yank bitch!"

Maggie looked at him through narrowed eyes. *I wonder if I could get that transmutation spell to work. How did that go again—a pillar of salt?* But instead she turned and walked out the door.

"You all right, Johnny?" asked the bartender to the little man.

"Aye, I'm damn well all right!" he yelled back. "Give me another bloody pint!"

Johnny sat down at the bar and snatched his beer from the bartender. He gripped it tightly and stared at the door where Maggie Devereaux had just exited, his chest rising and falling with his angry breaths.

The other patrons returned to their conversations, or to something else to distract their attention. But in the back of the club, sitting largely unnoticed by the other patrons, another man was also staring at the door where Maggie Devereaux had just exited. Unlike Johnny, his breathing was controlled and even as he stood up and laid several bills on the table. He pulled on a very stylish overcoat, which only punctuated the fact that he was dressed considerably better than the other regulars at the bar. In this way he seemed rather out of place. The only thing that would have indicated that this well-dressed man who was making his way to the exit somehow fit in with the pierced, tattooed and hardened crowd of the tavern, was the single untidy scar running down the length of his left cheek.

48. The Morgue

The 10:45 never came. Maggie had arrived at the bus stop well before then, and had waited until after eleven o'clock, but no bus. So she pulled her coat tight around her, swung her book-laden purse over both shoulders and started walking, her misty breath trailing behind her. She probably should have called for a ride, but how was she going to explain being down at the docks at eleven o'clock at night? Alex and Lucy were probably asleep. Iain was probably still mad at her. She could have called Ellen, she supposed, but again, how did she explain? It wasn't that long of a walk, and it would give her time to think.

She looked up. Still no moon.

She wasn't walking home of course. Not directly anyway. She didn't even know the direct way home. She had taken a bus from the college and so was following that trail back. Once at the college she would know her way home. Maybe she could call for a ride from there. The college was more centrally located, and it wouldn't seem strange at all for her to be there late on a Saturday night. She would reach the college no later than midnight, she figured. What with the stop by the morgue.

The morgue was close to the college. Close enough that she could swing by it on her way back. The bartender had said Annie Gwyer would receive a pauper's funeral tomorrow and her body was most likely housed at the morgue for the night. Maggie supposed she could stop by in the morning, but the funeral was probably pretty early. Even with no family to mourn her, Maggie still didn't think the priest would appreciate an ancient pagan divining spell being cast during his eulogy.

Of course, the morgue was probably closed. Although maybe not. Did morgues close? Hospitals don't, and she supposed the people who died there needed to be put somewhere. She really had no idea. So it was at least worth a try.

The walk alone in the dark was a bit spooky. More than once she thought she heard footsteps behind her, only to whirl around and face an entirely empty sidewalk. She was just a little jittery. The short man at the bar had gotten her worked up and she was a little nervous at the idea of going to a morgue in the middle of the night. If she hadn't been so sure the murder would happen the next night she never would have been outside alone. But she *was* sure, and whenever she got a little bit too scared, or started to think she was crazy for what she was trying to do, she just replayed Iain's voice in her head: '*Some poor girl's going to be next if they don't catch this lunatic soon. I think maybe you'd have that girl's death on your head a bit if you could've helped, but didn't.*'

* * *

The morgue was easy enough to find. The bartender, for all his angry demeanor and inquisition, had given her quite good directions. Not surprising that he had related its position to the police station. No doubt he'd spent some time at the police station. Of course, so had Maggie.

Any building can be scary enough at night, Maggie

supposed as she approached the structure. Even the warmest homes can take on a foreboding appearance in the elongated shadows and half light of the night. The Aberdeen City Morgue was no exception. The word 'MORGUE' carved above the doorway sent an involuntary shiver up her spine.

Maggie paused at the end of the walk.

What the hell are you thinking, Devereaux? The morgue? The morgue?! At night? She looked around. No one else in sight.

So why did she feel like she was being watched?

Probably just nerves. What with walking into a morgue as it approached midnight and all. She wondered: if they were open, would there be a receptionist? *What kind of weirdo could work as the night receptionist at a morgue?* She didn't want to know. But she was very likely about to find out.

Maggie climbed the seven stone steps to the heavy wooden door of the morgue. There were lights on inside, but they were dim. It looked more like the lights any business left on overnight; not the brightness someone would need to work by. Except maybe a weirdo night receptionist at a morgue.

Okay, Maggie took a deep breath. *You're freaking yourself out here. Just take a deep breath.*

She still felt like someone was watching her. Time to get inside. She put her hand on the doorknob. What if the morgue was closed? What then? Would she still try to force her way in? She really needed to get access to a sample from Annie Gwyer. But she wasn't sure breaking and entering was the way to go. It was important, but not that important.

Her hand still rested on the doorknob. She considered her alternatives.

Finally she decided to just turn the knob. If it opened, then she could go in. If not, then she'd come back first thing in the morning and hope she could see the body before the funeral. That would still give her several hours to convince Sgt. Warwick.

Maggie looked around. She took a deep breath. She tried not to think about the weirdo receptionist hiding behind the door. She turned the doorknob.

It was open.

Wow. She was genuinely surprised. The door swung open with a predictable groan and, after checking that no one was behind the door, she scurried inside. The heavy door closed behind her with a gentle thud.

Inside the morgue, the lights were on, but dimmed. The front desk was abandoned—apparently the receptionist didn't work nights after all. The hallways were green linoleum flooring with light green painted walls. Very institutional. It made Maggie's stomach queasy. That and a faint smell she couldn't identify and wouldn't have wanted to anyway. She just needed to get the samples and get out of there.

So if I were a dead body, where would I be?

Actually, the morgue wasn't that large. She wandered around the first floor and confirmed it held nothing but offices. There was a stairwell which gave her the option of up or down. She chose down. If she were in charge of the morgue, the bodies would definitely be in the basement, not upstairs. She wasn't sure why, but she knew that made more sense. She descended the stairs into the dark basement below.

The basement had even fewer lights on than the first floor. Only every third ceiling lamp was on down the long green hallway which stretched out to her right and left. Choosing at random, she turned right and walked toward the dimly lit room she could make out at the end of the hall. Her footsteps echoed off the walls, even in her soft-soled shoes. It wasn't that far to the end of the hallway, but it sure seemed like it to her.

The room turned out to be an examining room, if that's what they called it. Three metal tables stood side by side, like lifts at an auto-body garage. To one side was a tray with several brutal looking instruments lying on top of it. In the corner, Maggie saw a what looked remarkably like a chain saw.

Well, she supposed with a shudder, *it's not like they have to sew them up again.*

In any event, there were no bodies in there just then, and no personal effects either. Just the silver metal tables, the torture instruments, and a log book of some sort sitting on a small counter by the door.

Log book?

Maggie picked it up. She flipped through it quickly and confirmed that it appeared to be a record of each time they had removed a body from storage. The last page had the following entry:

'12/21. Gwyer. Out 1015. Returned 1145. C-3.'

C-3, huh? Sounds like a locker number.

She turned and headed back down the hallway.

Now, silence can play tricks on a person's hearing. It's not normal for the ear to pick up no sounds at all. It's designed to hear things, not to not hear things. That's why when it's really quiet, people hear a high pitched ringing in their ears. It's the brain trying to put a label on the silence the ear is hearing. And in the confines of a Scottish morgue on a dark night, a person's mind can play even more tricks with the silence. So when Maggie thought she heard the faintest muffled thud from upstairs, she stopped dead in her tracks.

Had she heard it? Or not? She stood stock still and strained to hear something, anything, against the silence. Nothing. She waited some more. Still nothing. Finally she decided that there had been no noise at all, that her ears had just been teasing her.

Either that or the weirdo receptionist forgot her purse.

Maggie finished walking down the long hallway, past the stairs—her only way out, she noted—and to the room at the other end of the hall. That strange smell was strongest here. It was obviously the storage room. One entire wall was filled with handled doors that looked remarkably like the fronts of file cabinet drawers, only larger. There were seven columns: A, B, C, D, E, F and G. And three drawers per column: 1, 2 and 3.

A brief scan of the wall quickly revealed drawer C-3: three columns over and nearest the floor.

She walked over to it and placed her fingers on the handle. It was cool to the touch. *Refrigeration,* she deduced. She couldn't believe what she was about to do. She strained again to hear any noise from out in the silent morgue.

Nothing.

Okay, then. Here goes.

She yanked on the drawer. It gave only slightly at first but then rolled all the way open with a low squeak. And Maggie stared down at a turquoise sheet that covered what must have been the remains of Annie Gwyer.

Maggie had expected a stronger odor somehow, but the combination of formaldehyde and refrigeration probably kept decomposition to a minimum. The coroner probably didn't enjoy the smell of rotting flesh either.

She crouched down next to the drawer. Pulling her purse around, she removed the spellbook and opened it to the divining spell. Might as well just do it now. She had privacy anyway. Taking a deep breath to steel herself, she pulled back the sheet covering the contents of drawer C-3.

When she had finished vomiting in the corner, Maggie

crawled back to the drawer, careful to keep her eyes fixed squarely on her spell book, the floor, or really anything other than the human remains in the drawer. Reaching a tender hand up to the retracted sheet, she pulled it again over the corpse's face. Refrigeration or no, it had been several days since the tissue had died, and in that time the coroner had obviously used several of his more invasive tools to inquire into the cause of death. Maggie sat down on the cool floor and tried not to vomit again.

After several minutes, she began to feel better. The silence was still ringing in her ears, so she tried to focus on that to distract her from the smell in her nostrils and the gory vision still dancing before her eyes.

Okay, Devereaux, she told herself. *Just hurry up and get it over with. Then you can go the hell home.*

She had deliberately not pulled the sheet all the way up again. The curly blond hair still stuck out from under the teal sheet. Hair had worked before; it would certainly work again. She grabbed hold of several hairs and tugged slightly. They gave way with absolutely no resistance, and a small wet sound. Maggie felt her stomach flip over again, but she managed not to have to return to the vomit corner. She laid the hair out in front of her and spoke the spell. Damn the black smear it would leave on the floor.

The vision rose quickly from the hairs. It was of Annie. And the short angry man from the bar. Somehow that didn't surprise Maggie. The two were arguing. Both yelling at each other, although Maggie could hear no words. She could feel the anger and the hatred and the jealousy and the feelings of inadequacy and fear which swirled around the two figures. It felt like love might have been there once but had been corrupted into something sad and hopeless. They were in the alleyway Maggie had seen the worker hosing down. It was dark out. They were still yelling. Then she reached out and slapped him. He returned the slap with a punch, right to her mouth. She fell down, but he picked her up by the shoulders and hit her again. She clawed at his face and neck and he grabbed her around the throat. And shook. And shook. And shook again. And she stopped struggling. She went limp. He stopped shaking. He lowered her body onto the ground, its weight pulling her down faster than he could help. He stood over her body for a long time, looking around fretfully and running his hands through his short blond hair. Then, finally, he reached into his pocket and pulled out a knife. He kneeled down and cut open Annie's shirt. Then he crossed himself and pushed the knife into her abdomen.

Maggie let the vision fade. It was clearly not the same as the other murders. The short angry man had killed her accidentally, and wanted to cover it up. Now she had proof there would be another murder. Now maybe Sgt. Warwick would believe her. She pushed drawer C-3 closed again. It was time to go.

Maggie looked over at her vomit in the corner. She really didn't want people to know that anyone had been there. She wondered whether her DNA would be present in it. And more than that, it was undeniably inconsiderate to vomit in someone else's place of employment and not clean it up. On the other hand, she wasn't really sure how to clean it up. She hadn't brought a mop and bucket, and the tissue she had in her purse would undoubtedly prove inadequate.

She looked at the spellbook. Now was as good a time as any to try that transmutation spell again. She had wanted to turn the short angry man into a pillar of salt. Maybe she could turn her vomit into salt instead. That would be easy to clean up. Hell, she wouldn't even have to clean it up. They would always wonder how a pile of salt had ended up in the storage room, but they'd never suspect the truth. She turned to the transmutation spell.

She was always surprised by how difficult the spell appeared at first glance. But she had been working on it and thought she might be able to pull it off finally. The levitation spell had been difficult at first too. Maggie looked at the vomit. She pictured salt in her mind. And then she spoke the spell aloud, shattering the silence of the morgue.

Nothing happened. That didn't surprise Maggie, though. She was expecting to have to try a few times. She readied herself to try again.

That's when she heard it. The noise. A kind of metallic scrape which echoed down the hallway. No ears playing tricks now. She knew she heard it.

She stood up and ran for the stairs, purse in one hand, spellbook in the other. Damn the vomit. She made it to the stairs and began running up them two at a time. She wasn't really tall enough to do that, but she was flushed with adrenaline. At the top of the stairs she bolted straight for the heavy wooden doors. She had no idea if anyone was behind her or not. It didn't matter. All that mattered was pulling that damn door open and getting outside. The door groaned on its hinges and swung open slowly. Maggie squeezed through it and bolted out into the cold dark night, not bothering to close the door behind her. She was three blocks away before she finally slowed down. And another two blocks before she returned to a walk.

Panting heavily, her side bursting, Maggie doubled over and looked behind her. No one. *Thank God.*

She started walking again. She wasn't exactly sure which way to go. She looked up to get her bearings. The lights from the business district by the college were behind some houses to her left. Otherwise the sky was cold and dark. And there was still no moon to be seen.

Then she heard the clocktower at the college begin its chimes. Twelve bells. Twelve o'clock. It was tomorrow already. It was Sunday. The winter solstice. And the day of the new moon.

And that's when she heard the footsteps behind her.

49. Be Traist

The footsteps were crisp and quick. Maggie turned to look over her shoulder, but she couldn't see anyone in the bulbous shadows engulfing the street behind her. She lowered her head and walked faster. Her side still hurt too much to just take off running. Besides, she had no idea where she could go.

There wasn't another soul around on the residential street. Why couldn't there be someone—*anyone*—out and about? Surely someone's dog needed a walk. But there was no one there. And the footsteps were getting closer.

She turned around again. The footsteps stopped. She thought she saw a shadow duck into some hedges, but she couldn't be sure. Then a chill ran up her spine and she felt even more vulnerable just standing there looking.

As she hurried down the street again, she heard the footsteps return. It was one of those long European streets that had previously connected two important points in the city without giving any thought to being able to cut over to any third, somewhat less important point. Like the college, which was just a few hundred feet to her left, but blocked by a row of townhouses, each connected to the next, without even the smallest side yards to cut through.

And she couldn't turn around because that was where the footsteps were coming from. Her only chance was to speed ahead and hope she came to an alleyway to the college, or some other sanctuary.

The footsteps quickened as well.

Maggie's hurried walk turned into a light trot. She was glancing around feverishly looking for some house that looked safe to approach. She wanted one where a light was still on, so she wouldn't be standing still on a porch while hoping that someone would be awakened her knocking. But there were no lights on. Everyone on this sleepy residential street had retired for the night. There was no one to help her.

And the footsteps matched her trot.

Then Maggie saw it. Up ahead. It was the Catholic church she had stumbled upon during her walk just a few days earlier. Weren't Catholic churches always open? For Vesper services or something? Especially in a predominantly Catholic area like the Scottish Highlands? She hoped so.

The church was actually several hundred yards away, facing the next street over to her right. Undoubtedly the street she had been walking on the other day when she'd first seen the cathedral. But behind the church, and between her and its promise of safety, lay a large graveyard encircled by the iron fence next to her, its back gate just ahead and opening onto the quay she was trotting down now, her heart pounding and her ears ringing with the rush of blood and adrenaline.

The footsteps grew louder. And closer.

All she had to do was cut through the graveyard and enter the church from behind. There must be some back door to the church which would be open. Maybe there were even parishioners, or at least some nuns, inside at this time of night? She didn't know. But she knew the footsteps were right behind her now—close enough that if she did turn around, she'd see who it was, but it would be too late.

She ran to the graveyard fence as fast as she could.

She quickly raised the iron bar on the gate and slipped through it, sprinting into the dark. The footsteps also turned into a run and then fell silent as they too stepped off the pavement and onto the frozen grass of the graveyard.

Maggie dashed toward the church. She managed to twist and dodge around the various gravestones that stood in her way. The ground shifted eerily beneath her steps, unaccustomed to anything more than the somber gait of the mourning. She raced past a small marble mausoleum, which couldn't have housed more than two people. Beyond that stood the church.

Then she hit it. The black iron fence cordoning off the cemetery from the rest of the churchyard. She hadn't seen its black bars in the dark, and she grabbed her nose and forehead where she had smashed into its unforgiving rods. Her glasses were bent, too, but had not broken.

Damn! I've got to get out of here!

Her head snapped back violently. Her throat was crushed shut. She grabbed feebly at the cord wrapped around her neck, but it was already burying itself into her flesh, and whoever was cinching it closed was clearly much stronger than she—especially as her arms grew weak, and her lungs started to burn, and her vision faded as her brain was deprived of oxygen. There was nothing she could do. She couldn't scream, she couldn't breathe, and she knew it was only moments before she wouldn't be able to do anything ever again. Her hands and feet burned as the spots flashed in front of her bulging eyes.

Then she saw the short angry man flying across the dirty bar, and she had an idea. With her last vestige of energy she flailed at the man behind her and thought the levitation spell, picturing her assailant thrown clear of her.

Deprived of the ancient Gaelic words which gave it focus, but amplified by Maggie's fear and adrenaline, the spell burst forth from her weakening limbs and the cord went slack. Her attacker landed on the ground several feet away with an unceremonious "Uff!"

The air rushed back into Maggie's lungs. She pulled the garroting wire from around her throat and turned to face her attacker. He lay on his back still—was just sitting up. He wore a long black overcoat, which even in the dark of the graveyard betrayed its stains of blood. His hands were sheathed in similarly stained black gloves. He leaned over to one side and pushed himself to his feet, and as he rose to his full height Maggie finally got a look at his face.

It was Iain.

Maggie sprinted back the way she'd come, her side bursting. There was no time to find the gate to the church. Her feet raced almost as fast as her mind.

Iain? she thought incredulously. *It can't be Iain!* She ran on. *Can it—?*

As she passed the small mausoleum on her left, a hand darted out and grabbed her forearm, pulling her off balance and wrenching her to the ground. A second hand quickly covered her mouth and Maggie's big brown eyes looked up at the stone-cold visage of Devan Sinclair.

"Don't scream," he instructed.

Maggie nodded.

Sinclair removed his one hand from her mouth and jerked her brusquely to her feet with his other. "This way."

They quickly crept around to the other side of the

mausoleum, their backs to the wall and Sinclair's grip still tight on her arm. He let go only to pick up a shovel which lay discarded against the mausoleum wall. Maggie stared at him, but he was busy trying to see around the near corner of the small structure, his neck craning and the shovel bouncing in his hands like the bat of an on-deck hitter.

"It's Iain," Maggie whispered, her throat stinging—the wire had hurt. "He's summoning a demon." She knew if anyone would believe this last part, it was Devan Sinclair.

Sinclair didn't turn around. "It's not Iain."

This was not a reply she had expected. "What are you talking about?" she asked again in a raspy, hushed tone. "I saw him with my own eyes."

This time Sinclair turned to face her. His expression was a combination of worry and impatience. "Think, Maggie," he said. "Who will benefit the most from the demon taking a human host?"

But before Maggie could answer, Sinclair's question was transformed from Socratic to rhetorical as his head hit the mausoleum wall with a sharp crack. The shovel fell to the ground and his arms and body went slack as he slid down the wall into an untidy pile of unconscious bookseller. Maggie looked up and saw Iain perched on the roof of the mausoleum, his hand still dangling below the roof line where he had reached down to grab Sinclair's head and smash it into the stone wall. Then Iain jumped down to the ground, well in front of the shovel, and stood to face Maggie.

"Iain?" she pleaded. "It's me, Maggie."

Iain's face bore no expression. His only response was to take a single deliberate step toward her.

Maggie looked at the slumped form of Devan Sinclair. He would be of no help now. She returned her gaze to Iain in time to see him pull a long knife from his coat pocket. Maggie looked down. She still held the wire in her hand. It was the same wire she had seen in her visions. The same coat and gloves. The same knife. She looked at it again: it was a surgical scalpel. *What would Iain be doing with a scalpel? He's not a doctor.*

Maggie tried to corral the thousand thoughts racing through her mind. Hadn't she encountered a doctor recently?

Iain took another step toward her and raised the blade slightly.

"Iain?" she repeated, hoping her voice might snap him out of whatever fever possessed him. But he was not to be deterred. He took another step, and in response Maggie took a tentative step backward on the slippery lawn.

This doesn't make any sense, Maggie thought. *Why is Iain summoning a demon? Or is he just a psycho, adding the ritualistic part for show—for some kind of sick kick?*

She looked again at the man she had kissed just days before. His expression was inscrutable as he raised the knife still higher.

Why would he have killed Annette Graham? Uncle Alex was the one whose wife was being blackmailed by Annette. But Alex can't be the murderer. He was with me when Fionna was killed.

Iain took another sure step toward Maggie. He seemed in no hurry; if she turned to run he'd be on her in a heartbeat. Maggie took another step back and almost lost her balance as her foot slid across the icy grass.

And why did he kill Fionna? Sean might have done it, incensed with his sister's pregnancy. And Ellen had even thought at first that Will might have done it. But Sean disappeared after Fionna's murder. Was he even in Scotland when Kelly was killed? And hadn't Ellen said Will had been in London then?

Maggie scanned Iain's face. His expression was still distant, holding no recognition of her, but she thought she detected the faintest smile hidden in the corners of his eyes. He took two bold steps toward her, causing her to back up yet again and have to put her hand against the mausoleum for support.

And what about Kelly? Macintyre seemed like the one. He'd had the affair with her and stolen her research. But again, Macintyre had said he was in Amsterdam when Annette was killed. He couldn't be the murderer.

Then Maggie realized something else, something that defied the image which filled her panicked eyes.

Iain can't be the murderer either! He was with me the whole day when Kelly was killed! He couldn't *have killed Kelly Anderson!* And yet she knew the murders had been committed by the same twisted soul.

Sinclair. *The murders in Glenninver eighteen years ago.*

The scalpel. *Sinclair had called the old man in the shop 'Doctor.'*

Annette Graham. *Uncle Alex had told Aunt Lucy he'd gotten so drunk the night Annette was killed that he couldn't remember where he'd been—or what he'd done.*

Fionna. *Sean had been enraged at her pregnancy by an Englishman—and her contemplation of an abortion—but did he really have it in him to murder his own sister?*

Kelly. *Macintyre had the most to gain from her death, but what evil force could have driven the ivory-tower academic to murder?*

And then Maggie finally realized who would benefit the most from the demon taking a human host.

She didn't know if it would work. It's wasn't a spell in the spellbook, but she had obtained a good command of the dialect, and the levitation spell had worked against Iain even when she had been unable to speak it. Maybe she could channel the magic directly; maybe she could craft her own spell. She took one more step back on the slick grass—not in retreat, but to solidify her footing. She raised her hands. Iain raised the knife. He was coming this time. It had better work.

"*Liàch ó chorp Iain!*" she cried out.

Iain stumbled backwards at the words, then righted himself again. His face finally bore a recognizable expression: surprise. And urgency. He raised the knife again and lunged toward Maggie.

"*Liàch ó chorp Iain!*" she repeated. 'Leave Iain's body.'

The spell burst forth and grabbed Iain by the shoulders, driving him to his knees. A brilliant crimson glow shot forth from his chest and a pained grimace flashed across his contorted face.

"*Liàch ó chorp Iain!*" Maggie commanded.

The scarlet light was pulled fully forward out of Iain's chest and his body fell to the ground like a sack of potatoes, unconscious and only a few feet from Sinclair's similarly helpless form.

The massive red glow hovered in the air for a moment, then flared and slowly coalesced into a semi-solid shape. Before Maggie's eyes stood the most vile thing she had ever seen. It was easily nine feet tall, with a torso that could barely be distinguished from the head atop it, a large saliva covered affair filled with literally dozens of six-inch long razor sharp teeth. At least seven arms protruded from the torso, each with a claw as long as Maggie's leg. The sinewy body sat atop too long bony legs which bowed back like a horse's, only to meet the earth in splayed hooves with uneven, spiked nails protruding from them. A long, thick, reptilian tail swished expectantly behind the beast and leathery folds of what Maggie could only suppose were wings hung from its back. The effect was terrifying, and was only made worse by the fact that the entire form was glowing red and transparent. She could see the gravestones through its ethereal body.

Who will benefit the most from the demon taking a human host? Maggie stared up at the monstrosity before her. *The demon, of course.*

The demon let out a long, loud laugh—one that gurgled and churned in its thick, spit-soaked throat, and one that Maggie felt more than heard.

"Congratulations, Maggie Devereaux," its voice seared into her brain. "You have deduced my secret." She didn't hear the words so much as sense their meaning in her mind, the ideas boring directly into the language recognition centers of her brain. "But you have also miscalculated."

"Is that why you came after me? Because I was getting too close?"

The demon laughed again. "Do not flatter yourself. I simply needed a final victim to complete the spell. A final victim so I could permanently graft to a human host."

"Like Sinclair." Maggie finally understood. "Eighteen years ago."

"Yes," said the demonic voice, "but he had been too strong-willed. He was able to wrest his body back from my control after watching his parents die in a blaze set by his own hand. I've had to wait eighteen years for the moon and sun to be properly aligned again. Eighteen years of impotence—condemned to stalk this plane only able to possess humans for short periods, and only then if they were angry enough to be able to receive me."

"Like Uncle Alex."

"And Sean FitzSimmons and Craig Macintyre," the monstrosity confirmed. "Even that doctor I obtained the scalpel from. And I kept my," an evil pause, "'tools' in a place where I could access them no matter whose body I possessed."

Maggie looked down at Iain's prone form. Had he been angry too? At her?

"So tonight..." she pointed weakly toward Iain.

"So tonight I possessed Iain Grant. And his body would

remain mine once the spell was completed."

"Why Iain?!" Maggie demanded. "Why steal *his* body forever?"

The demon sneered at this display of concern and defiance.

"Anyone would have done—any strong, young man." Frothy drool fell to the ground. "And earlier tonight, when it came time to select my victim and my new host, I sensed a confrontation. I was drawn to you and Iain in the pub. You were yelling at him, embarrassing him in front of everyone. And after he'd done so much for you: driven you across Scotland and back, skipped work to be with you, and never once questioned your motives. And then you went and yelled at him. He was very embarrassed. And very angry. And very vulnerable to me."

Maggie was numb. The thought that she had been partially responsible for Iain's possession—and current helplessness—made her nauseous. She had had no right to yell at him like that. But she had had no idea it would come to this.

"So you would be my final victim," the demon continued. "I would graft onto Iain Grant and I would be able once again to play with this world and its inhabitants. But now," the mouth curved into something disturbingly similar to a smile as more saliva fell to the ground, "now I do not need a weak human flesh-bag as a host. I will have my own body. Your magic will make my body solid."

Maggie shook her head in incomprehension even as the monster pounded mutely on its contorted, scarlet chest. "I can feel it. Your one spell has given my form semi-permanence. You are of this world but wield the magic from mine. You are the bridge. You will bring me here. I will be free." Another guttural laugh escaped its throat as it looked down at its glowing, horrific body. "I will be unstoppable!"

Maggie just stood there, frozen.

"Come, Maggie. Use your magic. Make me real." It raised its hand and looked through its half-corporeal fingers. "If you do not," it kicked at Iain, whose form was jarred only somewhat by the foot that disappeared into his torso, "I am already real enough to kill you where you stand. I will rip pieces of your body off one at a time until you beg me to let you use the magic."

Oh... My... God! What do I do? Maggie fought against the panic that threatened to enshroud her. Apparently she didn't dare use the magic, but she had no other weapons. *Damned if I do. Dead if I don't.*

"Maggie Devereaux," the demon's voice seemed to penetrate into her very soul.

"What?!" She was trying to think of something—anything.

"You know me." Another large piece of bubbling saliva fell from its glowing red lips. "You have visited me in your dreams."

And Maggie knew it was true. It was the demon from her dream. The one who had linked arms with her as they had drunk Iain's blood.

The demon held up a transparent crimson claw in invitation. "Join me."

Maggie was stunned. "Join you?!" she shrieked in panicked disbelief.

"You wield my magic. Make me real willingly and I will teach you to use it. I know the magic. You can know it too. Join me."

Maggie just stared at the demon, unsure what to think. Or say. Or do.

"I will teach you," it repeated, its evil voice echoing inside her head. "You will have whatever you desire. Money. Fame. Power." It looked through its leg at Iain. "Even him. Or any other mate you want."

Maggie was surprised by what she said next. "How do I

know I can trust you?"

The demon laughed. "You can't know that. But I will give you my word just the same."

Maggie blinked at the demon, her mind and heart racing.

"I know you want the full power of the magic," the beast coaxed. "I feel your desire. I can sate it."

Maggie couldn't believe she was considering the offer. But the demon was right: she did want the full power of the magic. And she knew there was so much more to it than was to be found in that one spellbook. Her last spell had confirmed that.

She didn't want money. She didn't want fame. She didn't want power. She wasn't even sure she wanted Iain.

But she wanted the magic.

And there it was, ripe for the taking, its full potential hovering and glowing before her face—just as the candle had done so many weeks ago.

What should she do? No one else was around. No one would know. Sinclair and Iain were out cold. Maybe she could talk the demon out of killing them. Maybe she could take the demon up on its offer, but then double cross it once she'd learned enough of the magic.

The magic.

It was as if her entire trip to Scotland had led her to this point. Stumbling across the spellbook, the chance meeting with Sinclair, the murders that spurned her into trying the magic. And the demon from her dreams who stood before her offering limitless access to limitless power. Had Grandma known all that? Could she possibly have wanted Maggie to ally with a demon? Finding the spellbook couldn't have been a coincidence. And the magic worked. And Maggie knew the demon was telling the truth when he said the magic was from his demonic world. It explained the horrific dreams which hadn't scared her quite enough. It explained the explosive anger which had seized her at any attack on her ancestry or her right to use the magic. And it explained the sweet rush which filled her veins at the slightest possibility of battle.

She remembered that day in the subbasement when she had first read the cover. 'The Dark Book of Rites and Damnation.' If she was supposed to find the book, didn't that mean she was supposed to learn the dark magic? And if she was supposed to learn dark magic, why not learn it from its source—even if that source was a terrifying nine-foot tall demon? Was that the NicInnes legacy? A healer wielding dark magic? Her daughter burned for doing the same?

Suddenly, Maggie really wished her grandmother were there.

She stared up at the crimson devil before her, his clawed hand extended so invitingly. It would be so easy to take a hold of it and finally learn all there was to know about the beautiful, glorious magic.

Then Maggie remembered her grandmother's last words: '*As long as you stay true to what's right, I will always be with you.*'

'*Stay true.*'

Be Traist.

"What say you?" The murderous claw stretched still further toward her own raised hand.

And Maggie Devereaux decided.

Then she saw a light open up in the sky behind the demon. At first she thought it was the moon coming out from behind clouds, but then she remembered there were no clouds, and the moon was new. The yellow-white light swelled and then diffused away, revealing the glowing form of a beautiful young woman floating in the sky behind the demon. It was the woman from the vision Maggie had seen spring forth from the clan crest pendant.

The woman's lips parted, and Maggie heard her grandmother's voice in her ears.

"Transmutation," was all she said.

Maggie's heart sank. *Anything but that.* She swallowed hard and looked again at the semi-solid beast before her. *But it might just work.*

"What will it be, Maggie Devereaux?" The demon took a menacing step toward her. "Power or pain?"

Maggie didn't say anything, but instead raised her hands and thought the simple levitation spell. She could feel the spell flow from her fingertips and watched as the demon rose only slightly off the ground, then flared a blinding red, before again lowering to the earth. Fully corporeal. Fully real.

"Ha-ha!" it shouted triumphantly. "Yes! I am real! I am here!" It pointed at Maggie. "You are wise."

"You are dead," she replied, and unleashed the transmutation spell.

There are times when one doesn't mind having to try something for the first time. And there are times when one doesn't mind trying something again which has failed in the past. Times when the stakes aren't very high. When failure means little more than a friendly chuckle and a pat on the back before turning off the grill and ordering pizza. But the stakes here couldn't have been higher. Maggie's very life was at stake. And the lives of her unconscious companions, and those of countless residents of Aberdeen and beyond, should this demon escape past her. But she had never been able to get the transmutation spell to work before. And she was terrified she wouldn't be able to now. Normally that doubt might have been enough to ensure failure. '*Ability to use the magic comes from belief in it.*' But the doubt was swallowed by the enormity of the stakes, and the knowledge that she had no choice but to succeed.

The spell sprang forth.

The demon cried out in agony. Its voice seemed to echo off the very sky itself. Maggie watched in victorious horror as smoke and fire flared from the sinews and bones of the hideous beast before her. The flames blinded her eyes. The smoke burned her nostrils. She turned away, the screams of agony still piercing her ears. There was one last scream, then it stopped. And then the crackling and popping stopped too. A final hiss dissipated into the black night. Maggie looked up.

Before her stood a nine foot tall stone statue of the demon who had tempted her. Whose presence had originally been summoned by the murdered children of Glenninver. Who had possessed Devan Sinclair. Who had murdered Annette Graham and Fionna FitzSimmons and Kelly Anderson. Who had possessed Iain in order to murder Maggie. Who had been drawn fully into this plane, his body made real. And whose flesh Maggie had just turned to stone.

Had it not been so large and so grotesque, it would have seemed as any other grave marker. And in a way it was a gravestone. For there died the demon who had terrorized two cities across two decades. And there ended the murders in Aberdeen.

Maggie sat down on the frozen earth and dropped her head into her hands. All was quiet for a very long time. Looking up again to the black sky, she confirmed that the vision of her grandmother was gone—although Maggie had no doubt she would see her again. Finally, she heard a groan and looked to see Sinclair stirring. He leaned up onto his elbows and rubbed the back of his head.

"M—Maggie? What—What happened?"

Maggie jerked a thumb toward the statue. "It's over," she

said simply.

Sinclair stood up slowly, his hand to the back of his neck, and just stared at the statue. Maggie watched him, but he was oblivious to her gaze. Eventually she saw his eye flash and a single tear traced the scar down the side of his face.

"The demon—" he started.

"Gone," Maggie answered. "For good this time. It's the same one you and Jared summoned?" she confirmed.

"Me?" Sinclair's moist eyes shot back to Maggie's darkened visage. "No. It was Jared. He—"

"Found a book," Maggie finished his sentence, thinking of the coffee—or blood?—stained text Sinclair had refused to sell her.

"Yes," Sinclair confirmed. "It detailed ancient demonological rites."

"Including summoning spells." These weren't really questions. Not anymore.

"Yes," Sinclair shook his head, "but they weren't supposed to be real, just an academic cataloging." He stared into the black toward the demon statue. "I remember when he first showed me the spell. Page 126. It was horrible. I laughed and told him it would never work. And he just looked down and said, 'Aye. But what if it did?'"

And then for the first time since she'd met him, Maggie saw Sinclair shrug. A defeated, tired shrug. "I found him, but it was too late. Too late for Heather. I ran at him, pushed him away—and that's the last thing I remembered."

"Until your parents died."

"It took the death of my parents," Sinclair raised himself up again, "their death at my own possessed hands, to rouse me into consciousness. I took back my body."

"Quite the feat." Maggie was sure it had been.

Sinclair didn't bother acknowledging the compliment. "The demon was trapped then. Trapped here, ethereal and impotent. It had no way back to its own realm, but it had no host either. And it would be eighteen years before the spell could be repeated."

"The moon cycle," Maggie said half to herself.

"Yes. The spell isn't for possession," Sinclair explained, his wet scar glinting dimly in the black. "It grafts a demon directly to a human host. Permanently." A smile played at his lips. "Or at least that's the intent. But to accomplish something like that, everything has to be perfect: everything must be aligned perfectly, and the spell must have had the time to ripen. It's the fourth sacrifice that completes the spell, and it must occur when the night of the new moon—completely lightless, dark as the soul being summoned— falls on the winter solstice. And that only happens once every eighteen years."

Sinclair closed his eyes and Maggie knew he was reading from memory the words which lay on page 126.

"Each victim is surrounded by the four elements, torn from her own corpse: earthy intestines; waterlogged bladder; fiery, acidic stomach; and air-pumping lungs. And each victim is oriented toward a different point on the compass, calling on the four corners of the Earth for power. The fourth victim is pointed south so that at the end of the night, when the moonless sky ends its reign over the victim's blood-drenched heart, it shines the last of its blackness past her lifeless face and into the empty carcass beyond—symbolic of the dark-souled demon coming to fill, like an empty vessel, the waiting human host."

Maggie shuddered. She was to have been the carcass; Iain the vessel.

As if perhaps sensing this thought, Iain finally stirred, twitching just slightly and let out a low "Hnnnhhh."

"Come on," Maggie urged Sinclair. "Help me get him to the church before he's fully awake."

She wasn't interested in trying to explain why they were in a graveyard in the middle of the night, who Sinclair was, or what was with the nine foot tall statue of a monstrous demon. Sinclair brought Iain to his feet as Maggie ran ahead to find the gate in the fence.

"Over here," she shouted finally, and Sinclair led the still groggy Iain to the sound of Maggie's voice.

"Thank you," she said, as Sinclair leaned Iain onto her shoulder.

Sinclair smiled. "Thank *you*, Maggie Devereaux."

"Will you be all right?" she asked.

Sinclair nodded strongly. "Yes. I've just one more thing to do." Then, as if reading her mind, he added, "I'll see you again."

Maggie was glad, and turned toward the church. Once through the gate, Iain started to wake fully.

"Hhnnh? M—Maggie?" he slurred. "Wh—Where are we?"

Maggie squeezed his hand as he stood fully under his own power. "What's the last thing you remember?"

Iain thought for a moment. "I was in the pub. Drinking. It was my third pint."

Maggie looked up at him, a friendly eyebrow raised.

"All right, maybe my fourth," he admitted. "Then that's it. I don't remember anything else. What happened?"

"Wow, you really did hit your head, didn't you?"

Iain raised his hand to his forehead and felt around a bit. "Hit my head?"

"Yeah," Maggie still held his other hand. "After I yelled at you, I felt bad. I shouldn't have talked to you like that. It wasn't fair. I was on my way back to the college when I ran into you. We walked along for a while, then I decided to walk through the graveyard."

"The graveyard? In the middle of the night?"

"Pretty scary, huh?" Maggie smiled. So far everything she had said had been technically true. "Well, anyway, you followed after me—of course. And I don't know, you must have tripped and hit your head on a gravestone or something."

Iain touched his head again. "I don't have any bumps," he observed.

"Yeah," she laughed. "Pretty weird, huh?"

Iain frowned at the mysterious young woman he'd befriended. "Aye. Pretty weird."

They had almost reached the church. Sure enough, the back door was propped open and light from the vestibule spilled out onto the stone path to the graveyard. As Iain hobbled inside the sanctuary, Maggie turned around and looked back to where she had left Sinclair. It was dark, but her eyes had adjusted and she could just make out the inky forms next to the mausoleum. What she didn't see was the figure behind her, standing in the shadows of the church. The figure of Elizabeth Warwick, who had been present and observing for some time now.

And then in the cold darkness of the black Aberdeen night, both women watched silently as Devan Sinclair raised the shovel and smashed the stone demon to bits.

Epilogue

Sinclair's bookshop was gone.

Maggie had seen him once more before he'd left, as promised. It was brief and awkward. They had chatted lightly, entirely avoiding the topic of that night. Then he left Aberdeen. He hadn't said where he was going. She hadn't asked.

Spring in Scotland suited Maggie. The days were long again and the rain was far less frequent. Taking advantage of a particularly sunny afternoon, she had led Iain to an outdoor café across the street from where Sinclair's bookshop had been. While Iain waited for the barista for their drinks, Maggie found a table outside and looked across the street. Workers were hanging a 'STARBUCKS' sign over the same wooden door she had walked through months before. It seemed so long ago. She pulled the clan crest pendant out from under her blouse and dangled it in front of her face. The transmutation spell mastered, she had finally been able to remove the black smudge that had defaced the clan motto.

Iain sat down with their drinks.

"Hmph," he said, glancing over at the workers. "It's a shame to see another one of those go in. And right across from this café. I mean, good for them and their success, but I don't want to see Scotland lose all her local charm."

Maggie laughed, half to herself. "Don't worry," she said as she pulled her cappuccino over. "I've found that Scotland has plenty of charms hidden away."

Her pendant flashed in the sun as she raised the cup to her lips.

"Hey!" Iain pointed at the silver crest. "You got the smudge off."

"Yeah." She glanced down with a satisfied grin.

"How'd you do that?" He looked her earnestly in the eye.

She met his gaze just as earnestly and smiled sweetly.

"Magic."

What follows is a preview of

BLOOD
RITE

the thrilling sequel
to *Scottish Rite*

1. Heir Apparent

He had no idea what was happening.

The year-old boy slept peacefully within his magnificent, solid mahogany crib, his opulent cotton sheets enveloping him in illusory protection. While across the impeccably decorated nursery, through the elegantly dressed window, silver moonlight streamed in over the child's angelic face. Indeed, so sound was the baby's slumber that he didn't stir at all as the watery light spilling across his soft features was blocked by the cloaked figure who stepped silently to the edge of his magnificent, solid mahogany crib.

A woman's strong, fine hands reached down and gently lifted the infant from his cotton womb, trading him his flannel sheets for the equally luxurious warmth of a waiting silk blanket. The boy cooed contentedly as he nestled against his kidnapper's breast and returned to whatever happy images fill a yearling's dreams.

Several silent moments passed. Then the happy images were sliced violently away. A muffled yelp, followed by a smothered wail, rebounded dully off the walls of the nursery; and a woman's fine, strong hand hurried to paint the words in blood on the wall above the crib:

'I AM RETURNED TO FULFILL THE PROPHECY'

And then, with even more haste, the same hand scrawled out another bloody phrase, this time on the polished wood floorboards next to the bleeding child:

'A THÁINMHNE NA DOHRGHATAS, SLÁINAICH AN LÁINABH A'SIO.'

'Forces of Darkness, Heal this Child.'

2. The First Hours

Inspector Robert Cameron stood motionless, his hands shoved deep into the pockets of his crumpled blue suit, and stared down at the bloody pattern etched at his feet. Again.

He was a large man, six foot three with broad shoulders and thick muscles beneath his forty-something skin, and he towered incongruously within the infant's nursery. Closely cut, snowy-white hair retreated sharply from either side of his furrowed scalp to an increasingly large bald spot at the back of his head. His tired blue suit dated from the Thatcher administration; his frayed red tie, hanging limply between his unbuttoned coat sides, from the one before. Intelligent blue eyes shone out from their recessed sockets as he stood in the middle of both the nursery and the cacophony which had seized the residence.

Officer MacGregor was sliding the diminutive baby furniture away from the walls for Officer Richards to peer behind. Flashbulbs from Officer MacAllister's camera lit the room repeatedly while Officer Henderson began to dust both the crib and the windowsill for fingerprints. From down the hall Cameron could hear the soft, choked sobbing of the nanny, being both half-consoled and half-interrogated by Officer Wilkins; he'd have to make sure Wilkins printed her before he let her leave. And Sergeant Willis was downstairs, undoubtedly failing utterly to prevent the lord of the house from leaving.

Cameron raised his gaze and stared several moments at the bloody phrase above the crib, drying brown, its drips extending almost to the floor. He was of the opinion that the gory script was just for show—to make the kidnappers appear to be more than just that, and to ensure the ransom would be paid quickly and without questions. After all, it was almost certainly not the boy's blood. Cameron doubted the body of a one year old even held enough blood to spell out the shocking graffiti on wall above the crib. But he had to concede that the lad's blood could well have been the source of the enigmatic phrase drying sticky to the priceless wood floor next to his own dull, worn black shoes.

Cameron rubbed a hand over his head and chewed his cheek contemplatively. Then he pulled his pipe from his coat pocket and lit the bowl, still packed with last night's tobacco.

He told himself it was just another kidnapping.

He told himself they'd get the ransom note within the hour.

He smacked disappointedly at his pipe and told himself to be sure to put some fresh tobacco in it once he was back at the station.

And then he told himself to wait until the end of the day for the ransom note not to come before calling her in on the case.

* * *

About the Author

Stephen Penner is an author and artist living in the Seattle area. He writes a broad variety of fiction, including thrillers, science fiction, and children's books. In addition, he enjoys drawing and painting.

For information on his latest books, visit his website: http://www.stephenpenner.com

RING OF FIRE PUBLISHING

www.ringoffirebooks.com